W9-BLA-261

The
IMPORTANCE
of BEING
KENNEDY

ALSO BY LAURIE GRAHAM

FICTION
The Ten O'Clock Horses
Perfect Meringues
The Dress Circle
Dog Days, Glenn Miller Nights
The Future Homemakers of America
The Great Husband Hunt
Mr. Starlight
Gone with the Windsors

NONFICTION
A Parents' Survival Guide
A Marriage Survival Guide
Teenagers: A Family Survival Guide

The
IMPORTANCE
of BEING
KENNEDY

A NOVEL

Laurie
Graham

HARPER

An Imprint of HarperCollins*Publishers*
www.harpercollins.com

HarperCollins books may be purchased for educational, business, or sales promotional use. For information, please write: Special Markets Department, HarperCollins Publishers, 10 East 53rd Street, New York, NY 10022.

FIRST EDITION

Designed by Mary Austin Speaker

Library of Congress Cataloging-in-Publication Data
Graham, Laurie, 1947–
The importance of being Kennedy : a novel / Laurie Graham. — 1st ed.
p.   cm.
ISBN: 978-0-06-117352-3
1. Kennedy family—Fiction. I. Title.
PR6057.R237I67 2008
823'.914—dc22
2007023964

08 09 10 11 12   OV/RRD   10 9 8 7 6 5 4 3 2 1

Author's Note

This is a work of fiction. While many of the c haracters in this novel are historical figures, many others, including the nanny, Nora, are fictional. The incidents and dialogues portrayed are also products of the author's imagination and are not to be construed as real, even though they are based broadly upon historical events.

To Jeremy Magorian,
Venice's very own Mrs. Thrale

CONTENTS

The

IMPORTANCE
of BEING
KENNEDY

Prelude

I happened to be in London in January 1970, when I got a call from my New York office to say my aunt Nora had died. We were just finishing up the photo shoot for a big piece on platform shoes for *Sassy!* magazine, so I was able to get away to Derbyshire in time for her funeral. Darling Aunt Nora, who started life three to a bed in Ballynagore, had a duke and a duchess at her Requiem Mass. If Aunt Ursie had lived to hear that, she'd have popped her corset bones.

I didn't really get to know Aunt Nora till she ferreted me out in Saks Formal Wear in 1947 and stood me lunch. She had a nifty figure and beautiful skin for a woman in her fifties. She was wearing an old-fashioned tweed suit, I remember, petrol-blue, fully lined, with a great corded buttonhole detail. Very classy.

"It's one of the perks of working for a lady who keeps up with trends," she said. "When the rest of the world won't be seen dead in a garment, it can always be passed along to the help."

We hit it off right away. She'd been a distant figure when I was a kid. "Your aunt Nora's with the Kennedys," Mom used to say, and as we had another aunt, who was a nun in Africa, I pictured Aunt Nora in a grass skirt and the Kennedys as some kind of tribe. In a sense, I suppose I was on the right track.

Aunt Nora was a blast. I relished the letter that came every year with her Christmas card, her annual report on life as a gardener's wife on the great Chatsworth estate of the Duke of Devonshire. "Another twelve months of 'tater peelings," as she described it. She outlived four of the nine Kennedy babies she'd raised. When Jack was killed in 1963, she wrote me that she hadn't watched the funeral. She said, "Stallybrass was glued to the telly all afternoon but I walked to Hassop and prayed the rosary till it was over. I don't care for the telly myself. They tell you the same thing over and over. I don't mind Walter watching it and I'll sit with him for company, but I turn my chair the other way and get on with my knitting. Anyway, I kept the death watch over Jack Kennedy more times than the sands are numbered and I could have swung for him once or twice too, little devil that he was. It's Mrs. Kennedy my heart goes out to now. This is surely too much even for that tough little nut to endure."

Bobby Kennedy's death, and old Joe Kennedy's, she hardly mentioned. Her own health was failing by then, though I didn't realize it. As her beloved Walter put it, "Nora were never one to skryke about her aches and pains."

I asked him if she'd believed there was a gypsy curse on the Kennedys. There were a lot of stories about that, after Jack and Bobby.

"Nay, lad," he said. "In fact it got on her pippin when folk brought it up. Nora always reckoned old man Kennedy didn't need any gypsy curse to bring him calamities. He brought them on himself, the way he thought he could buy the world, the way he pushed them lads into the spotlight."

When I mentioned to Walter how I wished Aunt Nora had written about her Kennedy years, he shocked me with his reply.

He said, "But she did write about them. That first cottage we had at Edinsor, she sat at the kitchen table and wrote it all down in exercise books. She called it her 'memoirs,' said she were only doing it to stop herself going round the bend with nothing to look at, only sheep and trees. She liked the city best, you know, Nora. She only endured all this beautiful countryside for me, God bless her. Should you like to see her writings some time? They're in the back of her tallboy."

So Aunt Nora's notebooks, with multiplication tables printed on the back cover and that old-lady smell of mothballs and dried lavender, came into my possession, and with them the story of how the Kennedy dynasty was planned and its legend created, step by careful step. Of how my aunt's loyalty to the family extended even to assuming the Kennedy name when English country house customs required it. The story of the altogether very great importance of being Kennedy.

RAMON N. MULCAHY,
NEW YORK 1972

1

Accidentally, Through the Keyhole

Herself came to the house at Smith Square. It was April 1948. She was meant to be going directly to Paris for gown fittings but then she announced she was coming to London first, to visit with Kick. Landed on us with all her bags and baggage as if it was the Ritz we were running. Now, I've seen Mrs. Kennedy walk away when her own child lay sick in bed, turn her back on him sooner than delay a shopping trip, so we knew she wasn't coming for the pleasure of it. There was trouble on the agenda.

Walter had to have the car at the aerodrome by eight in the morning. Too early for Kick to get herself out of bed and go with him.

I said, "I'd have thought you'd make the effort. Go and meet her, get off on the right foot."

"No fear," she said. "Talk about being trapped in a confined space. It could feel like a very long drive."

I was worried Mrs. K would start quizzing Walter about what had been going on, if she had him to herself. I said, "Just act dumb."

"Nay, Nora," he said. "I don't need to act. When you've been driving gentry for thirty-five years dumb comes natural."

It was about eleven when they arrived. Mrs. K looked as smart as a brass button, as usual. You'd never have guessed she'd been on an airplane all night. She walked right past me in the hallway, unsnapped the fox head on her stole, handed it to Delia and made straight for the drawing room, still wearing her little hat, one of those round wee chocolate box affairs with a bit of net veiling that came down over her brow.

"Kaaaaathleeen," she started. "We are going to have a very serious talk."

I don't care how many elocution lessons she's taken, she still has a voice on her that would clip a thorn bush. And it was something to see how that girl crumbled the minute she saw her Mammy. She was like a naughty child who knew she'd be getting the strap. It was all about her carrying on with Blood Fitzwilliam. It had finally dawned on Mrs. K that Kick wasn't as worried as she might have been about her money being cut off if she didn't stop seeing him, so she'd come in person to threaten her with the everlasting fires of hell. The lovebirds were in the country when the cablegram came, seeing his horses put through their paces on Newmarket Heath, but Kick came hurrying back to town as soon as she heard her Mammy was coming. She knew she was in hot water.

She said, "Mother can have my room. The guest room's too small for her. Give my room an extra spit and polish. I want everything to be perfect."

I said, "Then you'd better get yourself round to Farm Street and see Father D'Arcy, because the first thing she'll want to know is, have you been to confession? What bedroom we put her in will be the least of it."

She gave me one of her monkey faces. And that room of hers needed more than spit and polish. I've done my best with those children over the years but there's not a one of them ever learned to hang up a jacket.

I said, "What will we do about dinners? Will you have company in while she's here?"

She said, "If you mean Blood, no. He's going to make himself scarce. Maybe I'll invite Sissy though. Mother thinks Sissy sets the perfect example. Or maybe we should have tray suppers and I'll read aloud from *Lives of the Saints*. I just want to stop her ranting till Daddy's met Blood. He'll talk her round. I think Blood and Daddy'll really get on."

I didn't. No more than a pair of turkey cocks could be left in the same pen. Mr. K liked people he could order around and so did Lord Fitzwilliam. And as for anybody talking Herself round, the very idea was nonsense. There was only ever going to be one thing that would satisfy her, and that was for Kick to go home and marry a nice Catholic boy, if one could be found who'd overlook her history. I knew Kick would put up a fight but I was sure her Mammy would win the day and that'd be the end of that. Blood Fitzwilliam would be given his marching orders, Smith Square would be let go and so would we.

Well, then it started. All you could hear was Mrs. K's voice.

"Look at me when I'm talking to you, Kathleen."

"Perfect purity and self-control, that's what you were taught at Sacred Heart."

"After everything that's been done for you, Kathleen Kennedy. Every advantage in life you've been given."

The few bits I didn't manage to hear accidentally through the keyhole I could guess. Promises of hellfire and damnation. The threat of being cut off, not just from her Daddy's deep pockets. From the holy sacraments as well. As long as her Mammy was calling her "Kathleen" I knew she was holding out. They'd had no lunch, not even a glass of soda taken in, and it got well past the time when Mrs. K usually takes her afternoon rest. Then things fell quiet. Herself came out from the drawing room and told Delia she was going upstairs to nap and wasn't to be disturbed till five o'clock. Kick was asleep in an armchair when I went in, curled up in her stocking feet with a little sodden hanky balled up on her lap. Round one had gone to Mother.

Then it was my turn.

Delia said, "She's rung for a glass of milk, Nora, to be taken up by you, most particular. Thank God. She frightens the bejaysus out of me."

There she lay, waiting for me, in those old pink napping pajamas she's had for a hundred years and frownies stuck all over her forehead, to smooth out any lines the morning's shenanigans had brought on. She was a sight. You wouldn't have known her for that bandbox little body that had walked in from the limousine.

"Nora, dear heart," she said. Patted the bed for me to sit down like we were old pals. "What a to-do. Now, I need you to help me."

So it was "Nora, dear heart" for the time being. But I've been long enough around Mrs. K to know you can be a "dear heart" one minute and on the bus with your valise and no references the next.

She said, "This is a very grave situation. Kathleen still talks of marrying this person. Did you know? Has she talked to you about her plans?"

I said, "As far as I know Lord Fitzwilliam didn't get his divorce yet."

"Well," she said, "that's something. I wonder how it's being arranged. I wonder whether the wife could be persuaded to keep him. What do we know about her? Would she be interested in money?"

I said, "I believe she has money."

She said, "I'm sure she could use more. It isn't just the mar-riage, though that must be prevented at all costs. But talk can be very damaging too. I'm normally very attentive to these things, but I'm so far away, and then I was busy with Jack's campaign. It's difficult to manage these things from the other side of the world. You might have said something, Nora. You might have dropped me a little note. You've been treated very generously over the years. Allowed back on the payroll after an act of great disloy-alty. I'd have thought at the very least you'd have had Kathleen's well-being at heart."

I said, "I thought Jack would have told you. He heard all about it when he was here last summer. I don't see how it was my place."

"Jack's in office now," she said. "He's far too busy, though I'm sure he would have mentioned it if his health had been better. He came back from London with a tired liver. I had to find him a doctor and then get him back on his feet. It's all been such a worry. And now this. If I'd known when she arrived at Palm Beach what she'd come to tell us, I'd have had Archie Spellman down to speak with her immediately. She wouldn't have dared defy a Cardinal."

There was a lot I could have said. I didn't like Lord Fitzwil-liam, "Blood" as his pals called him, and I was certain Kick could have done better for herself, but I know there's no reasoning with the lovestruck. It was my opinion that if we left well alone it might not come to a marrying. For one thing he didn't seem in any great hurry to get his divorce. In fact there were quite a num-ber of people who said he wasn't serious about getting one. Why would he go to the expense of lawyers when his wife didn't seem to care who he saw or what he did? And they'd houses enough never to have to see one another. Obby Fitzwilliam was known to be a very devil for the drink but she had money, and a drunken old bird in the hand might be worth a lot more to him than a Kennedy cut off without a cent. I thought if he dragged his heels Kick might tire of waiting for him, or that someone else would come along and catch her eye. Sure, half of London was in love with her. But I didn't tell Herself any of that. I didn't approve of what Kick was doing but that didn't mean I had to do Mrs. K's dirty work for her.

I said, "I'd just like to see her happy. She's had enough sadness for such a youngster."

Mrs. K said, "We've all had sadness. And if it's happiness she wants she won't find it by breaking every rule she was raised by. Associating with a married man. That's not a path to happiness. And he's a Protestant. A married Protestant! I can hardly think of anything worse. It's her duty to set a good example, Nora, particularly now Jack's in Congress. We're all in the public eye, just as we were when we were Ambassador. What if Catholic girls start saying, 'Look at Kathleen Kennedy. She does as she pleases, so we'll do the same.'"

I said, "If she's here in London I don't see how girls in America will even know what she's doing. If they're interested in anybody it'll surely be Euny and Pat and Jean. And I don't see how it affects Jack. A congressman isn't like a monsignor, and just as well. Jack's no saint himself."

"Jack doesn't need to be a saint," she said. "Boys are different. They have to be men of the world to get ahead. But women set the moral tone."

I said, "Well, Kick's twenty-eight years old and a widow and a Ladyship, so I can hardly presume to catechize her now."

"Of course you can," she said. "That's precisely what you can do. It's never too late. You disappoint me greatly, Nora."

Then she closed her eyes, which is always her way of saying the conversation is over. That neat little foldaway face.

Four days we had of it. Threats and lectures and tears, and all the time I knew Kick was clinging to one silly thing her Daddy had said on the telephone. That if it could be shown Blood Fitzwilliam had never been baptized, then his marriage to Lady Obby wouldn't count and he'd be free to take instruction and marry Kick in a proper Catholic church. It was all moonshine, of course. The Fitzwilliams weren't the kind of family that would have overlooked baptizing their son and heir, but it was typical of Mr. Kennedy to dream up something like that, ducking and diving under the regulations until he found a wee hole to slip through.

I'll say this for him though. He just wanted his girl to be happy. He knew nothing she did was likely to harm Jack's prospects, nor Bobby's, nor Teddy's. He'd see to that. The boys were his affair and whatever happened, whatever trouble they got into or talk there might be about the family, he'd keep things on track for them.

Kick cried and begged but when it really came down to it she didn't care what her Mammy did. She absolutely would not promise to give up Fitzwilliam. So Mrs. Kennedy had Delia pack her bags for the onward journey to Paris and the car was ordered to take her to the aerodrome. It was an ugly leave-taking.

She said, "I won't stay another night in this house. You've fallen into bad company, Kathleen, and I rue the day we ever brought you to England. The Mothers at Sacred Heart laid out your path but you've deviated from it, and so deliberately, too. No one can ever excuse you; no one can say you weren't taught right from wrong. Well, if you really refuse to acknowledge your errors I shall see to it you at least don't ruin your sisters with your carrying-on. They'll have nothing more to do with you. Don't telephone, because they won't accept your calls, and don't send letters, because I shall have them burned. There's nothing more to be said until you're ready to repent."

I was just standing there like an article of furniture, holding that horrible wrap with the fox heads dangling over my arm. It seemed to me I didn't have a lot left to lose.

I said, "I never heard such a cruel thing. A girl needs her family, and the bigger the muddle she's in, the more she needs them, and sure weren't you the one always taught them to put family before everything else?"

"Nora Brennan," she said. "You should have been let go years ago. I wouldn't have kept you on, married in a town hall. Well, now we see what an influence you've been. Now we see it clear. I'll pray for your soul, Kathleen. I can't do more. Until you mend your ways I will not see you. You'll be dead to me."

She said it flat, with that darling girl standing right there. How does it sit with her now, I wonder, seeing the way things turned out. How many times has she wished she could take back those terrible words. Anyone might say a thing in anger, then wish it unsaid, but Rose Kennedy isn't anyone. I've been around her long enough to know. For a woman who's a Gold Star mother, she has a heart as hard as the hob of hell.

2

The Right Kind of Family

I came to work for the Kennedys in the spring of 1917. I'd been five years in America by then, come over to be with my two sisters. Marimichael Donnelly from across the lane was on the same sailing as me. They waked us two nights together with whiskey drummed up from somewhere by the Donnelly boys, telling us what a grand future the both of us had and then weeping and clinging onto us to keep us at home. We'd neither of us been out of Westmeath before. I'd never appreciated that sky and water could stretch so far, and I know they say the world's like an apple and doesn't have an edge you can tumble over, but I've never understood how they know. I was braced for the end all the way, till I saw the roofs of East Boston.

Marimichael had a sister who'd gone ahead too. That was how we did it in those days. The oldest one went, then she'd send the fare for the next and so on, till everyone was settled. It was the only thing to do. The factories were starting up around Tullamore, so the demand for hand-knitting was dropping off and there was no other way to make a living.

We were six in our family, one boy and five girls, except Nellie was in the graveyard, dead with the measles and only four years old. Ursie's the oldest. She left for Boston in 1909. Took a correspondence course in bookkeeping and taught herself the Pitman Shorthand and she was off. She got work in the office of Holkum, Holkum and Jauncey, and to hear her she ended up practically running the place.

Ursie always had ideas. Writing paper without lines was one of her things, not that there was a lot of letter writing going on in our house, but she said lined paper was common, and she used to have a fit if ever Mammy put the milk can on the table instead of the china pitcher. After she got to America and started earning, she'd send us marvelous things, not only money. Caramels and hatpins and silk stockings, and a beautiful handbag for Mammy one Christmas, real leather from Jordan Marsh, lined and with a big gilt snap. Dear God, we had everyone from Ballynagore come in to see that handbag. We should have charged for the viewings.

She must have had some courage to go off like that, not knowing a living soul in America. When they were handing out gumption, I reckon Ursie got Edmond's share. He's hardly been further than the foot of the stairs.

Margaret went out to join Ursie in 1910 and I cried myself sick. Ursie wasn't the kind of sister you missed, except like an aching tooth after it's been pulled, but Margaret had always been my pal. We'd shared a bed, even. When Mammy and Deirdre went with her to wave her off on the bus I couldn't bear to go with them. I was convinced I'd never see her again.

She kept saying, "You will too. I'll send for you and then you'll send for Deirdre."

But Deirdre could never have gone to America. She had a

sweet nature and the voice of an angel but she was the kind of girl that would easily be taken advantage of. She used to get confused enough in Tullamore market, so she'd have been lost in a minute in Boston. Anyway, Father Hughes said a girl like Deirdre would likely be blessed with a vocation, so we all prayed for that and our prayers were answered. She went to the Maryknoll Sisters, and then to Africa to teach little black children about our Risen Lord, which left just me at home and Mammy and my brother, Edmond.

Ursie kept writing that I should still think of going to America. *Mother won't stand in your way*, she wrote. She didn't call her "Mammy" anymore, since she worked for Holkum, Holkum and Jauncey. *She'll be a lot happier knowing you're making something of yourself. She has Edmond to take care of her.*

Edmond was supposed to be the head of the house. Dada had the Irish disease, and after we lost Nellie, he just turned his face to the wall and died.

Mammy used to say, "Edmond's a thinker. He doesn't rush into things. And did you ever see such a fine head of hair on a man?"

Well, that part was true. I believe it acted like a goose-feather comforter. It kept his noddle so warm and cozy his brain fell asleep.

I don't know whether I would have gone and left Mammy in his care, but anyway, as things turned out, it was Mammy who left us. She'd a growth under her left bosom that had eaten her away inside and she'd been too shy to say anything until it was too late.

"Never mind," she said. "I've had a good life. I've had my span."

But she'd only had forty-seven years and she could have had more if she hadn't been such a muggins about taking off her vest in front of the doctor. She died in the autumn of 1911 and, before the year was out, Edmond took off his thinking cap and announced he was marrying the Clavin widow from Horseleap and bringing her to our home. So my mind was made up for me. I couldn't have stayed in the house with that woman. She'd a face would turn fresh milk. Margaret sent me the fare and I was on my way.

Marimichael went into a cotton mill when we got to Boston, same as her sister, and Margaret could have got me a start at the grocer's where she worked, but Ursie had bigger ideas.

She said, "You've a brain in your head, Nora. Use it. Nursing would be suitable. The uniforms are very tasteful."

But I liked the idea of going into service, somewhere where I'd have my own room.

I said, "If I'm going to wipe BTMs and mop up dribble I'd as soon do it for a nice sweet little baby as somebody who smells of sickness or some grouchy old feller. I'll go for a nursery maid."

"Just be sure it's the right kind of family," she said. "A doctor, or a lawyer, like Mr. Jauncey. Cultured, professional people. There are people who have money to run a full staff but no breeding. You don't want to end up with a family like that."

I got a start with the Griffin family in Cambridge, Massachusetts, to look after Loveday, who was three, and the baby, who was on the way, Arthur. Ursie seemed to think they were good enough for me, even if they were a bit modern. Dr. Griffin was a scientist at the university but he thought nothing of pushing the bassinet out on a weekend. There was only me, a housemaid, a woman who came in on Mondays to do the laundry, and a man who helped with the garden. Mrs. Griffin did all the cooking and I had every Sunday off and one night a week. I used to meet Margaret at a soda fountain and she'd give out to me about Ursie while we watched the boys go by. That's where we met Jimmy Swords and Frankie Mulcahy.

It's a funny thing about boys. They go around in pairs, and if one of them is good-looking, the other's sure to be a poor specimen. That was Frankie. He always looked like he lost a dollar and found a cent, but Margaret fell for him, and Jimmy was keen on me. The only problem with Jimmy and Frankie was they worked as fish porters. They were always washed and shaved and dressed in a nice clean collar and tie when we saw them, but there was still that smell. You can never get rid of it. Jimmy seemed steady though. We never quarreled, and the Griffins liked him, because he used to bring oysters for them or a lobster, when he came to walk me out.

I had my nursery and my own room up under the roof and I had my beau. I was very suited, but then Dr. Griffin said he was moving to a different university, in California, and I had to decide whether to go with them. Ursie thought I should.

She said, "You've made a good start, Nora, now build on it. The Griffins think highly of you and you mustn't flit from position to position. It doesn't inspire confidence."

But Jimmy didn't want me to go.

He said, "I'm putting money by. Stay in Boston and we'll get married. Next year."

So the Griffins went off to California and I applied for a new position, in Beals Street, Brookline. The Kennedy family. They had a little one just walking, Joseph Patrick, and another one on the way.

I had to go to the house to be interviewed and inspected by Mrs. Kennedy. She's only a year or two older than me and people say she has the secret of eternal youth. To look at us now you'd think I could give her a few years, but that first day I met her she seemed quite the little matron. First thing she told me was how she had to be most particular about the help she employed, because of her position.

She said, "My husband is president of a bank."

The house was nothing to shout about and neither was the money they were offering.

She said, "And I expect you recognize me."

But I didn't know her from Atty Hayes's donkey. She laughed.

She said, "You're a newcomer. If you were Boston-born you'd know my face from the dailies. I'm Mayor Fitzgerald's daughter."

Well, you couldn't be in Boston five minutes without hearing of him, so that satisfied her. She rattled on, perched at her bureau like a neat little bird, telling me all about her travels and the big shots she'd met. She even had tea brought in, and I still didn't know if I had the job or not.

"I was my father's right-hand woman," she said. "My mother didn't have the nerves for public life so I went everywhere with him. But now of course I'm too busy running my own home. Mr. Kennedy works very long hours in business."

And that was the truth. I was there three weeks before I properly met him. He'd get home late and leave again early. He was a tall carrot-top of a man with a tombstone smile and ice-blue eyes. He came up to the nursery one Saturday morning and started throwing Joseph Patrick up in the air to make him squeal.

He said, "I'm Joe Kennedy. You have everything you need? Anything you need, tell Mrs. Kennedy. Money's no object. And make sure this boy of mine eats his greens. I have big plans for him."

Mrs. K gave me a book to read the day I arrived, on how a nursery should be run. Everything was to be done by the clock. When the new baby came, she was going to nurse it, but between feeds there was to be no picking it up or rocking the cradle. If it cried, it cried. And little Joseph Patrick wasn't to be played with, except for half an hour of nursery rhymes and physical training in the afternoon. He'd learn to entertain himself with toys, and the only time he was allowed to snuggle on my lap was for his bedtime story.

She said, "Too much petting makes a child fussy and it's a very hard habit to break."

"Yes, Mrs. Kennedy," I said.

Well, she didn't have to know everything that went on in my nursery. I had my rules and routines and she had hers. She'd walk to St. Aidan's every morning to early Mass, and then she'd do the marketing and write letters till lunchtime. Always a chicken sandwich and a glass of milk. In the afternoon she'd take a nap, and then have her hair done or go to the dressmaker's, and once a week Mayor Fitzgerald would come to tea. The way Mrs. K talked him up, "His Honor this, His Honor that," it was like expecting the President himself. It was such a letdown the first time I saw him. He was just a crafty-looking old knacker riding round in a limousine car, but Mrs. K thought the sun shone out of her Daddy's fundament.

Sometimes on a Friday night Mr. K would have some people in for bridge, business gentlemen and their wives, but otherwise she didn't see a soul. Her Mammy never visited, nor her sisters, and the neighbors on Beals Street kept to themselves.

The Ericksons' maid said, "She thinks she's the cat's pajamas, your missis, but nobody round here's impressed."

We knew war was coming. It seemed to have nothing to do with us back in 1914, but we could feel it just around the corner by the start of 1917. Mrs. K said it was a terrible, unsettled time to be bringing a new baby into the world, but at least Mr. Kennedy wouldn't have to go away to fight. She said he was too old, but he wasn't. He was twenty-nine, same as Jimmy Swords.

Jimmy and Frankie Mulcahy both volunteered. There were

a lot of the Irish who wouldn't, not wanting to take sides with the English, not even against that terrible Kaiser, but Jimmy said, "I'm an American now and Americans are going to fight, so I'm with them."

Not Mr. Kennedy, though. All of a sudden he got a management position at the Schwab shipyard in Quincy, reserved occupation, and when they drafted him anyway, he went to a tribunal to appeal and he won. Mrs. K said they'd made an error when they tried to draft him, because he was engaged in vital war work, but that was only because Mayor Fitzgerald had pulled strings to get him in at the shipyard. Whichever way you cut it, Joe Kennedy was a draft-dodger. But that's water under the bridge. God knows, we've had another war since then, and what he got away with in 1917 he's paid for in buckets since.

Jimmy went off to a training camp, but the doctors failed Frankie because of his chest, and he was sent to a uniform factory in Pennsylvania, as a machinist. Margaret thought we should have married them before they went, but Jimmy never offered it and I had my mind on my nursery. Mrs. Kennedy was very near her time.

A weekly nurse was hired and Mr. K moved into the guest room so we could get the big bedroom ready. All the little trinket boxes and hairbrushes had to be cleared off the dressing table, and the rugs lifted and the floor washed down with carbolic acid and boiling water, for reasons of hygiene, the nurse said. It made you wonder how the human race ever got to be such a thriving concern.

She came along to the nursery still in her bathrobe that morning. She said she'd had a few pains in the night but she hadn't wanted to say anything till Mr. K had gone off to business.

"This is woman's work," she said. "Now we'll get on with it. We'll have this baby delivered and everything tidied away by the time he comes home."

I took Joseph Patrick to the park and played with him on the teeter-totter, and by the time he'd had his soup and lain down for his nap, the doctor had been sent for.

I'd never seen a baby born. When Mrs. Griffin had baby Arthur, she went to the nursing home so they could give her the twilight sleep and then she had two weeks of lying-in before she brought him home. I knew the facts of life, and I'd seen plenty of sows dropping their piglets, but it was hard to relate that to Mrs. Kennedy. I'd heard it said that women screamed and cursed and that there was blood and worse, but she'd hardly a hair out of place. She just lay there with the ether inhaler over her face and Dr. Good fetched the forceps out of his bag and fairly dragged the poor mite into the world. John Fitzgerald Kennedy. Though as I recall, he was hardly ever called John. He was Jack right from the start.

The nurse told Mrs. K she had another boy, but she was too doped for it to register or even to hold him, so he was given to me to put in the crib. And it was a grand thing, to cradle him in my arms and see his surprised little face and his tiny fingers weaving in the air, to wonder what life had in store for him. I was the first to hold the next three Kennedy babies and every time it gave me that nice, funny feeling, like someone slipped a piece of velvet inside my tummy.

But by the time Mr. Kennedy came home from business, Herself was wide-awake, washed and powdered and sitting up in a new satin bed jacket. Then His Honor the Mayor turned up, with Mrs. Fitzgerald, who I'd never seen before, and a bouquet of carnations. They came to the nursery to take a look at Jack but they didn't seem very interested in him. He'd been given Fitzgerald for one of his names, so I'd have expected them to be thrilled.

His Honor said, "He'll do, for a spare. Now let me see my best boy."

And I had to go contrary to all Mrs. Kennedy's instructions and wake Joseph Patrick from his bed, to be petted and made overexcited by his grandpa.

"See this fine feller?" he said. "This fine feller is going to be president of the United States."

It's a funny thing, there's never been any love lost between Mayor Fitzgerald and Mr. Kennedy, but that's one thing they always agreed on. Joseph Patrick was going to be president.

3

The Trouble with Blood Fitzwilliam

The minute her Mammy was on her way to the aerodrome, Kick got the shine back in her eyes.

She said, "That was pretty gruesome, but Daddy'll fix everything. He can probably get us a special dispensation from Rome."

I said, "The Holy Father won't change the rules, not even for a Kennedy."

She said, "This Holy Father might. He's practically part of the family."

Part of the family, my eye. He paid a call once, that's all, long ago, when we were in Bronxville, and that was only because Mr. Roosevelt couldn't think what else to do with a visiting cardinal all afternoon, only send him to Mrs. Kennedy for a cup of tea.

She said, "And we had a private audience. He gave me a rosary."

I said, "I know. I was there. And so was Fidelma Clery. He gave us all rosaries. He gets them wholesale, I'm sure. But that

23

doesn't mean he hands out dispensations so a man can have two wives."

She got into such a paddy.

She said, "Why doesn't anyone understand? Blood married Obby in one of their churches, so as far as our church is concerned he's never been married. Anyway, the Holy Father can change anything he wants to. Especially if Daddy sends him a big fat check for a new altar or something."

There were cablegrams flying back and forth all that week, and then Blood Fitzwilliam turned up, like the bad penny. He was back in town and expecting to take her to lunch. When you're in service, you notice that the ones who're too grand to give you a "Good day" are not necessarily the ones with the biggest estates or kings in their family tree. Just a middling rip like Fitzwilliam can be full enough of himself to ignore the help.

As soon as she heard his voice, Kick was ready to grab her pocketbook and go.

I said, "Didn't you tell me Lady Ginny was calling for you?"

"Oh Lord," she said. "Well, she's late. Just tell her something came up, would you? She'll understand."

He'd picked up the telephone without so much as a by-your-leave, putting through a call to his club, tapping a cigarette on his silver case. Kick was watching me watching him.

She said, "Darling, no smoking in the hall. Nora's got her fierce face on."

"Sweetie," he said, "who pays Nora's wages?"

It was four o'clock when she came home, pink and silly from champagne wine.

She said, "Blood's going to take me down to Nice for a vacation, next month. Such bliss. We're going to stay with his friends at their villa, and then by the time we come back Daddy will be in Paris, so we'll be able to stop off and see him. It's all worked out perfectly. We can have a big powwow about asking the Pope and things, without Mother being there to have a fit, and Daddy and Blood can get to know one another."

I said, "Angel girl, will you listen to yourself? All this talk about marrying. Is the man divorced from his lawful wedded wife?"

"He soon will be," she said. "He just has to see the lawyers. Then it won't take long. Obby's going to cooperate. You know they haven't had a real marriage for years."

I said, "And what about his child? Where does she fit into a divorce?"

She said, "She'll be fine. I expect we'll live at Coolatin when we're not in London, and she'll be able to come to visit us and keep a pony there and everything. I'm sure she's an absolute sweetheart, and I'll bet she'd love to have some little brothers and sisters. I'm going to have dozens of babies for you to look after, Nora, and we'll all live happily ever after. Blood will charm Mother off her feet, and Pat and Jean'll come over for the hunting. We might even be able to have poor Rosie to stay."

Ah yes. Poor Rosie. Well, there was a name she knew better than to bring up with her Daddy if she wanted to get him on her side. We never mentioned Rosie anymore, except below stairs.

4

A Perfect Little Doll

Rose Marie was born in the September of 1918. It was a darker time even than when Jack arrived. We didn't only have the war still dragging on and our men far from home, we had the influenza too, and that was on our very doorstep. We hardly left the house. There was such a panic on that Herself didn't even go to Mass. Cook went out in a gauze mask to do the marketing, and the laundry woman was told not to come, for the duration, because she was in and out of different houses all the time. There was no telling what germs she might carry with her. Mr. K slept on an army cot at the shipyard most nights sooner than risk bringing the infection home. Some people said the docks were where it had started.

No one we knew in Brookline got sick, but the Ericksons' gardener reckoned there was a four-week wait for funerals in Boston, there were so many bodies to bury, and after it was over, I heard that Marimichael Donnelly had been one of them, ironing sheets in the afternoon and dead by midnight. Three little ones left without a mammy. To think she left Ballynagore to finish up like that. She was strong as an ox, Marimichael, but that was the thing about that influenza. It carried off the strong and didn't touch the babies and the old folks.

Before Rosie was born, Mrs. Kennedy decided she needed an extra nursery maid. She hired Fidelma Clery. Flame-red hair and terrible, crooked little teeth. I was glad of the help. Young Jack caught every cough and cold that was going, and Joseph Patrick had the very devil in him, always climbing into trouble and tormenting Jack and taking his toys.

"Why is he still a baby?" he used to ask. "When will he be big enough to fight me?"

His Honor was the one who encouraged fighting, play-boxing with him, showing him how to put up his little dukes.

Mrs. K gave Fidelma the gospel on nursery routines to read, but I know she never opened it. Fidelma was a bit hazy when it came to reading. Every time she told the story of the Gingerbread Man, it ended different. But she had enough common sense to get by, and the first time Joseph Patrick gave her any trouble, she picked him up, hollering and kicking, and carried him to his room like a roll of linoleum.

The weekly nurse came a few days before the baby was due, and Mrs. K started her pains right on time, same as she did everything else. Everything was going along nicely and I quite thought we'd be cleared away by teatime with the baby safe in her crib, but when it came time to send for the doctor, he couldn't be reached. He'd been called away to somebody with complications, and you couldn't send for any other doctor. They were all run off their feet with influenza cases.

I said, "It hardly matters. It's her third child. She knows what to do."

The nurse said, "It does matter. If the doctor isn't here when it's born he won't get his fee and then I'll be for it."

It seemed to me you couldn't do much to stop a baby if it was ready to come, but she was the nurse and I was only there to help. So we tied Mrs. K's knees together with a scarf and the nurse instructed her that whatever she did she mustn't bear down when she got one of her urges. She was a model patient. I never heard her cry out once. And that's how we kept Rose Marie from being born until Dr. Good arrived, bounding up the stairs with his ether mask.

I loved all my Kennedy babies for their different funny little ways, but Rosie was the real beauty among them. She'd a mop of black hair and big green eyes and she was so contented. She'd lie in her crib for hours, smiling at the world and playing with any little toy you gave her. Not like Jack, always crying. Not like Joe, always looking for trouble.

If I'd been Mrs. K I'd have been up in the nursery gazing at Rosie all day long. She was like a perfect little doll and Herself loves dolls. Sure she has a whole room full of them at Hyannis, all in their glass cases. But she didn't trouble us much in the nursery. She preferred to be down at her bureau, clipping out articles on how children should be raised and making lists of things that had to be seen to. Timetables, charts for their weight, charts for their teeth.

Joseph Patrick was forever asking why did I live with them.

"Don't you have a mother and a daddy?" he used to say. "This is my house. But when I go to school you can still stay here. You can look after Rosie."

I wasn't sure I would be staying, because me and Jimmy Swords were sort of engaged. Frankie Mulcahy was back from Pennsylvania and Margaret wanted us to name the day as soon as Jimmy came home. A double wedding at Most Holy Redeemer and then to Mazzucca for ice-cream sundaes. She had it all planned. But Jimmy didn't come back from Flanders in a marrying frame of mind.

He said, "What's the point? Bringing more kids into the world. Cannon fodder for another war. Factory fodder for the bosses. It's all shite."

He'd got in with a lot of socialists in his battalion, putting the world to rights while they were waiting to be sent up the line to fight the Bosch.

I said, "I thought we'd won this war so there won't ever be another one. And what'd happen if everybody had your attitude? There'd be no more babies. Nobody to look after you when you're in your bath chair."

He said, "I'm not going to be in a bath chair. I'll put a bullet in my brain sooner. And I'm not getting married. It's nothing personal, Nora. You can keep the ring."

Silly beggar. He'd never given me a ring.

I did wonder, had he met someone else, somebody prettier. One of those French mam'zelles. Mammy always said it was a good thing I had my health and strength, because my face would never make my fortune. I wasn't exactly heartbroken over Jimmy but I did stop looking in the mirror. Looking in the mirror could make a girl dissatisfied.

Ursie said, "Never mind. You're better off staying single. You've a nice little job and a roof over your head and that's more than Margaret'll ever have. Frankie Mulcahy isn't fit to mind a canary, never mind a wife and family. There'll be a baby every year and never enough money to pay the electric. You'll see. She'll be broken down and worn out. So don't break your heart over Jimmy Swords. You've had a lucky escape."

Margaret didn't have a baby every year though. Nothing happened on that front for a long time. And as for Jimmy, I don't know that Ursie was right. He was a good man. It was just that the war had chewed him up and spat him out, bitter and twisted. When Ursie said these things, you always had to keep in mind that she was probably a disappointed woman, on the quiet. She worshipped her Mr. Jauncey and yet all he ever did was say, "Take a letter, Miss Brennan."

Poor Ursie and her little two-cup teapot.

Rosie sat up at six months, same as Jack did, but she wasn't interested in walking or talking. She was happy just to sit and watch the world go by. Mrs. K said we were to stimulate her more, talk to her, and pull her up onto her feet to give her the idea of walking.

Fidelma said, "There's not a thing wrong with her. She only seems quiet because you're used to the boys racketing about. If you ask me we should be thankful. She never gives us a minute's trouble."

Mrs. K said, "I didn't ask you, Fidelma. And I want particular attention paid to Rose Marie's activities. We can't have her falling behind."

Well, Rosie got up and walked when she was good and ready, and she talked too. She just didn't put herself out. If you threw her a ball she'd pick it up and look at it, but it never occurred to her to throw it back. And when Mr. K came up to the nursery he didn't seem to know what to do with her. The boys would clamber all over him begging to be tickled to death. Rosie would just sit smiling at him, holding back.

Later on, Mrs. K made quite a project of Rosie, tutoring her for hours on end to try and get her up to the mark with her reading and writing, but in those early days Joseph Patrick was her big project.

"He's the foundation stone," she said. "If the oldest child is brought along correctly, the others will follow suit."

Everything she did was in aid of Joseph Patrick growing up the brightest scholar and a champion sportsman and a Light of Christ altar boy. She took him to the Franklin Park Zoo one afternoon to set the scene and tell him about the poor Christian martyrs, but when he came home all he did was keep springing out at Jack and Rosie, playing at killer lions. Well, he was only four.

She kept up with all the new books that were brought out, too, and fetched them from the lending library to read to them, but when I was left to read them a story they always wanted their old favorite, about Billy Whiskers the Goat. It had been given them by their aunt Loretta Kennedy and they loved that book, but Herself thought it was a dreadful story for children. She said it encouraged naughtiness instead of obedience and she threw it in the trash can. Fidelma slipped out the back and rescued it. It had a wee bit of bacon grease on the cover but we kept it for a special secret treat when Mother was out shopping.

After the Armistice, Mr. K had gone back to his own business. Import and export, according to Mrs. Kennedy, and finance. He was always up early. He'd do his morning exercises and then look in on the nursery on his way down to breakfast, showered and suited and ready for the off. Sometimes we'd only see him on Monday morning and then he'd be gone all week, busy with meetings in the city.

Herself used to say, "I sleep so lightly. My husband doesn't like to come in late and disturb the whole house. When you're in business, you see, you have to be prepared to put in long hours."

Fidelma reckoned it was showgirls he was busy with, though at the time he didn't seem the type to me. He didn't smoke and he never took drink.

She'd say, "Sure, the clean-living ones are the worst. There's one thing none of them will go without and I don't think Your Man gets much of that at home, do you? Only when she's ready to get knocked up again. Do you think she puts him on her schedule? Joe's yearly treat? The poor bugger. No wonder he works late."

She liked him back then. We all did. He was fair and friendly and you could see his children were the light of his life.

Whatever it was that kept him in town so much, he was certainly making money. Anything that took Mrs. K's fancy she could have. We were the first house on Beals Street to get an electric carpet-beater and a phonograph. I don't know that Mrs. K got much joy from it though. She reckoned she was the musical one in her family, and Mr. Kennedy bought her a grand piano, but you hardly ever saw her sit and pick out a tune. Fidelma was the one who sang to the babies. Mrs. K never had friends around for tea or went visiting with the neighbors. If she saw them in the street, a crisp "Good day" was all she ever gave them. I suppose she knew they looked down their noses at her. Brookline people didn't like flash. When they saw a big new icebox being carried up the steps, they thought it was a sign you had more money than sense.

The only company she had was Father Creagh from St. Aidan's, and Mr. and Mrs. Moore, an older couple who sometimes came for bridge on a weekend. Eddie Moore worked for Mr. K, as his right-hand man, and a sort of friend too. If Mr. K trusted anyone to know about his business affairs, it was Eddie Moore. And Mrs. Moore was a kind, motherly sort, quite happy to chat to Herself about the baby's new tooth.

Fidelma said to Mrs. K once, "You know, Mrs. Erickson gives tea parties and the nursemaids are all invited too, with the babies, so the children can mix and have company. Shouldn't you like to do that, Mrs. Kennedy?"

"No," she said, "I would not. My children have each other for company and I'm far too busy for tea parties."

But the busyness was all created out of nothing. She set herself a schedule the same as she did for the babies. She had a time for reading the newspapers, clipping out stories and underlining things with her fountain pen. "Conversational topics" she called them. Then she had a regular time for doing her exercises, to get her waistline back in trim if she'd just had a baby, or a brisk walk to post her letters, if she was expecting again.

She wrote a lot of letters, though I don't know who to, and she read French literature too, to improve her mind. And there was her hour in the nursery every day, bending my ear. She loved to talk about when she'd been her Daddy's First Lady, the places she'd been, the people she'd met.

"Did I ever tell you about the time His Honor and I had luncheon with President Taft?" she'd say. "The President said I was the prettiest face he'd seen since he entered the White House. He had me sit right next to him."

And if she heard Fidelma humming a waltz, "Oh Fidelma, dear heart," she'd say. "You quite take me back to Vienna. Did I ever tell you about my trip to Europe with His Honor? We were treated like royalty. Receptions, balls. I had so many beaux. I could have married a Count or a Lord. I could have had my pick."

Well, those days were over. She'd taken her pick and she had a model house and a nursery full of bonny babies to show for it, but I don't know how much pleasure it brought her. She never sat by the fire with a little one on her lap, just to enjoy the lisping and the softness of them.

Fidelma used to say, "She's a sad creature. I could feel sorry for her if only I didn't."

By the time Rosie had her first birthday, Herself was expecting again, due in February, but then just after Christmas something happened.

Mr. K was gone ten days straight, not even home for Sunday dinner he had so much business to attend to, and Herself was getting more and more quarrelsome, coming up to the nursery, wanting everything in the hot press refolded, picking over the layette and finding fault. Then two suitcases appeared in the downstairs hall and His Honor's car came to fetch her.

She said, "I'm going to visit with my family. The babies will have to stay here though. My sister's very sick so we mustn't take any risks."

And off she went. Mrs. Moore came round that evening and every other evening, checking that we hadn't burned the place to the ground.

I said, "When will she be back?"

She said, "Mrs. Kennedy's gone for a little vacation but you can call me at any hour. My husband is in contact with Mr. Kennedy."

Fidelma said, "This is some family. He's left her, and now she's left us. Let's go down and see what's in the liquor cabinet."

The Ericksons' cook said it was the talk of the neighborhood that Mr. K was probably in jail or on the run from somebody he'd scalped, but Fidelma was likely nearer the mark. She said, "There'll be a chorus girl at the bottom of this. And can you blame the man? Herself and her card files, they'd take the shine off anybody's day."

Whether there was a girl in the picture that time I never knew, but he'd certainly been in Florida and come back with a spring in his step and two sets of tropical whites to be taken to the dry cleaner.

"Palm Beach is quite a place," he said. "The weather's perfect and if you stand in the lobby of the Royal Poinciana, sooner or later everybody who's anybody'll walk by."

He didn't seem fazed to have come home to an empty house.

He said Mrs. K was taking a well-earned rest and would soon be back, but the days went by and there was no sign of her. The weekly nurse arrived to get things ready for the birth and we had everything she needed except the expectant mother. Mr. K was all smiles and sunshine with us, but I heard him on the telephone, giving out to His Honor.

"Did you put her up to this?" he said. "You must be encouraging her, Fitz. She's not an effing child anymore. She has responsibilities. She has three children here keep asking for her."

Which wasn't true at all. They never asked for her.

He said, "Now you listen to me. Tell her she has to come home right now. Whatever it is she wants, she can have. More help. A new car. She can go on trips. I don't effing care, just send her home before there's any more talk. Tell her Jack's not well."

Jack was hot and cranky, wanted to sleep all the time but couldn't settle. When Herself turned up in the Mayor's limousine, brought home like the Queen of Sheba, he wouldn't even get off the daybed to give her a kiss. Then the rash came in and he got hotter yet so that even the sponge baths didn't help. It was the scarlet fever. Dr. Good said the best thing, as there was a new baby due any minute, was for him to be nursed at the hospital. Fidelma was sent to sit with him, although I know he cried for me and that fair broke my heart. It brought back to me the time when Nellie had the measles, tossing and turning on her cot, with a blanket nailed across the window because the least bit of light hurt her eyes. We'd all had the measles. It didn't occur to us Nellie wouldn't get over it. Ursie and Dada were sitting with her when she slipped away. Me and Deirdre were out on the back step playing five stones and we heard Dada start keening.

Deirdre said, "I think the angel came for our Nellie." And she just carried on playing. Mrs. Donnelly crossed the road later on, to help wash Nellie and make her tidy and we waked her the whole night before they put the lid on her box. God, I willed her and willed her till I thought I'd bust to open her eyes and stop playacting. It was just Mr. Donnelly helped Dada carry her casket up to the graveyard. I suppose she weighed no more than a wren.

Kathleen Agnes was born on February 20, 1920. She had blue eyes and the Kennedy ginger hair, and she was born with no difficulties at all, which was just as well, because everybody's mind was on poor wee Jack. Mr. K got up even earlier in the morning, so he could get through with his business and then take a turn at Jack's bedside to relieve Fidelma. He was very good like that, for a man.

He said, "Damn it, Nora. The little feller just lies there and there's not a thing I can do to help him. It's more than I can stand. I'm used to being able to fix things for my family."

I said, "I'm sure it comforts him to see your face. And you can always say a prayer for him. God's help is nearer than the door."

"Is that right?" he said. "Well, praying is more Mrs. Kennedy's department."

5

A Washer and a Dryer and Separate Beds

Mrs. Kennedy had been promised anything at all she wanted if she'd only come home and do her wifely duty, and when she got up from her childbed she wrung the pips out of that promise. First she got a shiny new Packard sedan and her own personal driver. She picked out Danny Walsh from all the men who applied, and it must have been more on account of his height and his wide shoulders than his personal qualities. He was a bigger gossip even than Fidelma Clery and he'd a foul mouth on him when Herself wasn't within earshot. Then, after the car and the driver were settled, she went for a rest cure. Fidelma was up to Poland Springs with Jack, for his recuperation. She could easily have gone with them and given the child some attention, but she went down to Virginia instead, to the Greenbrier resort, just her and her sister Agnes and a pile of novelettes.

I thought, You're a queer fish, no mistake. Blessed with another bonny baby and the first thing you do is go away from her.

It was all I could do not to sit in the rocking chair all day with one or other of them in my arms. But not Mrs. K.

"And when I get back from Virginia," she said, "we'll be moving house. This place is far too small for us now."

We shifted only a few blocks, to Naples Road. We were still handy for St. Aidan's, and for Joseph Patrick to go to the Devotion School, and Mr. and Mrs. Moore moved into the Beals Street house, so it stayed in the family, in a manner of speaking. We had all the conveniences at the new house. A motorized washing machine and a hot-air clothes dryer just for the use of the nursery, radiator heating, the latest gas range, and nice big closets for all the toys and coats and boots. The garden was bigger and there was a wide stoop too, so the children could get their fresh air even on rainy days. And there were bedrooms enough for Mrs. K to have her own private accommodations. From the day we moved that's how they lived. Mr. K had his room and she had hers. She was expecting again though before the year was out.

Fidelma reckoned he had two appointments a year, like the children going to the dentist.

And that was about the size of it. I remember, years later, when Kick used to play with little Nancy Tenney up at Hyannis, she came home from the Tenney house one day scandalized.

"Nora," she said, "don't tell anyone, but Mr. and Mrs. Tenney have to sleep in the same bed! Do you think they're too poor to get a bigger house?"

God love her.

Once Joe started school, there were never enough hours in the day, taking him and bringing him home. We'd push Kick in the bassinet, with Jack walking and Rosie on her tricycle, but she'd forget to pedal and get left way behind. I thought the easiest thing was for me and Fidelma to take turns going to the school and for one of us to stay home with Rosie, but Mrs. K wouldn't have it.

She said it was for Rosie's own good that she be made to pedal and not just sit in the nursery like a pudding.

Once a week she'd go to the school herself and quiz the teachers on what Joe had been learning. None of the other mammies did it, but she said she had to know what he was doing in school so she could build on it at home.

"Joe's exceptionally bright," she'd say. "He needs more than the average child."

Well, Joe was forward in some respects, but only because he had it dinned into him night and day that he was the oldest and the others would expect to follow his lead. He was no great student. Euny turned out to be the only scholar in the family. But Joseph Patrick was talked up, no matter what little thing he achieved, and every drawing he did, Mr. K kept in a special folder.

He said, "Anything he brings home from school, Nora, I want to see it. These'll be of historical interest when he gets to be president."

Joe brought home more than works of art though. We went through all the diseases that first year he was in school. Measles, whooping cough, the chicken pox. Five minutes and he'd be on the mend, bouncing on his bed and shinning up the drapes, but Jack was laid low by everything. Even if it was just a head cold, Jack would end up with the bronchitis. I didn't spend many nights in my own bed. Whenever I smell friar's balsam I think of that winter of 1920, how bone-tired I was, nodding off in the nursery chair, one eye on the steam kettle and the other on little Mr. Congressman Jack Kennedy.

Straight after Christmas Mr. K took off for Florida again, with Mr. Moore for company. They were going on business, but it was the kind of business you could do on a golf course. In those days Herself never went with him.

She used to say, "I'd be bored. There's no culture in Palm Beach. Some women are content to play canasta and go to the hairdresser's, but that's not my idea of filling each shining hour. I've traveled to Europe, you see, Nora. I've seen rather more of the world than most."

She changed her tune about Palm Beach later on, of course. After they bought Gueroda, she never missed a winter, and anyway, whatever this "culture" was she said they didn't have, I don't think there was a lot of it occurring on Naples Road either. Ursie said it meant museums and concert halls. Well, there were enough of those in Boston, but Mrs. Kennedy wasn't a big attender. She stayed in her room, doing her waistline exercises and leafing through the magazines for Paris fashions she could get copied on Boylston Street.

Fidelma used to say if she had half Mrs. Kennedy's money she'd have been down to New York every week, buying furs and seeing the new shows, not sitting in Brookline, clipping articles out of the *Ladies' Home Journal* and going round turning off lights.

Eunice was born in the summer of '21, named for Mrs. Kennedy's younger sister. The sickly one. Herself didn't nurse Euny though. From Kick on, the babies had bottles so Mrs. K wouldn't be tied down. She started traveling, up to Maine or all the way to Colorado, and then when His Honor announced he'd be running for governor, she was off to his campaign rooms three or four days a week, with a real sparkle in her eye. I wouldn't have voted for him if you'd offered me a big gold watch, but you could see why a lot of people did. He wore a beautiful Crombie overcoat, to remind you he was a man who'd done well for himself, and a beaten-up fedora hat, so as you wouldn't think he'd grown too grand, and he was a master with the flimflam. He told me the Fitzgeralds were from dear old Westmeath, just like me, but then he told Danny Walsh they were from dear old Limerick.

Danny said, "Fidelma, tell him your name's Esposito. Let's see what dear old place the bugger claims he's from then."

But for all his patter, His Honor didn't get Governor. There had been gossip about backhanders and womanizing and other things that had happened in the past. I don't know. He probably wasn't any worse than the rest of the Boston pols. His grandbabies loved him, that's for sure, and there were weeks when they saw more of him than they did of their Mammy or their Daddy. He'd take the boys ice-skating in the winter and then to Durgin Park for a baked-bean dinner, and in the summer he'd take them to the Gardens, for a ride on a swan boat, or the whole tribe of us would meet him at Walden Pond, to paddle our feet and fish for perch. Never Mrs. Fitzgerald though. She hardly seemed to leave her house. But you could depend on having a good time if His Honor had organized things. Always a laugh and a song and plenty to eat and drink. It's funny a man like that should have produced a prim little body like Rose Kennedy.

The children saw Mr. K's folks most weeks too, driving out to Winthrop after Mass to have Sunday dinner, but I could count on the fingers of one hand the times any of the Kennedys visited with us. All I know is Herself hadn't an ounce of respect for her in-laws, and all because old Mrs. Kennedy had a tendency to stoutness. They say old Mr. Kennedy was cut from a very different cloth than Mayor Fitzgerald. He didn't have the blarney. He didn't find occasion to rub up against nursery maids, unlike His Honor, who was forever playing bumps-a-daisy if Fidelma Clery was to be believed.

I said, "I don't have any trouble with him."

"Well, Nora," she said, "that's because you don't have magnificent bosoms."

Maybe so, but that's no great loss I'm sure. Mammy always reckoned the world would be a calmer place if women didn't have so many curves. Anyway, I had my moments. Gabe Nolan, who drove for Mr. K, and Danny Walsh. They were both sweet enough on me. New Year's, St. Patrick's, I had my share of getting loved up.

6

Two-Toilet Irish

It had been good for Jack to have Joseph Patrick going off to school every morning. It left him cock of the walk for a few hours, with his sisters looking up to him. Once Jack started school, he was back in Joe's shadow. Mrs. K said it didn't matter. She said having an older brother who was strong and fast and smart would make Jack push himself all the harder to match him, but that wasn't how it worked. Jack was a lazy little tyke. He knew he couldn't beat Joseph Patrick, he knew all he was expected to be was the president's wee brother, so he hardly tried. Young Joe would pick a fight and they'd be like a pair of terrier dogs for five minutes till he had Jack pinned to the floor. The times I had to separate them, before bones got broken. You could have made two Jacks out of Joe. And Jack would never cry, no matter how much he was hurting. He'd wait till Joe was out of earshot and then say something about him, to raise a laugh from Kick and Rosie.

There was no new baby in '22. Betty, who came in to do the laundry, reckoned she always knew when romance was in the air, because Mrs. K would have a silk peignoir laid out on her day-bed, and that hadn't been sighted since before Euny. It seemed as if Herself had shut up shop, and who could blame her. As she said, she'd been blessed with two fine boys and two fine girls, and Rosie.

Rosie was always tagged on at the end.

We'd be getting out of the motor to go in to Mass and Herself would say, "Joe, you take Euny, hold her by the hand. Jack, you take Kick. Nora will bring Rosie."

"We're playing at Olympic Games," Kick would say. "Rosie can watch."

They sent her to the kindergarten at the Devotion School, but she'd have been happier left at home for another year, playing with her dollies. She couldn't get the hang of writing her name, nor even of holding the pencil properly. Mrs. K had her up to her room for an hour every day, writing out words for her to copy, but if you ask me, it made her worse. You could have her write out "cat" a hundred times, and by next morning, if you asked her what it said, she'd guess "dog" or "efilant," as she called it. "Efilant" drove Mrs. K crazy. She thought it was just a sloppy, baby way of speaking, but I don't think Rosie ever noticed how the rest of the world said "elephant."

Sure we all have our funny little ways. Fidelma always misses seven when she's counting. My sister Margaret still talks about "the electric gas lighting." But funny little ways didn't amuse Mrs. K.

We didn't get a new baby in '23 either. As soon as we were back from vacationing at Cape Cod though, Mrs. K did make an appointment to see Dr. Good, and he told her there'd be a new arrival the following spring. But 1923 was a year of funerals. Mr. K's mother's was the first. She'd just faded away with stomach pains, till there was nothing left of her. They said the procession brought the traffic to a halt in Winthrop, the biggest funeral there in living memory, and it wasn't for anything the old lady had ever done. They turned out as a mark of respect for old Mr. Kennedy and his loss. Ursie was very impressed. She cut the obituary out of the newspaper and sent a copy to Edmond and one to Deirdre, all the way to Africa. *Nora's people, Irish but very high up* she wrote on it, in red ink.

Then Mrs. K's sister Eunice passed over. It was the tuberculosis. She'd been up and down to a sanatorium for years, so it came as no great surprise and Herself hardly missed a beat. She went to the funeral in the morning and to the dressmaker's in the afternoon, and I never saw her shed a tear. Me and Fidelma did. We didn't know the poor creature, but twenty-three is no age, whoever you are.

My brother-in-law Frankie's mother was the final one, on Christmas Eve, of all days. Mrs. Mulcahy was always the one for the big entrances and exits. The day Margaret and Frankie got married she was twenty minutes late to the church, like she was the blushing bride herself, then she drank so much honey wine at the wedding breakfast she had to be wheeled home on a cart borrowed from the fish market and put to bed. She swore it had happened in error. Every time I saw her she said, "You know, Nora, I'm a total abstainer, so that wedding beverage must have been doctored."

Mrs. K gave me a half day to go up to Our Lady of Mount Carmel for the Requiem Mass. Margaret and Frankie had always had to make do with two rooms in Mrs. Mulcahy's house, so I thought they'd be thrilled to have the place to themselves at long last, but Margaret had already decided they'd take in lodgers.

She said, "The money'll come in handy."

So they let two rooms to a nice-seeming Italian couple but they didn't last long. Margaret couldn't stand the racket they made, shouting and banging doors and clattering pans, and then by the spring Margaret was expecting and she couldn't stand the smell of all the onions they cooked, so the Italians had to go.

Ursie said, "Well, now you're in a fine state, Margaret. How are you going to manage the rent on Frankie's money? Can you depend on his lungs not letting him down?"

Margaret said, "I don't know. No more than you know if your Mr. Jauncey is going to fall downstairs and break his neck and leave you out of a job. You could drive yourself into the loony bin thinking like that."

Ursie had got a new laugh since she left Ballynagore. Very quiet and superior, like there was a joke only she got.

They say it's a hard thing to be the eldest child, but it's never appeared to give Ursie any trouble. She bossed us when we were playing with our dollies and she bosses us still, putting us straight, or so she thinks. The only one of six to rise to a job with a desk. You'd think it was General Electric she was running. But what's more important, raising a new generation, rearing children like my Kennedys, who'll likely amount to something, or watering Mr. Jauncey's African violet and jumping every time he buzzes his buzzer? I'd not trade with Ursie for a pot of gold.

She said, "You must keep in mind, Margaret, I'm with the firm of Holkum, Holkum and Jauncey, established 1884, so my position is entirely different to yours. I just ask myself why you had to rush into bringing another hungry mouth into the world."

I said, "She's hardly rushed. Four years married before she started a baby. Look at my Mrs. Kennedy. She's the exact same age as Margaret and she's got number six on the way."

Ursie said, "Mrs. Kennedy is the wife of a wealthy financier, not a fish porter."

I said, "Well, this baby won't go short of fish suppers, and if things go bad, won't you and me throw in a few dollars? A pair of old maids like us, what else do we have to spend it on? And I think it's grand we'll have a little baby in the family. I only wonder you waited as long as you did, Margaret."

"Oh," she said, "it wasn't that I didn't want a baby, only I could never have done a thing like that with Mother Mulcahy in the next room."

Rudolf Valentino Mulcahy was born November 1. If he'd been mine I'd have given him a proper name, like John or Michael, but Margaret was crazy for the moving films. She'd have been down to the Diamond nickelodeon every night if she'd had her way, her and all the other women from Maverick Street. I suppose that's what Mr. K saw coming when he branched out from the medicinal liquors and started buying picture palaces. He seemed to have a nose for where the money would be going next. Gin, racetracks, talking pictures. Joe Kennedy had more schemes than Carter had liver pills. And the new businesses meant we saw even less of him. He'd be gone for weeks on end, to New York City or Miami, Florida, and whenever he was away we were guaranteed to see more of Mayor Fitzgerald.

The Dawsons' nursemaid down the street used to say, "I see the old crook was visiting again. I suppose that means the young crook's out of town."

I ignored her. Making money is no crime.

And when Mr. K did come home he did it in style, collected at the railroad station in his Rolls-Royce motor, with Gabe Nolan in a peaked cap and jodhpurs with a stripe down the side. There was a lot of snickering among the neighbors about Mr. Kennedy's car but it was nothing but jealousy. All those Fullers and Dawsons and Warrenders thought they were a cut above.

I used to say to Fidelma, "I've a mind to go out barefoot today. Wrap myself in an old shawl and give them snoots next door a good dose of the begorrahs, so."

"Two-toilet Irish," they called the Kennedys. Well, God may have been an Episcopalian on Naples Road, but it was a Catholic who had the gold Rolls-Royce.

7

Three Categories of Feeble-mindedness

Baby Patricia was born in May of 1924, but she was a month old before her daddy even saw her. We all went to meet him off the train from New York. Rosie with a painting she'd done for him, Joe tormenting Jack in the back of the car, arms and legs flying, and Kick and Euny hanging out of the window like a pair of ragamuffins, shouting, "Daddy! We got another sister!"

Rosie was being tutored at home at that time. They'd tried her at the Edward Devotion, where the boys went, and they'd tried her at the parish school, but she couldn't keep up. She got top marks for good behavior and effort and a special mention for her dancing, but it was too much for her. She'd toil home on her chubby little legs, dragging behind the bassinet, hardly able to keep her eyes open, school fatigued her so.

Mrs. K did a lot of reading up on slow children and then she took her to see a special doctor in New Jersey, the big expert, Dr. Henry Herbert Goddard. She came back wearing her tough-nut

47

face, the one I've seen on her a thousand times, when any other woman would break down and cry.

She said, "It isn't good news, Nora, but I'm determined we can beat this. We just have to make greater efforts with Rosie."

She had it all written down, what this Dr. Goddard had said. Three categories of feeble-mindedness. Idiots, who were the worst, then imbeciles and then morons. As far as he could estimate, Rosie was only a moron.

Mrs. K said, "At least she's in the top category. Dr. Goddard says idiots have to wear diapers all their lives."

Well, I had my Rosie out of diapers before she was two.

She said, "Morons are harder to deal with though because they look so normal. As they grow up they have to be watched every minute or they get into all kinds of difficulties. Do you see what I mean?"

I didn't see what she meant at all.

I said, "I know she's the sunniest child I ever looked after."

"Precisely," she said. "She's amiable and eager to please and when she's older men will take advantage."

I said, "Well, that's a long way down the road. She's only six."

"But something to think about nonetheless," she said. "We have to keep her safe from men because she must never have babies."

I couldn't see why. She was just grand with Euny and baby Pat. And if Herself was anything to go by, too much brains and education only made for a restless mother.

"We have to develop what little gifts she has," she said.

I said, "She has the gift of contentment and that's no small thing. It's like a monkey house upstairs when they come in from school, but Rosie'll sit in a corner and play for hours making a tea party with the dolly cups and saucers."

She said, "I know, dear heart, I know. But I'm determined to get her reading and writing, whatever Dr. Goddard says. Perseverance pays dividends. And you're very good with her, Nora. I don't know what we'd do without you."

Fidelma said, "You should have asked her for a raise."

But Mrs. K didn't give raises, only job security, and variety, because those Kennedy children were like a box of Candy Allsorts. Young Joe was tall and strong, like his Daddy, and Pat looked likely to turn out the same way. Kick was thicker-set, but she had Mr. K's freckles, same as Jack did. Euny was the one that most favored Mrs. K, especially when she smiled, not that that happened so often. She was as skinny as a string bean, wouldn't eat, couldn't sleep. Euny just lived on her nerves.

And Rosie was the beauty. She had milky skin and lovely dimpled arms you could just have taken a bite out of.

"Fat," Mrs. K called it. "We must watch Rosie's line or she'll end up looking like a tubby little peasant."

Mrs. K kept herself as trim as a candle and she expected everybody else to do the same. The children were weighed regular as clockwork and Rosie was the only one who ever got a black mark. Jack had to have extra malt and cod liver oil, to build him up, and Euny got extra bread and potatoes to try and put a bit of flesh on her, but many a time Rosie had her rations cut, to try and slim her down. I didn't approve of it myself. I like to see a child enjoying her food, not corrected just for the way God made her.

I had all the girls in matching outfits. They looked a picture, lined up ready to go to Mass on Sunday morning. Wool coats with bonnets and muffs for the cold weather, and cotton print dresses in the summer, with white ankle socks and Mary Janes. But when we went to the seashore, they wore any old rags, just shorts and vests, first up, best dressed, and they ran around barefoot, brown as tinkers.

When I first worked for the Kennedys, we'd go to a different place every year, but once we'd tried Hyannis we took the same cottage again and again.

Mrs. K's driver said, "Know why we're going to Hyannis again? Because Your Man was turned down for the country club at Cohasset."

I said, "And how would you know a thing like that?"

"Because Herself told me," he said, "when I was driving her into town. She said it was because the Cohasset doesn't take Catholics, but if you ask me it's more likely they'd heard about him running whiskey. And do you know why he got in at Hyannis? Because they're not so toffee-nosed down there. They saw the color of his money and didn't bother to inquire where he got it."

I said, "So they're no more particular than you are, Danny Walsh."

"No, well," he said. "I'm only saying."

You have to be very careful with hired help. I wouldn't want servants if they were giving them away with Oxydol.

8

Learning the Ways of the Enemy

Bobby was born eighteen months after Pat. He was another one looked like a skinned rabbit, same as Jack. We thought he'd be the last.

Fidelma said, "She'll tie a knot in her hanky now. Sure, she only kept going to get another boy."

I thought so too. She was tired of it all by then, even though she had me and Fidelma in the nursery and all the help she wanted in the house. Poor Bobby. He loved to be allowed up to her room, to sit on her bed and watch her get dressed for dinner, but there were times when I thought she'd forgotten she'd ever had him. Rosie was the only one in the family who ever petted him.

Kick was at St. Aidan's, in first grade, and Euny was just starting in the kindergarten. Joe and Jack were day boys at Nobles down in Dedham. Herself would have liked them all taught by the Sisters, but Mr. K said the boys had to go to a top-drawer school and start mixing with Protestants.

He said, "When you intend to go places it's never too early to study the competition and learn the ways of the enemy."

There was talk though that we might leave Boston altogether. Mr. K was doing more and more with the moving-picture business, on the train once a month to Hollywood, California. Danny Walsh said it was quite on the cards that we'd be shifting there, getting a house on the same street as all the movie stars.

He kept saying, "That'll give Brookline something to think about."

As if Brookline gave two cents about the Kennedys. The children were at the age when they should have been having friends round to play, but the neighbors were very standoffish.

Mrs. K always said they didn't need other children because they had each other, but it didn't seem natural to me. That's why I loved going to Hyannis for the summer. Every blessed minute didn't have to be regimented when we were there.

As long as they worked hard at their sailing lessons and their swimming, they were left to run free the rest of the time and they did mix with other children, Kick especially. The first thing she'd do when we got to the cottage was race round to see if Nancy Tenney was at home, and Rosie'd tag along with her. Mrs. Tenney might have been a friend for Mrs. K too. The Tenneys were a nice family, no airs and graces, but Herself wouldn't socialize. She'd get Danny to run her to early Mass at St. Francis Xavier, then she'd be reading in her room or going for her swim, no matter how cold the water. Two or three times a week she'd go to the golf course, but just to play by herself, for the exercise, not for company, as Mr. K did.

Danny said, "And do you know what she does? She slips onto the course at the seventh and plays the same half a dozen holes over and over. She seems to think she's saving money if she's not seen going out from the clubhouse. Worrying about green fees with all the money she's got."

That was her. Penny-mean. I know for a fact she spent five hundred dollars on her outfit for her sister Agnes's wedding but we were only allowed forty-watt lightbulbs in the nursery.

Very often Mr. Kennedy would be away a month at a time, but he'd write to the children, and always a proper personal letter to each of them, not like Herself, who sent them carbon copies when she went traveling. And then when the word came that he was on his way home, you'd have thought the president himself was expected, the children got so excited. They'd all go along to his dressing room, first thing, to watch him shave and tell him everything that had happened while he'd been gone, and then he'd read the funnies with them before they went down to breakfast. Captain Easy and Tailspin Tommy. It was like a holiday for me and Fidelma the mornings Mr. K was at home.

He always brought them presents when he came home from a trip, but only little things. A scouting knife or a Spaldine ball, or picture postcards of the movie stars. The only extravagance was the time he brought Tom Mix cowboy costumes, with the kerchiefs signed by the great man himself. They were intended for Joe and Jack, and they caused nothing but trouble, because Kick helped herself to one of the hats and wouldn't be parted from it. Joe usually behaved nicely around his sisters, but he lit into her as though she was some boy in the schoolyard and he wouldn't be pacified till he got his cowboy hat.

When Mr. K had been away, he'd want to know about what they'd been up to, chapter and verse. How they'd been getting on in school or at the sailing club if we were up to Hyannis. Joseph Patrick won at everything he turned his hand to and so did Euny. Kick just enjoyed herself. If she won anything it was a happy accident, and Jack was the same. He could never quite be bothered to make that extra effort, even though he knew exactly what his Daddy would say.

"Don't let me hear you bragging about getting second place," he'd say. "All second place means is you have to try harder. First place is the only thing that counts. You're a Kennedy, remember, and Kennedys are winners!"

That was what they had drummed into them and they'd knock you flying to be first over the finishing line. I used to enjoy a game of checkers until the children got old enough to play. They'd study the board and try to distract you while you made your move, as if their lives depended on beating you. Rosie was the only one who wasn't like that. She didn't have the cunning to put one over on you, and anyway, she didn't really care. To her a game was just a pleasant way to pass half an hour, but naturally she did want to please her Daddy. She'd have loved to go running to him, to tell him she'd won at slapjack.

I'd say, "For the love of God, let her win, why don't you? Just once in a while?"

"Why should we?" they'd say. "What's the fun in that?"

"I'll try harder, Daddy," she used to say when she could get a word in edgewise.

"Good girl, Rosie," he'd say. "That's the right attitude."

He loved her, of course, but you could tell it irked him to see a child of his so slow. Sometimes it took her a while to think what she was going to say and he didn't have the patience to wait while she got her words out.

When Mrs. K took her up to her room to make her practice her letters he'd say, "You're a saint, Rosa darling."

He always called Herself "Rosa darling."

She'd come down on a Sunday morning, wearing one of her new rigs. "Looking like a million dollars, Rosa darling," he'd say, and then he'd run off to make one more phone call before we went to Mass.

I never saw him take her hand, though. She'd hang on his arm, gazing up at him, but he didn't pay her that kind of heed and neither did the children. When they all sat down to dinner he was the one they attended to.

"Dad said this, Dad thinks that" was all you'd hear.

I said to Jack one time, "And what did your Mammy have to say on the subject?"

"Mother?" he said, as if I'd asked him what the cat's opinion was. "Mother doesn't know about world events."

Everything about Joe Kennedy was lickety-split. You could practically hear the wheels turning in his brain. He'd be out on his deck exercising with his Indian clubs and he'd have a faraway look in his eye. Then as soon as he finished, he'd be on the telephone, barking out the day's orders to Joey Timilty or Eddie Moore. Timilty was Mr. K's fixer, according to Danny Walsh. Always carried a big fat roll of dollar bills. Eddie Moore was different, a kind of general manager, in on a lot of the meetings and phone calls.

But Gabe Nolan drove Mr. K, and he reckoned there was only one person who knew everything Joe Kennedy was up to and that was Joe Kennedy himself.

Gabe said, "He's like a shark, cruising around on his own. He goes in fast, makes his kill, and he's gone before they know what hit them. And all his money's spread around. If anybody goes looking for an office with J. P. Kennedy on the shingle or a bank account they'll be disappointed because there ain't any such thing."

But Eddie Moore was on the payroll, and Mrs. Moore was expected to be on call too, in case Herself got the urge to go down to Sulphur Springs for the waters or we had any catastrophes in the nursery. It was through Mrs. Moore we first got wind of the move.

She said, "How will you feel about leaving Boston, Nora? You'll miss your sisters, I'm sure."

Fidelma said, "Is it Hollywood we're going to? Are we going next door to any fillum stars?"

She said, "No, no, not Hollywood. That's not a fit place to raise children. You're going to New York. My husband's down there right now looking for a suitable property."

Fidelma had been to New York. She'd traveled there with the first family she worked for.

She said, "You'll love it, Nora. There's railways rumbling in the sky and railways rattling under your feet and eateries that stay open all night and shows with tunes you can sing. Not like this dead-and-alive hole. Still, I wish we could have gone to Hollywood. I might have got myself discovered."

Mrs. Moore was right, up to a point. There was one sister I was sorry to leave.

Margaret was expecting again. I'd have liked to be around to give her a hand, and there was little Val too. I loved to go and see him on my day off. Three's a grand age. Old enough to walk and not break your arms anymore, and too young to break your heart.

When we were girls, me and Margaret were always good pals. Edmond had the Donnelly boys, used to go fishing with them and rabbiting. Ursie preferred her own company, and Deirdre was away with the fairies. The wind would whine in the chimney and she'd say, "Do you hear the angels singing?" And if you got out the checkerboard to give her a game, she'd say, "Budge over, Nora. St. Bridget wants to sit there."

They say she's happy in Africa, love her. Maybe they all hear angel voices over there.

Ursie said, "New York is a wonderful opportunity for you. I'll give you a list of museums you must go to. You see, you're drawing the dividend of loyalty. Your Kennedys can't manage without you. Just like me and Mr. Jauncey."

Ursie and her Mr. Jauncey. He was all she ever talked about. How she kept his appointment book and remembered every little thing for him, even his wife's birthday. How he was the most respected lawyer in Boston and trusted her to see all his papers.

"I'm privy to all kinds of delicate things," she used to say, "but of course I'd never speak of them."

Margaret'd say, "Oh go on, Ursie, it won't go no further than these four walls. Tell us about one of his murders."

"Mr. Jauncey," she'd say, "is not that kind of lawyer. Mr. Jauncey is corporate."

She was first at her desk every morning and the last to leave at night. She said he called her his "office treasure."

Margaret said, "Has he ever asked you to be any other kind of treasure?"

"Don't be coarse, Margaret," she said. "Mr. Jauncey is a member of the Harvard Club."

She colored up though, so I reckon Margaret had touched a nerve.

I said, "No, but you must like him. What if Mrs. Jauncey was to pass over? What if he made you an offer? You know all his little ways. How many sugars he takes. Or do you like being an old maid?"

She said, "Mr. Jauncey doesn't take sugar. And I'm certainly not an old maid. I'm a personal and private secretary, I'm a member of the Altar Guild, and I get a very generous bonus at Christmas."

Well, but what does a Christmas bonus buy you when you've to go home to a boiled-egg dinner for one?

Margaret said, "You're a fine one to talk about old maids, Nora Brennan. Thirty-four and you spend your nights off playing Wincey Spider with my Val. You ought to be over Jimmy Swords by now."

I was over Jimmy Swords the minute I saw how hard his eyes had turned.

I said, "I get offers."

I did too. There was the Dawsons' driver, in Naples Road. There was Mitch, who taught the boys sailing up at Hyannis. I had my moments. But I had my seven Kennedys to consider too. I wasn't going to get silly in the head over some man.

9

Another Little Blessing

Mr. Kennedy said, "I've had it with Boston, Nora. A man can't do business in this town. Folks here have money but all they do is take it out of the safe-box once a year, count it and then put it back. Well, the hell with it. It's time for a change."

We moved to New York in the summer of 1927, but there weren't any railways rattling under our feet or theater lights like Fidelma Clery had said there'd be. We were out in the country, in a big rented house in Riverdale. If you stood on a chair at my bedroom window you could see over the treetops to the Hudson River. We had lawns and flower beds and neighbors you never saw because they went everywhere by motorcar. I don't believe anyone in Riverdale ever snubbed us. New York folk were too busy to care what line of business Mr. Kennedy was in or where we went to Mass. But considering how much he was worth, Mr. K seemed to think people were looking down on him. He always had to make the point.

"I wasn't one of those trust-fund milksops," he'd say to Joseph

Patrick and young Jack. "Everything I've achieved, I've done by my own brains and sweat. I started off a poor barkeep's son."

"The bollix he did," Danny Walsh used to say. "His old man had a motorcar when most of the Irish didn't have shoes."

For once Danny Walsh had it about right. Old Mr. Kennedy did have a nice house in Winthrop and a respectable reputation. Mayor Fitzgerald might have been the one mentioned in the dailies all the time, but it wasn't always the kind of mention decent people would be proud of. I never heard any gossip about old Mr. K.

We moved in August, but it was October before I even saw the city. When you had a night off you couldn't walk out the door and jump aboard a tram like you could in Brookline. I could have been back in Ballynagore for all the entertainment there was in Riverdale. The only thing to do was cadge a ride into Yonkers with Danny Walsh and go to a soda fountain, but the trouble with Danny was he was liable to make himself cozy at the Piper's Kilt saloon and forget to bring you home.

They were busy days anyway, and I liked that. We had a mountain of jobs to do, getting the children settled and ready for their new schools. And we had Bobby to contend with, the most bad-tempered baby I ever knew. He was born looking peeved and he didn't improve, scowling out from his stroller with that cross, freckled little face. I've never worked out what rubbed him up the wrong way so early in life.

Herself wasn't much better either. She was expecting Number Eight, so the heat was getting her down and she missed the little bit of company she'd had in Boston. Father Creagh coming to tea. Seeing His Honor every week and hearing all the goings-on among the pols. She kept ringing for me to go to her room and there she'd be on the daybed, making more lists. *Get books on the history of New York suitable for an eleven-year-old. Try Band-Aids on Kick's fingernails. Ask druggist if Euny is old enough to take*

Pepto-Bismol. She wasn't even interested in her fashion maga-zines, she was feeling so swollen and dowdy.

She said, "God's sent me another little blessing, Nora, but I'm thirty-eight. I'm too old to be having babies."

She was the same age as our Margaret.

I said, "You look ten years younger than my sister and she's only having her second."

She lapped that up.

"Well," she said, "I put in a great deal of work to keep my looks. These things have to be worked at."

Of course, my Margaret didn't have staff and a husband with a million in the bank, but Herself thought she had a pretty hard time of it.

She said, "Men have it so much easier. They go to business, but when they come home everything else has been done for them. We women have to be wives and mothers and careful homemak-ers. We have to stay young and beautiful and keep our minds lively.

"And somehow we carry it all off. I never bother my husband with anything, you know?

"I deal with everything concerning the household myself. I had a college education. I could have done any number of things with my life, but being a good wife and mother, smoothing the way for a great man, those things are just as important, just as satisfying."

As I recall, she made that pretty little speech just before the gos-sip about her great man started buzzing. Mr. K got a new business partner—Miss Gloria Swanson, no less, who'd starred in *Zaza* and *Beyond the Rocks* and *The Untamed Lady*. Fidelma asked him if he could get her Miss Swanson's picture, autographed.

He said, "I can do better than that. When she comes to visit I'll ask her to sign it for you personally."

"When Gloria Swanson comes to visit" was all we heard around the house after that. Cook and Fidelma and the drivers were all aflutter, and Kick and Rosie too. They were quite fans of Constance Bennett till their Daddy took up with Miss Swanson. After that Constance Bennett was history.

Then he came home one weekend and said, "Nora, I want you to put on a Halloween party. Spooks and witches and all that business. Miss Swanson will be in town with her children. It'd be a nice thing to do. Invite some neighbors' kids in, fix up some pumpkin lanterns. Boy, that takes me back! That was one of my first ventures. I bought up a whole load of pumpkins one fall, paid my sister Loretta to scrape the flesh out of them, ready-made lanterns, you see? I sold them off a handcart and turned quite a profit."

We'd never had Halloween parties before, and Mrs. K didn't really hold with it, but she went along with it that year, as long as nobody dressed up as a demon. Euny and Patty went as leprechauns, I remember, and Kick was a phantom in a sheet, gave Bobby nightmares with all her flapping and wailing.

All the talk in the kitchen was that Mr. K was doing a lot more than putting up money for Miss Swanson's talking pictures.

Gabe Nolan said, "It's not talkies they're making. It's music. Know what I mean? I drive him round there and the Do Not Disturb sign goes up on her door. I've seen it. He's in and out in half an hour but that can be long enough for the pot to boil. Well, time's money. But if her old man happens to be at home he only stays five minutes and he doesn't come out whistling neither. I tell you, it's in the bag. He's diddling her."

If what Gabe said was true, you wouldn't have known it from watching Herself, not even the day he brought Miss Swanson to the Halloween party.

Cook was scandalized.

"That poor creature," she kept saying. "Having her nose rubbed in his dirty goings-on."

It wasn't like that though. I knew Rose Kennedy well enough to see the arrangement quite suited her. She loved Mr. K, in her own way. He was the big success story and he kept her in style, but she wasn't so keen on her duties in the bedroom, and who could blame her. Eight babies. She was worn out.

It's a different thing if you're single. If a man says, "Come outside, Nora, take a look at the moon," you can please yourself. But Mrs. K wanted to be a good Catholic wife and Mr. K was only forty. Somebody had to keep scratching his itch.

But I did think it was a terrible thing him bringing Miss Swanson into the house and showing her off to his children. I felt for her over that. But she held her head high. The world could be ending and you'd never know it from Mrs. Kennedy's face.

I'd always thought Gloria Swanson looked a fright in her photographs, with all that blacking around her eyes, so it was a surprise to see her in the flesh, quite natural-looking and nice. She was wearing diamond ear clips and a sable coat though, every inch the film star. Mrs. K had on a good wool dress and pearls, but the baby was showing well by then. She looked a prim little body beside Miss Swanson.

They had a cup of tea together and then Miss Swanson joined in the apple-bobbing and a game of Nelson's eye, all very jolly but that didn't stop the tittle-tattling in the kitchen. I had to tell Fidelma to watch her tongue. I didn't want the children hearing things.

I said, "There might be nothing more to this than there is to him playing a round of golf with Jimmy Roosevelt. It could be a business arrangement. Just because she's a woman. Women can be in business."

Danny Walsh said, "They can too. I wouldn't mind putting a bit of business her way myself. Did you see the pins on her?"

Miss Swanson had her children with her; the girl was Kick's age, the boy was a timid little mite, a bit younger than Euny. Our lot were polite to them but that was about as far as it went. The Kennedys never really warmed to outsiders. They had all the playmates they wanted in the family, and sometimes getting them to mix with other children was more trouble than it was worth. Joseph Patrick had come home from school with a fat lip, been in a fight with a boy he'd invited to the Halloween party. The boy said he wasn't allowed. His parents didn't think the Kennedys were suitable people. And somebody wrote on the chalkboard that Mr. Kennedy took women to hotel rooms.

He said, "What does that mean?"

I said, "It doesn't mean anything. People in business like your Daddy go to hotels all the time. There was no need to get into a fight over it."

"Well," he said, "he had a smirk on his face so I figured I'd wipe it off for him."

Herself got a new mink jacket for Christmas, picked it out herself from Jacoby's showroom in Manhattan, and when Christmas Day dawned, Mr. K had another surprise for her. He'd bought the cottage we'd rented the last two summers at Hyannis, so it would be theirs to go to every year. He was having it renovated and rooms added. He said we should hardly recognize it the next time we went up there. Mrs. K was thrilled. Of all the places they've lived, I believe it's still her favorite.

I got a letter from Ursie the first week of the New Year, to say Margaret had another baby boy, Ramon Novarro Mulcahy, mother and child doing well.

She wrote,

> *I did everything I could to get the poor child a proper*
> *name. She could at least have named him Desmond for*

THE IMPORTANCE OF BEING KENNEDY | 65

Dada, but her head is full of picture palace nonsense and
Frankie Mulcahy daren't say a peep to contradict her.
I hope there'll be no more after this one. Two is surely
enough for anyone in this day and age, especially for a
fish porter with asthma.

I'm certain Margaret didn't need advice from Ursie on how
to stop having babies, and I was glad she'd got the two. More
than the rest of us looked like having anyway. Edmond's Widow
Clavin was too long in the tooth, Deirdre was a Bride of Christ,
and Ursie had her old-maid dreams about Mr. Jauncey. As for me,
well, there was a time. But now I think of it, I've had the best of
both worlds. I've had more of their little smiles and kisses than
ever Herself has, and none of her aches and pains.

Ursie's letter went on.

I mailed Deirdre a box of initialed handkerchiefs from
Federated. Whether they'll ever reach her I don't know.
They'll probably end up in a mud hut somewhere, but
it's the thought that counts. Mr. Jauncey is visiting with
his in-laws in Nashua.

Every year Ursie sends handkerchiefs and if I know Deirdre,
she gives them away. I bet all her little pickaninnies are wiping
their wee schnozzes on hankies from Federated. I try to picture
Deirdre getting older. The last picture we got she was tubbier and
wearing spectacles, but she hadn't a line on her face. Still that big,
shining smile. "Did you hear the angels last night, Nora?"

Directly after the New Year, Mr. K was off on his travels, to
Florida first, to play a few useful rounds of golf, he said, and then
to California. The children hated to see him leave. The house
felt different when he was at home. Kick and Rosie loved mak-

ing up little dances to perform for him, and the boys liked to get him playing spit or concentration. That last evening, before he left for the train station, Herself even dusted off the pianoforte and played "Silent Night." Me and Fidelma sat on the stairs and listened.

She said, "Happy families, Brennan. Fair brings a tear to your eye, doesn't it?"

Mr. K was to be gone a month at least. He came up to the nursery to kiss Bobby good-bye, only Bobby wouldn't be kissed.

He said, "Nora, I may not be around much but my children are everything to me. If ever there's a problem, if ever there's anything you think I should know about, especially when Mrs. Kennedy goes away to have the baby, you can ask Eddie Moore to call me. I don't care what time of day it is. He always knows where I can be reached."

I said, "They like to get your little letters."

"And I like writing them," he said. "Regular correspondence is a good habit for a child to learn. It's been such a swell Christmas. I really hate to go, but when you're in business you can't turn your back for a minute. You have to be on the spot and on your toes."

After he left I heard Mrs. K back at the pianoforte. She was playing Mayor Fitzgerald's favorite, "Sweet Adeline," putting in all the twiddly bits, but when I looked in on her to say good night, her face was grim enough to stop a Waterbury clock. It was common knowledge, written up in the dailies, that Miss Swanson was down at Palm Beach too, and even a new mink jacket couldn't take the sting out of that. Rose Kennedy loved her husband. She just didn't care for all that pushing and grunting.

Danny Walsh drove her up to Boston the next week, to a nursing home, to get ready for her lying-in. There were to be no more home births. She said, "I can't get the rest I need with children running up and down the stairs, and it's not good for the baby to

have a mother with jangled nerves. If there are any problems you must call Mrs. Moore."

Mary Moore was very good-humored about taking over when Mrs. K was away. She even came down when Joseph Patrick made his first Communion, because neither his Mammy nor his Daddy could be there. But I didn't have to call upon her while Mrs. K was away to the baby hospital. Even Jack managed not to get sick, and we had a grand time. I gave Rosie a holiday from learning her letters and she helped me with Bobby and Pat, and when the others came in from school I left them in peace to play their own games. There were none of Mother's Quizzes to study up for. Joe was thirteen by then, so he thought he was too old for milk and cookies by the nursery fire. He liked to be out of doors, throwing snowballs at tin cans or polishing his ice slide. But Jack didn't care for the cold. He'd have his head in an adventure book or play a game of Chutes and Ladders with Kick and Euny.

It didn't worry us that Mr. and Mrs. K were both away from home. In fact we all preferred it. With Mrs. K you could never be sure where you stood. Little things bothered her. You could be getting the "dear heart" treatment, hearing how she could have married Sir Thomas Lipton, if she'd played her cards that way, and been a real English Lady; then she'd start going through the trash can and before you knew it you were getting a telling-off because you might have eked one more spoonful of malt extract out of the jar you'd thrown away. Left to ourselves, me and Fidelma could run that nursery blindfolded, and after Jean arrived we had plenty of chances.

Jean Ann was born on Kick's eighth birthday. We were having a little tea party for some of her friends from the day school when we got the telephone call. Mr. K was already on his way up to Boston to see the new arrival.

Joseph Patrick said, "Nora, do you think I'm old enough to be the new baby's godfather? I think I am."

He was a hard one to fathom. I'd had to read the riot act only half an hour before, because of his silly roughhousing, nearly pulling Jack's arm from its socket, and then there he was, talking about standing godfather to his new sister. And he did it too. Mr. and Mrs. K thought it was a wonderful idea.

Jean Ann was a month old before she was brought home from Boston, so Herself had been gone eight weeks complete.

"Milking it for all she's worth," Fidelma said. "Well, I suppose it'll be her last time."

We lined them all up outside the door like a guard of honor for her homecoming and young Joe carried baby Jean in from the car.

Danny Walsh said, "Mrs. K's done all right out of this. Your Man gave her a diamond bracelet, and when she feels up to it she's going on a trip, anywhere in the world she fancies."

Gabe Nolan said, "But here's the best bit. The lady friend only went and sent her flowers. A great big bouquet of roses that nearly filled the room. How about that for front?"

Fidelma said, "See what I mean, Brennan? They're the best of friends, Miss Swanson and Mrs. K. They're in cahoots."

I said, "I wouldn't believe everything Gabe Nolan told me. It could have been anybody sent her flowers."

She said, "Will you ask her or will I?"

We went up to the nursery to give Jean her bottle. The nearest I could say, she had a look of Kick about her. Poor Jean. That's how we always talked about her. "Like Kick but fairer, and a look of Joseph Patrick about her when she smiles."

Mrs. K said, "Now, dear hearts, I'm going to take a little nap, but later on I want to see the weight charts and bring my records up-to-date."

Fidelma said, "Oh Mrs. Kennedy, we heard you got roses after the baby was born. Is it true? Can you really get roses in February?"

"Yes," she said, "I did get roses, from Miss Swanson and her husband. It was a great extravagance but such a very kind thought. Of course I received letters and cards from so many of Mr. Kennedy's business associates."

Butter wouldn't melt.

We went in convoy to Hyannis as soon as school was out, to the "cottage," as Mrs. K called it, though it was hardly a cottage anymore. Two big new wings had been built on, and garages and an extra floor, with a deck. I was given the first weekend off, to go on up to Boston and see Margaret's new baby and little Rudolf Valentino, who we all called Val. They'd already shortened "Ramon" to "Ray," which Ursie said sounded common. She didn't approve of pacifiers either, but then Ursie had never walked the floor all night with a child cutting his first teeth. Margaret wanted to know all about Miss Swanson.

She said, "You've done all right for yourself, no mistake. I'm stuck behind Middleton's counter every afternoon, weighing sugar and slicing bacon, and you're rubbing shoulders with film stars."

Ursie said, "Just keep your feet on the ground, Nora. You know we get famous people coming to the office, senior figures from the business world, but I treat everyone the same."

Margaret said, "You kill me, Ursula Brennan. You're not telling me you get anybody to top Gloria Swanson coming into the stuffy old place where you work."

When Margaret and Ursie saw each other they never stopped picking.

I said, "I don't rub shoulders with anyone. There are days I hardly set foot outside the nursery. We've eight of them to see to."

Margaret said, "Eight. Sweet Jesus. Could you not take my two as well? Just slide them in on the quiet? I'll bet they'd never notice."

Mr. K was away in California most of the summer of '28, but when he did come home he arrived in style. Gabe Nolan would meet him off the train in New York City and drive him out to Queens, to where he kept his new toy. He'd bought himself an airplane that could land on water, so he could fly up to the Cape and land right on his own doorstep. The first time he arrived it caused quite a stir. People were running around, thought a plane had crashed into the sea, but after they found out who it was and what it was, they didn't pay any more attention. Hyannis folk were too dignified to get excited about Joe Kennedy and his trappings.

The house renovations were still going on and some of the new bathrooms had still to be finished, but the movie theater was ready, downstairs in the old furnace room. Danny Walsh was taught how to work the projecting machine and Mr. K kept us supplied with new movies, cowboy stories mainly, hot off the press. They'd arrive by special messenger once a week.

Fidelma asked him why it was always cowboys and Indians.

He said, "Because they're easy to do. I can make twenty of them for what those fur-hondlers spend on one movie, and folks are just as happy to watch mine. People in Scranton, Pennsylvania, would watch paint dry, they're so bored."

Danny reckoned we saw things before they were in the picture palaces even in New York City, and we were all allowed down there to watch, because as Mr. K said, he'd never allow a movie to be made in a studio of his that wasn't fit for his family to watch, and the help too. Mrs. K didn't care much for movies though. She'd sit at the back, and after half an hour or so she'd slip out. She was happier pulling on an old pea jacket and going for a walk along the strand.

She said to me once, "Movies are so noisy. I don't like all the shooting. Peace and quiet are what I like. That's why I go to first Mass. It's worth getting up early. If you go later, other worshippers can be so irritating. I love a room to myself, Nora, and stillness."

Well, she was in the wrong family for that.

10

Kennedys Everywhere, Like a Rash

The house in Riverdale was a rental. We knew Mr. K had told Eddie Moore to look out for a place to buy, and in the spring of 1929 we moved again, to Bronxville, to a villa standing in its own park, Crownlands. I suppose the money was fairly pouring in by then. He owned the companies that were making the movies and he owned the picture houses where they were shown. For all I know he could have owned the celluloid factories and the popcorn machines too. Not that any of the help saw much of the money he was making. You asked for a raise only if you were prepared for a big performance from Herself. To hear her, you'd think they were down to their last dime. She should have been on the stage, that one. By the time she was done with her sob story you felt you should maybe offer her a loan yourself.

So it wasn't the money that kept me with the Kennedys. I stayed because I liked the life and I loved the children. Anyway, blessed are the poor. As Mammy used to say, "If you want to know God's opinion of money you've only to take a look at them he gives it to."

People like me and Fidelma and Gertie Ambler, who cooked, and Danny and Gabe, we were the lucky ones, because we were permanent staff, kept on whatever the time of year. But the maids and the gardeners at Hyannis had to find something else when the house was closed up for the winter. Mrs. K didn't see why she should pay people when she was finished with them for the season. No Kennedys, no money.

Crownlands was our grandest house yet. We had beautiful grounds and every convenience, and yet Mrs. K didn't seem happy. Thwarted, I always thought. She'd had her education and been the toast of Boston, riding on His Honor's coattails. She had money and a fine family, but there was no joy in her. She could tell you the date of every doctor's visit and she could tell you to the last cent what we were spending on socks or baby bottles, but she didn't have a friend in the world, nor anything to occupy her that would use all her brains and foreign languages. She was more like a head housekeeper than a mother, and she was so restless. She wanted to go back out into the world and make her mark, you could tell, but she'd eight children, and her sacred duty hung round her neck like a sack of rocks. Mr. K did take her along with him to California one time, which was how she happened to miss Jack and Rosie's first Communion, but she never went again.

She said, "Mr. Kennedy is so busy with meetings all day when he's traveling, but I'm not the kind of wife who sits around waiting to be entertained. I shall take a trip to Europe."

Fidelma said, "Do you think we'd ever move, to save Mr. Kennedy all the traveling?"

"No," she said, "I do not. We're not California people."

Still, he was so tied up there he didn't even come back for the burying of his own father. I'd have thought they could have kept the old feller on ice until Mr. K had time to attend, but Mrs. K said it wasn't necessary. She said it was time Joseph Patrick started representing his Daddy on certain occasions, and his grandfather's funeral was a very good place to begin. He was bought a new black suit from Alexander's. Only fourteen, but he was already a head taller than his Mammy, quite the young man when he offered her his arm and walked her to the car. I told Mr. K when I saw him.

I said, "Young Joe did you proud. And my sister wrote me from Boston. She said there was a very big turnout for the funeral."

"So I heard," he said. "And I wish I could have been there, but I couldn't leave town. It's dog-eat-dog in the movie business. If you turn your back for five minutes those Jew boys rob you blind."

Herself went off to Paris, for culture and shopping she said, and she was hardly out the door before Miss Swanson came visiting. I thought it was highly irregular, and Jack didn't like it either. He stayed out in the bay in his sailboat after everybody else had come in, and he had a monkey face on him when it was time to go in to dinner.

I said, "What's eating you?"

He said, "How come Mother has to go sailing off to France just when Dad's come home and we can all be together for a change? What kind of a family is this, anyhow?"

Miss Swanson was very nice. She remembered all the children's names, and she went along to the movie star club Kick and Rosie and little Nancy Tenney had got up to swap photographs and act out scenes from the movies they'd seen. She climbed the ladder up into the attic over Mr. Tenney's garage to say hello to Nancy and sign her autograph book, like a regular aunt might have done. But it still wasn't right that she was in the house when Mrs. Kennedy wasn't.

Mr. K took her for a ride through town in his Rolls-Royce, but according to Gabe Nolan, nobody paid them any attention. If people in Hyannis had money, they never flashed it, and most of them wouldn't have walked to the foot of the stairs to see even Tom Mix. Kick was film star crazy though. That's where all her pocket money went. Rosie used to save hers to send to the missionary nuns and Euny just counted hers and then put it back in her piggybank, but Kick's went on movie magazines the minute the money was in her hand, and then she cut them up for photos of Douglas Fairbanks or Miss Greta Garbo to thumbtack to the wall.

Young Joe and Rosie both went away to school that autumn. It had been decided that Rosie would never catch up at the day school, so she had to be boarded, at a special place for slow learners. I knew that wouldn't last five minutes. It was out beyond Philadelphia, and it could have been the far side of the moon for all that meant to Rosie. She sat with the map Mrs. K had showed her, with her finger on the place, looking and looking at me, to see if I could save her from having to go.

Euny kept saying, "You're lucky. I wish I could go away to school."

But all Rosie wanted was to stay home and help me look after baby Jean.

"I'll try more hard," she said. Well, she managed one term at the school but she came home for Christmas such a wreck even Mrs. K hadn't the heart to send her back. She said there were other places that might be more suitable and God knows we worked our way through a long, long list of them before we were done. I could never see why it was such a crime for Rosie to be slow. Apart from Euny, they were none of them great scholars and Mr. Congressman Jack still can't spell for taffy.

Joseph Patrick went off to Choate School in Connecticut that October. He was raring to get there, although Herself would have liked to see him go to a good Catholic school. She was worried he wouldn't be allowed to go to Mass.

Mr. K said, "Of course he'll be allowed. I'll make sure of it. The main thing is I want my boy in a school where there's no funny business. You can spend a pile of money and end up with a sissy, but they guarantee there's none of that at Choate."

It was a top school. The kind top families had sent their boys to for generations. I wondered if they wouldn't look down their noses at a Kennedy, especially if Mr. K started throwing his money around and turning up in his gold limousine, but the thing about young Joe was, he was one of those people who expected everybody to like him, and if they didn't, he just chose not to notice. And he went right along with whatever his Daddy said he must do. Like the first term, when he wanted to take horse-riding lessons but it would have meant he couldn't go out for the football team and Mr. Kennedy put it to him, the football was more important.

He said, "Think of it this way. You can make useful friends playing in a team, and be good enough to win your football letter when you get to Harvard. Horse-riding you can do any old time."

And when it was explained to him that way, Joseph Patrick didn't argue. He knew everything he did was part of a plan. First Catholic president of the United States. He'd been hearing it since the day he was born.

Mr. K had come home from California in time to drive Joseph Patrick to his new school, and he wasn't going back.

Gabe Nolan said, "He's had enough of the Jew boys. He's branching out again. And do you know who his new best pal is? The Governor's boy. Jimmy Roosevelt. They've got a few little deals on the go."

Mr. Franklin Roosevelt was the new Governor of New York.

So we went from never seeing Mr. K to having him home every night, and the children loved it. Herself was hardly there, because if she wasn't in Paris buying gowns she was sightseeing in New Mexico or off to Maine to take the waters, and I can't say she was greatly missed. She was away the week the markets crashed, visiting with the Fitzgeralds in Boston.

I was bringing the children home from school, pushing Jean in her bassinet. Kick and Euny and wee Pat, who'd just started in the first grade. Fidelma was at home with Bobby, because he had the croup and I remember telling her I'd seen three limousines turn up driveways, bringing their gentlemen home in the middle of the working day. Very unusual. Then Mr. K came in and went directly to his study. He didn't come up to the nursery and he didn't eat dinner that night. All he had was a glass of warm milk. I could hear his great booming voice on the telephone until very late.

It was in all the dailies the next morning, of course, how stocks had fallen and people had been ruined. I didn't understand it then and I still don't. If you've money in the bank, how can it turn worthless overnight? But Danny Walsh took it upon himself to explain it to us. According to him, it wasn't actual dollar bills that had gone west, it was other pieces of paper, promises to pay, and notes about who owned what, complicated arrangements that were how men like Joe Kennedy made their fortunes. And lost them.

He said, "We'll all be let go. Your Man'll be shining shoes by Christmas."

But as was often the case, Danny Walsh was wrong. There were a lot of ruined men in the neighborhood, but Mr. Kennedy wasn't one of them. He'd gotten out of whatever it was had dragged them all under and put his money in safer places.

Fidelma asked him straight. She said, "Are we all right, Mr. K? Only if you'll be cutting back I'd like to know sooner than later."

He laughed. He said, "Do you think we can't afford you? No,

4

you're still in a job. Stick with Joe Kennedy, see? A blind man could have seen this crash coming. The only ones who lost are the fools who held out for the top dollar."

But they weren't the only ones who lost. Everybody who depended on them was hurt too. Businesses closed, people were laid off. A lot of the houses in Bronxville and Riverdale were put up for sale, and when they didn't sell they were just closed and shuttered and left empty. You didn't see so many limousines anymore. Children were taken out of school, just disappeared without any good-byes. Sometimes it felt as if we were the only survivors. And Danny Walsh changed his tune.

"Mr. Kennedy's nobody's fool," he kept saying. "I knew we'd be all right. He'd have sold his own mother if the market was right. Provided we keep on the right side of Herself we've all got jobs for life here."

A driver, maybe, but nursery maids lose their usefulness after a few years. I didn't think I'd be with them for much longer. Sometimes, on the way from school, Kick would say, "I wonder if there'll be a new baby in the nursery when we get home today?" Even when she knew her Mammy was away to Virginia for a little holiday she'd still say it.

But there wasn't. Not that year, nor the next.

Fidelma said, "No, but I reckon we're still pretty safe, Brennan. Now that Herself is gallivanting all the time she needs us more than ever. We've a good few years till Jean's all growed up and there could be a new bunch of them on the way by then. The next generation. They'll keep us in mothballs till we're needed for the grandbabies, like they used to do at the big houses back home, remember?"

It was a happy thought. All my Kennedys coming of age, getting married and having ten babies apiece.

I said, "Well, bags I get Kick's babies, or Rosie's, if she's allowed any. I'll leave the boys to you."

I could imagine how it'd be with the boys. They'd all get their wives chosen for them. Little replicas of Herself.

I said, "Eight of them. Just think of it. Even if they only have two or three apiece, that's still an awful lot of Kennedys. They'll be everywhere, like a rash."

Fidelma laughed. "Kennedytown," she said. "The old man'll buy a whole street of houses and even the dogs'll have ginger fur and big white teeth. See if I'm not right."

11

The Sacred Duties of a Wife

They say there were terrible sights to be seen in the city after the stock market tumbled. Businesses boarded up, men in good suits hanging their heads and waiting on line for a bowl of soup. Ursie said it was the same in Boston. Middleton's closed down, for one thing, because nobody could settle their accounts, which put Margaret out of work with two young mouths to fill and Frankie Mulcahy's chest not all it should have been. *I send her what I can spare,* Ursie wrote,

> *and I hope you'll do the same. Thank goodness you and I had the sense to tie our fortunes to men like Mr. Jauncey and Mr. Kennedy. Mr. Jauncey is as busy as ever with so many liquidations, and we seem to read more and more about your Mr. Kennedy. These are the people who will ensure America survives and comes back stronger than ever.*

It was true it would have to be some kind of calamity for lawyers not to do well out of it, so Ursie had no worries. But it tickled me to think of Joe Kennedy as a lifeguard, helping to keep America afloat and pull her safe to shore. He watched out for his own, plain and simple, and if your name wasn't Kennedy, he'd have the lifebelt off you before you knew it and sell it to the highest bidder. Anyway, Mr. K had a big new project. He'd palled up with the state governor, Mr. Roosevelt, learning the ropes of political office.

We were spared seeing the worst of things out in Bronxville, tucked away in our nice leafy garden. There was nobody panhandling on our street, no breadlines. Mrs. K's packages still arrived from Paris, with gowns she didn't have any occasion to wear, and Gabe Nolan still drove Mr. K around in the Rolls-Royce. He'd prospered. He didn't have factories or warehouses full of stock. He just moved around quietly, picking up all those worthless bits of paper. Then he waited for their value to climb back up. And it was the same story when we went up to Cape Cod in the summer of 1930. In Hyannis you'd never have known there was anything wrong in the world. The sun seemed to shine every day and even Herself was in a good humor. There were no more visits from Miss Swanson, and Constance Bennett's photo went back up on Kick's bedroom wall. Jimmy Roosevelt and his wife came to stay, and a wonderful singer, Mr. Morton Downey, moved into a house just around the corner, so some evenings, instead of the everlasting cowboy picture shows they'd have a little musical soiree. The help all sat with the kitchen door open so we could hear him singing in the parlor.

> 'Tis the last rose of summer
> Left blooming alone.

All her lovely companions
Are faded and gone . . .

Every day at Hyannis was filled. They all had a tennis lesson in the morning and sailing practice in the afternoon, with special instructors brought in, if there wasn't a regatta for them to race in. Mr. K organized swimming contests too, and running races and games of football, but Mrs. K had no part of any of that. She liked to swim, but just gentle paddling about, with Danny Walsh to accompany her. They were a sight to see, walking down to the water's edge together, Herself in a big rubber helmet to save her hair from the salt, and Danny in a woolen swimming costume, legs on him like a gray heron. His job was to bob around close by, in case a big wave swept her off her feet.

Fidelma said, "When you answered that advertisement, Danny, I'll bet you never thought the job would mean taking your trousers off."

He said, "Flexibility, Fidelma Clery, that's the answer to sur-vival today. You can't just be a driver. Nor a nursery maid, so you can wipe that silly smile off your face, Nora Brennan. Think how much more I'm worth to the Kennedys than you are. Driver, swimming companion, projectionist, handyman."

I didn't care. I still wasn't going into that ocean.

There were all the outdoor activities, but that wasn't all. The older ones were expected to prepare for mealtimes too. Mrs. K had a notice board nailed up for pieces she clipped out of the newspapers, conversational topics she thought they should know about, so they'd have something to say at the dinner table. It was for the benefit of Joe and Jack mainly, so they could decide what they thought about things and then listen to what their Daddy had to say, but Kick and Euny were allowed to join in as well. Not Rosie though. She was excused from conversationalizing, and from the sailing lessons.

Mrs. K had her up to her room every morning for two hours instead, to try and bring her along with her reading and writing. It was no vacation for Rosie. She'd have liked to sit in the dunes and play with her dollies, I know, but Mrs. Kennedy said she'd never improve if she wasn't pushed. And when her lessons were over she still didn't get any peace. The others would drag her off to play French cricket and yell at her when she dropped the ball. Eunice was the only one who had any patience with her. She'd take her out in her dinghy once in a while and show her how to tack and trim the sails and Rosie would come back with a smile that'd light up a Christmas tree.

"I've been crewing for Euny," she'd say, pleased as punch. "She said I did pretty good."

She was a help with the little ones too. She'd feed Jean for me and push Bobby on the swing. Sometimes he'd get mixed up and call her "Mother." He was a quiet one, Bobby. Always studying the floor, but then he'd up and do something to surprise you. I was sitting on the lawns one time with wee Jean on my lap when he came running up from the strand. He pushed a seashell into my hand, said "Love you," and ran off again, come over all shy. A Scotch bonnet shell. I have it still. And that was the summer he punched Joseph Patrick. Young Joe had taken the book Jack was reading and wouldn't give it back so Bobby landed him one with his little fist, and when Joe laughed at him he burst into tears and went and hid.

But he could be a grouch. Fidelma took to him more than I did. She says he's still the most prayerful of the lot of them, and he did used to screw his eyes up tight when he was saying his rosary at bedtime. You'd have thought that would have endeared him to Herself, but she was starting to feel her wings by the time Bobby came along. And none of them ever got paid the attention Joseph Patrick did.

Things were so sweet between Mr. and Mrs. K that summer, she even had her way over Jack's next school. He'd been intended for Choate, following in young Joe's footsteps, but he was sent to Canterbury instead, a proper Catholic school, right up by Candlewood Lake. He was in and out of the school infirmary all that first term, what with the batterings he took on the football field and his sore throats and stomach aches, so Mr. K said we'd all better go to Florida for the Christmas holidays, so Jack could get his strength up. Blue skies and palm trees on Christmas Day. Fidelma swore she'd died and gone to heaven. Ursie reckons Deirdre gets weather like that all the time in Africa.

But Florida didn't do Jack a lot of good. He'd only been back at Canterbury five minutes when he was rushed to the hospital with his appendix attack, and after his recuperation he never went back. Mr. K said he was to have private tutoring at home to make up what he'd missed and then go to Choate in September. He said Mrs. K could choose whatever schools she liked for the girls but from now on his boys were going where he decided, to mix with the crème de la crème. That was how Lem Billings ended up part of the family.

Jack brought him home from Choate on their first weekend break, and apart from the war, they've been joined at the hip ever since. They were a pair. Both growing too fast for their own good, both covered in pimples, both of them needing glasses. They found one another highly amusing, talking in silly voices, sniggering and making up names for people. "Nurse Strict," they called me.

I liked Lem though. He remembered his manners, and it was nice to see Jack with a proper friend. Those children had grown up too closed in, always playing with each other sooner than climb over the garden fence to find outside company. But in the end Lem hardly counted as an outsider anymore. He'd come to Bronxville every midterm break and to Hyannis too and leave half his belongings behind at the end of the vacation, that's how sure he was he'd be coming back.

Mr. K said, "There's a rumor that boy has family in Philadelphia, but I guess we've adopted him."

It was all said in good part though, and we had another golden summer. Mrs. K had a little cabin built in the dunes, a place where she could sit and read without a football knocking the book from her hand, and I remember her quite gay and smiling.

Fidelma said it was because the Holy Father had sent out a letter reminding wives of their sacred duties. We'd all had to listen to it read out at Mass, everybody shuffling and coughing and looking at their watches, I don't know if that was why Mrs. K came over all sweetness and light but anyway, when we headed back to New York in September she went up to Boston to see Dr. Good and she came home with the news that there was another little blessing on the way, Number Nine, due in February. In Ballynagore they used to say it was terrible bad luck to have three weans in a family born the same month.

I heard Mrs. Moore congratulating her.

She said, "You look wonderful, Rosa. You have the figure of a twenty-year-old."

Mrs. K said, "I know I do. But I'm too old for this, Mary. I'm forty-two and I'm tired. After this one there can't be any more babies. Joe will just have to realize."

Of course, Mr. Kennedy could have anything money could buy, including lady friends for his comfort and consolation, and there never seemed to be any trouble about that between him and Mrs. K. They got along just fine, and when he opened his mouth she'd gaze up at him as though the Golden Oracle had spoken. But that was twenty years back. The shine has gone off Joe Kennedy since then, and Herself has her darling boys to gaze up at now. I've seen her. She looks at Jack just the way she used to look at Mr. K. Pity help the girl he marries. She'll have Rose Kennedy for competition, fluttering her old eyelashes, hanging on his arm more like a sweetheart than a mother.

$$12$$

No Crybabies, No Losers

Teddy was born just after Kick's twelfth birthday and Jean's fourth. It had already been decided Jack and Rosie would be his godparents. Jack wanted the new baby to be called George Washington Kennedy, but Herself wouldn't hear of it. He was to be named Edward Moore, for Mr. Moore, who was like a special uncle to those children. When Jack had his tonsils out it was Eddie Moore who visited him, and when his stomach was so bad that he had to go to the Mayo for tests, it was Eddie Moore who took him, because Mrs. K was in Paris getting another dose of culture and Mr. K was up and down to Albany with Jimmy Roosevelt, visiting with the Governor. Mr. Roosevelt was intending to run in the presidential election and Mr. K had offered his services.

Gabe Nolan reckoned we could end up at the White House ourselves someday.

He said, "Joe Kennedy doesn't really have the time of day for Roosevelt. You know what he's like when he's around anyone born with a silver spoon, how he plays the barefoot Boston boy. And you should hear him go on about Mrs. Roosevelt. She gives him the hoohas. But he keeps writing the checks. He's backing him so he can get up close and study how it's done. You'll see. Next time round it'll be Kennedy who's running for president."

I said, "It's his boy he wants it for, not himself."

He said, "I know he wants it for the boy. But if he got it first, then he could keep the seat warm. See what I mean?"

I never heard anything so silly. Joseph Patrick was only seventeen. But Mr. K had started including all the boys when he gave his pep talks about the future, even Teddy, who was still in diapers.

He'd say, "You've heard of the Three Musketeers. Well, you'll be the Four Kennedys. When the time comes it'll be a team effort to get Joe the presidency, then after his eight years he'll pass it on to Jack, Jack to Bobby, and Bobby to Teddy. Once we've got it we'll keep it in the family, like Mayer and Goldwyn. I learned a few things from those pants-pressers out in Hollywood."

The girls he left to Mrs. K, which was how Kick came to be sent to the Sacred Heart Sisters. She was enrolled for Noroton, on the Long Island Sound, in the autumn of '32. She might have been allowed another year in the day school but boys had begun to notice her, calling her up on the telephone, inviting her to cookouts and football games. Herself soon put a stop to that. Kick was on her way to Noroton so fast I hardly had time to stitch the name tags in her clothes. She was to be kept pure, with her mind on her studies and wholesome pursuits, and no more silly talk about boys.

Mrs. K used to say, "When a girl loses her good reputation, Kathleen, she loses everything."

I don't suppose she thought it any of her business to worry about the ones who might lose their reputations on account of Joseph Patrick. He was a chip off the old block when it came to girls, always chasing them and then as soon as he caught them, giving the next one the eye. You hardly saw him with the same girl twice, but he always picked stunners. Mrs. K thought he should only walk out with Catholic girls but Mr. K said he didn't care if they were Seventh-Day Adventists, as long as they were pretty. I'd watch the old goat sometimes, especially up at Hyannis, joining in the football, showing off in front of Joe's girlfriend, finding occasion to bump up against her. And he always insisted on his good-night kiss, even if the girl had never met him before in her life.

Fidelma brought it up to Mrs. K one day. She said, "They don't like it, you know, being made to kiss Mr. Kennedy. And I shouldn't like it neither. Sixteen years old and you're expected to kiss some old man. It's not right."

Mrs. K said, "What nonsense. They're simply being made to feel part of the family, which is more than some of them merit."

They were just somebody else's daughters.

Kick didn't want to go away to school. She didn't think it was fair that Rosie was allowed to stay at home, but Rosie couldn't have managed the lessons at a school like Noroton. She was grand as she was, getting her own private lessons and helping me and Fidelma with the little ones.

Thursday afternoons Kick was allowed visitors. Mrs. K quite liked to go, being an old Sacred Heart girl herself, but when she was traveling, Rosie and I would go instead. They served you tea in a big visitors' room looking out across the Sound. It made a nice trip out, and when I couldn't be spared, like when Jean and Teddy had the chicken pox, Rosie would go on her own. When they say she was always an imbecile, that's what I bring up to them. If she was an imbecile, how could they have let her go visiting, all the way to Darien, with nobody but that fool Danny Walsh to keep an eye on her?

Mr. K was away all through that autumn, trailing around with Mr. Roosevelt on the presidential campaign, and Herself sailed to France and Italy, to recuperate from giving birth to Teddy and shop to her heart's content. That was the trip when she started buying the dollies, but not for Jean to play with. They were dressed in national costumes, beautiful, expensive things, to be kept under wraps away from dust and sunlight. Eventually she had so many she had to get a special room for them, up at Hyannis, and none of the help liked going in there to clean. There was a maid called Freda, who swore she saw one of them move.

We saw nothing of Mr. Kennedy till the week of the election. Mrs. K was sitting on thorns, wondering if she was married to the next president's right-hand man.

I said, "Will it mean moving again? Will we shift to Washington if Mr. Roosevelt gets in?"

"Very likely," she said. "Of course we don't know yet what position Governor Roosevelt has in mind for us, but we'll certainly need a home in Washington."

That was when we started hearing a lot of "we."

"We're throwing a party at the Waldorf, to celebrate our victory."

"We'll join the children at Palm Beach later, Nora. We're invited onto Vincent Astor's yacht first, as a thank-you for all we did to get FD elected."

Then it was, "We're waiting to learn what the President wants to do with us."

And then, when the President didn't appear to want to do anything with Mr. K, it was, "After all we did for that man. We should ask for our money back."

Mr. K hung around in Washington though. He rented a house, a great big spread, according to Gabe Nolan, with views of the Potomac River, and he had a little elevator put in, big enough for a bath chair and a bodyguard, to encourage the President to visit him.

Gabe used to say, "One thing about Joe Kennedy, he's a hard one to snub. The weeks pass by and the President keeps not sending for him, but still he goes back to eat more shite and still he keeps smiling."

But Mrs. K wasn't smiling. Everybody else who'd helped the President get elected had been given a payback, even that old swindler Jim Curley. There were new ambassadors being sent all over the world and I know Mrs. K would have killed to go to Paris, but it wasn't offered. Gabe said Mr. K had donated twenty thousand dollars to the campaign and it looked like he was getting nothing for his generosity but the brush-off. Danny Walsh said it was double that at least, and it wasn't a gift. It was a loan, which Mrs. K said should be called in immediately.

Whatever he was thinking, you couldn't read Mr. K. He went back to business, back to doing his morning exercises and quizzing the children every night, and he stayed thick as thieves with Jimmy Roosevelt, playing the long game. They went on a vacation together to England, with the wives along for company. I suppose if you can't have the President's ear, having his boy's is the next best thing.

We'd had two golden summers at Hyannis, but they were over. From then on it seemed that every year there was something to cast a shadow. In '33 it was the phone call that never came from the White House. It was Jack and Joseph Patrick forever sparring. And it was Rosie. Mrs. K had found a Sacred Heart school with Sisters who were willing to give private tuition. It was in Rhode Island. Rosie was enrolled there for September and it hung over us like a storm cloud all summer. I know Mrs. Moore pleaded for her not to be sent.

She said, "She'll be so lonely, Rosa. It'll be very hard for her to make friends when she's being treated as a special case."

But Mrs. K was determined. She said, "She has to go to school. I've really done everything I can. She needs to learn self-discipline and we're all far too easy on her at home. She doesn't always try her hardest, because she knows we make allowances. The Sisters will be good for her."

Rosie cried and begged not to go. "I didn't mean to dipsapoint you," she kept saying. "I'll try really, really. And I'll help Nora with Teddy and Jean."

She loved Teddy. Everybody did. He was a fat, smiling little body, always happy to be passed around and petted. I don't remember him ever getting a sharp word or a paddling from Herself, no matter what mischief he got into. He was her frost-blossom baby and he was let get away with anything.

Now I look back, Jean was the one who got the rawest deal. Patty was strong enough to tag along with Euny and Kick and keep up, and Bobby was away in his own little world, but Jean was left out on a limb. After Teddy was born Mrs. K didn't have any time for her.

I'd take her on my knee, but she wasn't my favorite and she knew it, poor wee scrap. I still feel bad for her though she's a grown woman now and making her own way well enough. It must be terrible to be lonesome with a great big family buzzing around you.

Outside of the nursery the only one who paid Jean any heed was Joseph Patrick. He took it very seriously that he was the big brother she looked up to, and her godfather too, but he was away to school. And when he did come home he and Jack were always fighting, particularly that summer. Joseph Patrick had won just about every sporting trophy going at Choate and all Jack had come home with was a set of arch supports for his shoes, recommended by a doctor who'd seen him about his back pains. He wore them, uncomfortable-looking things they were, and he did some special exercises too, but he got nothing but ribbing from young Joe.

"Jack," he'd say, "you been measured yet for the surgical boot?"

In the end Jack had his revenge. He told everybody at the dinner table how Joe had taken a drubbing from some senior boys at school, how he'd provoked them and taken them on and then they'd wiped the floor with him. He made everybody laugh, the droll way he told it, and Joe's face was like thunder. The rest of that vacation every time Joe was in earshot, Lem Billings would say, "Hey, roomie, that fight Man of Steel was in? Tell me again. How'd it finish?" and Jack would say, "Man oh man, they wiped the floor with him."

Joe and Jack had never been exactly best friends, and once they were grown men all they did was bicker and show off around each other. And Bobby, of course, wanted to keep up with both of them, to be a tough guy and a wiseacre. He knocked himself out stone-cold at Hyannis one time, smack into a tree, showing Joseph Patrick how fast he could run with a ball. He'd a bump on his head the size of a hen's egg. Even Mrs. K thought a doctor should take a look at him, but he wouldn't give in and admit to being hurt. He just chewed his lip and swallowed hard, acting the brave little soldier. He knew what the Kennedy rules were. No crybabies, no losers, and no sourpusses.

13

An Anniversary Trip for One

President Roosevelt did give Mr. K a job in the end.

The way it happened was, they finally got the invitation to the White House she'd been angling for, but it came out of the blue, with only a day's notice.

I said, "What if you'd been away traveling? I thought these affairs were planned weeks ahead?"

"Some of them are, Nora," she said, "but this is a mark of our closeness to the President. It's an invitation between friends."

Still, she had us in an almighty flap while she decided what outfits had to be packed. She wanted to be sure of out-swanking Mrs. Roosevelt, which can't have been any great achievement. Best clothes, for being seen in public, were the one thing Mrs. K wasn't cheap about. Her Paris gowns were stored in special tissue paper and cedar boxes to keep everything perfect, shoes on trees, lingerie in muslin bags.

It was a different story when she was at home with nobody but the help and the children likely to see her. Then she went around dressed in any old thing, the old pajamas she kept for afternoon naps, or a chain-store day dress, with memos pinned all over it, things she'd jotted down on the back of old envelopes. *Jack, Vitamin C. Lightbulb too bright, rear stair hall. Maupassant for Kick. Chicken cutlet missing from fridge.*

It was Gabe Nolan who'd taken that piece of chicken. Gertie Ambler warned him it'd be missed. Herself has no interest in food at all, but she counts every item in and every item out and if there's a spoonful of peas left at dinner she expects to see it used the next day. So when a whole cutlet disappeared that time at Hyannis, we all got the third degree. You'd have thought it was a diamond clip that was missing. If Rose Kennedy's the marker of what it is to have money, I hope to stay poor. We were always taught, better an open hand than a tight fist. Mammy used to say, "When your hand is open you can give and you can receive."

Mammy would have given you the coat off her back, and had more joy of it than Mrs. K with all her chicken cutlets accounted for.

Anyway, Saturday morning off she went down to Washington to join Mr. K and the Roosevelts at the trotting races. She'd three Paris dinner gowns in the trunk but they never saw the light of day. The President had to go to a special dinner that night, at the Gridiron Club, and he took Mr. Kennedy with him, which left Herself to have dinner with Mrs. Roosevelt and a few other wives. According to Danny Walsh, it was practically a tray supper and they were told not to dress. Mrs. R wore a tweed skirt and a cardigan set. He said all he heard on the way back to New York was how different things would be if ever she were mistress of the White House.

Fidelma said, "Let's guess. It'll be diamond tiaras every night, but Gertie Ambler'll still have to count out the peas."

The men had been out till very late at the dinner, but the President sent for Mr. K early Sunday morning, which was when he gave him the job. It was something to do with the stock market and, according to Gabe Nolan, not at all what he'd hoped for, but he took it anyway. And Herself was soon talking it up.

"It's a very prudent appointment," she said. "Of course, we should really have gotten the Treasury, but there are jealous people who have the President's ear. Never mind. It's a great honor. And this is just the start."

Not for her it wasn't. All it meant was more time on her own-some. Mr. K didn't appear to want her in Washington. He said it was no place for a family, a rented house without any cozy touches. The telephone ringing at all hours and men sitting around, stinking the place out with cigars. Her place was with the children, he said, providing them with a regular home life. But Gabe Nolan reckoned it wasn't so much the late-night smokers that wouldn't suit Herself, it was the pretty girls Mr. K had in, to help him relax. And as for giving the children regularity, that was what me and Fidelma were paid to do. There were times I'm sure Jean and Teddy thought I was their mammy, or Rosie, when she was let home from Sacred Heart.

The Sisters gave her a very fine report for her first term, A for effort, but they said she seemed in low spirits. They said she appeared to think she'd been sent to school as a punishment, and it was a shock to see her when she came for midterm break. She'd piled on the pounds, buying cake with her allowance and eating it in secret. Mrs. K flipped her lid when she saw her.

She said, "I'm putting you on a regime, Rose Marie. No bread, no potatoes, and no cookies and no cake. It's for your own good. When I get back I'll expect you to have lost five pounds at the very least."

She was just on her way out the door to Paris. It was a wedding anniversary trip, to celebrate twenty years of marriage, but she was going alone. Mr. K was busy with business.

I said, "Couldn't you go some other time? Isn't it a pity Mr. Kennedy can't get away?"

"No," she said, "it couldn't matter less. I'll be busy shopping and he'd be bored. He doesn't like Paris so very much and I'm not a sentimental person, you know? That's my secret for a happy marriage. I don't get upset about sentimental things."

So she went off on her anniversary trip for one and we could please ourselves for a few weeks. I even took Rosie up to Boston one Sunday to visit with my sister Margaret and see her boys. Ursie came over too, brought a great big box of blueberry muffins.

"Now, Ray," she said, "show Aunt Nora how you have your multiplication tables by heart."

He did too. He had them right up to twelve times twelve. I was worried for Rosie, that he'd ask her how far she could multiply, but then I realized: To him she was a grown-up. Margaret couldn't take her eyes off her.

"Not quite the ticket is she?" she said. "She's a beautiful-looking girl, and nice with it. There's no side to her. But she's not quite all there."

I said, "She's all right. She's as 'all there' as our Deirdre and look how well she's done. Got her own school and everything."

Ursie said, "Yes, but Nora, that's Africa. They're glad of what they can get there. It must be different for a Kennedy girl. They'll have hoped for her to marry well. I wonder what they'll do with her?"

I could see her out in the yard playing quoits with Val and Ray.

I said, "She will marry well. Her Mammy'll see to that."

We had a grand day. All the way home she kept saying, "I liked those boys. They didn't play rough. I liked those muffins.

Are they fantening, Nora? I wish we could get those sometime, if they're not fantening."

God knows we did everything we could to get her weight down before Herself saw her again. We had her pushing Teddy in his little pedal car, which was enough to crease anybody. Kick gave up cake, to keep her company. And when Euny and Pat played tennis they had her for a ball-girl, running up and down like a dog after a stick. We could all notice the difference in her, but when Mrs. K came home she wasn't satisfied.

She said, "Mary Moore gave me an article about glands. I wonder if Rosie might benefit from some pills to pep up her system."

So she was taken to see a gland doctor, but he couldn't find anything wrong with her that pills would fix. Rosie was just Rosie. Mrs. K said she was very disappointed that the Sisters at Sacred Heart hadn't regulated her diet more closely and it was decided to try the private tutoring again, but not at home. Mrs. Moore recommended a nice family back in Brookline, where she could have her own room and have her lessons from one of the grown-up daughters. It would be a sort of ready-made friend for her, as well as a teacher. She was to go the same weekend Kick and Euny went back to Noroton, and Mr. K drove up from Washington to see her off.

She said, "I'm sorry, Daddy. I'm sorry I ate too much cake."

"Now, Rosie," he said, "you know you're aces with me. You try your best. That's all that counts."

He held her in his arms and she was only half a head shorter than him.

He said, "What did I just tell you? What are you with me?"

"Aces," she said.

"That's right," he said. "And what's your name?"

"Rose Marie Kennedy."

"And if your name's Kennedy what are you?"

"I know what it is," she said, "but I forgot it."

He said, "You're a winner, that's what. Kennedys are winners! So you go do your very best with Miss O'Keefe. Rise early, huh? Say your prayers, study hard as you know how, take regular exercise. I'm going to have a set of Indian clubs sent up there for you. Best exercise a person can take. You do your damndest at all those things and you'll get no criticism from me. You got that, Rosie? You're one of Joe Kennedy's winners."

"Yes," she said, "I got that."

"I'm getting my own set of clubs, Nora," she said. "And I'm not going to dipsapoint Daddy. I'm one of Joe Kennedy's winners."

14

Something in the Blood

When Joseph Patrick went off to college, Jack was out from under his shadow at last, but it didn't improve him. He acted sillier than ever, neglecting his studies and getting into scrapes with Lem Billings. The pair of them nearly got sacked and Kick made matters worse, sending Jack a cablegram congratulating him on livening things up at Choate. Mr. K had to go up to the school and smooth things over. Herself laid all the blame on Lem, so he didn't get his usual invitation for the Easter vacation. Jack was sent on a retreat instead, him and Kick to Our Lady of Deliverance for all of Holy Week, and then he was made to do extra Latin, to catch up where he'd fallen behind.

From time to time Mrs. K hinted that the President had some higher position in mind for Mr. Kennedy and that the call might come at any time to up sticks and follow him. Gabe Nolan said it would likely be to Germany. He reckoned if anybody could get on the right side of Adolf Hitler and keep us out of another war it was Joe Kennedy. I prayed that wouldn't happen. I didn't fancy having to shop for socks and Gregory powders in a foreign tongue. Then we heard a rumor that he was going to be offered ambassador to Ireland. Fidelma was over the moon. She had her Daddy still living, and a thousand cousins, in Tralee, so she thought it'd be a chance to visit with them at Mr. Roosevelt's expense. She practically had her bag packed. But the weeks went by and we heard nothing.

She kept saying, "You ask. I'm always the one who asks. Ask Mrs. Moore."

But it wasn't me that was eager to get back to the old country. Fidelma had this notion about visiting graves and taking chrysanthemums in case your loved ones were feeling neglected, but in those days I wasn't one for graveyards. The day we buried my sister Nellie, it was blowing heavens hard. All I could think was how cold and lonely she was going to be. I decided there and then I'd just carry her memory back home in my heart, and that's how I've tried to think of the dead ever since. I did get back to Ballynagore eventually, to take a last look round, but that was nothing to do with Mr. Roosevelt.

Anyway, when Mrs. K got back from her travels Fidelma asked her right out if it was true we were going to Ireland.

"No," she said, "we are not." And her face snapped shut.

But Fidelma Clery had the pluck of the foolish, so she didn't let it rest. She brought it up with Mr. K as well, the next time we saw him.

She said, "We heard a whisper you might be asked to go to Ireland, sir."

"Indeed I was asked," he said, "but I turned it down. My people left Ireland to make a better life for themselves, so why would I take my children back there now?"

"Well," she said, "so they'd know where they came from?"

"Load of applesauce," he said. "My boys know their history,

and they know it's not where they come from that matters, it's where they're going."

As soon as he said that I knew why Herself was so upset.

He'd had the chance to be an ambassador and he'd turned it down because he didn't think Ireland was good enough for him, and Mrs. K was madder than a hornet in a jam jar.

Fidelma was disappointed too. She'd been buying bits and pieces to take for her folks, convinced that's where we'd be going. It was no loss to me though. The only kin I had left in Ballynagore was Edmond, and I hardly ever thought of him. Being the only boy, he'd always been given the top of the milk. It was always Edmond got the buttered heel of a fresh-baked loaf, but it didn't appear to have put much spine in him. It must have been the Clavin woman who proposed marriage, because he'd never have thought of it for himself. If it wasn't for Ursie, I wouldn't know if he was dead or alive.

Ursie's the great correspondent in the family, tapping bits of news out on her typewriter and sending me the snippets of the news she got back.

"Deirdre's mission had a lovely visit from a Vatican monsignor," she'd tell me. "But monkeys had got in and ruined a pile of missals and her bunions were bad."

Or Edmond had been to Tullamore for dentures, cost a fortune but he couldn't get along with them so they sat on the mantel shelf reproaching him. Two boys drowned in Lough Ennell. The Clavin widow wanted to move back to Horseleap.

That got Ursie all steamed up.

She said, "He can't just go off."

I said, "Of course he can. They could put all their stuff on a handcart and be there in two hours."

"But what about our house?" she wanted to know. "What if he leaves it to rot? That's our inheritance too. We're entitled to a say."

That's what comes of working around lawyers. As far as I was concerned they could dynamite the place. Tiny windows and low ceilings, and that everlasting damp striking up through the floor. If Edmond was threatening to shift to somewhere more comfortable, all I could say was "about time too."

But as I recalled, there was an ocean of difference between what Edmond talked of doing and what he actually did. Anyway, we weren't going to Ireland and that was that.

Joseph Patrick was in London, taking a year away from his classes at Harvard College. Mr. K had sent him there to study under a famous professor, and when school was out he and Jack sailed for England, to meet up with young Joe and go traveling, Germany, France, Russia, father and sons together. Which left us in peace at Hyannis, because Herself was gone too, touring in Switzerland and then taking Kick to her new school, near Paris. She wanted Kick to have the same education she'd had, guided by the Sacred Heart Sisters but made to speak foreign languages too and mix with girls from good families. Kick wasn't keen. She had her friends at Noroton, and France was too far away for her to come home for vacations.

Mrs. K said it wasn't called "vacation" in France. It was called "congé." And she said it didn't matter that Kick couldn't come home, because she'd go to her and take her on trips, to stay in fancy hotels and visit all the famous churches and ruins. She was trying to turn her into a refined young lady, but that would have been a lifetime's work. Kick never had the naturalness trained out of her, I'm glad to say. She'd say the first thing that came into her head. She'd kick off her shoes and sit on the floor sooner than a chair, anytime. So for all Mrs. Kennedy's efforts I couldn't see anything different about her when she came back from France, except that she'd had a permanent wave.

"Had my culture shot, Nora," she said. "Now it's Euny's turn. I'm just going to sit on the swing seat and read *Moviegoer*."

Jack was meant to be following Joseph Patrick to Harvard but Lem Billings was down for Princeton and Jack didn't want to be parted from him. Mr. K agreed to his going to Princeton too, but he warned him, if he wasted his time he'd be out of there quick sticks. And when it came to it, he'd no sooner arrived but he fell sick again. Mr. and Mrs. K were both traveling, so Eddie Moore went with him to the Brigham hospital in Boston. They said there was something wrong with his blood and the situation gave cause for concern, so Mrs. Moore expected Herself to sail home immediately. But Mrs. K never appeared. She cabled to say she'd only just arrived in Vienna and she was sure Jack would be over the worst by the time she could get back.

I don't believe it bothered Jack. They were all accustomed to her absences. But the doctors had him in isolation, so he missed having visitors. *Some kind of Darling Nora you are*, he wrote.

> *I'm suffering up here and all you send me is fruit. I need company and sympathy. How about sending Euny? Lem would drive her. Tell her to bring me magazines and candy bars and a back-scratcher. The quack says there are two kinds of cells in blood, red and white, and I'm short on the white ones. I should have 10,000 but I'm down to 3,500. Get to 1,500 and you're road meat. Pray to St. Jude for me, DN.*
>
> *Your loving "3,000 white cells and counting" Jack*

He was suffering from something called neutropenia. They said it had more than likely been brought on by the medicine he'd taken for his stomach aches. He was in the hospital for weeks but he climbed back, bit by bit, and then he was home, sunning himself on the porch and eating ice cream by the gallon when Mrs. K finally showed her face.

"Just as I thought," she said. "He's better already. I expect he'd been eating too much rich food. Or it could have been bad water. I'd have cut short Vienna and come hurrying back for nothing."

I said, "It didn't seem like nothing. The first two weeks we thought we might lose him."

"What nonsense," she said. "Jack's suffered from these little setbacks all his life but he always overcomes them. You of all people should know that."

Well, so I did, but even though his blood got back to normal he was still full of aches and pains. His back hurt, his knees hurt, and he stayed thin as a lath no matter how much ice cream he ate.

I said, "If you were mine I'd send you to the knackers."

"You're right," he said. "I reckon they just better shoot me."

Euny was no great specimen either, though she at least didn't have the knee trouble. If she couldn't have played tennis she'd have made life miserable for all of us. With her it was stomach trouble and nerves. She couldn't sleep, couldn't sit still, couldn't put on any flesh. Mrs. K thought she had the makings of a perfect figure, but we called her "the greyhound." She was a fast study though. She did so well in school Mr. K said it was a pity she was a girl because she looked like she'd make a smarter president than Jack or Bobby.

Euny couldn't compete with Joseph Patrick though. He was still the star attraction, back from London, looking so debonair in a drape-cut suit and his tie in a Windsor knot. Mr. K treated him man-to-man from then on. He even put up with his smoking, though he'd implored all the children not to take up such a silly, wasteful habit. And for his part Joe put up with his Daddy slavering over the girls he brought home. There was a beautiful redhead, all legs. Danny Walsh nearly broke a blood vessel watching her climb on a bicycle. Then there was a blonde called Mitzi, when the redhead fell out of favor. Herself said Mitzi wasn't a proper name. As a matter of fact, she found something wrong with every last one of them. If she has her way, those boys will all stay bachelors.

When Mrs. K was a girl and she'd had her year overseas at the Sacred Heart, she'd come home a gold medal Child of Mary, but none of that had rubbed off on Kick. All we heard from her when she came back was a list of the beaux she'd met, brothers of her new friends mainly, all very proper, but still, she was boy-crazy. And Rosie was just as bad. That was the first summer we had any trouble with her and it was all because Joe and Jack both brought girls home and Kick was getting letters every day, but Rosie didn't have a beau.

She'd been getting along just dandy living with the O'Keefes. She'd joined the Girl Scouts and learned how to pitch a tent and fry sausages over a campfire. And she concentrated better, so if you sent her to fetch something she didn't always forget what she'd gone for. But she was betwixt and between. Not a child anymore but not really a woman either. She loved to watch the Laugh-O-Grams with Teddy and play dollies' tea parties with Jean, but she was eighteen years old and when there was a dance on in Osterville she expected to be treated like a grown-up.

Joe and Jack and Lem Billings were under instructions to dance with her and keep an eye on her at all times, but of course she didn't want to be supervised. She wanted to dance with any boy who asked her and go outside for a soda if she was invited. We had a scene or two over that.

She'd say, "I want to dance with real boys. Why can't I? Kick does."

And Lem used to say, "Real boys? Gee Rosie, thanks for the compliment."

Sometimes she'd laugh and tell him his feet were too big. Sometimes she'd boil over. She'd start screaming and stamping, and when that happened Fidelma was the only one who could do anything with her. Mrs. K would just turn on her heel and go for a walk along the strand, and Fidelma would take Rosie to her bedroom and stay with her, sing to her, till she calmed down and fell asleep. And when she woke up the storm would have passed. She'd be her usual smiling self, as if nothing had happened, and Mrs. K would never mention it.

In the summer of 1936 we suddenly had three extra heads to count. Mrs. Kennedy's sister Agnes had a seizure of the brain and died, so her children were brought to Hyannis, three young Gargan cousins, with their world turned upside down.

Mrs. K said, "Fit them in where you think best, Nora dear. And we'll look through the boxes in the attic. There may be some of Jean's old things that would do for the girls."

"Extra work for no more money," Fidelma said, but we hardly noticed we had them. When you've had nine, what are three more? And they were lambs compared to the shenanigans the Kennedys got up to, climbing out onto the rooftops, purloining things from the candy store, chasing across neighbors' gardens like a bunch of hoydens. Joey Gargan was barely two years older than Teddy, so they paired off and Teddy padded around behind him like a day-old chick.

"What shall we do next, Joey?" he'd say. And whatever Joey suggested, he went along with. To watch them you'd never have thought Joey was the orphan.

The two wee girls didn't settle so easily though. They wandered around trying to fathom out where they were and why. They knew Mrs. K was their aunt Rose, but of course she didn't look like a child's idea of an aunt. She had no lap to sit on, for one thing. Still, she gave all our children a lecture about treating the Gargan cousins nicely and remembering their recent misfortune. But one morning I heard Jean say, "I'll play with you, Anne, but only for a little while. I can't be friends with just anyone, you know. I'm a Kennedy."

When Mr. Roosevelt ran for another term we wondered whether Mr. K would be so generous again with his time and money. He didn't seem any nearer to getting offered a plum job, and, according to Eddie Moore, the President didn't particularly like Mr. K any more than Mr. K liked the President. But they found each other useful. Like when the Holy Father sent Cardinal Pacelli on a visit to America. The President had him up to Hyde Park, but Mrs. Roosevelt was out of town and nobody could think what to do with him after the luncheon. Mrs. K was roped in, which thrilled her to bits. She said, "Why, he'll come to Crownlands for tea, of course."

Danny Walsh drove her to the station to meet him. I'll bet Danny's still getting free drinks on that story. "The Pope, is it? Oh I knew him when he was Cardinal. Had him in my car, as a matter of fact."

Mrs. K was in her element. She said, "Nora, those Roosevelts know nothing about Mother Church. They should have consulted with me from the very start. I'd have organized a wonderful program for His Eminence."

I was instructed to wait half an hour after their arrival and then bring Jean and Teddy down to the sitting room. There sat His Eminence, gaunt as a death's head, picking at a slice of Gertie Ambler's apple Johnny cake. He had beautiful scarlet piping on his cassock. Well, Teddy did no more than take a running jump and land on his knee and Mrs. K never corrected him. That chair the Cardinal sat in was kept roped off ever afterwards, so no ordi-

nary backside should ever sit upon it again, and when the Bronxville house was sold, it was taken up to Hyannis.

"What a fortunate boy you are, Teddy," she kept saying. She
was like the cat that had had the cream.

She said, "This is a day you'll remember all your life. We must
write and tell Grandpa Fitzgerald how you met the Holy Father's
very special Cardinal."

"Yes," he said. "And he told me I was a real smart little feller."

Mr. K would do anything to keep his children in the front
row. He told the President that Bobby had started collecting
stamps, and the next thing we knew Bobby got a personal letter
with some stamps enclosed from the President's own collection.
And then, after he was reelected, all the children were invited to
go to Washington for the Inauguration.

Herself was away on a shopping trip and Mr. K was in the
presidential party, of course, so me and Fidelma got to chaperone
them on the train, along with Mrs. Moore. Joe and Jack couldn't
come, because of their classes, but the others were all given leave
from school and Rosie was fetched down from Boston for the
occasion. She looked so stylish, with a new beaver trim on her
coat and a little felt hat. It's times like that I'd like to bring up to
them when they say she wasn't safe to be let out. If that was the
case, how come she was allowed to go to a reception at the White
House and shake hands with the President himself and talk to
both the Mrs. Roosevelts? Nobody can ever answer me that.

15

The Queen of Bronxville, the Queen of England, and Walter Stallybrass

Gabe Nolan was the one we depended on to know how things stood between Mr. K and the President. "Very cordial," he said. "Like clock hands at quarter past three. He came over to the house last week and watched a movie."

Then Danny Walsh would give us the version according to Mrs. K, which was that putting on private movie shows for the President was all very well but it didn't appear to be leading anywhere.

He said, "She reckons there's somebody on the inside keeps queering things for Your Man. She's not happy."

That was what I thought. I'd heard her giving out to Mr. K while we were packing to go down to Florida for Christmas.

"Another year wasted," she said. "Call him up. Just tell him what we want."

She'd been clipping pieces out of the dailies, about Mr. Bingham who was the ambassador to London. He was very sick, com-

ing home for an operation and not expected to go back to his
work for a long time.

She said, "Tell him you have to see him before the holidays.
That job has our name on it. Bob Bingham's on his way out and
if you don't step forward and claim what Roosevelt owes you,
you're a fool."

We were still down at Palm Beach when we got the word. Mr.
Kennedy called from Washington to say he was the new American ambassador to the Court of St. James's in London. I thought
Mrs. K would die, she was so happy. She called us all together
to tell us Mr. K was to be referred to as "Ambassador," from that
moment on. And she still calls him that, when he's in her good
books, though the job was a flash in the pan and it's a very long
time since he was any such thing.

"Once an ambassador, always an ambassador," she says.

The household maids were the first to be given notice.

Fidelma said, "Here we go. We'll be on the scrap heap, Brennan, just when things are getting interesting. I tell you what. If
they don't take me with them I'm going to hide fish trimmings in
with her ball gowns."

Gabe Nolan was convinced Danny would be let go, because
the Kennedys would need a driver accustomed to VIPs and high
levels of personal security.

Danny said, "And that's you is it, you bandy-legged little whippet? What are you going to do, carry a BB gun? Your Man'll be
getting an English driver, Nolan, that knows the rules of the road.
And Mrs. K will take me, because I'm more than a driver to her."

Fidelma said, "You are, Danny. You're an arse-wiper. You've a
job for life, I'm sure."

Gabe said, "And what do you mean, 'knows the rules of the
road.' I've drove on the left. I was driving in Ireland when you
were still sucking on your Mammy's tit."

Danny said, "The bollix you were. Driving what? A horse and cart?"

And so they went on. But Danny Walsh came out ahead. He was kept on to drive for Mrs. K, Gertie Ambler was kept on to cook, and me and Fidelma were told we'd both be required.

Herself said, "The Ambassador and I will have very many social obligations. I expect there'll be weeks when we hardly see the children."

As Fidelma said, "Nothing different there then."

Our passage was booked for February and we were all in an uproar, steamer trunks everywhere and Herself running round with so many lists pinned to her skirt and blouse you could hardly see what she was wearing. Seven children to pack for, and all their appointments to be kept before we left. Eyes to be tested, teeth to be checked, hair to be cut, confessions to be heard.

Then she got stopped in her tracks. It was one of the maids who found her. She was curled up on her daybed, gripping her pillow, she was in so much pain. She wouldn't let anyone touch her.

They all said, "You go in to her, Nora. You know how to handle her."

"Such a nuisance," she kept saying. "I have so much to do. But I'll be perfectly well in a minute."

Then she was sick and she was feeling so rotten she didn't even give instructions how the mess was to be cleaned up.

I said, "I'll send for the doctor."

"No, no," she said. "I'll just have a glass of hot water. It's sure to pass."

But I didn't like the look of her so I sent for the doctor anyway and just as well. It was her appendix and she was in hospital within the hour. That threw a spanner in the works. Mr. K said he couldn't delay getting to London, so he'd sail as planned, and maybe take Kick with him, to stand in for Mrs. K in case he needed anyone to throw an urgent tea party. Well, Herself may have been just out from under the surgeon's knife, but she was in her senses enough to put the kibosh on that little plan. She said it would get the Ambassador's tour of duty off to completely the wrong start to have an eighteen-year-old girl acting as his hostess, and anyway, no tea parties were to be given until she'd inspected the hollow-ware.

So our tickets were changed and we sailed in March instead, except for Danny Walsh, who took Mrs. K's limousine over on the same boat as the Ambassador, and Fidelma, who was on unpaid leave, to get off at Queenstown and to go to Tralee to see her folks. Herself should have recuperated another week or two at least but she was determined to get to London. Even before she was up from her bed she was trying on different hats, deciding which one to wear for the farewell photographs when we went aboard.

"All the dailies will be there," she said. "And you children must all prepare something to say. They're sure to ask you how you feel about going to live in London, so each of you think of something bright and interesting, and practice saying it. No mumbling. You must smile and speak up."

We were taking Teddy, Jean, Bobby, Pat, and Kick. Joe and Jack were to come over in the college vacations, and Euny was to follow on at the end of the spring semester, with Rosie chaperoning her and Fidelma hooking up with them again when they docked at Cork. And that's another thing. When they say Rosie was always backward and incapable, I'd like to remind them, in 1938 she wasn't considered incapable. She was allowed to cross the Atlantic Ocean with nobody for company but a sixteen-year-old sister. In 1938 she was capable of going to curtseying lessons and passing with flying colors and being presented to Their Royal

Majesties at Buckingham Palace. But how people can change their tune.

We might have been film stars, the send-off we got in New York. Ursie clipped a whole pile of photographs and sent them to Edmond and Deirdre. I'm not rightly sure where Nyasaland is, but it's funny to think of me and my Kennedys pinned to a wall somewhere in the middle of the jungle. Mrs. K was in her element, yammering away to the reporters.

She said "I'm no stranger to London, of course. As Mayor Fitzgerald's daughter, I traveled extensively and I received much of my education in Europe. As a matter of fact it feels more like going to my second home than a voyage into the unknown. And of course I'm greatly looking forward to working alongside the Ambassador."

We'd been told Prince's Gate was a very good address, with views onto a carriage drive and a big green park. We'd been told we'd even have our own ballroom.

She said, "The timing couldn't be more perfect. The girls will be able to make their debut in great style. I was twenty before I had my coming-out, you know. I'd been too busy with my studies to have it sooner. Most girls had their parties at hotels, but mine was held at home. It was more appropriate for the Mayor's daughter. We had dinner and a ball and the house was filled, just filled with carnations and sweet peas. And the next morning my picture was on the front of every newspaper in town. It was the most important debut of the year. But things will be even better for Rosie and Kick. The Ambassador's daughters."

We docked at Plymouth and Mr. K met us with even more cameras and reporters than had seen us off in New York.

Somebody shouted out, "You all look the same. Which one's the mother?"

She loved that, waving and smiling and posing for more pictures.

Somebody else asked how Mrs. K could look so young and slim when she'd had nine children. Mr. K said, "We had the stork deliver them from Barney's."

We went in convoy to London. It took all day and when we got to Prince's Gate there wasn't even hot water for baths. Nor towels fit for anything but cleaning rags, nor a mirror you could see your face in. We had twenty bedrooms and ten bathrooms and a gas range that wouldn't light and then, when it did, it took your eyebrows off. Gertie said either it went or she did, so there was no dinner cooked that night. We had sandwiches and lemonade and Teddy and Jean rode up and down in the elevator till well past ten o'clock, driving the butler and the maids demented.

Mrs. K came in to me after I'd got the young ones to bed. She looked exhausted.

I said, "You never got your nap today."

"No," she said, "and it takes a great deal of energy to put on a good show. But never mind. We did it. And now we really have our work cut out. Tomorrow, dear heart, as soon as the Ambassador has gone to his office, we'll make a start. There are things that need to be repaired, things that have to be replaced. I have to hope we're not called upon to receive anyone important just yet. The residence of the United States Ambassador and not two matching glasses in the house. Can you imagine?"

I'd never known her to take any great interest in furnishings. She'd spend on hats and gowns and then have rugs darned and sheets turned sides to middle till there was nothing left to turn. But Prince's Gate was different. She seemed to think the whole world was watching to see what kind of figure the Kennedys cut in London. She bought a Royal Worcester dinner service and new table linens. She had paintings brought round from the embassy in Grosvenor Square to cover the grubby patches on the walls, and two water geysers replaced before we were all gassed in our beds. She had carte blanche. Mr. K never minded her spending. For days she had me follow her round the house writing down what needed to be done and I thought how small she looked in those big, grand rooms. It was one thing to be the Queen of Bronxville, but Prince's Gate was something else, even if it did have a cracked toilet bowl.

Pat and Jean started at the Sacred Heart School in Roehampton, as weekly boarders; Bobby and Teddy went to Mr. Gibbs's School, only ten minutes walk away on Sloane Street; and as soon as they were all settled she started planning for Kick and Rosie's debut. It was called "the Season."

They didn't really know anyone in London, of course, but the way it worked was the debs' mothers gave afternoon teas, to introduce their girls to one another and pass around the names of boys suitable to be dancing partners. There were girls down from Yorkshire and Scotland and all over, so the Kennedys weren't the only new faces in town, and Kick being Kick, she soon had a hundred new friends. Ginny Vigo, Sissy Lloyd-Thomas, Minnie Stubbs, Sally Norton, Pamela Digby, Susie Frith-Johnstone, Cynthia Brough, Caro Leinster, Debo Mitford.

Once the Season got started there were parties every night of the week, except Fridays, when everybody went off to weekends in the country. So they needed stout shoes and good warm tweeds as well as party dresses. There were hair appointments and gown fittings and curtseying lessons at Madame Marguerite's, as well as all the teas and luncheons and balls. It was a full-time job for any deb, and Kick was more in demand than most. Then, after Rosie and Euny arrived, Rosie was included in a lot of the invitations. She was old to be making her debut and Mrs. K decided against her having her own ball, for the excitement and worry of it would have been too much for her, but she went with Kick to selected parties and one of our new drivers, London Jack, was deputed to keep a special eye on her and dance with her if nobody else had filled her card.

Danny Walsh said, "I could have done that. Why didn't they ask me?"

Fidelma said, "Because you're a big ugly lummox and London Jack looks like Johnny Weissmuller."

London Jack was probably the undoing of her. Mrs. K danced with him herself, to try him out, and she said he led very well. And poor Rosie was ripe to be led. I don't believe London Jack ever did a thing except make her feel she was a normal girl, but after that summer of dancing night after night she was never the same. She'd throw a paddy if Kick was allowed to go somewhere and she wasn't, if Mrs. K said it wasn't suitable for a person of her abilities.

"Damn it, I am suitable," she'd say.

Mrs. K told Fidelma off. She said she'd obviously been using language in front of the children.

Fidelma said, "The bloody cheek of her. It's not me Rosie's learned it from. Joe Kennedy needs his mouth washed out and Danny Walsh could curse for Ireland."

Rosie would get the very devil in her sometimes when she was thwarted, but you couldn't help but feel sorry for her. Kick would be invited to Hever Castle or Cliveden, and be gone all weekend. Euny and Pat went off to tennis parties, and Bobby would take Jean and Teddy across to the Serpentine Lake or riding their bicycles through the park. And Rosie would be left, trailing around after me, romancing about London Jack.

"I love him," she'd say. "I'm going to marry him."

I said, "You'd better not let Mother hear you talking like that. If she does, London Jack'll be getting his cards."

"Damn Mother," she'd say. "I like the trotfox best. Dancing up close. Close, close, close."

I didn't know what to do for the best. I thought London Jack was trustworthy. He had his position to consider. But there'd be other boys. She could get a reputation. She and Kick were going to be presented to the King and Queen with all the other debutantes in June, the kind of occasion a girl would look back on for the rest of her life. I didn't want Herself deciding Rosie had better not go.

Fidelma said, "Leave her be. She just wants a bit of a cuddle. Sure I wouldn't mind one myself."

I said, "Years ago, one of the doctors told Mrs. K that Rosie must never have babies."

Fidelma said, "You don't get babies doing the foxtrot, Brennan. Just leave her be. We'll have a quiet word with London Jack."

He swore he hadn't encouraged her.

He said, "She's not quite the full shilling, is she? She gets pretty fresh though, and I don't want any trouble. I mean, I don't mind a bit of dancing but driving's my trade."

Fidelma said, "That's all right. Just bear in mind she still plays with her dollies. No good-night kisses. If it's good-night kisses you want, apply to me."

Mr. and Mrs. K went to Windsor Castle, weekend guests of the King and Queen. I thought we should never hear the end of that.

"The Ambassador sat next to Her Majesty," she must have told me a hundred times, "and I sat beside the King, and there was an orchestra playing through dinner, all tricked out in scarlet jackets. They made such a gay picture. We met the little Princesses, of course, after church on Sunday. Adorable. Princess Margaret Rose would make such a perfect playmate for Jean. We went to their private quarters on Sunday afternoon and one of the guests had a seizure, right in the middle of tea, but you should have seen how the Queen reacted. She set the most wonderful example. She remained perfectly calm and just carried on passing the cups. It prevented an embarrassing atmosphere while the woman was being helped from the room. One could learn a great deal by studying Her Majesty."

They'd had sheets of the headed royal notepaper provided in their accommodations and Mrs. K wrote a special keepsake letter to each of the children, and probably to every Tom, Dick and Harry she ever met, so the whole world would know she'd been to Windsor Castle. It was funny to see how thrilled she was to be mixing with royalty. I'd have thought it would take more than that to impress Mayor Fitzgerald's daughter, but her head was turned.

"His Majesty has so taken to the Ambassador," she said. "They're firm friends already. And the Queen loves to talk about the children. She can't wait to meet them."

Well, she was about to meet Kick and Rosie, or at least see them in a sea of other girls with feathers in their hair.

It was a big production, getting two girls ready to be presented at Buckingham Palace. Mrs. K was to go with them in the limousine and she had to wear a diamond tiara and white kid gloves with twenty-one buttons, no more, no less. She said you could be turned away if your gloves weren't right. The things the English dream up to keep you in your place. The main worry though was the curtseying. The girls had to go to special lessons. They'd to practice walking up the red carpet until they had it off pat. Curtsey, step to the side, then glide away.

We all went downstairs to see them off. Herself was in a gown made by Mr. Molyneux, white satin with tiny gold beads stitched all over it, and a tiara borrowed from Lady Bessborough. Kick and Rosie had white tulle with a silver thread, Prince of Wales feathers pinned to their veils, and lily-of-the-valley nosegays. Kick looked pretty, though we'd had to wrestle with her hair, and Mrs. K looked a million dollars, but it was Rosie who stole the show, with her beautiful creamy shoulders and her dimples when she smiled. As Danny Walsh said, she was a grand doorful of a girl.

It was after midnight when they got home, because the limousines had been backed up along Constitution Hill. I took them hot milk and bread after they'd put on their pajamas, and there sat Rosie in tears.

She said, "I tumbled, Nora. I didn't do the curtsey thing right."

Kick said, "You didn't tumble, you noodle. You stumbled. And absolutely nobody noticed. Gracious, the King and Queen had probably nodded off, sitting there for hours just being curtseyed to. And you looked ravishing."

"Thank you, Kick," she said. "You looked nice too. But I think I dipsapointed Mother."

Kick swore it had only been the tiniest stumble, at the end, when she was meant to glide away.

She said, "Know what, Nora? It was all a big zzzzz anyhow. The best bit was waiting in line to get in. There were all these people peering into the car. They wait for hours, apparently, to see if they can spot any really famous debs. Just think, there are people going to bed happy tonight because they saw Kick and Rosie Kennedy."

Their pictures were in the papers the next day, along with Minnie Stubbs and Debo Mitford and Cynthia Brough. And then we had Kick's ball to get ready. She had eighty coming to dinner and three hundred more for the dancing afterwards, with Ambrose's Band brought in for the evening and all the help invited to the buffet supper later on. I don't know if Billy Hartington was there that night. Kick danced every dance with a different beau and there was nothing about Billy that would make you remember him. He was just a tall, soft-faced English boy. But she did meet him that summer. He was the Duke of Devonshire's eldest boy and Kick was invited to their house in Sussex, Compton Place. There was going to be a big house party for the horse racing at Goodwood and I was sent along as chaperone. Kick had never been interested in horse racing before, in fact she only had to look at a horse for her wheezing to start up, but she was very keen to go.

She said, "Billy's a Marquess. Isn't that a scream? Doesn't it sound like an old guy in a velvet cloak and a wig?"

I wasn't sure what a Marquess was, but Lord Billy certainly had a big name for one so young. He was Lord William Cavendish, Marquess of Hartington and heir to the Duke of Devonshire. I've never understood the Devonshire bit either. They none of them live in Devonshire. They live in Derbyshire.

Danny Walsh said, "Devonshire, Derbyshire, what's the difference. It's all robbed from the poor saps who work on it."

He was just put out because he wasn't the one going to Compton Place. He had to drive Herself to Hertfordshire instead, to see a special school she thought might be a suitable place to keep Rosie occupied, helping with a kindergarten class.

Kick was in a tizz, wondering what outfits to take. All she knew was there'd be tennis and drives out to the racetrack and dancing at night, to phonograph records. She didn't think the Duke would be there. Lord Billy had told her his father didn't care for the racetrack and parties. But she was worried about meeting the Duchess.

I said, "You've been presented to Their Majesties, so a Duchess can't be anything to worry about."

"No," she said, "but what if I have to talk to her? Caro Leinster says I sound like Daffy Duck."

I said, "Pay no attention. Most of those English girls sound like donkeys. Now what about this Lord Billy? When did he catch your fancy?"

"He didn't," she said. "I mean, he's cute, but he's just Billy. His sisters are fun though."

We went on the train and a driver collected us from Eastbourne station. Middle-aged, with a dove-gray livery and a Clark Gable chin.

Kick started straight in, tried to sit up front alongside him but he wasn't having that.

She said, "I'm Kathleen Kennedy."

He said, "I'm relieved to hear it, Miss. I try not to make an error when I'm meeting guests."

She said, "I guess you know the Duke and Duchess."

He said, "I've worked for the Devonshires twenty-five years."

She said, "So if I meet them, what do I have to do? Do I have to call them Your Graciousness or something?"

He said, "You call them 'Your Grace,' but you won't meet them. They're not here."

She said, "But just say I did, do I have to curtsey or anything?"

"Nay," he said. "No curtseying. But you won't see them, because they're at Chatsworth. I can vouch for that. You're an American, if I'm not mistaken, Miss Kennedy."

She said, "My Daddy's the American Ambassador. His Excellency Joseph P. Kennedy."

I could see him studying me in his driving mirror.

He said, "You from America too?"

Kick said, "Of course she is. She does that funny kind of Irish talk, but she's American really. Nora's been our nanny for centuries."

He said, "Has she? She's wearing well."

Compton Place was a low, square house, covered with Virginia creeper. It had lawns and flower beds and a little kitchen garden but inside it was nothing grand. It was just a comfortable house, perfect for a crowd of youngsters on a summer weekend.

There were two other cars being unloaded as we pulled round onto the drive. Kick spotted a girl she knew and went running off, laughing and squealing.

Our driver said, "If you hop back in, Kennedy, I'll run you round to the servants' entrance."

I said, "My name's Nora Brennan."

He was lifting the valises down off the dickey.

"Well, Nora Brennan," he said, "you'll find you'll be known as Kennedy here. That's the way we do things in Devonshire houses. Lady's maids go by their lady's name. But you weren't to know that."

He had a funny, flat way of talking.

I said, "Anything else I should know?"

"Yes," he said. "Your Miss Kennedy. She's a bit free and easy, you know, gabbing to a driver? Generally speaking, I drive people all day long and don't get two words out of them."

I said, "Then it must have made a pleasant change, to meet a natural, friendly American girl."

"Aye," he said. "A nice, natural young lady. But she'd like to fit in, I daresay? She'll want to know the ropes."

I said, "Anything else?"

"Yes," he said. "You've very bonny hair, Kennedy. Very bonny indeed."

And that was the start of me and Walter Stallybrass.

Billy Hartington's people lived in a different world from Kick, even if her Daddy was a millionaire. They had the houses and the servants and ancestors hung on the walls in big gilt frames, but they'd had it all so long they didn't appear to notice. They carried it lightly, just nice, polite people who'd give you a "Good day" whoever you were.

I'd been so long around Mr. and Mrs. Kennedy I expected everybody to be like them, always calculating and maneuvering and expecting to be stabbed in the back. The Devonshires treated people right and so I don't suppose it ever occurred to them that people wouldn't treat them right in return. Good food, too. Me and Fidelma generally ate in the kitchen with the drivers, and the rations weren't generous, everything counted out. One chop, two potatoes, one spoon of beans. But that weekend down at Compton Place we had big rib roasts and Yorkshire pudding, and pies filled with gooseberries fresh from the garden, with clotted cream.

The youngsters all motored across to another big house on Sunday evening, for a treasure trail, so I tagged along with the other lady's maids, for a walk along to the bandstand and a glass of ginger beer.

Minnie Stubbs's maid said, "You've not been a lady's maid long, have you?"

I said, "I'm not a lady's maid. The nursery's my province. I'm just here to keep an eye on things, with all these young men around. Miss Kennedy's only five minutes out of Sacred Heart."

She said, "What's Sacred Heart?"

Caro Leinster's maid said, "A nunnery. They're Catholics, Stubbs. American and Catholic."

Stubbs said, "Well, you needn't worry about any of the gentlemen. They're all very high up. You won't catch any of them getting serious about an American girl."

Ginny Vigo's maid said, "Can't they afford a lady's maid for her then, your people?"

I said, "Her Daddy's one of the richest men in America."

"Well then," she said, "she ought to travel with somebody who knows to put her shoes on trees before they're sent down for cleaning. That's how we do things over here."

I was getting tired of hearing how things were supposed to be done in a Devonshire house.

And on top of everything else, they didn't believe I'd met Gloria Swanson.

16

The Fox Supervises the Henhouse and
Mr. Chamberlain Goes to Munich

That summer of '38 Prince's Gate was always full of young voices. Joe and Jack came over as soon as college was finished. Jack was as yellow as a ragweed and still getting his stomach attacks, but he wouldn't slow down. Kick was the toast of the town, so they were all invited to half a dozen parties every night and they'd take Rosie with them too, as long as she promised not to get overwrought when it was time to come home.

I told her she was lucky to have two handsome brothers willing to dance with her.

She said, "They don't always. Sometimes they go off."

I said, "You're still lucky. My brother hardly danced a step in his life, only at his own wedding, and then he looked like he had concrete in his boots."

She said, "Sometimes Joe and Jack don't dance. They take girls in the dark and squeeze them. Squeeze them and squeeze them to make them feel nice. They give them kisses and do things you're not supposed."

I said, "You'll be for it if your Mammy hears you talking like that."

"She won't hear," she said. "She's gone to tea at Lady Bossyburgh's."

It was a good thing they were sending her to Belmont after the summer, to keep her mind occupied.

Fidelma said, "Do you know what I'd do with her if she was mine? I'd marry her off quick. Let her have what she's longing for."

I knew Mrs. K wouldn't wear that. She'd always said Rosie mustn't have babies, in case her slowness could be inherited, but I agreed with Fidelma. Rosie would have made a very contented wife. You don't need to be a scholar to keep a man happy, and from some of the marriages I've seen maybe it's better not to have too much going on up top. And as for babies, I never did believe Rosie's funny little ways were the kind that could be passed on.

When Mrs. K was at home she'd come down and take tea with any of Kick's friends who called by in the afternoon, but in the evenings she made herself scarce. If she wasn't going off somewhere with the Ambassador, dressed up in her jewels and spangles like a circus pony, she'd have an early dinner with the children and then go up to her rooms to read. Conserving herself, I always thought, for when she was in the public eye.

So Mr. K was the one who did the evening socializing. He never touched liquor himself but he kept a very lavish bar and he liked to hold court. He loved showing off in front of all those pretty girls, and some of them encouraged him. Pamela Digby was the worst, cheeky little minx she was, the way she joshed him. If I'd been Kick I'd have dropped her. I wouldn't have felt right watching my father making such a fool of himself, but Kick could never see any fault in her Daddy. He liked to hear what the young men thought about the situation in Germany, too. The newspapers were saying Hitler might invade Czechoslovakia, the same way he'd helped himself to Austria, and then we'd be obliged to go to war again.

Mr. K didn't think so. He said, "Nobody's ready for another war, except Germany. Why would anyone in their right mind risk everything to save a few Czechs? And save them from what? They'd probably be better off under Germany anyway."

But Kick's friends thought there would be a war, and when it came they were ready to fight. I could see Kick didn't know what to think. Usually whatever her Daddy said was holy writ, but she was impressed with those boys, not twenty years old, some of them, and talking about fighting, willing to risk their necks.

She said, "Gosh, Nora, they're so gung ho. But Daddy says they only talk like that because they don't remember how awful the Great War was."

Of course Mr. K didn't exactly have personal memories of the Great War himself. And a lot of those boys were in the Reserves already.

Mrs. K had rented a villa in the south of France for the month of August and we were all going, except for young Joe. His Daddy said it would be good for his future career to travel to places where history was being made and he sent him to see at first hand what was going on in Germany and in the war in Spain. I wasn't sorry. Joseph Patrick had been a bit of a handful while he was in London. He'd turned out so tall and manly, a real lady-killer, but Kick had it from a couple of her friends that he was liable to forget himself, especially after a whiskey or two. NSIT was what they whispered about him. Not Safe in Taxis. Her friend Caro Leinster wouldn't even come to tea, in case Joe was there.

Kick brought it up with him and he turned on her, rapped her on the nose with his finger. "Keep it out, Little Sis," he said. "Just keep it out."

Kick would never tell on him. They all looked up to Joe, and they were raised not to tell tales. No snitching, no whining, no moping. But that didn't mean I couldn't say something. And anyway, Rosie was going around shouting, "I know what you did. You did a sin with a girl and that's how you get babies."

So I mentioned it to Herself. We were doing the school uniform lists for Bobby and Teddy.

She said, "I don't want to hear servants' gossip. My sons behave correctly, Joe especially. He knows he has to be an example to the others."

I said, "He does. But there's more than one story going round, so I thought you should be told. There's too much smoke for there not to be a bit of a fire."

She said, "And we both know what kind of girls allow stories like that to be spread. Girls that don't deserve a man's respect."

I said, "Well, Caro Leinster's highly respectable and she won't come to the house anymore, in case she runs into him. And Minnie Stubbs seems like a very nice girl. She told Kick he tried to get into her drawers going home the other night."

"Nora!" she said. "I don't believe Kick said that."

She hadn't, not in so many words. Kick was a Sacred Heart girl through and through. No vulgarity.

I said, "She didn't need to. I'm reading between the lines. The word's getting round that Joe takes liberties."

She laughed.

She said, "Do you think so? The scamp! And of course, these girls throw themselves at him. He's so handsome and vital. You know, he looks very much like the Ambassador when he was a young buck."

I said, "I love Joseph Patrick dearly, but if I had a daughter I'd be warning her off him. That's the thing. I wouldn't want Kick getting into the hands of a boy like that."

But she wasn't listening to me. She was off down memory lane.

She said, "It was love at first sight, you know? My father sent me away to Europe. He didn't think a Kennedy was good enough for me, but I was determined. I knew Joe was the one for me. And he's always treated me with respect, Nora, because I commanded respect. My husband has always been a perfect gentleman to me."

See, it was all forgiven and forgotten about Miss Swanson and his other lady friends. I never met anyone quite like Rose Kennedy for ignoring an ache in her heart and soldiering on.

She said, "A man must do what men do, obviously, but he'll only take liberties where he sees them on offer. Decent girls have nothing to fear. Certainly not from my son."

I said, "Well, he likes to get his own way, that I do know, and he's a powerful strong boy. They get a glass or two of whiskey inside them and who can say what might happen. It would be a terrible thing if there should be a misunderstanding. If the Kennedy name should get dragged in. It could ruin things for everyone."

That made her think.

She said, "I won't have anything spoil Euny's debut. I think Kick should distance herself from these girls. She has plenty of other lovely friends. And I'll get the Ambassador to have a word with Joseph Patrick."

Well, there was a brilliant scheme. As well ask a fox to supervise the henhouse.

All the time we were in Cannes there were cablegrams being delivered and sent. Danny Walsh said they were likely about the

Herr Hitler situation. Neither Mr. Roosevelt nor Mr. Chamberlain wanted to get into a fight with him, but they didn't want him thinking he could go around helping himself to countries either. Then there was Mr. K, who thought everybody should mind their own business, and Danny Walsh, who thought Mr. K should be sent to Germany to straighten things out.

He said, "I'm telling you, leave it to old man Kennedy. There won't be a war if he has anything to do with it."

Fidelma said, "And there we were thinking Danny Walsh was just Mrs. Kennedy's pool attendant. Isn't he the regular kingmaker!"

Danny said, "You can laugh, but I get to hear a lot of things."

He did too.

"Danny, where's my scarf? Danny, how much are we paying for gasoline? Danny, did you see those awful Reagans? They grab the front pew and throw dollar bills on the collection plate and they're nothing but bog Irish when you look at their faces. They have no refinement. People like that quite ruin Mass."

At the end of August Jack went back to Harvard to his studies and me and Fidelma and Mrs. Moore took the children back to London, ready for the new school year. Mary Moore was given the job of taking Rosie to the Belmont School, to start her teacher training. It wasn't any old school. The children were allowed to pick and choose what they did and all in their own good time. It was called the Montessori method and it sounded right up Rosie's alley. They said if she settled down and learned all about it she'd have a certificate at the end of it. She'd be able to go to a Montessori school anywhere in the world and teach kindergarten.

"Teaching college," she called it. "I'm going to get a certificate like Jack and Joe. I'm going to be a Tessymori teacher."

She went off in a new straw hat, all smiles. Rosie would do anything to please Mrs. Moore or Fidelma, but if her Mammy tried to get her to do something we'd hear language and all sorts, so Herself stayed on at the villa for another month, with Kick and Euny for company. They missed all the excitement of war nearly breaking out.

While we'd been gone from Prince's Gate there had been trenches dug in Hyde Park and gas masks issued. Mr. Stevens, the butler, said we should have a practice, in case of gas attacks. He pretended to be the siren and we all had to see how fast we could get our masks on. Teddy took his everywhere the first week, even into bed, but then he lost interest. We all did. We'd heard Herr Hitler on the wireless, railing and screeching at one of the big rallies, but he seemed a very long way off from London, SW1.

Bobby asked Mr. K if there was going to be a war.

He said, "If I thought that, son, you'd be on your way home to New York. All these preparations are just for appearance's sake. They don't want Hitler to get the impression he can help himself to any little country without anyone lifting a finger. They have to show a bit of solidarity with these Czechs. He'll get what he wants in the end, but it'll just look better this way."

Bobby said, "Does that mean he wants this country?"

Mr. K said, "I guess he does, but there doesn't have to be a war over it. Nobody wants a war."

Gertie Ambler started stockpiling canned goods though, and then sandbags appeared around the embassy doors in Grosvenor Square. Anybody could get sandbags if they were willing to fill them. We took a walk one day, across the park towards the Bayswater Road to see a great pit they'd opened. There was a long line of trucks waiting to back up and take on a load of sand, and ordinary people too, come in from miles around with trailers hooked onto their little cars. The military were in Hyde Park that day, too, practicing raising a barrage balloon and getting in a right old tangle, too many chiefs and nobody listening to orders. We had quite an entertaining afternoon out.

Mrs. K and the girls were supposed to be going to Paris on the way home, to shop for clothes, but Mr. K sent them a wire to come back to London directly, "because of the worsening situation," he said. He was on the telephone to the President at all hours and round to Downing Street to see the Prime Minister at least once a day. Then Mr. Chamberlain went by airplane to meet Adolf Hitler face-to-face and we all held our breath.

Three times he went. "Like a poodle dog," Danny Walsh said. "Adolf Hitler must be laughing up his sleeve."

I just felt sorry for poor Mr. Chamberlain. Travel's a curse and he didn't look a well man. But just when things looked so bad Herself had ordered the trunks brought down from the attics ready for packing, he came back from Munich with an agreement that saved us from war. Hitler could have the bit of Czechoslovakia he wanted, which was only the part where a lot of German people lived anyway, and in exchange he'd leave the rest in peace. We could put our gas masks away and the trunks were to be hauled back upstairs.

Billy Hartington came round that evening, I remember, and Richard Wood and Tony Erskine, as well as Cynthia Brough and her crowd. As soon as the word was out that Kick was back in town, the boys were buzzing around. Mr. K came back from the House of Commons. The Prime Minister had just spoken about the agreement that had been reached with Germany. Mr. K said it had been a very stirring speech and when it was over everyone had stood on their seats and cheered enough to raise the roof. But it didn't sit well with some of Kick's young men and they told Mr. Kennedy so.

She said, "Things got a bit sticky last night. The boys were all saying Hitler should be taught a lesson, but Daddy said Mr.

Chamberlain's done the right thing because England's in no shape to teach anyone anything. Daddy says Germany would win a war in five minutes and he's in a better position to know than someone like Harry Bagnell. Daddy had luncheon with Colonel Lindbergh so he knows how many bombers and things Germany has. Daddy has all the facts."

And whatever the facts were, they seemed to be robbing Mr. K of his sleep. He was fifty years old and London had taken the bounce out of him. Mrs. K reckoned it was all the grand dinners he had to go to affecting his ulcers, and it was true all he took at home was warm milk or a bowl of chicken soup. But it wasn't only his health. He wasn't really suited to his position. Stevens had been butler to Mr. Bingham before him and to Mr. Mellon and Mr. Dawes before that and he said he'd never known an ambassador like Joe Kennedy. He spoke his mind instead of telling everybody what they wanted to hear. He didn't know how to sweeten things and he didn't have a lick of patience. He wanted things done his way and fast. Joe Kennedy wouldn't have gone three times in an airplane for the sake of somebody else's country. "Leave me and mine alone," he'd have said, "and we'll say no more about these other little places." And then he'd have sent Adolf Hitler a case of whiskey.

They'd hardly finished cheering in the House of Commons when Hitler marched into Czechoslovakia anyway and the dailies that had said what a marvelous thing Mr. Chamberlain had pulled off said that was what came of trying to strike a bargain with a dictator. Kick had words with Lord Harry Bagnell. He told her if America really thought Hitler was none of its business it had a shock coming, and if it didn't think that, then it should sack its ambassador for saying so. We didn't see him at Prince's Gate again after that, but Kick wasn't grieved. Richard Wood and Billy Hartington were her favorites.

She had two invitations for the first weekend of November, to stay at Susie Frith-Johnstone's house in Leicestershire and go to a costume pageant at Belvoir Castle, or go to Chatsworth House for Lord Billy's sister's birthday tea.

Fidelma said to her, "Go to the pageant. I would. A castle has to be better than a house. There'll be ghosts and turrets and all sorts. Nora can run you up a costume. Stevens'll give you a loan of his flashlight and you can go as the Statue of Liberty."

"No," she said, "I'm going to Anne's birthday. I promised her. And you know Chatsworth may not be a castle, but I don't think it's just any old house."

I should have gone with her, of course.

Mrs. K said, "Now, Nora, I want you to make sure Kick gets to Mass on Sunday morning. The Devonshires are very highly placed people and I'm sure like to do things correctly but they're Protestants. They may just not think of it. When the Ambassador and I spent the weekend at Windsor Castle details like that were organized to perfection. A car was sent to take us into the town. Of course that was royalty. They don't overlook a thing."

But I didn't get to Chatsworth. I missed my footing, running down the back stairs where Herself had said a twenty-five-watt bulb gave brightness enough, and turned my ankle so it blew up like a watermelon. Fidelma went in my place and I wasn't sorry. I had two days of peace, reading Mrs. K's magazines with my foot raised on a stool while London Jack kept Teddy and Bobby entertained, and Fidelma got to deal with the whys and wherefores of being a lady's maid.

I said, "Remember, they'll call you 'Kennedy.'"

She said, "They can call me Tallulah. Doesn't mean I'll answer."

But she came back whistling a different tune.

"It's bigger than Lady Astor's place," she said. "Bigger than

Buckingham Palace, if you ask me. And you should see how many staff they have. The help have help. And land. There's hills and woods and farms as far as the eye can see."

Kick said, "And we saw your favorite driver, Nora. The one with the dint in his chin."

I said, "He's no favorite of mine. I hardly spoke two words to him."

Fidelma said, "What driver?"

Kick said, "The one who drove us to the station. Stallybottom or something. He liked Nora. He remembered you from Compton Place, Nora."

Fidelma said, "His name was Stallybrass. And he has no business liking anybody. He's got a wife. She's the pastry cook at Chatsworth. We had steak pies, Nora, with onion gravy, and the crust was so light it nearly floated away."

I said, "I hardly even remember him."

Kick said, "Well, he remembered you. He sent you his best regards."

17

Other People's Babies

Mr. Kennedy went back to America for Christmas. Herself said he needed to see his ulcer doctor in New York, but they had plenty of good doctors in London and anyway, Washington was where he went first. Danny Walsh predicted he was getting the sack for speaking out of turn, but I didn't see why the President would send for him if that's what it was. All he had to do was pick up the telephone and we'd be on our way back to Bronxville.

As soon as it was known Mr. K would be away from home, Mayor and Mrs. Fitzgerald announced they'd pay us a visit. Then Jack decided he wouldn't come to London for Christmas. Jack found His Honor hard to take, especially if Joseph Patrick was around getting the My Grandson the Future President treatment. Behind his back Jack and Lem Billings called him Grampy O'Blarney.

So Jack decided to go down to Palm Beach instead with a crowd of friends from college, and it was while they were there that something happened. It was Christmas Eve. They were trimming the tree when Eddie Moore telephoned from New York, wanting to speak to His Honor. All night the phone was going and by the time we went to Mass Mrs. K had her buttoned-up face on.

Fidelma said, "Everything all right, Mrs. Kennedy?"

"Perfectly," she said.

A sure sign there was trouble.

Danny Walsh said that piecing things together from what he'd been able to hear, Jack had gotten into a bit of a scrape and strings were being pulled. That was where Mayor Fitzgerald came in. He knew even more useful people than Mr. K did.

A motor accident, I thought, and so did Danny. Joseph Patrick and Jack both drove like loonies. But Fidelma reckoned there had to be a girl in the picture.

"He's knocked a girl up," she kept saying. "I'll bet you. Or he got too fresh and now she's made a complaint."

Fidelma tried to get something out of Mayor Fitzgerald. She was always a trier.

She said, "All those telephone calls, Your Honor, and at Christmas too. No rest for the wicked, eh?"

"Oh you're right, dearie," he said. "But what a wonderful thing, to be able to talk to a person in Boston as if he's in the next room."

It was to be a long, long time before I got to the bottom of what all that had been about. The phone calls stopped, Jack was apparently out of the doghouse, and then Mrs. K got a cablegram to tell her that Associated Press had voted her Outstanding Woman of the Year 1938. All her troubles were forgotten then. She was so happy she dusted off the pianoforte and played so that Mayor Fitzgerald could sing.

Sweet Adeline, my Adeline,
All night, dear heart, for you I pine.

In all my dreams, your fair face beams.
You're the flower of my heart, Sweet Adeline.

It seemed to be the only song he knew, so he sang it over and over and he was no Morton Downey. That's more than twelve years ago and I'm not ready yet to hear it again.

Right after the New Year we were going to St. Moritz so the children could ski. I went in to see Herself about the packing and there she sat with a pile of 1938 calendars she'd bought in Woolworth. They sold them off for practically nothing at the end of the year. She was scribbling out the days of the week and writing in the changes.

I said, "That's a fearsome job. Is it worth the bother?"

"Yes," she said, "it is. Take care of the cents and the dollars will take care of themselves. Now, dear heart, I'm just wondering whether we'll need both you and Fidelma in Switzerland. I'm wondering if one of you might not stay in London and do something with Rosie. It's such a waste of money to take her skiing."

She often went into one of her economy drives at the start of a new year.

I said, "Well, you know I don't mind. Skiing's just wet clothes and frozen feet to me."

She said, "Being Ambassador has been a terrible drain on us, you know? People think everything is provided but that's not the case at all. We've been put to enormous expense."

I said, "Were you thinking of letting me go?"

"No," she said, "I wasn't thinking that at all. I depend upon you greatly, Nora, but we do have to reduce our expenditure. Shoe repairs, for instance. I believe you'll find the charges are much lower outside of Kensington."

That was her mentality. She'd have you wear out your shoe leather walking to save sixpence.

She said, "Last year was a particular burden, of course, bringing out two girls. I think we won't give a ball for Eunice this year. A small dinner will be quite enough. Euny isn't a ball kind of girl."

I said, "So will I stay behind while you're skiing?"

"Yes, dear," she said. "Do something nice with Rosie. Take her to the Wax Works or the Zoological Gardens. She's trying so very hard at Belmont, I'd like to encourage her with some little treats. Let her choose for herself. Within reason."

I knew what Rosie would want if she had her druthers. A kiss and a cuddle from London Jack.

I was half out the door. She said, "Nora dear, please don't worry we'll be letting you go. This is going to be a busier year than ever and I shall absolutely depend upon you. I think we can anticipate a Royal visit to Prince's Gate this year. Their Majesties are going to America, you know? And it'll be for us to give them a great send-off. They'll come to dinner. That's something you won't have seen in your future when you came to us at Beals Street."

I said, "We'll be staying on then?"

"Yes," she said. "Why?"

I said, "The Ambassador never seems to stay anywhere long. You know, always on the go."

She laughed. "Well, dear," she said, "we're certainly here for the foreseeable future. But who can say what exciting things next year might bring."

The White House, Danny Walsh reckoned.

He said, "Your Man's going to run, it's as clear as day. And that costs a small fortune. That's why she's tightening her belt."

Fidelma said, "That's it, Brennan. She wants the shoes heeled in Notting Hill from now on so there'll be more money to put in the First Lady Gown Fund."

Me and Rosie had a fine time while they were all gone skiing. I fetched her into town on a bus and the underground train, and we both had our hair done and tea in Marshall & Snelgrove and tried on a load of hats we had no intention of buying. She told me all about this Montessori teaching.

"There's no shouting," she said. "I like it. You can do painting or clay or weighing and measuring. All kinds of things. It doesn't matter if you're slow."

She'd filled out again, a guaranteed sign she was happy, and her Mammy was hundreds of miles away so I wasn't going to put her on any silly regime. Me and Gertie Ambler took her to Drury Lane to see *Dick Whittington* and we had wine gums and choc ices and joined in with all the singing and booing and hissing. We were going along just dandy till the interval. She needed the powder room and I trusted her to go on her own. The bell was ringing for the second half and she hadn't come back. Gertie went searching in one direction, I went the other. I found her in the Stalls Bar, the only one left in there, smoking a cigarette and talking to the man who was putting up new bottles.

I said, "Did you serve her drink?"

"Bar's closed," he said.

She had a pack of Park Drive, nearly full, but there wasn't a cigarette left whole by the time I'd finished with it.

I said, "What has your Daddy always told you about smoking? Hasn't he told every one of you he'll give you extra money if you don't start with cigarettes? Nearly twenty-one and you start a daft habit like that."

"Joe smokes," she said.

I said, "Then Joe's a fool. Is that what you're doing now? Copying fools? Why are you doing it?"

She said, "It looks nice."

I said, "Well, it doesn't smell nice. How can you teach nice little children smelling like an ash can? And boys won't want to dance with you."

"I've got gum," she said. I could tell she was going to go straight back out and buy more smokes.

The curtain had gone up. We had to push along the row to get to our seats, treading on everybody's toes. Dame Trot was singing.

Other people's babies, that's my life.
Mother to dozens, but nobody's wife.

Gertie whispered, "That's your song, Nora."

Mother to dozens was about right. I suppose I'd taken it for granted I'd have weans of my own someday, and when you're young, the ticking of the clock doesn't bother you. Later on, it was one of those things, if I stopped to dwell on it I'd get a funny old ache in my insides. "A touch of the what-ifs," I always called it. But life rolled along and there's nothing like keeping busy to get rid of the what-ifs. All those fine places I visited with my Kennedys. I'd never have seen the half of them if I'd married Jimmy Swords. I'd have sat at home darning socks while he was in the pub planning a revolution.

Fidelma and Mrs. Moore brought the children back from Switzerland while Herself continued her vacation. "Traveling throughout the Mediterranean," according to Mrs. Moore.

She was in Greece when the Holy Father passed away and she went directly to Rome, so she'd be there when the new Pope was named.

This is an opportunity to be part of history, she wrote to Bobby. *Be sure to keep all my letters. They will be a precious memento of this important time in our lives.*

It meant she missed Teddy's birthday and Kick's and Jean's and not for the first time. We made them a little tea party though, and Mr. K arrived just in time for it, and Jack with him. He was looking better. He was through the spots and pimples, finally, and carrying himself like quite the smart young buck.

I said, "And what was all that commotion about over Christmas?"

"Don't know what you mean," he said. "What commotion?"

Kick said, "Oh come on, Jack. Even Grandpa looked pretty mad about it. Did you rear-end somebody's car?"

"No," he said. "Oh, yeah. It was nothing. Busted taillight."

She said, "Well, was it, like, the Governor's car or something? It didn't seem like nothing. The phone calls must have cost more than the damage."

He said, "You know what, Kick? You need an interest in life. You get way too excited about every little thing goes on in mine."

Teddy said, "Was Daddy mad? Why didn't you make Lem say he did it?"

Bobby clipped his ear. He said, "Because that's not what you do, Ted. Thou shalt not bear false witness."

Teddy said, "But he could of. And then made an act of contrition."

18

Our Pope

When the new Pope was elected I thought Mr. K would turn a cartwheel. It was Cardinal Pacelli, who'd been to tea at Bronxville and allowed young Teddy to sit on his knee.

"*Our* Pope," Mr. Kennedy called him. "Now we have ourselves our own Pope."

He said all the children were to go with him to the coronation. Only Joseph Patrick was traveling and couldn't be contacted. Mr. Moore said there might be a problem, because seats were hard to come by and the invitation was really only for Mr. and Mrs. K, so they could represent the President.

Mr. K said, "Eddie, you know that's not the way I operate. If you want something, the thing to do is just step forward and stake your claim. There'll always be people ready to tell you why you can't have what you want, but once you've grabbed it they'll think twice about taking it from you."

Danny Walsh went to Belmont to bring Rosie home and Mrs. K sent me my orders. The girls were all to have new wool coats and lace mantillas, white for Jean and black for the others. Mr. Moore took care of the boys, black single-breasted for Bobby and a dark blue knicker suit for Teddy.

Fidelma said, "That chair the Cardinal sat in when he came to the house, it'll be under a glass dome the next time we see it. There'll be nobody allowed to breathe on it, never mind rest their behind."

We caught the Golden Arrow boat train to Paris and then the Rome Express, and I didn't get a wink of sleep what with the rattling and the swaying and men coming aboard to check your papers and Jean and Teddy in and out of their beds all night long, fiddling with every little gadget. I was afraid they'd open a door and go tumbling out, or pull the cord that stops the train. The conductor said there wasn't a hotel room to be had in Rome, but we were fixed up. Mrs. K had got us four suites at the Excelsior and limousines to meet us at the train station.

She hadn't seen the children in six weeks but she started straight in. Bobby needed a haircut, Rosie was carrying too much weight, Kick's nails were chewed to the quick. Where had I bought the girls' stockings? How much had we paid for Teddy's suit?

Poor Eddie Moore was sweating over the seating arrangements for the coronation. He kept saying, "They'll never get in. It's two tickets per country." But they did get in. The cars came for them early and they got front-row seats. There were eight dignitaries bounced from their seats so the young Kennedys could have a grandstand view. And some black looks, too, according to Kick.

She said, "I'd sooner have stood and so would Euny and Pat. And Teddy could have sat on Daddy's lap. But Mother said we were entitled. It was kind of embarrassing."

Mrs. K was certainly full of herself. She'd come a long way from that retiring little body in Beals Street.

She said, "It was the most beautiful occasion I ever saw, Nora, and particularly wonderful for us because His Holiness is a personal friend. But it isn't over yet. On Wednesday Teddy will receive his first Communion, and tomorrow we're all going to visit with the Holy Father, for a private audience. And that includes you and Fidelma. I'll lend you each a piece of lace for your head, but you must promise to be very careful with them. They're handmade Venetian."

"Now, Brennan," Fidelma kept saying, "pass me that old rag would you while I shine my shoes."

I said, "My guts are churning already. What are we supposed to do when we get in there? Do we have to say anything?"

She said, "Of course we don't. Won't it all be in Latin? Just don't look at me else I'll burst out laughing."

But we didn't feel like laughing when it came to it. We walked miles down corridors to get to the room, and there were guards posted all the way. Nobody said a word. All you could hear was Teddy's new shoes squeaking and Herself tap-tapping along in her high heels. Mr. K went in first and after five minutes the doors opened to let the rest of us inside.

I'd expected the Holy Father to be on a throne, with his vestments on, but he was sitting in an ordinary chair in just his house cassock and his little white cap. He'd looked more impressive the day he came to Bronxville. He remembered Teddy, of course, and he allowed him to take a picture with his Kodak camera, and then he gave us all rosaries. He was dishing them out from a big box on his table. The children went up first and then me and Fidelma. I wish now I'd dared take a close look at him but my heart was in my mouth. Christ's Vicar on Earth giving me a rosary. Everyone who went up, he said something. Fidelma said it sounded like "Pay for three."

I said, "I think it was 'Pray for me.'"

"That'd be it," she said. "Because he only gave me the one rosary, and I'd no money on me anyway. God, Nora, I was all atremble. I couldn't think straight."

Me neither. I wished I could have it all over again, so I could pay proper attention.

When the audience was over we were taken to the Sistine Chapel, to see where the cardinals sit while they're deciding on a new Pope; then Mr. and Mrs. K went off to a reception and to a dinner at the American Embassy, which left us in peace. Mr. and Mrs. Moore took the children for a spaghetti supper, "bisgetti," Rosie called it, and me and Fidelma tried our luck with the old parley italiany. Sure they're a friendly, helpful people, the Italians, and saucy too. I reckon we could both have gotten ourselves husbands if we'd put our minds to it and told Mrs. K where to stick her Venetian lace.

We did a bit of pointing and playacting till they brought us a dinner and I don't know what half of it was, but we'd a lovely drink called Chianti wine that went straight to Fidelma Clery's head, and ice cream to finish, though it was bitter cold outside.

We had to have the children dressed and ready to go by seven for Teddy's first Communion, which was no easy thing, because Rosie kept disappearing, hoping to see a bellhop who'd caught her eye, and Teddy was lolloping around, complaining his collar was too stiff and his pants were itchety.

Jack said, "Ted, you're a pain. If I were Nora I'd put you in a hair shirt."

"Nora has to be nice to me," he said. "Or I'll tell Mother and then she'll be let go."

Jack said, "You're the one should be let go. I reckon the Moores should adopt you, Teddy Baby. I'm not sure we want such a whining little brat for a Kennedy."

The Mass was held in the Holy Father's own chapel, just a plain little place, although Our Lady did have the electric light in her crown, which Fidelma thought was a very miracle. And when it was all over Teddy tried to give me his candle, sidling up to me, calling me Darling Nora, trying to make amends for his cheek.

Herself said, "Oh no, Teddy. You must keep the candle. It's a souvenir of a very special day."

"Sorry," he whispered to me. "Sorry, sorry, sorry."

Mrs. K traveled back with us as far as Paris and there we left her, with more shopping to be done. She was going to America to help with the King and Queen's visit and she wanted to be sure of turning heads with her gowns.

Mr. K said, "Spend as much as you like, Rosa. I want you to show those snoots back home the Kennedys know how to do things. And if you run across that bitch from Baltimore, don't curtsey to her."

She'd been invited to dinner at the American Embassy in Paris and the Duke and Duchess of Windsor were going to be there.

She said, "Now, Joe dearest, I'm not going to create a scene. The Windsors are just a pair of has-beens, and if a little curtsey makes them happy I'm not going to ruin their evening. I'll just bob a little bob."

He said, "Well, I'd be happier if you didn't. I begrudge them even a nod of the head. We have our friendship with Their Majesties to think of. And I'd never have taken this damned job if I'd thought it would oblige you to curtsey to a tart."

Jack said, "So now it's 'this damned job'? Not all it's cracked up to be, eh, Excellency? Ambassador to the Court of St. James's not so great, hunh?"

Mr. K said, "I tell you, it's a thankless posting. You end up out of pocket and the papers are always hoping you'll goof, that you'll speak out of turn or do something you shouldn't have, good news being no news. I'll finish my time here, but frankly I can't wait to go home."

Jack said, "But you're definitely not going to run next year?"

"No," he said, "I'm not. Your mother would like it, I know, but I've worked out a little agreement with FDR. If he runs for another term, I'll back him. Then he'll back Joe for governor of Massachusetts in '42."

Jack whistled. He said, "Does Joe know?"

Mr. K said, "He knows I'm working on his future."

We were no sooner back from the boat train than Billy Hartington was on the doorstep looking for Kick. There was a cocktail party at Ginny Vigo's that evening and then everyone was going on to the Café de Paris for dancing.

Kick said, "I don't know. We've been traveling all day. My hair's a real mess."

"Is it?" he said. "I think it looks rather wonderful."

Rosie said, "I'll come. I haven't been dancing for ages."

But Kick wasn't having that. "No, Rosie," she said. "You're not invited this time. I can't drag you everywhere with me."

Rosie's eyes filled up.

Billy said, "Oh but it'd be fine, Kick. Why not? Ginny absolutely wouldn't mind."

"No," she said, "she'll make a pest of herself wanting partners. You don't know what she's like. She won't sit out a single dance. And anyway she has to go back to Belmont. Go get your things ready, Rosie. Danny's taking you first thing. And if Mother were here she'd agree with me."

Billy felt bad about it, you could tell. He was a proper young gentleman.

"Well then," he said. "Well then. But another time, I'm sure."

That was the night Rosie broke a water glass. She picked it up from her night table and hurled it at the wall.

"Kick's a bloody, bloody bugger," she was shouting. "A bloody, bloody bugger."

It took two of us to hold her still until she calmed down.

Fidelma said, "Nice kindergarten teacher you're going to make, using words like that."

Rosie said, "I wouldn't have been a pest. I only wanted a dance."

Fidelma said, "I know you did, darling. And you'll have plenty. You heard what Lord Billy said. Another time. But you do have to be up early, to get back to your studying."

I said, "Think of it, Rosie. You'll be a certified teacher and all Kick'll have will be a pair of worn dance shoes."

Kick had half a dozen invitations to the country for the Easter holidays, but it was Billy Hartington's she accepted, to go to Chatsworth. She said of all the boys he was the only one who had sweet sisters and a nice house.

Mrs. K said I was to go with her.

She said, "I know you'll make sure she goes to Mass, Nora. When Fidelma went with her she allowed her to sleep in late like the Protestants."

Chatsworth is in Derbyshire, plumb in the middle of England. We took the train, along with Minnie Stubbs and Cynthia Brough, and we were met at a town called Bakewell. Lord Billy's brother Andrew was there in an open-top roadster to pick up the girls. A shooting brake had been sent for the luggage and the maids. The driver looked only about sixteen, a skinny kid, in a livery that swamped him.

Cynthia Brough's maid said, "You're new. What's your name?"

"Wildgoose," he said. "I were on boilers but I put in for a change."

She said, "Stallybrass usually collects us."

He said, "No telling who you'll get this weekend. We've a right houseful."

Minnie Stubbs's maid said, "I hope that doesn't mean the maids have to double up. I'm accustomed to my own room."

Brough said, "Perhaps Wildgoose here'll double up with you."

Poor lad. His ears turned bright red.

He said, "You've been here before then?"

Stubbs said, "I've lost count. I hate these country weekends. They're forever changing their clothes. And if you do get five minutes to yourself there's nowhere to go. Where's your nearest picture house?"

He had to think. "That'd be Chesterfield," he said.

"See what I mean?" she said. "Nothing out here but cows and sheep. And trees. Look at them."

I said, "I haven't been here before."

Brough said, "This is Kennedy. She's American."

"Aye," he said, "they told me there was more Americans arriving. We've Mr. Fred Astaire arrived last night. Very nice gentleman."

Fred Astaire's sister Dellie was married to Billy Hartington's uncle Charlie Cavendish.

We drove up from the town, thick hedgerows on either side, and then as we came out of a bend in the road he slowed down, nearly to a halt.

He said, "Are yer set? Look out yer winder an' you'll get a treat."

Brough said, "We know. We've seen it."

He said, "I were talking to Kennedy."

And there it was, across the river. A great square stone house built on a rise, with East Moor rolling away behind it, and sheep grazing in the park. Chatsworth House. I'd have sworn it was pink, but on Sunday morning when I saw the same view, it was more the color of honey.

"One hundred and seventy-five rooms," he said. "I'll wager you haven't got nowt like this in America."

Stubbs said, "Blenheim's better."

"Nay," he said. "Bonniest house in the land, this."

Chatsworth was a bit of a shambles, truth to be told. They'd closed it up the previous year when the old Duke died, and Billy Hartington's folks were only just getting round to moving in. They'd been cozy down in their own little house and loath to leave it, I suppose, for such a palace of a place. It had a nice atmosphere though, and it was well run, considering the miles you had to walk to get anywhere. They needed skates on to get dinner served before it was cold on the platters. In those big houses you did better below stairs. You got your food hot, and you could eat it wearing proper clothes, not filmy little dinner gowns and your arms covered in gooseflesh.

We had roast pork with cracklings and applesauce, that first night, and Bakewell puddings, with jam from Chatsworth strawberries. That was the first time I saw Hope Stallybrass. Tall and stout and red-faced from the ovens. She was giving orders, counting out the savories that were to be carried upstairs, watching so everything for our dinner would be ready at the right moment. There was an empty chair across from me until Walter Stallybrass ran in, smoothing down his hair, just as grace was being said.

"How do again, Kennedy," he said.

Mrs. Stallybrass never cracked her face even after she'd sat down, never spoke. She just shoveled the food in like it was another job that had to be done. She seemed older than Walter.

He said, "Your Miss had a different maid when she was up here last back end. She said you'd busted your ankle."

"Sprained it," I said.

"That was it," he said. "Sprained. You getting used to English ways, you and your Miss?"

He held his knife and fork cack-handed.

I said, "We can't be doing too badly. She still gets invitations."

One of the kitchen maids said, "Why? Are you foreigners?"

He said, "She's from America, Florrie. This is Miss Kennedy's maid."

"Never heard of her," she said.

He said, "You have. You've seen her in the papers. Miss Kathleen Kennedy. She were presented last Season."

That was the first time Hope Stallybrass looked up from her plate.

The maid said, "Do they allow Americans? I thought it were for English girls."

Hope said, "It is. It's for English roses."

I said, "No. There are American girls presented every Season. It beats me why anyone would want to, but as long as they do, it must be a treat for Their Majesties to see a nice sparkling American smile."

Everything went quiet.

When the plates were being cleared Walter Stallybrass leaned across to me. He said, "Is your Miss fixed up for her corsage, for the dance?"

I said, "I don't know. Is there an order going down to the florist?"

Some of the maids started tittering and Hope Stallybrass hauled herself to her feet.

She said, "Why Lord Billy invites these people I shall never understand."

Walter said, "We do our own flowers here, Kennedy. I'll pick her out a nice camellia if you like. What color's her gown? Come down to the glasshouses tomorrow morning. I'll be there while ten."

When Walter Stallybrass wasn't required for driving, camellias were his specialty. He showed me how they had them trained against walls and clipped into hedges. There were some in flower beds and some in big earthenware pots ready for taking up to the South Front.

He said, "They're not difficult, as long as you've the right soil. The only thing they don't like is hot weather."

I said, "Like me."

"Is that right?" he said. "Then you're in the right place up here. Where are you from, Nora?"

I said, "New York. Boston before that."

He said, "But where are you from?"

I said, "I'm from Westmeath, but I've been gone longer than I was ever there."

"Westmeath?" he said. "I've never heard of it."

Nobody ever has.

He said, "We've got a place in Ireland. Lismore. Where Lord Charlie lives. Beautiful parks around it. Prime salmon fishing. You probably know it?"

I said, "Until I went to America I'd never been further than Mullingar. Where is Lismore exactly?"

He said, "I don't rightly know. I haven't been."

He picked out a bloom for Kick.

He said, "How's that? Will that do for American royalty?"

That was what they called the Kennedys in the dailies.

I said, "She's a nice girl. Why are you all so against her?"

"Not me," he said, "I've nowt against her. She's a bit of a novelty, that's all. You must pay no heed to Hope. She's stuck in her ways. She were just the same when Lord Charlie married Lady Dellie. Thought it were the end of the world and we'd all be eating them frankfurter hot dogs. See? I speak the American lingo."

I said, "Well, I don't care to hear my young lady picked over by kitchen help. If she comes up here again they can send Fidelma Clery with her."

"Nay," he said. "Don't say that. I were right pleased to see you sitting there when I come in last night. I've often thought of you, Nora, since Compton Place. Did you ever think of me?"

He was nothing to look at really. His hair was thinning on top.

I said, "Somebody better turn that hosepipe on you. You'll be for it if Mrs. Stallybrass catches you talking like that."

He said, "Mrs. Stallybrass? You mean Hope? What's she to do with it? She's busy with the breakfasts. I could steal a kiss and nobody'd know, only you and me."

I said, "I thought it was the Lordships who took liberties, not workingmen who ought to know better. No wonder your wife has a face on her would stop an omnibus."

He didn't say another word. Just looked at me and walked away into the glasshouse.

I took the flower that he'd cut for Kick and she was the belle of the ball in her sky-blue silk with that bloom pinned to her shoulder. It was so perfect you'd have thought it was made of wax. And later on, when I went to turn in, there was a soup plate on my night table, with another camellia floating in water, red and white stripes, and a note underneath. It said, *She's my sister, you muggins. Stallybrass, bachelor. P.S. This one's called Yours Truly.*

Dear God, how my face burned when I read it. First time in my life a man ever gave me a flower. All I wanted to do was sit on the bed and think what it might mean, but there was no chance of that.

I was sharing with Lady Blundell's maid.

She said, "If you don't mind my asking, Kennedy, how old are you?"

I was going on forty-five but she was just a slip of a girl. To her I must have looked a hundred.

She said, "You and Stallybrass, are you carrying on?"

I said, "We are not. There was a misunderstanding, that's all. They have marvelous gardens here. You should take a walk and see what they've got down there. Not only flowers. Whatever this house needs, they grow it. Apricots. Asparagus."

She said, "I know that. Every big house grows apricots and asparagus. Where have you been all your long life?"

She was scandalized, I could tell, me in my dotage getting a flower and a billydoo. I never slept that night, going over it and over it how I'd got the wrong end of the stick and I owed Walter Stallybrass an apology.

It was mizzling rain when the car came to take us to Mass the next morning, and it wasn't Walter who came trotting up with the brolly. It was Wildgoose.

I wasn't sorry. My hair was destroyed in the damp.

He said, "Her Grace said to have you at the church for eleven. And would you kindly mind waiting on another car to bring you back, because we've a great number of comings and goings today. Driver Stallybrass'll likely come for you."

And Driver Stallybrass did. He winked at me in the mirror, but we didn't speak till he'd dropped Kick and swung round to the stable yard.

I said, "I've been a bit of a chump."

"Nay," he said. "Not another word. Did you like your flower?"

I said, "It's beautiful. It'll be all over the servants' hall, you realize? Blundell couldn't wait to tell somebody."

He laughed. He said, "Let's give her summat to get her teeth into then, Nora. I think it's time I showed you my potting shed."

There was a deal of smirking when we all sat down to luncheon.

One of the kitchen maids said, "I wish I was a Catholic. You can get up to all sorts if you're a Catholic and then just go to church and get the slate wiped clean."

Hope said, "I shall be glad when it's Tuesday and we can get back to regularity. All these outsiders coming in, creating extra work, causing distraction. Soup plates turning up in bedrooms. It would never have happened in the old Duke's time."

So Hope was his sister, and a spinster, like Gertie Ambler, though they both went as Mrs. It seemed if you were a Stallybrass it went without saying that you'd work for the Devonshires. Hope and Walter's Mammy had been a sewing woman and their Daddy had been a groom. They'd an uncle who'd been a boiler man and another had had charge of the Lily House. There are sisters and sisters though, and Hope Stallybrass seemed cut from the same cloth as my Ursie. Bossy as a nanny goat.

I got the third degree from Mrs. K about Kick and Lord Billy.

I said, "His Lordship didn't make anything special of her. In fact, that Sally Norton was there and they reckon she's his favorite. But her dance card was filled. And she went to Mass. She was up and dressed before anyone else had appeared. You'd have been proud of her."

Mrs. K said, "I'm so glad. It's a great opportunity for her, our being Ambassador. I'm sure the Devonshires are very fine people. The Duchess is a close friend of Her Majesty, you know. Kick can make friendships here that will take her far in life, but one still has to be on the alert. We don't want any silly romances that can only end in tears."

It wasn't long after that she met the Devonshires for herself, at a dinner at Lady Astor's house.

"Most charming people," she said. "His Grace is very reticent, but I drew him out and we had such an interesting talk. It's a great pity Billy won't do for Kick. If it weren't for his church it would be a rather wonderful match."

Kick didn't appear too concerned about Billy Hartington. She was such a popular girl. She went to Lady Airlie's party with Tony Erskine, and to a horse show with Lancelot Wemyss. And then Joseph Patrick came home from his travels, so all those London beaux had to take a backseat. She loved being squired by her brother.

As she said, "He's good-looking, he can dance and Mother approves of him. I'm all for the simple life."

The Kennedys were all like that. They had their friends and their admirers, but when it came down to it they were happiest in each other's company. Kennedys stuck together and you had to pity anyone who tried to break into that tight little circle. Lem Billings was really the only one who ever managed it and I think they just felt sorry for him, with his father dying and his not having a proper family life.

May 4, 1939, was a real red-letter day for us. Their Majesties were coming to dinner at Prince's Gate. Gertie was so excited. She went through her recipe books and brought up all kinds of suggestions for the menu. She wanted to make a turtle soup, which takes days, and a turkey stuffed with a chicken stuffed with a pigeon, but Mrs. K wasn't having any of that.

She said, "We're going to give them good, plain American food. The poor dears go to so many banquets, they must long for a simple meal. We'll give them shad roe and then a baked Virginia ham and strawberry shortcake."

We had to get in extra help for the evening, borrowed from Buckingham Palace, because they knew how everything had to be done. But first the police came. They went over the house from the attics to the cellar, with a dog that could sniff out gunpowder, and there were questions asked about me and Fidelma and Danny Walsh. How long had we been employed by the Ambassador? Were we known to the police in Ireland or the United States? Who did we associate with on our days off?

Fidelma said, "What days off?"

The bobby said, "I'm only doing my job, miss. Haven't you heard of the Irish Republican Army?"

She said, "I have heard of it. But if you work for Mrs. Kennedy you don't have time for joining armies."

The day of the dinner it was one flap after another. First the fishmonger sent sole because he couldn't get shad roe, and the menu had already been printed. Then the flower people were late coming and Teddy broke a dining chair bouncing on it. Herself was still running around in her frownies and her day dress. It was nearly six o'clock and the stylist was waiting to finish her hair. But what a transformation once she was dressed and ready. She'd chosen aquamarine satin, fitted to show off her slim line, and a suite of brilliant-cut diamonds.

Jean and Pat had special leave from school, as it's not every day your Mammy and Daddy have the King and Queen to dinner.

Jean said, "I think Mother looks like a beautiful princess."

Mrs. K said, "Thank you, dear. Well, anyone can keep their looks if they're disciplined about it. You know, when we were shopping in Paris one of the vendeuses thought Kick and I were sisters."

Patty said, "Why isn't Rosie here? She'd have loved to have dinner with the King and Queen."

Jack and Rosie were the only ones to miss the big occasion. Jack was at school and Mrs. K had decided the excitement might be too much for Rosie.

She said, "Seven youngsters will be quite enough for Their Majesties, and Rosie doesn't do well at dinners."

Patty said, "She loves dinners. Specially when there's baked ham. She could have had my place. Then I wouldn't have had to cancel my tennis game."

Joseph Patrick and Kick sat at the main table, and the younger ones were at a side table, with Euny in charge, so that they'd be able to look back and say they'd attended a dinner with the King and Queen of England. If it had been up to me, Rosie would have been there too.

They say the mark of a queen is that she can talk to anybody, and from what I've read there are persons in the Royal Family as slow as my Rosie, if not slower.

We were allowed to watch from an upstairs window, to see the King and Queen arrive. Their limousine pulled up on the very stroke of eight.

Fidelma said, "God Almighty, will you look at that. They must have been waiting round the corner, watching till the big hand was on the twelve."

Mr. K went striding out to meet them and brought the Queen in on his arm. She was in pink, with sparkles stitched all over her gown and a white fichu round her shoulders. Too many frills, in my opinion, for a woman with her curves. She reminded me of the little doll our Ursie used to have, to cover up the spare toilet roll and keep the lav looking genteel.

After the dessert had been taken in we hung about on the top landing and eventually we heard the ladies leave the dining room to go powder their noses and take coffee. Then Euny brought the juniors up to bed. Teddy was in a sulk. He was still hungry, because everything had been served very dainty, and he thought he should be allowed to stay down and watch the cartoons with the grown-ups. Danny Walsh had the projector set up in the family room, with a couple of funnies and a new Robert Donat movie the Royalties had particularly asked to see.

Fidelma said, "Will you get into your pajamas, Teddy Kennedy, or do I have to paddle your backside? You've school in the morning. And you should write your diary too, before you go to sleep, so you remember everything about tonight."

He was moaning and groaning, swore he wouldn't be well enough for school because he'd a stomach ache and a sore throat and his legs felt wobbly. The banana sandwiches revived him though, and the chocolate milk. We listened to *The Laughing Policeman* three times on Kick's phonograph and then he went to bed like a lamb.

They'd had photos taken to commemorate the occasion and Herself was thrilled with them. She had nothing but nice things to say about Her Majesty, but I know Rose Kennedy. The reason she gazed and gazed on those pictures and had copies made and sent to every mortal soul she'd ever met in her life was that they made her look younger than the Queen. Younger and slimmer and more vivacious.

"Ten years older," she kept saying. "And I've borne seven children more than Her Majesty. But we can't all be blessed with a brisk metabolism."

19

The Season at the End of the World

Jack came home for the summer vacation and Mrs. K went off to Washington, to make sure everything was in place for Their Majesties' visit. We loved it when she was gone. It was like ripping off your corsets.

Me and Fidelma would take turns walking Bobby and Teddy to Sloane Street. Teddy was always dreaming up ways to cut school. Monday mornings he'd be hobbling about with a bone in his leg or croaking with a pretend sore throat. One of his new pals at Mr. Gibbs's had had his tonsils out and Teddy thought living on nothing but ice cream for a week sounded just the thing. Bobby was different. He went off to school without any trouble. It was just the cricket he hated.

"The rules are stupid," he'd say. "And the ball's too hard. It can really hurt."

Our other job while Mrs. K was in America was to keep things on track for Eunice's debut. She had tea parties to attend and fittings to go to for her gowns. Peach tulle for her own party and ivory for her Presentation at the Palace, and she wanted everything to be perfect. As a rule she went around looking like Raggedy Ann. She'd as soon have had a tennis party, with everybody wearing canvas pumps, but being presented was something else. There were rules about everything. How long your veil had to be, how many feathers in your hair, the color of your gloves. It was the kind of thing that worried Euny until she was sure she'd gotten it right.

The balls had started already. Langrish House, Brayfield Court, Queen's Deerhurst. The newspapers said there had never been such a Season. The boys were the handsomest bunch ever, the girls the loveliest, the parties the most lavish, and the ball that topped them all was the Spencer-Churchill girl's at Blenheim Palace. Jack went with Euny. Danny Walsh drove them and Fidelma went as lady's maid.

She said, "You never saw anything like it, Nora. They must have had six hundred there, could have been more, pouring drink down their throats and eating like there was no tomorrow. And then there was all the help, and the bands, and special dance floors that had been put down. What they must have spent. It's a wonder this country's not had a revolution."

Danny said, "They did. Only it went off at half cock. Typical."

We saw a lot more of Billy Hartington while Mrs. K was in America, but he always dropped by with a crowd of friends. Then Kick was invited to another house party at Compton Place and the question was, who would go with her? Kick wanted me. But I'd promised to visit with Rosie that weekend. She was going to show me the classrooms at Belmont and then we were going to go into Watford to get tea and buns and see Irene Dunne in *Love Affair*.

Kick said, "Oh please. Rosie'll understand. You know why I want you to come. It's not for me. It's for you. You know why."

I said, "I do not know why. And I can't break a promise to Rosie."

She said, "What if I tell you a certain driver is keen to see you?"

I said, "I don't know anything about any drivers."

"Oh Nora," she said. "What a whopper. What about camellias and love letters on night tables?"

It must have come from the Blundell girl's maid.

Fidelma said, "You should see your face, Brennan. You're the color of pickled beets."

Kick said, "I just don't know how I'll face Mr. Stallybottom if I have to step down off that train without you."

I said, "Stallybrass. And I'm too old for such silliness."

Fidelma said, "God in heaven, go, why don't you. He might be your last chance of a man without a white stick. I'll go to Belmont. It's all the same to me and Rosie won't mind."

Everybody always said "Rosie won't mind," but they didn't see how she looked forward to her little treats. They were all taking off, traveling and making new friends. Pat would be the next one. And Rosie was left behind. She wanted to go out dancing with London Jack and get married and have babies, but all she was safe for was playing pickup sticks with Teddy. And she did mind.

So even though I did go to Compton Place, I felt ashamed of myself every inch of the way, for letting Rosie down on account of a silly man. And then he wasn't even there to meet us from the train. Lord Billy collected Kick and Sissy Lloyd-Thomas and Ginny Vigo, but the maids all had to wait, sun blazing down and not a spot of shade, till a station wagon could be spared and when it came it didn't have Walter Stallybrass at the wheel. I was crushed in the back with the bags, nobody speaking to me, and by the time we got to the house Kick had already disappeared, gone out for a bicycle ride in her traveling suit and left a tap running in the bathroom and towels on the floor.

I'd just got back from laying out her dinner gown when he came tap-tapping at my door. Five strawberries on a saucer.

I said, "I'm in a bad mood."

He said, "Me too. They fetched me down here to be an extra driver and they've had me hanging curtains all afternoon. How have you been?"

I said, "I'm grand as long as I'm not running around being a lady's maid. It's not what I'm used to. I like my charges young enough that I know where they are and what they're up to. And I don't like sleeping in strange beds."

He said, "I hoped it'd be you they sent this time. I thought to bring you a camellia. I had a dark red double ready for cutting, but it wouldn't have lasted the journey so I picked you the strawberries instead."

They were still warm from the sun.

He said, "Well then."

I said, "How's your sister?"

"Champion," he said. "She's champion. I shouldn't really be up here. Maids' quarters. I'll get shot."

I said, "You'd better be off then."

"Aye," he said. "I'll see you at dinner, though?"

I said, "I don't want any talk."

He said, "There's always talk, Nora, in a big house. Tonight they'll be talking about Lady Vigo's brother getting sacked from Oxford University. And why Lord Bagnell's selling off his grouse moors. They won't be talking about you and me."

I said, "There isn't any you and me."

He said, "But there could be. You're a very handsome woman, Nora Brennan."

And then he ran off down the back stairs.

There must have been something in the sea air that weekend. Things had changed between Kick and Billy too. I could tell it when I was doing her hair before dinner on the Saturday night. I was chattering on to her about Euny's debut and she wasn't listening to a word I said.

I said, "What's on your mind?"

"Nothing," she said. "What exactly is the difference between our church and the one the Devonshires go to?"

I wasn't the one to ask. I knew they didn't pray the rosary and they didn't think anything at all of the Holy Father, but there had to be more to it than that.

I said, "All I can tell you is you shouldn't be thinking about it. There are plenty of boys who'd make you a suitable sweetheart, but Lord Billy isn't one of them."

"Sure," she said. "I was just wondering."

I said, "Well, don't wonder anymore. Your Mammy would have a fit."

"I know," she said. "Unless Billy converted, of course. Then she wouldn't mind."

I said, "Yours wouldn't but his would. Now stop this, before you get your heart broken."

She said, "Don't worry. It was just a crazy idea. Anyway, a Marquess's wife is called a Martian or something and who'd want to be one of those."

Perhaps if Jack had been there, or young Joe. Perhaps if I'd been sharper with her. But I had a few things of my own to wonder about. Every chance Walter Stallybrass got he wanted to walk me round the kitchen gardens.

I said, "What am I doing down here, if people ask?"

He said, "I'm showing you the black fly on the broad beans. Would you ever think of getting wed? If we did, there could be a position for you at Chatsworth."

I said, "What position? They've no babies."

He said, "No, but they will have. Any road, there's other work. Laundry. Kitchen work."

I said, "What, work under your sister?"

He said, "All right then, not kitchen work. But sewing. There's always plenty of work for sewing women. And we could get a cottage."

I did quite like him. It was nice having a man tuck your hair behind your ear. But I had my Kennedys to think of. When you're in service it's not just a job, it's your home too, and your family, if you've had charge of the children.

He was forty-nine and never been married. He said, "I did have a sweetheart. I was walking out with Mary Fantom before the war, but she didn't wait for me. She went off to Sheffield to do war work. Ended up marrying some old pawnbroker. Well, I were in no state when I come home. I had mustard gas on my chest. And now I look back, I don't know as me and Mary were that well-suited anyhow. I reckon she were too interested in brass. She wouldn't have been contented on what I make."

I said, "What makes you think I would?"

He said, "Well, if you'd wanted to be Mrs. Vanderbilt you wouldn't have stayed a nursery maid all those years. Anyhow, if you turn out to be a scold I can still enjoy looking at you. Your chin's a bit lopsided, did you know? And you wouldn't be half as bonny if it were perfectly straight."

I said, "I've been twenty-two years with the Kennedys."

He said, "I know. You keep saying. But will you think about it? Getting wed, I mean. Then when you come north for His Lordship's birthday party, you can give me your answer."

I said, "As far as I know we're not coming north."

"Oh you're bound to be," he said. "In August, for Lord Billy's twenty-first, belated. They didn't do anything for him at the time because the old Duke had just died. But now the mourning's finished they're having a circus and a ball and all sorts. You're sure to be coming. If you ask me, your Miss is Number One with Lord Billy."

Well, I knew we had a villa to go to in France, same as the previous summer, and I doubted Herself would allow Kick to travel all the way back to Chatsworth to be Lord Billy Hartington's Number One. But I didn't tell him that. I didn't have the heart. His face was so bright, as if I'd already said yes.

I said, "I'll think about it."

"Do, Nora," he said. "I'm in earnest, you know? I wouldn't have spoke up if I weren't."

I didn't know what to think. Surprises always make me feel giddy. Specially the touch of a man.

I said, "You'll find me a slow thinker."

"Oh aye," he said. "Well, you'll find me a patient waiter."

And that was how we left it.

20

Keeping Going with a Cheery Smile

It seemed like everyone was summering in Cannes. The Duchess of Alba, Miss Marlene Dietrich, the Duke and Duchess of Windsor. Mr. and Mrs. K were out to dinners and parties every night, and so were the youngsters. Jack was supposed to be working but I didn't see much sign of activity. He had to write a paper, a kind of composition, to finish his studies, and Mr. K had said if he made a good enough job of it he'd have it turned into a book.

He said, "Dad says a published book is a great thing to have if you're going into politics."

Kick said, "What a draggy old way to spend a summer. How come Joe hasn't had to write one?"

He said, "Well, I guess Dad thinks Joe can get by on charm and good looks. I'm going to need a few bonus features. Like Jack Kennedy, the intellectual."

I said, "Like Jack Kennedy who wears odd socks. Jack Kennedy who can't spell for taffy. How can you write a whole book?"

He said, "It's a lot easier than you'd think. I had to write this paper anyway and Dad's got people who can pad it out a bit, tidy it up, check the facts, correct the spelling. It's a great idea. When it's published I'll give you a signed copy."

Teddy wanted to know would he get money for it.

Jack said, "I guess not. It won't be that kind of book. We'll just send copies out to useful people."

Kick said, "All those words. How can you think of what to say?"

I said, "I could think of plenty to say. I reckon I should write a book. Jack Kennedy as I knew him. My life with the Kennedys, before a one of them learned to close a door or slide a drawer shut."

Bobby said he thought I bettern't. He said, "Mother would never allow you to do that."

Kick was invited to Lord Billy's birthday as Walter had predicted, but she didn't argue when her Mammy said it was out of the question for her to attend. We were in the South of France and that was where we were to remain.

Mrs. K said, "There'll be plenty more parties in the fall."

But she was mistaken, of course. Adolf Hitler put paid to that.

Kick settled down though, and she seemed happy enough to swim and play tennis and go shopping with Pat and Rosie.

She said, "August was a crazy time to have a party. I'm going to send Billy a wire and tell him so. And I'll bet it rains. Any messages for Walter Stallybottom?"

I said, "It's Mr. Stallybrass, and don't make fun of your elders."

After Neville Chamberlain went to Munich we'd stopped talking about whether there'd be another war. Just before we'd left for Cannes we'd had pamphlets delivered, reminding us about gas masks and blackout precautions and the difference between the

Take Cover siren and the All Clear, but they'd all been pushed into a drawer. And Mr. K had come with us to France. If he'd thought war was in the offing he'd have stayed at his desk, I'm sure.

But then the calls started. Two or three a day at first, and cablegrams arriving, too, and then round about the third week in August there was a day when he hardly left his rooms. He was talking on the telephone to the President. It was Jack who told us what had happened. The Russians had come to an agreement with Germany and left everyone else out in the cold.

He said, "Dad says it looks like war. He's flying back to London first thing and I'm going with him."

Mr. K came up to say good night to Teddy and Jean.

He said, "You'll have to close up the villa and follow me to London. Ted, you and Bobby are going to be the men of the house. No idling. I want my team on its toes and ready for action."

Teddy wanted to know if he could have one last swim before we packed and would he have to carry a gun.

Mr. K said, "No, no gun. We're not at war yet. Just be a good boy and do everything you can to help Mother."

Fidelma caught him on his way downstairs. She said, "Is it very bad, sir?"

"Bad enough," he said. "If it's war and America goes in, I have two boys old enough for the draft."

Mrs. K was worried about shortages, so she stopped off in Paris for a day's shopping and then flew to Croydon. The rest of us caught a boat train, lucky to get places. Everybody was cutting short their vacation because the latest was that the German army was on the move, lining up along the frontier of Poland.

Kick was very subdued.

She said, "When the boys talked about volunteering and going to fight and everything, I didn't think it'd really happen."

I felt the same. I'd thought as long as all those clever people in government kept talking and sending messages and flying to meetings we'd be all right. But all of a sudden it seemed Adolf Hitler was determined to have a war. Danny Walsh said it was just another flap.

He said, "Remember last summer, how they were digging trenches in the park? It all blew over and it'll be the same this time. Poland's nothing to do with us."

Fidelma said, "Where is it exactly?"

"Near Switzerland," Danny said.

But Euny said it was between Germany and Russia, and when it came to facts learned out of a book you'd trust Euny over Danny Walsh anytime. She'd been given the brains intended for all nine of the Kennedys.

And Danny was wrong on another count. It wasn't just a flap. The minute we stepped off the train in London you could tell it was something serious.

Everybody was carrying gas masks. There were sandbags along the front of Prince's Gate, and queues at Bourne and Hollingsworth to buy blackout material. Even Teddy could feel the difference, spinning out his questions when it was bedtime.

"What did Germans look like?" he wanted to know. "Would there still be school if a war started? Could a bomb knock down a whole house?"

Mr. K drove to the aerodrome to collect Mrs. K, and when they got to Prince's Gate she came straight upstairs to see me and Fidelma.

She said, "The Ambassador has taken a house in the country while this grave situation continues. We'll begin the move in the morning."

Fidelma said, "What about their schools?"

"We'll see how things develop," she said. "Rosie will go back to

Belmont as planned. I see no sense in disturbing her routine. But the most important thing now is to get the rest of the family out of London. I don't want them alarmed, though. There's to be no talk of gas attacks or air raids, especially in front of Teddy."

The house was out in Radlett, not far from Rosie's school. Wall Hall. It belonged to a friend of Mr. K's, Mr. J. P. Morgan Junior, but he hardly ever used it. It was perfect for us. Big grounds, so you didn't feel cooped up, and yet handy for London. Beautiful yellow stone, with little turrets and mullioned windows. I don't know why we hadn't stayed there all along. It was a great deal nicer than Prince's Gate. Mrs. K could have had a grand old time there playing Queen of the Castle if the circumstances had been better. As it was, we had one golden week. September 3, everything changed.

It was a Sunday. We were all going into town for ten o'clock Mass, but just as we were leaving, Mr. K was called to the telephone. Lord Halifax wanted to speak to him. We sat with the engine ticking over until Mrs. K told Danny he was wasting juice. Then we sat in silence. I couldn't think of anything to say that didn't have the word "war" in it.

Mr. K came loping out eventually.

He said, "Rosa, go to Prince's Gate directly after church. And tell the Father to hurry things along. The Prime Minister's broadcasting to the nation at eleven fifteen. People are going to want to get home in time to hear him."

She said, "Perhaps we shouldn't go to Mass?"

"No," he said, "take the children. It's important. Just don't stay for the Dismissal. Jack, when you get out of church come straight round to Chancery. Joe's going to ride with me now. Danny, when you've dropped them off, go to Prince's Gate and make sure the wireless receiver's working."

It was such a grand morning. It seemed too fresh and sunny

for anything bad to happen. There was hardly anyone at the Oratory and Father Minns served Mass faster than anything I ever saw in Ballynagore. With Father Hughes you could be in and out in twenty-five minutes, before he got his bad hip, but Father Minns beat that the morning war broke out.

We could hear the bells ringing down at St. Mary Abbot's when we got to the house. Everybody hurried up to Mrs. Kennedy's sitting room and the staff came in, Danny Walsh hovering there beside Herself, in case the wireless signal went wonky and an expert was required.

Mr. Chamberlain said he'd warned Germany they had till eleven o'clock that morning to stop threatening Poland, and if they didn't promise to pull back their troops, we'd be at war.

He said, "I have to tell you now that no such undertaking has been received and that consequently this country is at war with Germany."

He sounded like a tired old man. He said we'd be fighting against evil things but right would prevail. "God bless you all," he said, and Fidelma Clery wasn't the only one who had to wipe away a tear.

Kick said, "What happens next?" and the very next minute the air-raid sirens started.

Mrs. K made us all put on our gas masks and sit on the floor, away from the windows. London Jack and the pantry boy went up to the roof to watch for bombers. They said the barrage balloons had gone up over Westminster and St. James's, but there was no sign of any planes. A false alarm. It was a shock though. Even Teddy wasn't doing his usual larking about. He stuck close to Mother until she got a call from Mr. K. He was taking Joe and Jack to Parliament to hear the Prime Minister speak and he wanted her along too.

"Cook, dear," she said. "Make a little lunch for the children.

Nora, I expect we'll drive straight back to Radlett this afternoon. There'll be arrangements to be made."

Kick shot me a look. She'd never said anything about wanting to stay on, if it came to a war, but her face said it all. I went down to the kitchens to help Gertie Ambler and she followed me.

She said, "We're all going to get sent home, aren't we?"

I said, "Of course you are. To be kept safe from German bombs."

She said, "Maybe Daddy'll let me stay if I say I want to do war work."

I said, "You're dreaming. You can do war work in New York, isn't that what he'll say? Fund-raising. Red Cross parcels."

She said, "All my friends are here."

I said, "Eighteen months ago you didn't know a soul here. Is it Billy you're thinking of?"

"Not only Billy," she said. She was picking at the crust on the bread.

"Well, actually," she said, "we are kind of engaged."

And the first terrible thought that came into my mind was that Adolf Hitler and his war might just have spared us a big drama.

She said, "I know, I know, don't look at me like that."

I said, "You may think you're 'kind of' engaged, but your Mammy and Daddy'll have none of it and neither will Their Graces, so if you've an ounce of sense you won't even bring it up."

She said, "I know Mother'll fuss, but she just needs to get used to the idea. She really likes the Devonshires. It's just the church thing, that's all. And Daddy'll understand. He'll be able to get me a position somewhere. You know, typing at Army Headquarters or something. Take a top-secret letter, Miss Kennedy!"

I said, "You can't type."

She said, "You're splitting hairs. Okay. I can make tea."

She couldn't, of course.

They came back from hearing Mr. Chamberlain's speech and Mr. K looked like a specter. As the butler took his coat he said, "It's the end of the world, Stevens. It's the end of our world."

Then he had the whole family assembled to hear what had to be done.

He said, "You'll go back to the States, but tickets are hard to get because everybody else has the same idea, so you may have to travel in twos and threes."

We all knew the real reason though, after the Germans torpedoed the *Athenia*, with women and children aboard, American citizens who weren't even in the war. He was afraid if we all sailed together we might all go to the bottom of the ocean and that'd be the end of the Kennedys.

Minnie Stubbs dropped by, and Susie Frith-Johnstone, both abubble about volunteering. I thought Kick might say something about her own crackpot scheme, but she didn't. Only that war sounded like it might be fun.

Good girl, I thought. Keep your head screwed on.

Our whereabouts at Wall Hall was meant to be a secret. An important ambassador can't live out in the sticks where any madman can walk up to his front door. But Billy Hartington knew where to find us. We were just back from Prince's Gate when he came looking for Kick. The Guards' Reserves were being called up, so he'd come to say good-bye.

Then Danny Walsh came into the scullery. He said, "Nora Brennan, you're wanted. At the tradesman's door."

Fidelma and Gertie Ambler were all ears.

Walter Stallybrass was out on the doorstep, mangling his driver's cap like it was an old cleaning rag.

He said, "War's broke out."

I said, "I'll bet I knew before you did. How did you know we were here?"

"Lord Billy made inquiries," he said. "Are they leaving, your Kennedys?"

I told him what had been decided.

He said, "Don't go, Nora. Stay here. Did you think about what I said? We can get wed."

I said, "I can't. How can I? I've got obligations."

"Nay," he said. "You're not obliged. How old are those kiddies?"

Teddy was eight, Jean was eleven.

He said, "They can't expect to keep everybody on. There's a war on now. Everyone that can be spared'll have to do war work, till we've beat them Germans."

I said, "We're Americans. America's not at war."

"Oh," he said, and he took a step back. "Is that how you see things?"

It wasn't, not really. I felt sorry for England. It wasn't as if they'd started it. But I didn't want to be bothered with another war. I'd been supposed to marry Jimmy Swords and it was the war that scuppered that. I wanted everything to stay as it was.

I said, "My head's spinning, Walter. I got up this morning, put my best hat on and went to church, and now all of a sudden the Germans are coming and you're talking about getting married."

He said, "It's not all of a sudden. I asked you when you were down at Compton Place and you didn't turn me down. You said you'd think about it. Well, thinking time's up. Why not grab a bit of happiness? There's hard times ahead, Nora, and I reckon we could be a bit of comfort for one another. Stay here. We can volunteer together."

I said, "You're too old for the forces."

"Plenty else I can do," he said. "You too. It's called the home front."

Then Fidelma put her head out the door.

"Inside, Brennan," she said. "Excuse me for interrupting. We've got a situation on our hands. And you'd better get round the front, Romeo, fast as you like. Lord Billy's sitting in his car wondering what happened to his driver."

I said, "It's all too rushed."

He started to walk away.

I said, "We can't leave it like this."

"Up to you," he said. "I'm at the Devonshires' house in Carlton Gardens. Don't know how long for though. We could all be dead by morning."

There was a shouting match going on between Mrs. Kennedy and Kick.

"But I love him" was all we could hear from Kick. Mrs. K was doing most of the talking, rapping out the words she wanted to drive home.

"Be *still*, Kathleen. You must *master* your feelings. No more *foolish* threats. You'll *do as you are told* and not cause your poor father further anxiety. On this horrid day of all days. Remember what the Sisters taught you. Bear the small trials of *daily discipline*. Develop fortitude. Now be *silent*, Kathleen. I won't listen to another word. Go and contemplate the Sacred Heart."

Kick went to her room and Mrs. K went back to her lists and the whole house tiptoed around them, waiting till Mr. K drove home and they came out of their corners for round two. I was darning socks, trying to think straight. Danny Walsh was cutting out pictures of German bombers and English bombers, making a chart so we'd know the difference.

Fidelma said, "Well? Spit it out, Brennan. That driver you've been pretending not to like comes looking for you, you must have something to tell us."

I'd practically never mentioned him.

I said, "We were just talking. Wondering how long this'll go on."

She said, "Poor bugger looked like you were making him sweat. What's up?"

Gertie Ambler said, "You're not in the family way, are you?"

Danny said, "She's too old for the pudding club."

I said, "No, Danny. Too smart."

Fidelma said, "Did he propose?"

I said, "Sort of. He wants me to stay on. Volunteer for war work."

She said, "What is he? A recruiting sergeant?"

I said, "Well, he did tell me he liked me before. He said they'd probably find something for me at Chatsworth. If we got married."

She said, "That's a proposal, you chump. What do you expect at forty-five, a moonlight serenade?"

Danny said, "Mrs. K won't like it if you give your notice. She's having a very bad day."

I said, "I'm not giving my notice."

Fidelma said, "Mrs. K doesn't need to hear about anything, Danny Walsh, and if she does we'll know which blabbermouth told her. Now why don't you go out and scan the skies for Stukas. This is girl talk."

He went.

"Well," she said. "Are you going to accept him?"

I said, "I hardly know him."

She said, "That's not such a bad thing. My cousin Tula's been engaged nineteen years to Declan Mulherne. She knows every last thing about him, so it doesn't seem worth the bother of a wedding now. And he'll be nicely fixed, this Walter. He'll have a job for life up there. Does he live in?"

I said, "He said there might be a cottage."

"Well, there you are then," she said. "And he's not bad-looking, Brennan. I'll have him if you won't."

I said, "This is a good position to give up."

"It is," she said. "There's fools lined up all the way down the road, waiting to jump into your shoes."

I said, "And Danny's right. Herself'll have a fit if I give my notice at a time like this."

Fidelma said, "She will not. All she's interested in is getting her gowns home safe and keeping Kick from running off with Lord Billy. And she's in a better mood now than she'll be once she gets back home. God in Heaven, Bronxville's going to feel like a comedown after London. One minute she's getting her photograph in the dailies and having dinner with the King and Queen of England, the next she's back on Pondfield Road playing bridge with Joey Timilty. She's not going to like that. You'll be well out of it. And you don't have to give your notice now. Wait till we see who's traveling when. She might go on the first sailing. Then it'd just be Mr. K. I'd sooner face him any day."

Mr. K didn't get home till gone eleven that night and he looked all in, but Mrs. K insisted he speak to Kick.

She said, "I want to stay here and do my bit, Daddy."

Over his dead body, he said.

She said, "But all my friends'll be doing war work. I can't just run out on them."

He said, "It isn't our war, nor ever will be if Roosevelt listens to me, and I didn't raise this fine family to see the Luftwaffe use it for target practice. You're going home, Kick, away from the damned stupid war."

Mrs. K said, "And away from Billy Hartington."

Kick said, "I won't go. I just won't. I love Billy and I'm staying where he is. We're engaged."

Well! Mrs. K wanted to telephone Their Graces, to get the

affair nipped in the bud from both sides, but it was nearly midnight, and anyway Mr. K said he didn't need help from any Devonshires in taking care of his family. Truth be told, I don't think he minded the idea of Kick being a Ladyship someday. It would have been quite a feather in his cap. But when it came to anything to do with the girls or the Church, he always allowed Mrs. K to have the last word.

He said, "Your mother's upset by this, Kick, and if she's upset, I'm upset. Now go to bed. I have graver things than this on my mind, young lady. We could wake up tomorrow to find Germans at our door."

Mrs. K sent for me. I was in my nightgown and she was in hers.

She said, "Dear heart, I'm worried she'll try to elope. When she's gone to sleep, take her shoes and bag away."

I said, "If she was set on doing that, she'd go whether she had her bag and shoes or not. But Lord Billy's not that type. I'm sure Devonshires don't run off to get hitched. They've their own chapel up there, you know? And he'd want everything done by the book, I'm sure."

"Yes," she said, "I expect you're right. But then, it would be *their* idea of 'by the book.'"

She looked so tiny and tired.

She said, "Kick can be so headstrong, but Billy must know his people would never agree to the match. The Devonshires have always been the most stubborn kind of Protestants. I'm just worried this declaration of war might have prompted him to suggest something crazy."

I said, "I'll sleep with my door open. I'll hear her if she makes a move. But I doubt she will. We're all worn out by what's happened."

"We are," she said. "Oh Nora, what a long day it's seemed.

All that effort Mr. Chamberlain put in and it's still come to this. Everything's changed, thanks to those Germans. And it was going so well for us here. The opportunity of a lifetime for the children, and now we won't be able to stay on for Pat to have her debut."

I said, "How soon do you think we'll be going?"

She said, "The sooner the better. There could be gas attacks and bombs. The Ambassador has his people getting us onto the earliest possible sailings. We might not be able to get staterooms, of course. We'll just have to take what we can get and consider it part of our war sacrifice. And I have to think of this setback as a blessing in disguise. I've been so busy and distracted while we've been Ambassador. I believe this may be God's way of telling me to pay closer attention to my children. We have to keep Kick occupied. When we get home she must take some classes. And we'll invite some nice Catholic boys down to Palm Beach for Christmas. She has to put this Billy Hartington episode right behind her."

I looked in on Kick. She was still wide-awake.

I said, "Do you have your sneakers on under those covers? Are you thinking of running off?"

She laughed.

She said, "I'm not that dumb. It's not fair though. I mean, Mother's so upset about Billy, but he's a good, sweet person. His folks are just in the wrong church, which is hardly his fault. And now he'll have to go off and fight. I don't know when I'll ever see him again. It's all so not fair."

Yes, I thought, and if it's anything like the last lot, there'll be a lot more unfair things before we're finished. Plans ruined. Lives snuffed out like candle ends.

I said, "Look at it this way, when the war's ended you and Billy will be old enough to please yourselves, if that's still what you want."

She said, "When the war's ended? It only started this morning. Daddy says it could last two or three years."

I said, "So you'll be ancient. You'll go up the aisle in your bath chair."

She said, "We'll be older but nothing else will have changed. He'll still be expected to do what Devonshires do and I'll still be a Kennedy. We have talked about it, you know? The church thing? Billy thinks we can work something out. Like our boy babies could be brought up Protestant and our girl babies can be Catholic, or something like that. I don't know. Sounds pretty weird to me. I'd sooner join his lot. How bad can they be? They say the Our Father. The only thing they don't have is the Hail Mary, and I can always say that under my breath."

I said, "Do you love him?"

She said, "I think so. I don't know what being in love feels like. But I really, really like him. Isn't that how it starts?"

I was a fine one to ask.

I didn't sleep that night for thinking about Walter Stallybrass. I surely wasn't in love with him. He was an oddity, old-fashioned in some respects, stuck in his Devonshire ways. But he made me laugh with his funny flat way of speaking, and he'd had some guts to stand on the doorstep and ask me like that. I like courage in a person.

The way I looked at it, there was going to be less and less for me to do with the Kennedys. Bobby was going to board at Portsmouth Abbey as soon as we got home. Then Jean would board at Noroton, and eventually Teddy would be sent to Choate, and where would that leave me? Mrs. K sometimes wondered aloud what she'd ever do without me, but her heart was really ruled by her billfold. She didn't believe in keeping help on the payroll a minute longer than she had to. There was Rosie, of course, but she was doing so well. It looked like she'd be nicely set up to go to a convent and teach kindergarten, and be safe from unscrupulous men.

I knew I could get another position, but it would be hard starting over with a new family. And then there was this new war. Nobody could say how that was going to pan out. Round and round it all went in my mind. I got up in the end and went down to the kitchen to make a pot of tea. Fidelma was down there, couldn't sleep either.

She said, "I thought we were supposed to have had the war to end all wars?"

I said, "I feel too old for another one."

"Me too," she said, "and I'm only glad the wheel came off when I was expecting, because if I'd had that baby he'd be of age by now. He'd have been another one for the draft, because it'll come to it, you see. America'll have to go in before it's over."

I said, "I never knew you lost a baby."

"Lost a baby, lost a husband," she said. "Keeping going with a cheery smile, that was my war work the last time around. This time I reckon I'll just roll a few bandages."

Nearly twenty years I'd known her and she'd never spoken of Noel Clery before, nor ever spoke of him again. He was killed at Cantigny in May of 1918, six months before she came to Beals Street.

I said, "All those English boys are going off for training. Lord Billy and his pals. I suppose they think it'll be a bit of an adventure."

She said, "One thing, if America goes in, you can be sure there won't be any Kennedy boys get drafted. Your Man'll have them slipped into reserved occupations before you can say 'Heil Hitler.' Are you going to accept Walter then, Brennan? Is that why you're pacing the floor? Are you thinking about wedding gowns?"

I said, "It seems like madness. I've never thought of marriage, not since Jimmy Swords let me down. It's suited me, the way things turned out. I've had the joy of the babies without the bother of a husband. I mean, Walter's all right. Quite nice, actually. But marriage. And I can't face a scene with Mrs. K. She's depending on me to keep Kick in order and help her get them all safe back to Bronxville."

She said, "Will you listen to yourself. She's depending on you till it suits her not to anymore. What do you think she's going to keep us on for once Teddy's away to the big school? Nothing, that's what. We'll be out on our ear. Unless His Honor's moved in by then and he's in diapers. Anyway, it's Adolf Hitler you want to be scared of, not Mrs. Ambassador Kennedy. We'll likely all end up bombed to kingdom come, so what are you worrying about? I know what I'd do. I'd get cuddled up to Walter, before them sirens start wailing."

21

Future Prospects Unknown

The sirens did keep sounding but there were never any bombers. Every time it was due to something different. Electrical malfunction. Testing the system. False alarm over friendly planes. But it got to your nerves just the same.

Mrs. K sent for me. She said, "Now, Nora, here's the plan. I'll be sailing on the *Washington* with Kick and Euny and Teddy and Cook. Fidelma will bring Pat and Jean and Bobby, with Danny Walsh to help her. I want you to stay here with Rosie until she gets her teaching certificate. The Ambassador will get you on the first sailing after that. You'll still be home by Christmas. You do understand, dear? This is so important for Rosie. It'll be her first big achievement."

I said, "Does Rosie know the rest of you are leaving?"

She said, "I'll see her if I have time before we go. But you know she doesn't really pay attention. If I tell her we're going she'll have forgotten it five minutes later."

But Rosie knew all right. I took Teddy and Jean out to visit with her before they all left and she was full of it. Proud as a princess.

"I'm staying on," she kept saying, "because Daddy's going to need help and I'm the oldest girl. I can make tea parties for him if he likes. I can come at weekends and play checkers with him. That'll help him to relax."

England and the war might have started the undoing of Kick, but I could see it might be the making of Rosie. The rest of the tribe was going to be out of her hair and she was going to have her Daddy to herself for five minutes.

Two days before the first sailing we drove to Prince's Gate to finish up the packing.

Mrs. K said, "Nora, I want you to go to Rigby and Peller to collect my new brassieres."

Kick said, "I'll go."

"No," she said. "You're to come with me to say good-bye to Lady Bessborough."

Maybe she guessed what Kick had in mind. Billy Hartington was at the Devonshires' town house in St. James's, waiting on orders from his regiment. Kick came running after me with a letter for him.

"Please, darling Nora," she said.

Ink on her fingers. Smudges all over the envelope.

I said, "You'll get me shot."

She said, "Please don't tell. I've written Billy that I'm going to do everything I can to come back. I've asked him to wait for me. If he really loves me, he will, don't you think?"

There was no arguing against that. If she'd been mine she'd have had my blessing anyway. I thought the likeliest thing was, when she got back to New York she'd fall back in with her old crowd and Billy Hartington would be forgot. It's hard to keep love warm when you're half a world apart. That was what I had in mind to write to Walter Stallybrass. I'd promised Mrs. K to see Rosie safely home and that was that. But that note never got written. When I turned in to Carlton Gardens, Walter was there in the street, polishing the Daimler with a wash leather.

First thing he said was, "Where's your gas mask?"

I'd forgotten it. It was such a damned nuisance to carry.

He said, "Nay, you must keep your mask handy. Gas is no joke. I'd hate for anything to happen to you."

It was nice to have somebody looking out for me.

I said, "Is Lord Billy at home?"

He said, "I knew you'd come. I had a feeling today would be the day."

I said, "I've a letter for him. Miss Kick sails on Thursday."

He said, "Are you going with them?"

His face lit up when I told him I wasn't sailing. He didn't give me time to explain I would be going, just later.

He said, "You've made me a very happy man, Nora. And I promise you won't regret it."

They were grubbing out the railings across the street, taking them away to turn them into guns.

I said, "The thing is, Walter, if I leave the Kennedys all I'll have is what I stand up in. Nowhere to live, nothing to live on. The mood Mrs. K's in I might not even get a testimonial."

"Oh well," he said, "that changes everything. I thought you were a woman of means. I were looking forward to a life of leisure. Well. Cancel everything. The wedding's off."

I said, "I'm forty-five."

"Aye," he said, "and you've got the bonniest pair of lips on you. Anybody ever tell you?"

And he kissed me, right there in Carlton Gardens.

He said, "Stand here and don't budge while I give Lord Billy his love letter."

I said, "I can't wait. I've to get along to South Molton Street for a parcel. If he wants me to take an answer he'll have to write it quick."

He said, "I'll walk you. Never mind about His Lordship. He's got all the time in the world. We're the poor old buggers as haven't got time to waste. I'm taking you round to the pop-shop in Whitcomb Street. I'm going to put a ring on your finger, Nora Brennan, before you change your mind."

I was late getting back to Prince's Gate but nobody noticed. Herself was still out doing the rounds with her good-byes and Fidelma had taken Teddy to get the retainer on his front teeth tightened. Lunch was sandwiches, left under a damp tea cloth, for people to help themselves.

I tucked Lord Billy's letter under Kick's pillow and went up to wash my face, to sit quiet for five minutes and look at my ring in private. A real diamond set in filigree gold, a bit worn on the band, but it was the prettiest thing anybody had ever given me. I put it on the chain with my crucifix, until the time was right. Teddy was the one who found it. He was sitting on my lap, big lump that he was, giving me farewell cuddles.

He said, "I wish you were coming with us on the boat. Why can't you come with us?"

I said, "I've to wait behind while Rosie gets her certificate. She can't stay all alone."

"Pooh," he said. "Rosie's lucky. Why have you got a ring? Who gave you this ring?"

"Nobody you know," I said.

He said, "Did you steal it? I'll bet you did. Oh do come with us, Nora. Lovely, lovely Nora. We can play quoits on deck. I promise I won't tell Mother you stole a ring."

Covering me with his slobbery kisses.

Fidelma pulled his hair. She said, "It's not the help that steal around here. It's little Kennedys that go into candy stores and forget to pay. Now you apologize to Nora."

He said he was sorry. He said he just thought maids were too poor to buy rings.

He said, "How much do we pay you? How much did that ring cost?"

I gave him a cookie. A cookie was guaranteed to take Teddy's mind off anything. Not Fidelma though.

"Out with it, Brennan," she said the minute we were alone. "So you've accepted him. Let's see the goods."

I said, "But I'm not going to tell Mrs. K. I'll stay and keep an eye on Rosie like I promised, but then somebody else'll have to take her home. Mrs. Moore maybe. I'll wait till you're all gone, then I'll tell Mr. K."

"There you are," she said. "Didn't I tell you it'd be easy? But I'll miss the wedding. Who will you have for your maid of honor if I'm not here?"

I hadn't thought about anything like that. I couldn't see any further than the day the last of them sailed. Everybody knew what they were going to be doing. Teddy to day school, Bobby to his new boarding school, Pat and Jean to Sacred Heart. Euny was going for a student, to Manhattanville College, and Kick had her name down for the Finch School the very minute she got home, to study fashion. I could see her coming bottom of that class. Kick would wear the first thing she picked up off her bedroom floor. She'd go out wearing one black shoe and one brown if you didn't watch her. But the idea was to get her in with a nice crowd of girls and take her mind off Lord Billy and all the friends she'd left behind.

I waved them off at the station, first Kick, Euny, Teddy, and Herself, and then, a week later, Fidelma, with Jean and Pat and Bobby. Both times I felt full of dread. I was convinced they were going to get torpedoed and I'd never see any of them again.

Fidelma said, "All the best, you jammy beggar. When you get up to that Chatsworth House, won't you see if you can't find a man for me too? Not one of them pansified footmen, but an outdoors type. A stable hand would do me, or a carpenter. With a house, though. I wouldn't want to live in. I'm a natural redhead, tell him, with collar and cuffs to match, and a very sweet nature. If you find me one I'll be back like a shot, U-boats or no."

I said, "Look after my Kennedys for me."

"Brennan," she said, "don't you know the Kennedys will always look after themselves?"

Joseph Patrick went next, on the *Mauretania*, to get back in time for the start of law school, and then Jack, on the new Clipper flying boat. Which left me and Mr. and Mrs. Moore and Ambassador Kennedy rattling around in that great big place, with Rosie out at Belmont House and only home on the weekends. The Ambassador had been offered another house, at Sunningdale, near Windsor, not such a great barn as Wall Hall, but far enough out of London that it should be safe from bombs. Not that anyone had seen any bombs so far. The weeks went by and there was no sign of any Germans. It was a terrible letdown. A lot of people had had their little dogs put to sleep, thinking there wouldn't be food for them. And the children had been sent out into the country, to be safe from the raids, but there weren't any raids, so most of them came home again. They weren't scared. Joe Kennedy was though. Worried about all the conniving and philandering he'd done in his life, maybe. Worried he might not make it through the Pearly Gates. According to Mrs. Moore, he needed a pill to make him sleep.

I liked Mrs. Moore. I believe she loved those children as much as I did, though she'd grown-up children of her own. She was a more motherly type than Mrs. K.

She said, "You don't seem your usual self, Nora. Are you anxious to be getting home?"

I said, "No. It's not that. Though I'm wondering what we're supposed to do if there's an invasion while Rosie's still here. They say they do terrible things to the women."

She said, "Well, Joe doesn't think an invasion's likely just yet. And it'd be such a shame to take Rosie away from school when she's so close to finishing. My goodness, she's done well. We'll have her graduation and then we can all go home."

I said, "The thing is, I don't think I'll be going. And I'm only wondering, should I tell Mr. Kennedy now when he has so much on his plate?"

She said, "Are you thinking of volunteering?"

I said, "I am."

"Oh," she said, "I should so love to volunteer, but I'm far too old."

I said, "They say they'll find something for everyone, even if it's only making tea. I haven't done anything about it yet, till I know what I'm doing. That's the other thing. I had an offer. I'm getting married."

I don't know who was the more surprised, her or me, to hear myself say it out loud.

She said, "But why didn't you tell Mrs. Kennedy?"

I said, "Because she wouldn't have liked it. It would have been an inconvenience."

"What nonsense," she said. "She'd have been very happy for you. Rosa's a real romantic."

Well, Mrs. Moore saw Mrs. Kennedy from a different point of view than I did. We'd all heard the stories about her beaux. How Sir Thomas Lipton would have followed her to the ends of the earth. How she was determined to have Joe Kennedy whatever her Daddy thought. But Mrs. K didn't think of nursery maids as having a life like that.

I said, "Do you think I should tell Mr. K?"

"Of course you should," she said. "I'm sure he'll wish you well. And there'll probably be a little something for you too. Twenty-three years you've been with them. I'd say that's worth a little wedding bonus."

But I knew better than that.

"Married?" he said. "Nothing to do with me. Talk to Mrs. Kennedy when you get back."

I said, "I'm not going back. That's what I'm saying. I'm staying here and getting married."

He said, "The hell you are. You came over single at my expense and you'll go back single. You'll take Rosie home."

Mrs. Moore said, "Joe, I can take Rosie, when the time comes. Don't be so hard on the girl."

"Girl?" he said. "She's no girl. She's old enough to know when I pay people I expect the job done."

I said, "I'm old enough to have seen all of your children into the world practically. Old enough to have been there for every tooth they've cut."

He said, "Help are like those insurance shylocks. Always hanging around underfoot when you don't need them and then gone the minute you do. Well, I'll just look at it as a mouth less to feed. It'll be a berth less to pay for."

I'd guessed it would be like that. I had my bag packed, ready to go to Walter.

Mrs. Moore said, "Pay no attention, Nora. *I'm* glad you've found happiness. I think we must all grab our blessings while we may. And I'm sure Mr. Kennedy would have been more gracious if he didn't have a hundred worries on his mind."

She was a steadfast friend to the Kennedys, Mrs. Moore. I doubt they really appreciated her.

When I stepped out of Prince's Gate for the last time I felt like I was walking naked down Knightsbridge. No children, no lists, no timetable to stick to. Just my one valise and Walter's ring on my finger for the first time. Stevens, the butler, saw me out.

He said, "All the very best, Miss Brennan. It's going to be a desolate house now you've all gone. We've never had anything quite like the Kennedys here."

I got a bus as far as Hyde Park Corner and then walked the rest of the way, up Piccadilly, to give myself time to think. Nora Brennan, spinster, lately of 14 Prince's Gate, formerly nursery maid to the family of Ambassador Joseph P. Kennedy. Future prospects, unknown.

The Devonshires' house was going to be used as a billet for army officers, with Walter living in as caretaker. He'd tried to enlist again, in the Sherwood Foresters, but they wouldn't have him because he was getting on for fifty and he had asthma brought on by mustard gas during the last lot. The Civil Defense had snapped him up though.

He said, "Civil Defense'll take anybody. You should see us. Talk about the bottom of the barrel. Talk about the broken biscuits."

They'd made him an Air Raid Precaution Warden, assigned to Lord Melhuish's depot, just along the street.

When I got to Carlton Gardens there were two faces I hadn't expected to see. Lord Billy's brother, Lord Andrew, in town for a night or two before he went back to Cambridge University, and Hope Stallybrass, sent down from Chatsworth to be cook and housekeeper.

The first thing she said to me was "I knew you were trouble the first time I clapped eyes on you."

Walter said, "Nay, Hope, stop that. You promised you'd give it a chance. You promised you'd be nice."

She said, "I never promised. I said I'd try. But now I see her I'm all roiled up again."

I said, "What is it you're supposed to be giving a chance? Me? What do you think I am, a stray dog he's taken in?"

I felt like the floor had fallen away under my feet.

She said, "We were champion till you turned his head. Taking up with women at his time of life. He's forty-nine, you know?"

Walter said, "Pay no heed to her. She's just got to get used to the idea."

I said, "No, she doesn't have to. I won't stay. I won't live with atmosphere. I've given up everything to come to you, but I'll go back to Mr. Kennedy cap in hand if I have to. I won't put up with this."

He had his arm round my shoulder.

"You're too old, Walter," she kept saying. "You never needed a wife before. Why now?"

He said, "Because I never met Nora before. Now give over, Hope. Stop being so hurtful. It don't make any odds to you. It's my bed she'll be sharing, not thine. And I'd have thought you'd be glad of the company. I'm not going to be here to listen to your yapping. I'm going to have my air-raid duties."

She was standing at the kitchen table, scowling, folding and refolding the same few tea cloths. I'm not a crybaby as a rule but I'd had a terrible day, and when I started so did she.

"That's it," he said. "Two women blarting. I'm off out."

I said, "Will I make a pot of tea?"

"Aye," she said. "Go on. Make it strong."

Nothing more was said till the kettle had boiled and I was stirring the brew.

She said, "I've always looked after him."

I said, "He asked me to marry him. I thought he'd have told you."

"He did," she said, "but I thought it were one of his phases he were going through."

I said, "Has he had a lot of phases?"

"Oh yes," she said. "Before camellias it were hydrangeas and before that it were motorbikes. I've nowt against you as a person, Nora. But it's a big upheaval. And there'll be shortages, likely. You'll be an extra mouth to feed."

I said, "I have my ration book."

"Well then," she said. She cut me a slice of sponge cake.

She said, "But what will you do all day? There's nothing here for a lady's maid."

I said, "I'm not a lady's maid. I was the Kennedys' nurse and dogsbody and spare aunty and now I'm going to do war work."

She said, "I can't have interference in my kitchen, that's all. Just so you know."

And she poured me another cup of tea.

I went to the Women's Voluntary first thing the next morning and they sent me directly to a transit canteen in a temperance hall near Waterloo station, me and a girl called Hilda Oddy. Hilda had been working in a tobacconist's in Lambeth Palace Road but she thought she'd be able to get something a bit more exciting seeing we were at war. The Navy was her first choice. The Navy was everybody's first choice. Hilda's trouble was she was walleyed. My trouble was I was old and I was a foreigner. Spreading margarine onto sliced bread for hungry soldier boys, that was our first strike against Adolf Hitler, and when there was a lull in convoys they had us unraveling old woolens so the yarn could be used for servicemen's socks.

Walter wanted to take out the marriage lines right away, but I wanted time to smooth the rough edges off Hope. I knew what a life my sister Margaret had had living under the same roof as old Mrs. Mulcahy.

I said, "When Hope stops sighing every time you call me 'darling,' you can go to the Town Hall."

He kept saying, "Don't dilly-dally too long, Nora. I might get snapped up."

And then, when I was ready, there was a wait for wedding dates. Everybody was scrambling to get wed before the world ended.

A note came from Mrs. Moore. Rosie was to be awarded her teaching certificate and Mr. K wasn't able to attend, so she wondered would I think of going, with her and Mr. Moore? They picked me up on the Saturday morning.

Mrs. Moore said, "Well? Let's see the wedding band?"

I said, "I'm still a single woman. We're trying to get a date before the end of the year. I'd have loved Rosie to be there."

"Can't be done," she said. "We're taking her home, sailing on Wednesday. But I brought you something. I was packing and I thought you might like to have it. You'd suit it better than I do."

It was a little blouse, oyster silk with mother-of-pearl buttons.

She said, "It could be your 'something old.'"

Rosie was looking a picture, twenty-one and in full bloom.

I thought, You'll turn a few heads when you get back to New York. I wasn't sorry it wouldn't fall to me to keep her on a short tether, for my heart wouldn't have been in it. Safeguarding her from admirers was going to be a full-time job for somebody.

She'd had her hair cut shorter, as a lot of the girls were doing.

She said, "It's the War Effort. I want to do everything I can for the War Effort."

Sister Isabel presented her with her certificate, with a special mention for perseverance.

She said, "You're a credit to your family, Rose Marie. And you'll be a great gift to little children, wherever you teach."

There was talk that there might be a job for her at St. Gertrude's when she got home, helping with the kindergarten class.

Rosie said, "We're going home, Nora."

I said, "You are, sweetheart, but you know I'm not coming with you this time? I'm staying here and getting married."

She covered me with kisses. "Nora's getting married," she kept saying. "Nora's getting married."

She'd bought little Christmas gifts to take home for Teddy and Jean. They were all wrapped up but she insisted on getting everything out to show us.

She said, "Getting married is nice. That's what I'm going to do. When you have babies, Nora, I'll come and help you. Then when I have babies, you'll come and help me."

I said, "I don't think your old Nora will be having any babies."

"Yes you will, yes you will," she said. "That's what happens after you get married. He squeezes you and squeezes you and makes you feel nice and then you get a baby."

I said, "Well, don't you be in any hurry to do that. You've all the world to enjoy first. Now, will you write to me? Will you remember to do that?"

"I'll try," she said. "I might put the dots in the wrong place, but I'll try."

Sister Isabel laughed. She said, "That's been my only failure with Rose Marie. With the full stops it's either feast or famine."

We brought her away with us in Eddie Moore's car and they dropped me off. When it came to it I hated to let her go. Since the day she was born I'd always known where she was and when I'd see her again. But standing there in Carlton Gardens it was a different kind of good-bye. Like the real end of me and my Kennedys. The fog hadn't cleared all day and it was starting to get dark though it was barely three. Walter came out to say good day to the Moores and he kissed Rosie on the hand, very gallant. She loved that. She was hanging out the back window, smiling and waving as they drove away.

"Don't forget," she shouted. "It's the squeezing that gets the babies."

I don't know what the neighbors must have thought.

Me and Walter were married the week before Christmas. There was a young Guards' major, billeted at Carlton Gardens, came with us for a witness, and my new pal Hilda from the canteen. Hope stayed home, to boil a corned beef for the wedding breakfast, she said, but I think she was making her little point.

I wore my good tweed traveling suit and the blouse given me by Mrs. Moore, and the Devonshires sent me a silk rose to pin to my lapel. It broke Walter's heart that I couldn't have a Chatsworth camellia, but those days were gone. The big house had been requisitioned, and anyway, men couldn't be spared to grow flowers.

As we went into Caxton Hall there was a young couple coming out, him in his regimentals, her in a mink car coat. She looked at me.

"Is it Kennedy?" she said. It was young Ginny Vigo, just got married to Lord Balderston. She said, "Gracious, everyone seems to be getting hitched. Pam Digby's marrying Randolph Churchill, you know, and they've practically only known each other five minutes. Do send my love to Kick. Tell her I'm in the ATS now, driving army brass around. Such a lark!"

I did write to Kick, and to Ursie and Margaret and Deirdre, but Ursie was the only one I heard from in a long, long time.

If you must marry, she wrote,

> you at least seem to have chosen a man who has a steady
> position with a good family, unlike Margaret whose hus-
> band can't hold down any position. Mr. Jauncey looked
> up the Devonshires and they appear to go back to the
> 17th century.
>
> They say this will be a long war. I just pray they're

wrong and that we don't get dragged in. If Margaret's boys had to go away I don't know what she'd do. Val does deliveries for Pinckney's Dry Goods after school and keeps himself and Ray in shoe leather.

I'd never known cold like that winter we were first married. We had stores of coal and wood, but nobody could say when we'd be able to get any more, so we had to be careful with it, huddling round the kitchen range at night, putting off going up into those frozen beds. I was glad to be out of the house first thing. If I walked fast enough, across Horse Guards and over Westminster Bridge, I was warm by the time I got to the Women's Voluntary.

We were a mixed bag there. You could find yourself cutting sandwiches with a ladyship or just somebody normal like Hilda. They were all friendly though, until the IRA started setting bombs. Then I got a few remarks, especially after the one that went off in Park Lane, but then they died down when the refugees from Belgium started coming through. They soon forgot to knock the Irish once they had the Belgians to complain about.

It's a funny thing, but I remember it as a grand time, those first few months of waiting for the war to get going. I was newly wed, of course, with sloppy little billydoos left for me, in my dressing-gown pocket, or on the saucer with my first cup of tea of the day. *Good morning, Beautiful,* he'd write. And they were always signed, *Stallybrass.* He had a nice hand, for a man who hadn't had a lot of schooling.

But it wasn't just that I was happy with Walter and happy to be doing my bit. London felt different too. Nobody was using their motors, conserving whatever juice they had left, so the streets were quiet, as though they'd been cleared for a big parade. Everybody was on foot and people gave you the time of day. And then there was the blackout, with every little chink and crack of light covered so the Germans couldn't see where to bomb us in the dark. When they first brought it in you couldn't even use a flashlight without you put paper over the end, to dull its light. A house the size of Carlton Gardens took near enough half an hour to get the blinds up every afternoon and I was never convinced it was worth it. They reckon the Thames shines so silvery the only way the Germans would have missed London was if you could have blacked out the moon itself. There was a lot of cursing about the blackout, people feeling their way for lampposts and the edge of curb, banging their shins and turning their ankles, but it didn't bother me. When we were weans there was many a time we walked home from Grandma Farley's, all the way from Ennell to Ballynagore with nothing to guide us but the moonlight on the lough. We Brennans all had eyes like farm cats.

I almost even liked London being blacked out. It reminded you that something very big was afoot, that the world had changed and there was no turning back. It was exciting, though it hardly seems decent to say so now. A real adventure. But we weren't even into 1940.

22

Everything by the Book

Mr. Kennedy went home for Christmas, as I learned from Kick's letter. After all that fuss about who would travel with Rosie, she could have sailed with her Daddy and saved Mrs. Moore the bother. They were all down to Palm Beach for Christmas. I dreaded the day the war stopped letters getting through. Those weans might not have been my responsibility anymore but there wasn't a day passed when I didn't think of them.

Mother's very cross with you for running out on us, Kick wrote,

> *but I think it's so romantic. Maybe I'll come back*
> *and marry Billy and then we'll both be Devonshires,*
> *kind of!*

But in the next line she told me she'd been out dancing, to the Stork Club with Laurence Babb, and to the Plaza with Clarke McGill, so she seemed to be getting over Lord Billy.

Euny's doing brilliantly in school needless to say but she's gotten so thin Fidelma says she must have a tapeworm, [it went on]. *Rosie's going to St. Gertrude's. She's trying to write you a letter too. Mother's going traveling, to South America or South Africa or South somewhere. She says she can't stay at home vegefying just because horrid old Hitler ruined things for us in Europe.*

I miss London like crazy. Sally Norton's working in an airplane factory and having such fun, and Sissy's getting married to David Ormsby-Gore the first furlough he gets. By the time you get this they'll probably have done the deed. And is it true Ginny Vigo married Chick Balderston? Gosh, the war must really have gone to her head. She used to say he had hands like dead fish. I guess he must look pretty good in his uniform.

It's such a bore being stuck over here. When I get back to school we're meant to be putting on a fashion show. Yawn, yawn!!!

Kick wasn't the only who was bored. Walter wasn't accustomed to sitting idle, but they didn't have much to keep them occupied at the ARP post except do their blackout rounds and get a load of cheek if they caught anyone showing a light. "Little Hitlers" one housekeeper in Angel Court called them. That's how soon people forgot we were at war and all supposed to be pulling together.

Being called names didn't bother Walter.

He said, "Never underestimate the ignorance of folk, Nora. People like her'll be the first to start skriking if Jerry drops a bomb on her. Hitler's playing a canny game, mind. If this drags on much longer people'll get careless. He'll be able to walk right in and catch us napping. It weren't like this last time. There were no sitting around waiting for something to happen."

Walter volunteered in 1915, him and all his pals together down to a recruitment post in Bakewell. They joined the Sherwood Foresters and got assigned to a battalion called the Robin Hoods and the first place they were posted to was Dublin. He cracks me up with that story.

"See?" he says. "I were on the lookout for a nice black-haired colleen even then."

He was too late for this colleen. I was long gone to Boston by the time Walter Stallybrass arrived to put down the rebels. The Easter Uprising, as it was called.

"We were at Watford, doing basic training," he tells it, "then all of a sudden we were on a train to Liverpool and shipped out, no idea where we were going. They don't tell you anything in the army. When we landed, a lot of the lads thought we must be in France. Started giving the local girls the old parlyvoo. We had it easy that time. But of course we had Passchendale coming to us, did we but know it. That were a real war."

And we had another real war coming to us, gradually getting closer while people were complaining about having to black out their windows. First Norway fell, then the rest went like dominoes. Denmark, Belgium, Holland. Walter said it looked like we couldn't help but play in the Cup Final. There'd be nobody left, only England and Germany.

We were run off our feet with refugees at the Women's Voluntary. Every day new trainloads, from different countries, and yet somehow they all looked the same. All beat, all just getting through life an hour at a time. The time flew and you never knew when you turned up in the morning what you'd be asked to do. You might be on delousing heads, or sorting secondhand shoes that had been donated. Palm Sunday of 1940 me and Hilda Oddy spent all day washing beer bottles so they could be used for baby milk.

Lord Billy's brother Lord Andrew got engaged that Easter, to Kick's friend Debo Mitford. She was one of Lord Redesdale's girls. Everybody said it was a very nice match, but there was no celebration. Lord Andrew had to go straight off to training camp. Lord Billy had already been posted, France, we thought, though nobody knew for sure. You had to feel sorry for anyone who had a son old enough to fight in those days. When France fell and the lucky ones came straggling home we expected to see Lord Billy's face any minute, but the days passed and there was no sign of him. Nobody said anything but we were all thinking the worst. He was in the Guards and they'd suffered heavy losses in the retreat.

Then in the middle of June he turned up at Carlton Gardens. His Lordship and an Easter card from Rosie both arrived the same day.

Darling. Nora I miss. you, she wrote.

> *Do you have baybies.yet. I got a new. gridle. Mother.*
> *says I am FAT. Your.loving Rose Marie Kennedy.*

According to Kick, Rosie had been playing up. *She wants to go dancing,* she wrote,

> *and she doesn't have any partners except Jack and Joe.*
> *She threw a scent bottle at Mother because she wasn't*
> *allowed to come to the Hunt Club ball and even Fidelma*
> *couldn't calm her down. Went to Jack's graduation with*
> *Mother, Euny and Bobby. The Commencement speech*
> *was about the war and Americans having to be pre-*
> *pared to fight and a lot of the boys boo'd and hissed. It*
> *was beastly to think of all my friends in England. Went*
> *sailing with Win Rockefeller. Also to Mary O'Keefe's*

wedding where I was bridesmaid, taffeta dress, kind of
candy pink, GRUESOME, and to Anne McDonnell's
where I was just a regular guest. Henry converted so
they could be married at Sacred Hearts of Jesus and
Mary. His folks are the Fords, I mean THE FORDS,
and they didn't like him doing it but he did it anyway.
Everyone seems to be getting married except KK. Have
Andrew and Debo named the day? I expect Billy will be
next. I'll bet Sally Norton's pulled out all the stops to get
him now I'm off the scene.

Well, I thought, that didn't sound like a girl who was breaking her heart over Billy Hartington. And it would all be grist to
Mrs. K's mill, that a good Catholic girl like Anne McDonnell had
landed herself a Ford and stayed true to the faith.

All through that summer the Germans did nighttime raids
along the south coast, but we still didn't see anything to worry us
in London. September 7 it started. The day before my birthday.
Seeing it was Saturday Walter said we should get out of town for
some fresh air. We took sandwiches and a bottle of lemonade and
went for a bike ride in Richmond Park. We both fell asleep under
a tree and we didn't start back till getting on for five.

As we turned towards Chiswick Bridge I heard Walter say,
"Oh my Lord," and when I turned to look, the sky over to our
right was packed with Jerry planes, wave after wave of them heading in towards the West End, or so it seemed. We were too far
away to hear their engines, but then we saw smoke from the first
hits. We'd ride a bit, then stop and watch and everybody you
spoke to had a different opinion about where the bombs were
falling. Nobody seemed in any rush to take cover. "They're miles
away," some people were saying. But it wasn't until we got to Hyde
Park that we started to get the facts. It was Rotherhithe that was

burning, far down the river, nowhere near the West End. The Surrey Docks had been hit.

Hope was in a state by the time we got home, shaking and sweating. She kept saying, "Where were you? I thought you'd been blowed up. I thought I'd never see you again."

Walter said, "We were miles away. We had a lovely afternoon out. Take an aspirin. Have a cup of tea."

"I can't drink tea," she said. "They'll be back. They've only gone home to fetch more bombs. They'll be back to get us next."

She wanted the three of us to go down into the shelter with a carboy of water and some tins of chopped ham.

Walter said, "I've to get to my post. But you go down if you'd feel happier. Take your knitting. Nora'll go with you."

I thought, Nora won't.

She said, "You shouldn't have to go to any post, Walter. You did your bit last time. They shouldn't expect you to do anything at your age."

"Hope," he said, "at my age I have to do what I have to do so the ones who aren't my age can go up the line. If there's another war after this, I'll sit it out. You have my word. Now give me my flashlight."

I left them arguing. The ATS girls who were billeted upstairs had all been called in for duty, so I changed into my uniform and went straight out again, to the depot, to see what had to be done. They sent me out to Bermondsey with Lady Baxendale and a mobile canteen. "Call me Lally," she said. We were brewing tea for firefighters and stretcher-bearers and anybody else who looked in need of a breather.

Things eased off for an hour or two during the evening and Lady Lally thought maybe we should head back to the depot to replenish stocks, but before we could shut up shop the word came that enemy planes had been sighted again, heading our way. Then we heard them. They came in low, bombers and fighters, wingtip to wingtip, making a horrible German droning noise. Our planes had a much friendlier sound. And you felt as though every one of those Jerry planes had a bomb with your name on it. It came into my mind, what Mammy always said:

"Nora, God won't let you hang if he means you to drown."

But that was the rub. The not knowing what God had in mind for you.

I wondered if I'd ever see my Walter again. Her Ladyship kept us going though.

"This is more like it," she kept shouting. "Now Jerry'll find out what the British are made of."

It was five in the morning when we got back to the depot, and we only went then because we'd run out of tea. The heat from the fires had scorched the paint along one side of the van, and the girls coming on duty said we looked like chimney sweeps.

"Go home if you can," Lady Lally said. "Clean up, get a spot of shut-eye and report back here for more of the same."

Hope was frying bacon and kidneys for herself and her officer gentlemen when I got home. Her stomach seemed to have settled down.

"We've had a very bad night," she said. "There was a bomb fell on Pont Street. You missed all the excitement."

Walter said, "Aye, Nora. Missed it all. By the look of you you've been holed up at the Ritz, getting your nails done and drinking them champagne cocktails."

I said, "You should see the fires around the docks. I'm supposed to take a break and then go back. There's hundreds homeless."

He said, "I've got something for you, sweetheart. I were thinking about it all night. It's very perilous what you're doing, going in while there are raids on and buildings burning to the ground. I want you to wear this, in case you get buried alive. Happy birthday, darling. Now give it a try, give it a toot."

A tin whistle on a length of clothesline. That was what I got for my birthday in 1940, and I have it still.

We read in the newspaper that a new American ambassador had arrived in London, Mr. John Gilbert Winant. He and Mrs. Winant had been met at Victoria station by the King himself. It was the first I knew that Mr. K had been replaced.

Recalled, Walter reckoned, because of his opinions.

Walter said, "He's nowt but a defeatist. We don't need his kind."

Mr. K had been going around saying England didn't stand a chance against Hitler and might just as well surrender.

I said, "He's worried America will get dragged into it. He's worried for his boys."

He said, "It shouldn't be a question of getting dragged in. America should step forward and volunteer. They were late enough turning up last time."

I didn't rise to it. All I know is, when we did turn up we made short work of it, and a lot of poor doughboys paid the price. A hundred thousand of our boys never came home after the Armistice, so nobody can say America didn't do her bit.

I said, "Well, I'll shed no tears over Mr. and Mrs. K, but it does make me sad to think the children won't be coming back. I had some good times with them. And everybody loved them over here."

"Not everybody," he said. "All that bloody commotion when they arrived. Photos in the papers. The Emerald King and his family. Emerald King! King Yellow Belly if you ask me."

The report said the retiring Ambassador had been no stranger to controversy but had enjoyed cordial relations with Neville Chamberlain. So that must have been in October, because poor old Chamberlain was dead by the start of November. Some said he'd a cancer but most people thought he was just plain worn out and brokenhearted.

It was a funny thing, but when I heard Mr. K had gone I felt different, as if I could settle down to my new life. My Kennedys wouldn't be coming back and I'd burned my bridges, so I just had to get on with it. It was for the best, really. Walter was a good man. It wasn't fair on him to be pining for the past.

Lord Billy was stationed just outside town in Elstree, so we saw him once in a while, when he had a night off. One time he brought Sally Norton back to Carlton Gardens, so she could change into her dance gown. She was a beauty, I must say, even in her factory boiler suit. My Kick was natural and pretty but she was a girl still, and a tomboy. You could see Sally Norton had the makings of a real lady. Everybody said she could easily have gotten into the Women's Royal Navy, because Lord Mountbatten was her godfather and he was head of Combined Operations, but credit to her, she stuck at the factory work until they found out she spoke the German lingo pretty well. Then they packed her off somewhere top secret.

I had all the Kennedy news with Fidelma's Christmas card, but it didn't arrive till March.

Everything's in the doldrums here, she wrote.

> *The Ambassydor resigned, I suppose you know. Mrs. K reckoned it was because of his stomick ulster but that's her story. The dailies said he jumped before he was pushed because the President had had enough of him saying Germany's going to win the war.*
>
> *Herself's got her brave smile on but she's simmering, you can tell. She loved all that Excellency business, having tea with the Queen, wearing a tarara five nights*

a week. Well now it's finished and it's all Mr. Ks fault because he couldn't keep his trap shut.

Teddy has a new brace on his teeth. Rosie's been teaching Jean to knit so she can make a scarf for her war effort. Kick's seeing the Killefer boy and the Macdonald boy but she's away to Long Island just now, to be brides-maid again. Bobby has had boils, brought on by to many new schools if you ask me. Mrs. K thinks he might have a vocation for the Church. She wants him schooled by the Brothers but Mr. K wants him tuffened up and got ready for Harvid college.

Herself was tidying her linjery drawer and gave me some of her old stays, but she asked for them back the next morning. She said, "Fidelma dear heart, on second thoughts I'd better keep that corsylette. There may be shortages." It was a terrible worn old thing. She was lucky I hadn't firebacked it because that was all it was fit for. I said, "That's all right, Mrs. Kennedy. I never use the things myself."

"Oh but you should, dear," she said. "Once a woman has let her line go she can never get it back."

She's a riot, that one, strapping herself into corsets when she's nothing but a bag of bones, and Euny's going the same way. She doesn't have an ounce of flesh on her. Poor Rosie had better watch out. She'll be back on short rations once we get up to Hyannis again and Herself sees how her bozzoms are tumbling out of her swimming costume.

Don't know what's to become of us, Brennan. Jean's going to Noroton and Teddy won't be long till he's a weekly boarder. You did the right thing, marrying your man. Does he have a brother?

There had been a lot of talk about being prepared for whatever Jerry threw at us, plans for this, plans for that, but it was a different matter when it really came to it. There was no rest from the raids, day after day, and whatever was being tried to stop them, it didn't appear to be working. The barrage would go up, but the bombers still got through.

And down at the Women's Voluntary we didn't always know what we were doing. We made it up as we went along. We were sent out with a soup kitchen one morning, over to Millwall, where whole streets had been flattened, but when we got there they already had a soup kitchen, organized by one of the vicars. What they really needed were baby napkins and blankets, and a bath chair or two for the old folk who'd been bombed out of their houses and were too frail to walk.

People were nice enough to us. They seemed glad to see friendly faces even if we hadn't turned up with what they needed, and ladies like Lally Baxendale cheered them up.

"Not to werry," she'd say. "The impossible marely takes a little longer."

The local pols were a different matter. Their names were mud. All that huffing and puffing and promises they'd made, but when it came to it, there weren't shelters fit to be used nor provision made for the homeless.

Hilda Oddy used to say, "Never mind Hitler. If it carries on like this there'll be a bloody revolution. Some of those councilors could find themselves strung up."

But the pols fought back, of course. Some of them put it about that it was only the working people who were getting bombed. That the toffs had their houses marked with special paint on the roofs so they wouldn't get hit. That they were just waiting for the Jerry bombs to get rid of the lower classes and the Socialist troublemakers, then they could carry on as before, only under new management. King Ribbentrop and Queen Wally Windsor.

Anybody talked like that around me, I told them. We had raids on the West End too, and casualties, but there are always the ones who'll never allow the facts spoil their argument. Walter was shaken, some of the stories I came home with. The thieving and the lying and the profiteering. Just because we were fighting a war didn't mean everyone was behaving as if they were out of the *Boy's Own* comic. But Hope and Walter had been raised to believe a councilor knew better than a constituent, same as a Duke knew better than a gardener, and only God, the King and Winston Churchill knew better than the Duke of Devonshire.

Sometimes I think Walter wondered what he'd taken on with me, but once the Blitz got serious neither of us had a lot of time for wondering about anything. He was out on ARP patrol every night, and if I wasn't working I'd be in the scullery with Hope, helping her with the mending, half dead on my feet.

Hope wasn't quite the termagant she'd have liked you to think. She'd scowl at her sewing basket, scowl at the milk jug, but it didn't signify anything. It was just the hang of her face, and anyway she mellowed with me when she saw I hadn't ruined Walter or tried to step into her size sevens. We grew to be quite companionable.

Breakfast was about the only time me and Walter had together. A pot of tea and a slice of bread and pork dripping, and then he'd walk me partway to work, hand in hand as far as Westminster Bridge, like Darby and Joan. We were crossing the Mall one morning early, drizzling rain and the sky still dark, when we heard the sound of hooves, and blow me down if a zebra didn't come trotting through Admiralty Arch, heading up towards Buckingham Palace. We'd heard on the wireless the Regent's Park zoo had taken a hit that night.

I said, "We'd better herd him back."

"No," he said, "it's none of our business. That's a job for the zoo people."

I said, "But how will they know he's here? If they've been bombed out there could be lions and tigers and all sorts on the loose. They won't be worrying about one harmless little zebra. We should at least shoo him back to Trafalgar Square. See if we can find a policeman."

"Nay, Nora," he said, "you must stay away from it. It's a wild animal."

It was a dear little thing, shaking its head, swishing its tail.

I said, "It's only like a horse with a striped cover. I thought you knew about horses."

He said, "I do and this is nothing like a horse. It's from tropical climes for one thing. It could be full of disease. Now steer clear of it, I beg of you. Leave it to the zebra people. It's their job."

That was the difference between us. Apart from the army, all he'd ever known was the Devonshires, and in those big houses everybody has their place and keeps to it. The pastry cook doesn't make gravy and a button can't be stitched on till the sewing woman's been sent for. Well, if I'd kept to my place I'd still be in Ballynagore being lorded over by Edmond and the Clavin widow. Surplus to requirement was my place there, sleeping on the pullout in the kitchen. But you learn different ways in America. You learn to make your own place and use your head. Me and Walter have had more than a few words on that topic over the years.

And I've often wondered what became of that little zebra. I hope he didn't end up as horse steaks. When people are on short rations there's no telling what they might do.

23

An Insult of a Cake

Me and Hope saw in 1941 sheltering under the kitchen table with a bottle of Wincarnis Tonic Wine. The All Clear had sounded but we'd made ourselves comfortable and neither of us could be bothered to move.

She kept saying, "It'll be different this year. Walter says there'll be a big push and it'll all be over by summer."

As if Winston Churchill kept Walter Stallybrass informed of his plans. Hope was missing her Derbyshire hills and her kitchens and her big pantries full of meat and eggs and fruit put up in bottles. Every night she dreamed about food. Rationing wasn't such a hardship if you'd worked for Rose Kennedy, but Hope's belly was rumbling all the time.

"I dreamed I was making a pork pie last night," she'd say. "It was a beauty. Six pounds of boned shoulder, six trotters to make the jelly. That's the first thing I'm going to do after we've beaten Hitler. Make a big pork pie."

214

It was a good thing we didn't know then how long we'd have to wait for that pie.

The firebombs had started right after Christmas and we didn't get much respite till May. People in the East End thought they were the only ones to suffer, but we had our share. Jermyn Street, the Admiralty, and then there was the terrible night the Café de Paris was hit, the Caff, as Kick and her pals called it. It was their favorite place to go dancing, and Jack and Joe's too, when they were in town. If Mr. K hadn't stood firm about them all going home we might have had three of them to bury, which doesn't bear thinking of. We've had tragedy enough, as things have turned out.

I was out in Poplar with a mobile canteen, serving tea and sandwiches after a dive bomber attack, and I heard an old boy saying that the people caught in the Caff had had it coming to them.

I said, "Oh yes? And how do you make that out?"

"Toffs' kids," he said. "Parasites."

I said, "They were just youngsters in uniform, taking their sweethearts dancing. Nobody deserves what happened to them."

"Glugging champagne while the workingman suffers," he said. "Well, now they've had a waking-up."

Nasty old beggar. I'd have spat in his sandwich if I'd had prior notice. Hilda Oddy's brother had been on fire watch in Shaftesbury Avenue the night the Caff was hit and he told her that by the time he got to Leicester Square to see if he could help there were people going through handbags and taking jewelry off the corpses. They say war brings out the best in people, but the bombing of the Caff didn't. When I was out with the Women's Voluntary there were things said I wouldn't have credited if I hadn't heard them with my own ears. How we'd be better off if Hitler won. How British kiddies were starving while we were feeding foreigners and refugees who were likely to turn round and stab us in the back. Well, I never saw any kiddies that were starving. There were plenty of them needed their heads disinfected and their necks scrubbed, but a peck of dirt never killed anyone. The worst I heard though was about the Jews.

Wherever you went you'd meet someone who knew for a fact there was no room in the air-raid shelters because the spaces had all been taken by Jews. How they never left when the All Clear was sounded, just stayed down there like troglodytes, saving their places and keeping normal Christian people out of a place of safety. Then the next minute somebody else would say, "It's all right for the yids. They've all gone. Taken their money bags and scarpered to somewhere that's not getting bombed."

So far as I know I never met a Jewish person. There weren't any in Ballynagore and Mr. Kennedy wouldn't have them in the house, but I'm sure they can't be as bad as they're painted. Actually, Joe Kennedy doesn't like anybody very much, except his own flesh and blood. He thinks everybody's out to snub him or rob him blind.

Lord Andrew was in barracks at Regent's Park, waiting to ship out, so it was decided he and Miss Debo would get married while they had the chance. The marrying was at St. Bartholomew's and then at her people's house in Rutland Gate, even though they had bomb damage. Their Graces dropped by at Carlton Gardens after the wedding breakfast to tell Walter they'd managed to get a few camellias from Chatsworth and to bring Hope a slice of the cake. No frosting, because you couldn't get the sugar, not enough sultanas or candied peel, and made with beer instead of brandy. Altogether an insult of a cake, according to Hope.

She said, "When Lady Elizabeth gets married and Lady Anne, I'll supervise the cake."

She was sent down to Compton Place to cook for Lord Andrew and Lady Debo while they had a few days' honeymoon, and that trip was an eye-opener to her, getting out of our little corner of London, seeing troops on the move and Jerry bombers flying right over her head. When she got back from Eastbourne she couldn't settle.

She said, "I think I should like to do some war work too. It don't seem right, sitting here darning socks."

I said, "Come with me to the Women's Voluntary. We have grand times. You never know what you'll be doing from one day to the next."

But Walter said, "Nay, Hope, you're already doing war work, running this house. Feeding the military's important work. You stick to what you know."

I said, "We can't all stick to what we know, Walter. If we did that there'd be no munitions made, for one thing. There'd be no buses running. We're crying out for girls like Hope."

"Girl!" he said. "She's no girl. She's fifty ruddy five. What's she going to do, drive a tank?"

He hated the way the war turned everything topsy-turvy. He's a man who likes regularity. He likes to know who's who and what's what, which is why the army should have taken him. They'd never have got any talking back from Walter Stallybrass.

Hope said, "You only don't want me to volunteer in case I have to stop out late and your tea's not on the table."

He said, "Don't talk so wet, woman. I don't need anybody to put my tea on the table. Any fool can brew a pot of tea and slice a bit of bread."

"Then let any fool do it," she said. And she put on her navy straw and went out.

He said, "I suppose you put her up to this."

I said, "No, Walter. Hitler put her up to it."

She was gone more than an hour. Came back with a quarter pound of premium butter and a smile on her face.

She said, "You'll all have to do your own breakfasts from now on. I've got a milk round for Vincent's Dairy. It'll free up that boy with the clubfoot. He wants to go to Hatfield, to the airplane factory."

Walter said she should have asked Her Grace's permission first.

He said, "This is still a Devonshire house."

She said, "Her Grace has a husband and two boys in uniform, so I'll not be bothering her when I know what her answer will be."

He said she'd never get up in time for a milk round, but she did. She had to be at Appletree Yard by four to load up the pony and trap and she was finished by ten, so it was no great inconvenience to anyone who was billeted with us. Then he said it was all very well during the summer months but she wouldn't stick at it when the weather turned cold. But she did. It made a new woman of her. And she came home with all the gossip. Who was closing up their house. Who'd got rabbits or eggs to trade. Who'd received a telegram.

The middle weekend of May we had a bad time of it. It was full moon, so we were quite expecting a big raid, but it still shook us when it came. Parliament was hit and Westminster Abbey, the Strand, Russell Square, Waterloo. I had to walk to Vauxhall Bridge before I could get across the river to work, and when I got there, the depot and the yard where we parked our trucks were lying under a mountain of rubble.

A few of the regulars were there already, milling around, wondering what to do. Then Lady Lally arrived. She stood up on a milk crate and told everybody to gather round. She said we mustn't let a little setback stop us when all over London there was work to be done. She said her sister, Lady Billie, had a depot near King's Cross station and the best thing to do was go and offer our services to her. Then she requisitioned a ragman's horse and cart and drove us all the way to Pentonville Road. We had such a laugh, seeing people's faces as we passed by, jogging along with a big dented soup kettle and Lady Lally in her felt hat, sitting up on the box, cracking the reins.

There was plenty needed doing at Lady Billie's depot and I drew a nice number. They sent me to a school hall to help with mothers who'd been bombed out with their babies and toddlers. They all got a hot dinner and clean nappies for the babies and milk bottles. We even played some games with the little ones, oranges and lemons, the farmer's in his den, to give the mammies a rest. I had such a grand day. It didn't feel like war work, jiggling babies in my arms again. Not like poor Hilda. They sent her to the morgue, to give people sweet tea and a cigarette after they'd been in searching for their loved ones.

She said, "I don't know what was worse, Nora, when they found somebody or when they didn't. Because there'll be some that'll never be found."

She reckoned she cried all the way home that night.

It was late when I got back from Pentonville Road, and Walter was fretting. He'd heard the Waterloo depot had been flattened and he didn't want to go out on his blackout rounds until he knew I was safe. That was the night we really started having words. It must have seemed to him I was having a better war than he was. When people saw you in your WVS green they were respectful. They thanked you for what you were doing. But the ARP people came in for a lot of lip. They say an Englishman's home is his castle, and round St. James's they didn't take kindly to being told to get off the streets and take cover, or being prosecuted because they had holes in their blinds.

It was a shame the army wouldn't take Walter. He was a patriotic soul and still in his prime, apart from his bad lung. A man doesn't feel right, I'm sure, when the whole world's in uniform and all he's got is a tin helmet and an armband. Even Joseph Patrick had volunteered, who'd always listened to what his Daddy said about America minding its own business and staying out of other people's wars.

Darling Nora, he wrote me,

> I'm at Squantum doing basic training, then I'll be off to Florida, learning to fly, so say a prayer for me when you get down on your creaking knees. Dad's not happy I dropped Law School but I can always go back when the war's over. The way things are shaping up I don't see how America can stay out of it much longer, and I didn't want to wait for the draft. When he heard what I'd done Jack tried to get into the Navy too but he failed his physical big time he's such a pipsqueak, so now he's doing squat jumps and stomach crunches day and night to try and get himself into shape. Dad could get him a desk job at the Naval Reserve but I guess that would stick in his craw, having to stand by and see me get my wings while he's pushing a pen.
>
> Rosie's still acting up. She doesn't understand she can't always tag along when we go out. You know how she is. A guy who didn't know her could take her for normal. She just wouldn't know what she was getting into and neither would he. We took her to a hop in Osterville and to a clambake and she was no trouble but she told Euny she wants a beau or ten, like Kick has. Well, she just has to realize. The worst thing was she hit out at Grandpa Fitz. All he did was kid her about

*the way her fanny has spread and she went crazy. Even
Fidelma couldn't calm her. Mother doesn't know what
to do. I wish you were at Hyannis to help her, but seeing
as you've run out on us I'll settle for you doing your bit.
Any Hun come your way I hope you'll give them some of
those worm powders you always keep handy.*

    Your ever loving Joseph Patrick, Seaman Second Class

I couldn't believe Rosie had hit His Honor on purpose. He
was an oily old devil and there had been times I could have clocked
him myself, but Rosie loved her Grandpa. I could only think he'd
gotten in the way of her arm when she was in a paddy so he'd only
himself to blame. Sure, when the other pols were flinging mud up
in Boston he was quite the expert at ducking out of the way.

The next I heard Rosie had gone away to a school near
Washington, to teach kindergarten. I had a darling note from her.
The Sisters are all right, she wrote.

> *Sister. Clara is best. Not best as you thow. Mother says I
> am fat STILL. and I am traying not to be. A man said
> I am cute. He is cute to. That is hour secret. Angel Nora.
> Miss you. millions.*

Washington sounded like a good move. She'd be spared Herself's nagging and Mayor Fitzgerald's teasing, and she'd be handy for
visiting with Kick and Jack. Kick had got herself a little job, writing
pieces for one of Mr. Kennedy's newspaper friends, and Jack had
taken that desk job in the Naval Reserve. I was glad he'd been man
enough to do it. I knew he'd have had Joe needling him but Jack
can't help being sickly. It's not everyone can be a hotshot aviator.

Kick wrote me that she and Jack had rented a little apart-
ment together, with just one spare room for Rosie to visit at

weekends and no help except a weekly domestic. I could imagine what the place would be like after five minutes. They all leave a trail wherever they go, and Jack and Kick had to be the messiest of them all.

Greetings from your Washington correspondent! she wrote.

> *You practically wouldn't know me. I come into work nearly every day and get to write up all the important parties and any new plays. It says "by Kathleen Kennedy" at the top of the piece. Isn't that wild! Mother says I should have my photograph next to my name too. Actually Mother says she's the one should be writing for newspapers because she's a better speller than I am and she's had an interesting life people would like to read about.*
>
> *Rosie's being SO naughty since she came back from London. Twice she went out at night without telling anyone. She says she was just walking around but Sister Philomena at the school says she smelled of cigarettes when she came back and won't be able to stay on if she keeps this up.*
>
> *I'm palling around with some nice boys but nobody special. Do you ever see the Devonshire girls? I should write to them. I heard from Minnie Stubbs. She's a VAD, apparently, at a special hospital for people who got burned. She has to empty potties and stuff. It sounds pretty vile but she's terribly jolly about it. Cynthia Brough is having a much better time. She's flying new Tiger Moths from the factory to the airfields, ALL ON HER OWN. I wish I'd learned how to fly.*
>
> *Jack's "in lurve." He's dating a really great girl called Inge. She's Polish or Russian or something and speaks a*

hundred languages, but she's d-i-v-o-r-c-e-d, so it has to
be kept hush-hush from Mother.
    Miss you heaps,

she signed off, then

P.S. Sissy and David have a baby boy, Julian. P.P.S.
Lem failed his medicals because he has to wear those
thick geeky glasses but Dad put in a word and got him
into the Ambulance Corps. He's waiting to be posted.
P.P.P.S. Give my love to Billy if you see him.

So Lord Billy had become one of Kick's P.P.P.Ses. And, according to Lady Debo, it was quite on the cards that the next time Lord Billy was home on leave he'd get engaged to Sally Norton. Lady Debo was expecting. She'd fallen for a honeymoon baby, but then it came too soon and she lost it. Loss seemed to be all we heard about in those days. Hope heard on her milk round that Lord and Lady Melhuish had had a telegram. They had two boys in uniform and then we found out it was the young one who was missing. The battleship he was on had been sunk by the Japs. That was December, not long after Pearl Harbor. Rory Melhuish. He was a nice young man. Always gave you a wave and a "Good day" if he saw you in the street.

All we seemed to hear was bad news. The only hope we clung to was that it would make a difference that America was fighting too. That it would soon be over, before too many more fine boys were cut down.

24

A Broken Doll

His Grace used to look in at Carlton Gardens from time to time and it was him suggested Walter should try for a position at the Royal Botanical Gardens at Kew. He said there was special war work going on there and they needed experienced gardeners.

Walter wasn't sure at first. He said, "It doesn't seem the kind of work a man should be doing. They've got Land Army girls for things like that."

I said, "Perhaps they need somebody who can tell the Land Army girls what to do. And perhaps they won't even take you. Why don't you find out? I won't think any the less of you if you're wearing gum boots instead of that tin helmet."

So the Duke placed a telephone call and Walter was on his bicycle and off to Kew like a shot. He seemed to get his old bearing back after that. He held his head higher.

"Top secret," he said. "We're engaged in work of national importance, but I'm not at liberty to say what it is."

And neither me nor Hope got it out of him till after VE day.

They'd been growing things that could be used to make up for the shortages. Milkweed was one, and nettles and all different kinds of herbs, for remedies. The milkweed was useful because you could make rubber from the milk and flying suit padding from the floss inside the pods. The nettles were for a kind of flax. I knew about nettles. Grandma Farley had a nettle tablecloth, better than linen she reckoned. It was the cloth she kept for funerals. Walter said you could make good strong twine from nettles too.

I don't know how much difference it made to the war effort, but I believe Kew Gardens was the saving of me and Walter. I'd been getting to the point where I thought I wasn't cut out for marriage. I wasn't accustomed to having a man watching the clock till I came home, wanting to know where I'd be every minute and who with.

I'd have a busy day, out with a soup kitchen, or cleaning up urchins that had been bombed out, first bath some of them had ever had in their lives. Time would just fly and I liked meeting all those different people. Then I'd come home to find Walter pacing the floor. Before he had his top secret gardening to think about, he didn't seem to understand that I couldn't keep to a timetable. You didn't leave till the job was done, and then you never knew how you'd get home. I had three bicycles purloined. After that, it was Shanks's pony.

"I just worry you'll come to harm, Nora," he'd say. "When you're late I worry you're lying under a pile of rubble and nobody knows you're there."

I'd say, "Well, if it happens, either I'll blow my whistle and they'll find me, or they'll send what's left of me home in a carrier bag."

He'd say, "I suppose that's what passes for humor in America." And then we'd have words.

But once he started at Kew he was too busy to fuss about me.

He'd dash home, grab a slice of bread and scrape and go out directly to do his blackout rounds. We got that we hardly even met in bed.

"Stallybrass, reporting for duty," he'd say if we did both happen to slide between the sheets. "Permission to come alongside?"

He could be an annoying old fusspot, always tidying the spoon drawer and putting my shoes in a row, but he did make me laugh, and as Fidelma Clery always said, it was nice to have a body to warm your feet on. I still don't know if it's what the story books call love.

At the start of 1942 I got a new job.

"Nora," Lady Lally said to me one morning, "you must know how Americans do things. Why don't you pop along to the Red Cross at Piccadilly and give them a hand. They're getting complaints about their coffee."

London was filling up with American military. You heard their voices everywhere. When I walked in to the Rainbow Corner and saw all those bright smiling American boys it made me realize how much I missed my Kennedys. I hadn't seen any of them in two years. The young ones probably hardly remembered me, and I might not even know them anymore. Teddy especially. There's a big difference between a boy of eight and a boy of ten. Rainbow Corner brought something else home to me too. How worn out we all were in London. The Americans were fresh and ready for anything, but we'd already had two years of it and that's a long time to be braced for disaster. They reckoned General Monty had the Germans beaten in Egypt, but we didn't feel like we'd beaten anybody. There was greenery springing up on the bomb sites, Mother Nature moving back in. That made you realize how long things had dragged on. And when I heard some of the GIs talking about what they intended doing after the war it dawned on me I'd stopped imagining any "after the war." I couldn't imagine how it was ever going to end.

It got to the middle of March and I still hadn't had my usual little homemade Christmas card from Rosie, but I didn't think anything of it. We hardly marked it ourselves that year. Pilchards on toast, that was Christmas dinner.

Then, just after Easter, I got a letter from Kick. Jack had been accepted by the Navy and was off to midshipman school on Lake Michigan and he'd asked her to let me know. *Daddy put an end to Jack's pash for Inge,* she wrote.

> *He said she's most probably a Fifth Columnist and it had to stop because when the war's over Joe'll be running for Congress and we can't have his chances ruined by any skeletons in the family closet. Also, the d-i-v-o-r-c-e thing would break Mother's heart.*

The Bronxville house had been closed up and Herself had taken a suite at the Plaza Hotel, so I guessed Fidelma was out of a job, though Kick didn't mention her. Teddy and Jean were shuttling between Palm Beach and Hyannis, Pattie was off to college in Philadelphia, Euny was in California for her health and her studies, and Kick was still writing her newspaper pieces, quite the career girl.

Mother keeps calling the Editor with ideas for articles, she wrote.

> *I wish he'd give her my spot. I'd much rather be in London doing something exciting. Also she called Joe's commanding officer because Joe got a demerit for having a messy bunk or something and Mother told them they shouldn't be so petty when a boy had volunteered to put his life on the line. Word got round and now all the other guys are joking about it. Joe is SO ticked off with Mother.*

Washington is really depressing. The only men around are old timers or wounded or 4Fs so there's not much dancing to be had.

Darlingest Nora, I have something to tell you. Rosie isn't so hot. You mustn't worry about her because the Sisters are taking the very best care of her, but she had a little operation back in the fall and it didn't go quite as well as expected. I didn't write you before because I hoped she'd start feeling better but I don't think it's very likely now. Dr. Freeman said the best thing would be for her to have complete rest and not see places that might upset her, like Hyannis, so she's gone to a nursing home in Beacon, on the Hudson. It's called Craig House and Mary Moore says she's settled in just fine so you're not to worry about her.

Miss you a million. Jack and Joe send kisses.

P.S. Nancy Tenney got married. He's a navy aviator like Joe. At this rate I'll be the only one left on the shelf.

I wrote to Rosie at Craig House, Beacon, but nothing ever came back and it wasn't till I heard from Fidelma that I really knew what had happened.

They've runed our darling girl, she wrote, *and broken my heart.*

Mr. K was looking into opyrations you know for people with over-exited brains. I told him and told him all Rosie wanted was a natural life. Sure when it comes down to it she was only longing for the same trills the old billygoat expects for himself. I don't know how far things went. She did go missing a couple of times and somebody may have given her strong drink but there was still no call to do what they did and Mister and Mrs. Moore agree with me.

The doctor said he had plenty of satysfed customers. Ladies who had low spirits or given to tantroms. Mr. K got sent testymonals. But it was still wrong what they did.

It was done at the Goerge Washington. Just a wee cut they said to take away the troublesome part of her mind. It's called lowbotummy. Kick came with us to the hospital, and Mrs. Moore. Herself was up to Poland Springs taking the waters.

Rosie went to it like the lamm she was. Smiled and waved as they weeled her out to the opyrating room. They shaved away a lock of her hair but that was easy covered by a headscarf when they'd done, and she'd to wear a sunshade, because her eyes were a bit bruised but that wasn't the sum of it. She was runed. They said she wouldn't feel a thing and afterwards she'd just be nice and carm, and stop her night time wanderings and all that talk about boys and squezing but that wasn't the way she was at all. She couldn't speak. I don't think she knew who any of us was not even when her Daddy came in. He was shaken to see her. Serve him right.

But then he said it was likely just the carming pill they'd given her before the opyration and she'd be all right later. He told Mrs. Moore to bring her to the Sisters at Craig House for a holliday.

Kick said What'll we do Daddy if it doesn't wear off?

He said Hellfire and damnation it will wear off. And if it doesn't well we gave it our best. At least she won't be going around queering things for Joe's future.

Well then he had to go tell Herself what had hap-

pened and I prayed she'd kill him when she got up to the nursing home and saw the dammidge. But she didn't go to the nursing home and so far as I know she still hasn't. The only visitors Rosies had are me and Mrs. Moore and the pill didn't wear off. They meddled where they shouldn't have and now she's like a poor broken doll.

Herself said the Ambassydor only tried what had been hily recommended and no-one was to blame if it didn't work on Rosie. She said every family has its cross to bear and Rosie was theirs and she said there was to be no talk, particly not in front of Teddy and Jean. There doesn't need to be talk. They know she's not coming home. Teddy cried himself sick when she didn't come for Christmas. So that's how things stand. And then I was let go because they can't keep Bronxville going when help is so hard to get.

I purely hate them Nora the both of them. They couldn't make a winner of Rosie and they couldn't just leave her be. I'm glad to be out of there.

I'm back up to New York, learning riviting at the Brooklyn shipyard. Still looking for a husband. Make a novena for poor Rosie.

Rosie was kept at Craig House till last year, then Mr. K decided to move her out west, to a convent in Wisconsin where there's space for her to have her own little house and a Sister to live in with her. And now they've started putting it about that she was mentally deficient from the start and was bound to have to be put away sooner or later. Well, that's not my recollection, nor Fidelma's. I still have her little letters, and that picture of her, dressed up in her silver thread gown and her ostrich feathers, off to curtsey to the King and Queen of England. I know what I know.

Kick never mentioned Rosie again in her letters though she was a good little correspondent and kept me up-to-date on the rest of them. Jean and Teddy were forever moving school depending on whether it was the season for Palm Beach or Hyannis or New York. Bobby was getting ready to go to Harvard, Pat was at Rosemont, and Euny was out at Stanford in California with Herself tagging along, attending the classes, going to the teas and socials and having a dandy time, according to Kick. Dandy for Mrs. K maybe. It's no wonder Euny's such a nervous wreck. When you're twenty-one years old, you don't want your Mammy perched on your shoulder all the time, bragging how her waistline's no different after nine babies, blowing her trumpet about the weekends she spent at Windsor Castle. All that time on her hands, she could have been doing war work, using that Kennedy name for something useful, not crowding in on the children.

Jack finished his training and was posted an ensign, out to the Pacific, and Joseph Patrick still hadn't gotten his wings. Jack had overtaken him. Young Joe wouldn't have liked that. He was based at Norfolk, Virginia, so Kick saw quite a bit of him when he got time off.

Must close, she wrote one time. *I'm having dinner with the future President.*

Every letter I had from her she complained her Daddy wouldn't allow her to come to London and help win the war, but early in '43 she finally wore him down with her begging. The American Red Cross was recruiting girls to come to Europe and Mr. K said if the Red Cross could use her he wouldn't stand in her way. Of course Joe Kennedy being Joe Kennedy, he couldn't keep from pulling strings. He didn't want her posted to any old job in any old dump. He fixed up for her to get a posting to London.

Clear the decks, she wrote. *I've done my basic training, had my shots and I'm on my way.*

I quite thought she might turn up at the Rainbow Corner. There was plenty to do, taking care of all those American boys, in a strange country for the first time. I was the one they applied to if they had something needed mending, but you weren't just a seamstress at the Red Cross. You had to be a mother to them too. "Aunt Nora" they called me. They'd show me pictures of their folks, tell me about their sweethearts, read me their Dear John letters sometimes. We were there to give them a home away from home and serve it with a smile. You couldn't stop to think what might happen to them once they saw action.

It would have been grand to have a girl like Kick around. We were mainly older women working there and the boys would have loved to see a pretty young face, but Mr. K didn't want her hobnobbing with the ranks. He made sure a job was found for her at the Officers' Club in Knightsbridge, so she was back on her old stamping ground, just along the road from Prince's Gate.

Her first Sunday in town she came round to Carlton Gardens to see us, dressed in her glad rags, ready to go dancing with Tony Erskine. She looked grand. Her face had lost some of its puppy fat and she was wearing her hair softer. She'd rinsed it in vinegar to bring out the color and give it a nice shine. Still that same old ragamuffin grin though.

She came knocking at the tradesman's door.

"Hey, Nora," she said, "how's married life?"

She sat at the scullery table, back under a Devonshire roof, and Hope made a pot of tea.

I said, "I can't believe you're here. I never thought your Mammy and Daddy would let you come."

"Well," she said, "Mother's kind of busy, working on Euny and Pat, seeing as how she failed to turn me into a swan, and Daddy's easier to get around these days. He's tired, you know? He's really kind of low in spirits. Joe says it's because of the way Roosevelt's treated him."

I said, "And he likely has Rosie on his conscience too."

She didn't like that. She said, "But that wasn't Daddy's fault. He went into it with lots of different doctors and he got a top, top man to do the procedure. It should have turned out fine. And he did it for the best, before she got into trouble. You don't know what she was like after she came home from England."

I said, "What was she like?"

She colored up. "Not in front of Walter," she whispered. So Walter remembered he had boots to polish.

"Well," she said, "she just ran wild. She was boy crazy. The Sisters said at night they daren't let her out of their sight. She wanted to go out dancing."

I said, "Then why didn't your Mammy fix her up with a dancing partner, like she did when you were here? She was all right as long as she had London Jack to give her a twirl."

She said, "But it wasn't just dancing she wanted. It was, you know, the other thing. I think she may have done it, Nora. The thing we mustn't do till we're married. She seemed to know an awful lot about it all of a sudden."

Hope sat there, turning a sock heel and wheezing like an old geyser.

She said, "Nowt new about that. Sexual intercourse. They all do it, married or not. Specially now we might all wake up dead tomorrow."

Kick looked at her. She said, "Kennedys don't. We're Sacred Heart girls."

I said, "But why did they tamper with her brain? They must have known it could go wrong."

"Oh no," she said. "The man Daddy got to do it had operated on loads and loads of people. It was just bad luck, what happened to Rosie. Really, really bad luck. But you know what? I don't think she remembers anything about it. I don't think she remembers anything about anything."

And then her eyes filled up. "I really miss her," she said. "She was such a klutz. But nice. It's like she died. Only she didn't."

Oh then we had a good old weep together. Crying was something else Kennedys didn't do, but she knew she was all right with her old Nora. It was a good job Stallybrass had left the room. He can't be doing with waterworks and we both ended up with noses as red as her dance gown. Even Hope joined in and she never even knew Rosie.

She said, "The thing is, she might have gone with a man and gotten a baby. Then what would we have done?"

I said, "It would just have been another little Kennedy. Fidelma would have loved it."

"Maybe so," she said. "But Mother wouldn't. It could have been a baby from any old unsuitable type. Rosie would have gone with anyone."

I said, "And how did your Mammy take it, about the operation?"

"Went for lots of walks at first," she said. "You know how she does. Went to Mass and then for long, stomping walks, on her own. But then she decided to go to California and keep Euny company in college. She reads all the books and goes to the lectures and everything. She's quite the perfect student, except she doesn't have to take the tests."

I said, "And what does Euny think about that?"

"Gosh, I don't know," she said. "But I don't think she's wildly happy at Stanford anyway. She doesn't seem to have any new friends, and she looks terrible. She just gets thinner and thinner."

There never was an ounce of fat on that one. Euny could eat like a cart horse and the grass still wouldn't know where she was treading.

I said, "And have you seen any of your old crowd yet?"

She said, "Well, I'm going to the Florida Club tonight with Tony Erskine, except he's now Earl Rosslyn if you please. But if you mean have I seen Billy, no. He's in Herefordshire at the moment. Or is it Hampshire? In camp, anyway. But I've seen Sissy. She's got another tiny, tiny baby, such a sweetie, and I saw Ginny Vigo, now Lady Balderston of course. I wish I could be in the ATS. I love those furry coats they get to wear. And we'll probably see Caro Leinster and Harry Bagnell tonight. They're engaged, you know? Imagine! And I'm going to try and visit Debo. It must be the absolute worst thing, not knowing when she'll see Andrew. Not even knowing where he is."

Lady Debo was expecting again, due any day.

Kick had sailed with a big contingent of new Red Cross girls. Most of them had been sent out on the road with mobile canteens for the GIs, trucks rigged up to serve doughnuts and real American java, but not Kick. Her job was to show the officers around London and keep them entertained, fix them up with tickets for a show or find them a card school or a nice English family to have them round for tea. As war work went it was a nice little number. She was living in, at Hans Crescent, so the late nights didn't matter. She seemed to get plenty of time off and she hadn't been back in London a month before Billy Hartington was squiring her again and all the competition fell by the wayside.

His battalion was stationed in Hampshire, awaiting orders, and he came up to town to see Kick every minute he could. Sally Norton was history and so were all Kick's beaux. She fell like a ton of bricks. Walter reckoned it was the captain's pips that did it. Hope thought it was visiting Lady Debo and seeing her sweet little Devonshire baby that put ideas in her head. I don't know. They dropped by Carlton Gardens one night, on their way to the Embassy Club, Lord Billy and Kick, Lord and Lady Balderston,

Minnie Stubbs, Cynthia Brough. They all had their war stories, but to me they were no more than infants. They looked like children who'd been playing in the dressing-up box.

Walter said, "There'll be ructions, you know, if Their Graces find out this romance has started up again. Can you not have a word with her?"

I said, "I've nothing to say that she's not heard before. And it hardly seems right, laying down the law to them when they're both old enough to be in uniform. They'll have to work it out for themselves."

I did speak to her though.

I said, "There'll be tears, young lady. Your Mammy didn't approve of Lord Billy for one simple reason, and nothing's changed."

"I know," she said, "but other things have changed. People are different since the war. Daddy is. He's not so definite about everything. And if we can get Daddy on our side, he'll talk Mother round."

I said, "So you're serious about each other."

"Pretty much," she said. "Billy's going to talk to his folks. See how things could be worked out."

I said, "You mean so you can be married?"

"I guess," she said. "We're both of age."

She sat at the scullery table, chewing her nails as usual.

I said, "You may be of age, but I've still a mind to paint your fingertips with mustard."

She said, "Sissy and David got married and that was dead easy. They're raising their babies Catholic. I mean, as long as they're something I don't see it matters what."

Hope said, "In our house it matters what. Devonshires are Church of England. Always were, always will be."

Kick said, "All right. Then we'll just have to have Church of England babies."

I said, "And your Mammy will cut you dead if you do."

"Well," she said, "I figure if I just keep saying my prayers every-thing will turn out dandy."

I'm sure she did too. It didn't matter how grown up my Ken-nedys grew, they still got down on their knees every night and prayed their rosary.

25

Girl on a Bicycle

We didn't hear the news about Jack until weeks after it had happened. His patrol boat had been sunk with two of his crew lost and the rest had ended up stranded on a desert island. They were there for days, sitting under palm trees, watching for a passing boat and writing messages on coconut shells, just like in the comics. There was a little piece about it in the *Daily Mail*.

Lieutenant John Kennedy, it said, son of the former American Ambassador to London, has been commended for bravery following an incident in the South Pacific. Kennedy, a college swimming champion, swam through treacherous currents to rescue eleven crew members.

Swimming champion, my eye. With those spindly arms and legs! When Jack was in the water he made more splash than progress. Joe was the swimmer. But that's newspapers for you. Kick said her Daddy had had the story written up much bigger in the *New York Times*. She was so proud of Jack, and so was I. No one knows better than I do how he's struggled. If there's a sickness that boy's not had, I can't call it to mind.

I heard from him eventually, laid up in a hospital bed. His back had been hurt when the boat was sunk.

Darling Nora, he wrote,

> *Please excuse the scrawl. I'm lying here in nothing but my skivvies, back in the land of the free and the home of the brave which I didn't believe I'd see again. I managed to keep a good attitude most of the time but there were bad moments when I thought we were all goners. Joe's really itching to see a little action himself since Dad got my name into the papers, and so is Bobby, though I can't believe that shrimp's old enough for anything more than a Wianno Junior regatta. I hope for both their sakes they don't draw the South Pacific. It's not all it's cracked up to be. All the time I was there I hardly met a single dusky maiden willing to coat me in coconut oil. I don't know what the Navy has in mind for me next. I guess it would have been quite a boost to JP's great future career if he'd had a kid brother die defending Old Glory, but he's just going to have to get along on his own considerable talents and I'm going to have to get out and find myself another piece of war to fight.*
>
> *Wish you were here to cool my fevered brow. Some of these nurses are cute but many of them are not.*
>
> *Your ever loving Silver Star, Jack*

As the summer wore on Kick seemed to get more days off than she did days on, and she never worked a weekend. Come Friday afternoon she'd be off to see Sissy Ormsby-Gore and her babies, or down to Compton Place. The *Daily Mail* newspaper had a picture of her in her Red Cross uniform, riding a bicycle along Basil Street, to show how American girls of every rank were doing their bit. Mr. K made sure it got published in America too. "Girl on a Bicycle" it was called, but I heard people call it "Girl Getting a Free Ride."

It didn't buy you much to be a Kennedy by 1943.

But came September we had another Kennedy in town. Joseph Patrick's squadron was posted to England, to a base in Cornwall, and he came up to London, on a forty-eight-hour pass. Kick brought him round to Carlton Gardens, made me close my eyes.

She said, "You have to guess who it is. You can feel but no peeping."

I knew by her giggling it was one of the boys and the smell of tobacco gave him away, but I let them string me along.

He'd brought us nylons and tinned fruit. He looked so natty in his flying jacket. He wasn't allowed to say where he'd be flying or even exactly where he was stationed.

"We're just here to whup the Germans," he said.

I said, "And how about Jack? Didn't he do well?"

"Yes," he said, "all of a sudden the little punk's a great big hero. Hell, if he keeps this up they'll be naming a street for him."

He said it so sour.

I said, "Now, Joe. He did well even to get into the forces when you think of all the sickness he's had. Those Navy doctors must have winked at his medicals. And you were always his champion, you know. So don't begrudge him this."

He said, "I don't begrudge him. Anyhow, there's still plenty of war going on. I'll top him yet."

Kick said, "Jack's gone back to finish his tour of duty, Nora. They patched him up at Guadalcanal and he's gone back on patrol.

And Daddy wrote me that Bobby's volunteered for the Reserve too. Just think. I'll soon have three brothers in Navy blues."

Joe said, "Bobby just better get a move on before Jack wins the whole damned war for us."

He was smiling, but I knew he was rattled. When you've known them from a wean, you read them like a book.

Walter didn't warm to Joe. "He's full of himself for a youngster," he said.

Well, not such a youngster. Joseph Patrick was twenty-eight, and full of himself is only what a Kennedy boy is raised to be.

I said, "He's a good lad really. A rascal for the girls, but you should see him with Jean and wee Teddy, how he watches over them. He's the grandest big brother to them. And you know he's had his Daddy and his Grandpa Fitzgerald cooing in his ear since he was in his crib, telling him he's going to be president of the United States, so you can't expect him to be a shrinking violet."

He said, "Lord Billy's known from the cradle he'll be the Duke of Devonshire but he don't saunter around like he owns the place."

Wherever Joe was flying, he headed back to London when he was on leave, always in his precious flying jacket, always puffing on one of those nasty little black cigars. Every time we saw him he had a different girl on his arm, every one a beauty, and he always brought something for us. Hand cream, fresh eggs. Onions, he brought one time, all the way from Scotland in his kit bag. And a piece of parachute silk for Hope to make us new bloomers.

There were times when you felt you couldn't stand another day of war and there were times when life didn't seem so bad. Perhaps you can get used to anything. Perhaps we were just getting cleverer at making do. Walter's Pig Club made a difference, that's for sure. There had been one started on a bomb site in St. James's

Street and Walter had tried to join that, but they said it was for Fire Service members only.

He said, "Ruddy glamour boys, they think they're God's gift because they can go through red lights. Nobody appreciates the ARP. They think you're a joke. But we should be entitled to affiliation, the kind of work we do. We get involved in fires. I'd like to see what it says in their constitution."

I said, "Why don't you start your own Pig Club. You've acres enough at Kew."

"And every inch put to good use, Nora," he said. "It could be tricky. Permission might take some getting. It'd have to go through channels. Ministry of Food, probably."

I said, "That's not the way. Get the pig, then ask permission. It's all part of the war effort. They can't shoot you for it."

"I don't know about that," he said. "They can hang you for looting."

I do believe if Adolf Hitler hadn't invaded Poland, Walter Stallybrass would still be in Derbyshire, doffing his cap to the assistant under-gardener and scared of his own shadow.

I love a pig myself. For looks I'd have a big ginger one, but they're slow growers. We could still have been waiting for our Christmas roast come Easter, and gingers are very prone to wandering as well. Our Margaret forgot to latch the gate on a ginger we had one year at Ballynagore, and he turned up the other side of Kilbeggan with a twinkle in his wee eye. Well, they couldn't have any escaping pigs at Kew, not with all those top secret crops of national importance. Anyhow, the head man, not such a flutter-guts as my husband, said, "Bugger permission. People have to eat," and they got an Old Spot, which is a nice-mannered, home-loving type of pig, and when his time was up they turned him out onto a patch of kale for his last supper and then shot him with a rifle. He'd had a good life, doing his bit against Jerry, and we had our first taste of pork crackling since 1939.

Kick flew home for Christmas so she could go to Palm Beach and see the family. It must have been something her Daddy fixed. No one was supposed to go anywhere, wasting precious fuel, if it wasn't for war work, but Mr. Kennedy's dollars still opened doors and freed up seats on transports.

She said, "Say lots of prayers for me, Nora. I'm going to talk to Mother about marrying Billy."

I said, "Then you'll need someone who's better at praying than I am. You know she'll never countenance it."

"Well," she said, "it'd mean I'd be a Marchioness and then a Duchess eventually. I think she'd like that, don't you? And Billy's going to talk to his Mama and the darling Dookie. We could maybe do something like bring our boys up as Protestants and the girls as Catholics. Don't you think?"

I said, "What I think doesn't signify. If your Mammy is against it as well, try to change the direction the wind's blowing."

"The thing is," she said, "Billy reckons the invasion'll happen in the spring. And then, who knows? It's not like ordinary times. We really don't want to wait."

I knew what she was thinking. That Herself might be softened, now she had boys of her own in uniform and it had become a regular thing to marry in the heat of the moment. But Mrs. Kennedy didn't think that way, war or no war. She harped back to her "duties," drummed into her at Sacred Heart, and she planned for the future, how her boys would run America and the girls would make good Catholic marriages. She didn't have a peck of sentiment in her.

I said, "Will you visit Rosie while you're over? Will you take her some candy from me?"

"Sure," she said. "If I have time. If Mother thinks it's a good idea."

26

A Trainee Duchess

The air raids started up again after Christmas, firebombs mainly. Walter was tearing his hair out. Instead of taking cover, folk stayed out on the street, watching the fires. I could see why. People had grown accustomed to the raids, and anyway, a lot of the shelters were smelly and dirty. And the ones that were clean only stayed that way because they were kept locked, so it didn't matter how much the sirens wailed, you'd to wait till a warden came with a key. Walter said they'd had to do that because of people thieving the lightbulbs.

"No sense of right and wrong," he'd say. "No sense of pulling together. In 1940 all you thought about was beating Hitler. Now it's every man jack for himself."

He had a point. We had bus strikes that winter too, fired up by the unions. We'd gone through the Blitz and we'd gone without food and none of that got me down the way those bolshies did, sitting at their bus depots spouting about revolutions while hardworking people walked home. We were rushed off our feet at the Rainbow Corner, there were so many GIs in town. The word was they were getting ready for the big invasion into France, but the invasion kept not happening.

Kick came back from Palm Beach without any joy. Mrs. K had been so worried she'd gone to the expense of placing a telephone call to the Duchess, and Her Grace had agreed with her that it was out of the question for Lord Billy and Kick to get married. The Devonshires didn't want it and the Kennedys wouldn't allow it, so that should have been the end of that, but Kick always was a tryer. She went off to Farm Street to see Father D'Arcy. And cold comfort she had of him too.

He said if she married in the English Church it would be no marriage at all in the eyes of the Catholic Church. She'd be living in sin and headed for eternal damnation, unless Lord Billy died first and she had time to make an act of contrition before her own death. As a matter of fact, I thought Father D'Arcy was wrong, because Our Lord would never have been so petty-minded over two good Christian souls, and even a man who's been to the seminary can make a mistake, but he threatened her with the terrible wrath of God and that was something her Daddy's dollars couldn't buy off. That had been her last big hope, but Mr. K was dead against the match too. He was building his empire, laying the foundations ready for his boys after the war, and even the girls had their place in his scheme.

As Joe explained it to us, when the time came for him to run for office he'd be depending on the Catholic vote.

"The way it is," he said, "if the first Kennedy to get married does it with an Episcopalian, it's liable to split the vote. There'll be Catholics who'll say, so much for the Kennedys being our kind. I love you, Sis, but not enough to let you lose me my first election."

We were on pins. You could see Lord Billy loved Kick to distraction and a man can't be blamed for the church errors of his forebears, but I truly wished Mr. Churchill would get a move on with the invasion and cancel all leave, before there was time for them to do anything rash. May 1 she came round to see me.

"Behold, I bring you tidings of great joy," she said. "Debo's had a baby boy. And Billy and I are engaged. Really, properly, officially engaged. You're the first to know."

Well, a baby's always good news, maybe specially a war baby. Lord Andrew was serving overseas and Kick said the baby was his double, so it was a comfort to Lady Debo. And lots of people get engaged without anything coming of it. Getting unengaged isn't so difficult. I thought she'd be brought to her senses once Mrs. Kennedy's cablegrams started raining down damnation on her and the Devonshires pulled Lord Billy back into line.

We had a good old hug, just like the old times. She said, "I'm so happy, Nora. Billy's just the sweetest boy I ever met."

Then she said, "Can you get time off on Saturday, you and Walter? We're getting married at Chelsea Town Hall."

That was the Monday. Walter said Their Graces would never wear it.

He said, "It cannot be, Nora. She's a nice enough lass, but it cannot be."

We heard nothing more till Thursday night. When I got home from the Red Cross young Joe was waiting for me, sitting in the scullery, turning the charm on Hope with a bar of soap and a bottle of OK sauce.

"Compassionate leave," he said. "I'm here to stand up for Kick on Saturday morning."

He'd been that afternoon to see the Devonshires' lawyer, with a message from Mr. K about money.

I said, "Does that mean they have your Mammy and Daddy's blessing?"

"Not exactly," he said. "Dad told me to pull out all the stops and give her the best wedding I can, in the circs. But Mother, well, I'm afraid she's taken it very badly. She's gone to a clinic. The quack says she needs complete rest."

He'd brought some clothes coupons for Kick.

He said, "The guys on my station rustled them up, like a kind of wedding gift. Is it too late to get a dress made do you think?"

It was all hands to the pump. We had a volunteer at the Rainbow Club who'd been a finisher at Molyneux. She spent all day Friday running up a little sheath dress, pale pink moss crepe, very simple, and Hope baked a cake with the last of our cocoa powder. Kick had rings under her eyes. After she'd had her first fitting, Joe took her horseback riding in Hyde Park, trying to get her to relax.

She kept saying, "I don't want this to kill Mother."

And Joe kept saying, "It won't. Mother's made of reinforced steel."

The Duke and Duchess had asked the Archbishop of Canterbury if he'd give them a blessing after the registry office, and then he asked the Bishop of Westminster if he'd like to come along and give them a Catholic blessing too, but he wouldn't of course. He said either they were married in the sight of God or they weren't and it wasn't for him to change the rules.

A box of camellias was sent down from Chatsworth.

"Such as they are," Walter said. "Nobody's kept the roots aerated, Nora. It's a wonder to me they've not rotted in the ground."

It grieved him to see such poor specimens used for a Devonshire wedding, but Kick was thrilled to have them, and the bottles of champagne wine brought up from the Chatsworth cellars and a diamond bracelet that had been in Lord Billy's family for centuries. Their Graces might not have approved of the match, but once they knew there was no stopping it, they did everything they could to give them a happy day.

Walter said, "That's because they're highborn people. They know how to behave."

I said, "I suppose you mean, not like the Kennedys."

He said, "All I'll say is, Kick's done very well for herself and your Mrs. Kennedy has no occasion to be so standoffish. From what I hear her people still have the bog sticking to their boots."

I said, "They do not. Mrs. K is a Fitzgerald and they're quite the Irish gentry in Boston, and old Mr. Kennedy was very well thought of. Anyway, it's easier for Protestants to give way over things of the faith. They don't have so much to lose. And I'm sure one of the reasons Their Graces are being nice about it is they've grown to love Kick."

She was a girl who was very easy to love.

Saturday morning Joe brought her to the Town Hall in a hackney cab. He was in his dress blues and Kick had borrowed a little ostrich feather hat with a bit of pink veil to match her dress. Joe led her in on his arm and we followed behind, with Sissy Ormsby-Gore as a kind of matron of honor. None of her other friends had been able to get away at such short notice. When I think what a splash we'd all looked forward to when the Kennedy girls got married. Every one of them would have been the wedding of the year. But Kick ended up with a little hole-in-the-wall wartime wedding, and it wasn't just Hitler they were up against. Herself was across the ocean, covered in frownies I'm sure and praying for a last-minute cancellation.

Lord Billy was waiting inside with the Duke and Duchess and his sisters. He had young Lord Granby for his best man. Lady Astor had turned up too, said she wanted to show solidarity. The old crackpot would never have come if we'd had a real wedding with a Nuptial Mass, of course. Wild horses wouldn't get her into a proper church, but I reckon she liked the idea of Kick defying Mrs. K. Anyway, she brought rose petals to throw, so she helped to take the bleakness off the occasion.

It was all over in ten minutes. William John Robert Cavendish, Marquess of Hartington, and Kathleen Agnes Kennedy. There were photographers waiting outside from the dailies, and after they'd snapped them we walked to Eaton Square to a house belonging to one of Lord Billy's uncles. All the Red Cross girls from Hans Crescent were there, and some of the officers too, come to toast the bride and groom.

A cablegram arrived just as they were cutting Hope's austerity wedding cake. It was from Mr. K. It said,

My Darling Kick, Remember you are still and always will be tops with me. Love, Dad.

There was a separate one arrived from Herself, but Joe tucked it in his pocket and let it slip his mind until after they'd left for the honeymoon. Then he showed it to me.

Heartbroken, it said.

You have been wrongly influenced. Mother.

Seven little words that took all the joy out of the day. Oh I wished Rose Kennedy ill when I read that wire, though I'd never have said so to Joseph Patrick. He'd really done his level best, for Kick and for his Mammy and Daddy.

I said, "It's early days. Maybe she'll come round."

Joe said, "Yeah. Maybe. And at least she didn't manage to get the Town Hall struck by lightning."

Lord Billy had ten days' compassionate leave, so they went down to Compton Place, to where it all started that weekend back in '38. And not only for Kick and her Lord Billy. That was the first time I met Walter too, studying me in his rear mirror as he drove us from Eastbourne station.

I said, "Remember when we came down for the horse racing? She was worried about how to carry on if she met Their Graces, when to curtsey and all that, and now she's on the way to being a Grace herself."

He said, "I do remember. Not as much as I remember her lady's maid, mind. She was a cracker. I wonder what ever became of her."

Walter had grown fond of Kick, never mind what he thought of the rest of her family. He called her "my lady" when it was time for us to wave them off to catch their train. Oh and how she covered me with kisses.

She said, "I'm so happy I could burst. And you know, after Billy's gone back to camp, I'm going to write to Mother again. I think she just needs time to get used to the idea. I think she'll rather like having a trainee Duchess in the family, don't you? It'll be a kind of talking point. And once she realizes nothing else has changed, that I still say my prayers and everything, I think she'll come round. God is good, Nora. He won't punish me for marrying Billy, and I'm sure Mother will dote on our babies, as long as they're baptized Christians."

Mrs. Kennedy dote on Protestant grandbabies! Well, God may be good but still, no sense in dancing in a small boat.

27

The Beginning of the End

We knew something was up. The last week of May the military were all on the move, heading out of London. Rainbow Corner was nearly deserted. There was so little for me to do there, I took in a pile of Walter's socks to mend. Everything was quiet but not a nice kind of quiet. They'd warned us we might have to clear the lounges and the canteen ready to set up hospital cots, to be prepared for a flood of casualties, though it never came to that. I walked home down the Haymarket and Pall Mall one evening and it was like being in a ghost town. I didn't see a single uniform. It was the night before D-day, except we didn't know it at the time.

Kick was down in Hampshire, billeted at an inn so as to be near where Lord Billy was stationed. She'd heard from all her pals when they read about the wedding, and Nancy Tenney even asked her if she'd turned Episcopalian enough to be godmother to her baby girl, but from Mrs. K and the rest of the family she heard not a thing. I knew Euny and Pat wouldn't dare write, not as long as Herself held out, but Jack was down at Palm Beach recuperating from the operation on his back, and Lem Billings was there to keep him company, invalided out with shrapnel in his legs. It wouldn't have hurt the pair of them to drop her a line and wish her well. Young Joe was the only one to really stand by her.

I said, "You did the right thing."

"You reckon?" he said. "Well, I hope so. Mother's still steaming and I'm not exactly in Dad's best books. First I drop Law School, then I connive with the Devonshire Prods. So there goes the first Catholic presidency. I'll be lucky to get elected borough councilor now. Maybe I'll go into the movies instead."

He could have done. He was the handsomest of my Kennedys by far. Jack and Bobby were too scraggy and Teddy was like a suet dumpling.

Joe's tour of duty was nearly over, but he was very smitten with a girl he'd met, so he wanted to stay on. Patricia. He showed me her picture. She was older than him, married, with children. There was a lot of that went on in the war. Lonely women.

He said, "Don't look at me that way, Nora. Her marriage wasn't happy even before she met me."

I said, "And where's the husband?"

North Africa, he thought.

I said, "And what do the children call you? Daddy the Second?"

He said, "They call me Joe. It's no problem. They don't all have the same father anyway. The girl's from her first marriage."

She was nice-looking, but I'm sure he could have done better than steal a fighting man's wife, and a secondhand one at that.

I said, "So what's to be done? Your Mammy'll be back in the convalescent home if she hears about this."

"I'm working on it," he said. "Main thing is, I want to stay here. I've volunteered for another tour of duty."

They said we'd made great gains on D-day, that the tide had turned and Jerry was on the run. Well, he might have been on the run, but that didn't stop him pausing to send those doodlebug rockets to torment us.

It was a Sunday morning when the first one came to London. I'd just got back from early Mass at Farm Street and Hope had set me scraping carrots for a pie. We didn't hear a plane because there was no plane, just a big vibration that made the milk pitchers dance on the dresser. Then the two Joans, ATS girls who had a room on the top floor, came thundering down the stairs. They said there was black smoke rising from over by Buckingham Palace. That got Stallybrass out from behind his newspaper.

He grabbed his helmet and his bike and he was off down the Mall, didn't even wait for orders. The Joans gave us a running report. Sirens, more smoke, then Lord Melhuish in his shirtsleeves and three more of his ARP men setting off on their bicycles. It was the barracks chapel that had been hit, in Birdcage Walk, packed to the doors with guardsmen and their loved ones, singing the first hymn.

We didn't see Walter again till nearly midnight. He came home covered in brick dust and soot, fit to drop, but he couldn't sleep.

"The roof fell on them, Nora," he kept saying over and over. "It's a bomb with an engine and when it runs out of juice it just glides down and explodes. It brought the roof in on them. What kind of folk bomb churches?"

I don't know that they had picked out a church, though. I'm not making excuses for Jerry, but bombs fall where they fall, especially the doodlebugs. But Walter had it in his head that it had been done out of spite.

"Nay," he kept saying. "Bombing on a Sunday morning. That's not decent. That never should be."

He cracked me up. He never sets foot in a church.

The guards' chapel was the start, pretty much, of the rocket bombs. It didn't flatten the altar, nor the bishop. He lived to tell the tale. But there were plenty of others not so lucky. One hundred and fifty dead, they reckoned, people at prayer, just minding their business on a beautiful summer morning. They said the rockets flew on their own all the way from France though how they did that nobody could ever explain to me.

Everybody seemed to know what should be done except Mr. Churchill. Walter said they should send ack-ack units down to Kent and Sussex, to catch the rockets before they crossed the coast and bring them down into the sea, and eventually they did just that, but we took a beating in London first. Five years of war and I'd never had hysterics, but I came close to it the night a doodlebug hit Victoria railway station.

There were a lot of GIs expected by train and they were shorthanded at the Donut Dugout so I was asked to work a late turn, serving them coffee and smokes. I'd just turned on to Wilton Road when I heard it pop-pop-popping, like a motorbike in the sky. I couldn't see it. Then the noise stopped dead, as if a plug had been pulled out, so I guessed what it was.

Walter had been telling me all week what I had to do if I heard the noise stop.

"You must take cover, Nora," he kept saying, "because if the blast doesn't get you the flying glass will."

But my legs wouldn't carry me. I was frozen to the spot and God knows what would have happened to me, but a big Polish soldier boy pushed me inside the doorway of the Grosvenor Hotel, and then the blast came and blew in all the lobby windows. We stayed crouched down together for a long time. I could smell his breath, like sausage meat. Then we heard people starting to move about in the street again and when I stood up I realized I'd wet my drawers. I thought, well, I can't work in these all night, so I wriggled them down and kicked them into the doorway of the movie theater. I suppose whoever found them must have thought they were all that was left of somebody. Tragic, mystery drawers.

There was glass underfoot, like gravel, and a bit of dust, but it was business as usual at the canteen. And all through the night, as well as the smell of java, there was a wonderful fragrance in the air, like new-mown hay. It was leaves, an ARP warden told us. The smell of thousands of leaves that had been stripped off the plane trees by the blast.

I worked my turn, did whatever I was asked, though I don't think I was much use to anyone that night. I even smoked a cigarette, my first and my last, nasty, choking thing. I'd seen things in the Blitz, and been out in the middle of raids and firestorms, but nothing had frightened me like the doodlebugs. And that one down at Victoria was only the start of it.

All that summer they tormented us and the casualties were terrible. Lady Melhuish was one of them, who lived just along the street in Carlton Gardens. She was an American lady, but very highly connected. She had an office job in the Wrens and she was just taking a walk along the Aldwych, out on her lunch break, when a rocket hit the Air Ministry. A body fell on her, sucked out of the building by the blast. Walter came home from his rounds with the story.

"See, Nora," he said. "You think I make a fuss, but the point is she didn't take cover. If people had seen what I've seen, bits pulled out of the rubble down at Birdcage walk, they'd be more cautious. I had to take charge of rounds tonight. His Lordship came down for the roll call, but he was in no state to do anything else. He held up very well when they lost their boy, but I reckon this has rightly finished him."

Young Joe came and paid us a call the first weekend of

August and brought Kick with him, Lady Kathleen as everybody was calling her now. Lord Billy's regiment had been posted overseas, to France she thought, so she'd decided to come back to town and see if the Red Cross could find anything to keep her occupied. She was staying at Cynthia Brough's in Cheyne Walk. Lady Cynthia was in the Air Transport Auxiliary, gone for days on end flying new Spitfires from the factory line out to the air bases, then having to wait for a ride back. She'd adopted a little terrier dog, but she didn't like to take him up with her, in case something went wrong and she had to bail out and leave him to perish, so she was glad to have Kick stay at her flat to look after him.

I quite thought Joe had come to say good-bye. He'd served his turn and he could have gone home.

But he said, "I'm not going, Nora. I've volunteered for a new assignment, so I'll be staying on."

As Kick said, staying on meant he could carry on with his married lady friend too, but it wasn't only love that was driving him. I knew it still niggled him that he hadn't sunk any U-boats while wee Jack had got a medal and a hero's welcome. Kick kept trying to get out of him what his new assignment was, but of course he couldn't tell us. All he'd say was that it was something big, something that could be the big turning point in the war.

"It could mean the beginning of the end," he said. "You'll hear all about it soon enough."

And so we did.

It was a Sunday afternoon, gray and muggy. Hope was putting up a few jars of carrot jam and Walter was resting his eyes. I was pressing my skirt, ready to work an early-evening turn at Rainbow Corner, when there was a rapping at the front door. We hardly used that entrance anymore. We spent near enough all our time down in the scullery and used the tradesman's door.

It was Lady Cynthia, very smart in her dark blue serge and her aviator wings, though I didn't know her for a minute, she'd had her curls cropped so short.

"You won't remember me," she said. "Cynthia Brough. Is Kick here by any chance?"

But I hadn't seen Kick in nearly two weeks.

She said, "I've had U.S. Navy brass on the blower, trying to track her down. Any idea where I'd find her?"

All I could think was she might have gone down to Compton Place. She liked to spend time with Their Graces when she could, learning all about the family and the estates and everything she'd need to know for when she was Duchess of Devonshire. "Studying graceship," as she called it.

Cynthia said, "I'm afraid it must be about her brother. He must be missing or wounded."

I don't imagine they even knew yet up at Hyannis. It was morning there. Herself would have been on her way back from Mass. Jean and Teddy might be out to Osterville for a regatta. Pat and Euny would likely be on the tennis court and Mr. K would be up on his veranda reading the Sundays. I could just picture them. And then any minute that telephone would start ringing.

I went to St. Patrick's on Soho Square and lit a candle, but I didn't learn any more till Tuesday night, when a note was delivered by hand.

Joe killed, she wrote.

> *Going home. Darlingest Nora, pray for the soul of the best brother in the world.*

I had a photograph of him, I know I did. It was taken on the strand the first summer we went to Cohasset, Mr. K with

Joseph Patrick in one arm and Jack in the other, both in their wee sailor suits. Well, I searched everywhere for that picture the night I heard Joe was dead, but I couldn't find it. As the family grew, he wasn't my favorite, but those first few months he was my only Kennedy and such a handsome child. Those were happy days. And when Jack was born Joe didn't like sharing me. "Mine," he'd say, and he'd try to push Jack off my lap.

When a serviceman was killed you got no details. We didn't hear until after V-day exactly what had happened, but I knew Joseph Patrick well enough to guess. He was the kind of lad who was never satisfied till he was doing the daringest stunt, till he'd given Jack and Bobby and Teddy something crazy to beat. And that was the sum of it. There'd been just a few of them, a select band who'd volunteered for something that hadn't been tried before, to try and knock out the doodlebug launchers over in France. Flying a bomb was what it amounted to, a Liberator airplane packed with dynamite. They had to fly it so far, to set it on the right track, and then parachute out before it blew up. Except that the first few they tried blew up while the aviators were still inside so there was talk of calling the whole business off. There would have been no dishonor in devolunteering until they'd made it safer, but if you advised Joe against doing a thing it only made him the more determined.

Kick wrote again when she got home.

> *Things are just too awful here. Daddy doesn't leave his room. Mother's hardly speaking to me because of Billy and everything. She's given orders that everyone has to carry on as normal because as you know, Kennedys don't cry. And now Nancy Tenney's husband is missing in action and he hasn't even seen their little baby yet.*

I'm afraid I AM crying. Seems to me I'm not a hundred percent Kennedy anymore. I'm a Devonshire too and I think Devonshires are allowed a little weep.

I reckon Rosie's the lucky one now. She doesn't even realize all these terrible things are happening. They say Joe's likely to get the Navy Cross at the very least. Mother's talking that up but who cares about a stupid medal when we've lost Joe.

I'll be back to dear old England as soon as I can get on a transport. Have to keep busy or I'll go crazy.

When first I heard what Mr. Kennedy had had done to Rosie, all I could think was what a monster he'd turned out. He couldn't stand to be beaten, he wouldn't have anything stand in the way of his big plans, not even one of his own darling girls, and he thought everything in the world could be fixed by pulling strings and spending dollars. I'd felt sorry then for Mrs. K, because he'd likely waited till she was up to Maine for a rest cure and then sneaked Rosie away to the hospital. Mrs. K might have despaired sometimes of teaching Rosie her letters, but a mother's love is a mother's love. That's what I'd thought. But when I heard how she was after Joe was killed, I changed my mind. Not speaking to her own daughter, when she'd flown across the ocean to be with them and share in their loss. If losing that boy didn't soften her heart, if it didn't make her treasure Kick and count her blessings, then what kind of mother was she?

Walter said we shouldn't judge people like the Kennedys by our lights.

He said, "Folk who've come up fast the way they have, they'd never have got where they are if they acted sentimental. Empire builders, Nora. They don't tick the way we do."

I said, "That's the way men think. I'm not talking about Mr. K. I'm talking about Herself. She's not the empire builder."

"If you say so, sweetheart," he said. "If you say so."

And it wasn't long anyway before another blow fell that made me think Walter might have the measure of Mrs. K better than I did.

28

A Real Winner, with a Bit of Grooming

Mr. Churchill said we might be over the worst, because our boys had flattened most of the places those terrible doodlebugs were launched from, but he spoke too soon. Jerry had something else up his sleeve and we got our first taste of it at the start of September. Walter's Pig Club had slaughtered Hermann Goering that week and we'd got the head as part of our share, so Hope had made a lovely brawn. We'd just sat down for tea when we heard an explosion, quite far off, and then another sound, like a great thunderclap that shook the whole house and set a load of soot tumbling down the scullery chimney.

Walter was on his feet. He said, "That was a big one. I'd best get round to the telephones."

Since Lady Melhuish died, His Lordship had left more and more to the men under him, and Walter loved manning the telephones. I don't believe he'd hardly seen one before the war and he still hasn't got the hang of talking into them in a normal way. He shouts so loud you might hear him in Bakewell without his even using the telephone. He went round to the ARP and later on he came back with the news that some kind of rocket bomb had hit a street in Chiswick, just across the river from Kew Gardens. He wanted to cycle over there directly, to see if the greenhouses were damaged, but Hope wouldn't let him.

She said, "I haven't gone through five years of war for you to go wobbling down to Chiswick in the blackout and get run over by a bus."

He said, "I do not wobble."

He did though.

He said, "What if there's a frost tonight? What about my plants?"

Well, there wasn't going to be a frost. It was as hot as blazes. Sometimes Walter takes too much upon himself. Anyway, he didn't go, because Hope hid his bicycle pump. Doing Vincent's milk round had put a bit of spine in her.

Well, that was the start of the V2s. They said they were worse yet than the doodlebugs, because you didn't hear them coming until after they'd arrived, but they didn't frighten me the same. Perhaps it was because they never hit anywhere near us. Perhaps it was because I was tired of being scared. From then on I was just plain worn out and heartsick.

The news came a week after the Chiswick bombing. It was Saturday night and Hope was alone in the house. Walter was doing his blackout rounds and I was working an evening turn at Rainbow Corner. When I got home I could hardly make sense of what Hope told me. Every time she started she couldn't get it out for her tears. One of the Duchess's relations had come from Eaton Square to tell us Lord Billy had been killed. They'd buried him where he fell. In Belgium, she thought.

Hope didn't go to bed that night. She sat at the scullery table stitching black armbands, so people would know we'd suffered a loss. I didn't see the point. I'm sure by 1944 everybody had lost somebody. Walter sat and watched her.

He said, "Lord Andrew'll be the next Duke now."

Hope said, "Not if Lady Kathleen's in the family way, he won't be."

He looked at me. He said, "Is she?"

I said, "How should I know? And even if she was, it'll be a miracle if she still is, with all these shocks, and flying in airplanes."

He said, "Well, let's say it'll be Lord Andrew. But then he might cop it too. Then it'll be Lady Debo's new little baby. What a thing to happen. They should bring him back though. When all this is over, they should bring him home and bury him at Edensor. That's where Devonshires should be laid to rest."

I went to bed but I didn't sleep, wondering if Kick knew yet, wondering what would become of her, widowed already and her Mammy still in a sulk over her marrying.

She was in New York when she heard the news, in Bonwit Teller, buying stockings. A cablegram had come to Mr. Kennedy at his hotel and he'd sent Euny out to the shops, to try and find Kick. She told me all about it when she came down to London after Lord Billy's memorial service.

"I knew," she said. "Euny didn't actually tell me. She just said I should go see Daddy because he needed to speak with me, but I knew. Poor Daddy. He said, 'I don't know how to tell you.' And it was such a silly thing, the way it happened. I got a letter from one of the platoon commanders. He said the company was moving out on patrol and it was raining, so Billy put on that awful old canvas waterproof over his battledress. I don't know why he liked that coat. It always smelled of dogs. They lost lots of men that day, but Billy must have been an easy target in that silly coat. He was shot through the heart."

She was still a child to me. She sat there in her best black suit, shoes kicked off, fiddling with her lace gloves, rolling them and unrolling them.

"No hugs, please, Nora," she said. "I'm trying really hard not to blub any more today."

I said, "Not on my account, I hope."

"'Course not," she said, "but I think they were finding the blubbing a bit of a bore back home. Time to move on and all that. You know? It probably didn't hurt, do you think? The bullet? It would have been over quickly, wouldn't you say?"

"Like the lights going out," I said.

What did I know.

She said, "I'd just like to know it didn't hurt."

I said, "What will you do? Will you stay on?"

"Oh yes," she said. "I want to be where the war is, not stuck in New York going to fund-raisers. I'm a Devonshire now, Nora. I want to be around people who loved Billy. I want to see Andrew and Debo's children grow up. Being Duke will fall to Andrew now, you see, because I didn't get a baby by Billy. I wish I could have done that at least, but I didn't. Nancy Tenney's got her little girl. But all I've got are memories. Anyway, I can't face going back to the States again. Do you know what Mother said when we heard Billy had been killed? She said, 'Bow your head to God's wisdom, Kathleen. God took Billy to put right the terrible wrong of your marrying.'

"She said all I have to do now is make an act of contrition, then I can receive the comfort of Communion again, but it'd be a lie, Nora, because I'm not contrite. I'm absolutely not. I'd marry Billy again in a heartbeat."

Well, there it was, as clear as day, the kind of mind Mrs. Kennedy had, catechizing and lecturing when her girl was hardly five minutes a widow. I don't care how many Masses she has said for the departed, she's not my idea of a good Christian soul.

The weight had dropped off Kick. She said nothing tasted of anything anymore. Their Graces had been kind to her though. They'd told her she should always find a home with them, although the title of Marchioness would pass to Lady Debo. Kick could still be Lady Hartington, but she'd be the Dowager Marchioness.

She said, "I guess I'll carry on at the Red Cross. One thing about a war, there's always something for a girl to do. I'll stay at Cynthia's for a while. If anyone can cheer me up it's Cynthia. She's such a stitch. She had to bail out of a plane last week and she swears the only thing that worried her was whether people on the ground would see her bloomers."

Kick reckoned Jack looked like death warmed up, what with the shock of Joe and the pain from his back. The Navy had tried to fix him up but he was still in pain, and the fevers had come back. They'd told him it must be malaria, picked up from those tropical waters, but Jack had fevers even when we lived in Bronxville.

She said, "He probably won't be sent back into action, but he's working hard to get fit. Now Joe's gone he's the one who'll run for office."

Well, then I'd heard it all. Twenty-seven and a walking wreck.

I said, "Jack hasn't the strength to run to the corner of the street."

"Oh but Daddy's organizing it," she said. "He says the voters'll love him because he's young and he won a war medal. And Grandpa Fitz says the injuries could be a real asset, with the women voters. Plus, Jack comes across better than Joe did, kind of funnier, easier-going. Grandpa thinks Jack could be a real winner, with a bit of grooming."

They were a scheming pair of devils. Mr. K and Mayor Fitzgerald couldn't stand the sight of each other, but they were willing to team up to get Jack into politics. They knew they could get more done together than they could on their own and there they were, moving the children around like checkers on a board.

She said, "So you see, that's another reason for me to stay here. They won't want me around besmirching the family record. I told Euny, as soon as the war's over she'd better find herself a nice Catholic boy so Mother can go to town with a big wedding at St. Patrick's. Or maybe Bobby'll go to seminary. That'd do it. A priest in the family would just about make up for the scandal I've created."

We were into the fifth year of the war. It was hard to remember what normal life felt like. But then it was announced that we could ease up on the blackout regulations, because the only attacks we were getting were the rocket bombs and they were as liable to come in broad daylight as any other time. I think Mr. Churchill understood how we were all feeling, sick of the cold and the dark and never really getting enough to eat, but Mr. Churchill didn't have to live with ARP Warden Stallybrass. Walter said we wouldn't be taking our blinds down until Germany surrendered or His Grace gave the order.

I said, "His Grace has other things on his mind than our blackout curtains. He just lost a son."

"Nora," he said, "you'll pardon me, but you don't understand the ways of a big house. There's a chain of command and you don't just take it into your head to move the furniture or change the timetable. You wait to know the pleasure of your betters."

There was a time when Hope would have backed him up. When I first knew them they were like Tweedledum and Tweedledee, particularly with anything concerning the Devonshires.

But she said, "Nay, Walter, I think Nora's right. If Mr. Churchill says we can do it, I don't think Their Graces'll take exception."

That's what a milk round can do for a woman.

A week or two after Christmas I was in the kitchen at Rainbow Corner, washing coffee cups, when one of the girls said I was being asked for at the information desk. We got a lot of people wandering in, girls especially. They'd go with a GI, then find out they were expecting and turn up looking for him. Half the time they weren't even sure of his name.

"I think he was called Mitch," one poor scrap said to me. "He was from America."

But this wasn't a girl that was asking for me. It was a soldier, wearing service ODs. I didn't remember his face, but there was something familiar about him, just the way he stood.

"Aunt Nora?" he said. "Is it you?"

It was Margaret's boy, Val. Private Rudolf Valentino Mulcahy, Eighty-fifth Infantry.

I said, "What are you doing here? You're never old enough to be drafted."

"I am too," he said. "Volunteered the day of my birthday. I was worried it'd all be over but looks like they saved me a bit of war."

It was our Dada he reminded me of, the way he folded his arms and rocked on his heels as he was talking, though where he learned it from I can't think, because he never knew his Grandada Brennan.

I said, "I'm surprised your Mammy allowed you. She must be sleepless with worry."

"Well," he said, "she's still got Ray at home and I doubt the military'll ever be desperate enough to take him."

I said, "Why? Does he have your Daddy's chest?"

"No," he said, "he's just a regular faggot."

"Faggot" was the kind of word Mr. Kennedy was liable to use. Men who never married, and theatrical types. He didn't like his boys mixing with anybody like that. He seemed to think it was catching.

I said, "Who calls him a name like that?"

"Nobody exactly calls him that," he said. "We don't need to. It's in the bag. Ray's a fag."

I said, "Does your Mammy know?"

He said, "I guess. See, he's the real helpful type, so Ma don't mind. A momma's boy. Good-looking too. He's got those long eyelashes girls really go for. Kind of a waste if y'ask me."

I said, "And what does your aunt Ursie say?"

He had Dada's quiet laugh.

He said, "Aunt Ursie says she knew something bad would come of naming a boy Ramon Novarro. 'Course, army life ain't exactly peachy if guys find out your name's Rudolf Valentino. What time do you get off? Can we go get something to eat?"

I took him home with me to meet my Walter. He was in London for forty-eight hours, on his way couldn't tell us where but he was with a special unit called the Mountain Infantry. He'd been trained to fight in snow and all sorts at a camp in Colorado. Hope made a Woolton pie in his honor and almond shape, and we were just clearing away when Kick turned up.

I said, "This is Lady Hartington. Lady Kathleen Kennedy Hartington."

He stood there, mouth open, catching flies. "Wow," he said. "I never met a real live Kennedy before."

She said, "I don't know about 'live.' I'm dying of boredom. My housemate's flying a Spitfire to Scotland and I'm supposed to stay home like a good widder woman, but I'd really love to go dancing. I'm sure Billy wouldn't mind."

So our Val squired her to Frisco's, took her jitterbugging two nights running, before his division was shipped out.

He said, "She's cute. And she must be worth millions."

I said, "Well, don't get any ideas. We've had trouble enough already. If the Marquess of Hartington wasn't good enough for her, Mrs. Kennedy won't want her walking out with the help's relations."

He said, "I took her dancing is all. And I like older women. But you know how it is, I'm young, I'm getting sent into action, there might be a Jerry bullet has my name on it. I guess it wouldn't be right to make her any wild promises."

I said, "No. And don't talk like that about bullets."

"Hey," he said, "I don't believe in all that jinx stuff. I just say my prayers and follow orders."

He shipped out in the middle of January, to Italy, Walter surmised. He reckoned units like the Eighty-fifth must be going to clear the mountains of Germans. But a lot of the GIs were talking about the war moving east, to hammer the Japs, and for all we knew they had snow and mountains over there too.

We went right through from Christmas to April without any air raids. Walter still went to his post every night, but there wasn't much for them to do except practice bandaging and drink cocoa. He was in very low spirits.

Every night he'd say, "The war's not over yet, Nora. It don't feel right to be sitting idle."

Then they started hauling away the barrage and filling in the trenches in Hyde Park and we were busy again at the Rainbow Corner, but not so much with new boys. Mainly we were taking care of GIs just back from fighting in France. Things were turning our way, they said. Hitler was on the ropes and it could only be a matter of time. The Pacific was where they all expected to be sent next.

We should have been over the moon, knowing it was nearly over, and yet a lot of us felt like flat beer. Hilda Oddy kept saying, "It's been the best time of my life. What am I going to do when it's over, go back to selling Woodbines?"

And then there were a lot of people who'd have reckoning up

to do. Girls left with little babies, gotten while they were living for the moment. Men coming home and finding another man's hat hanging on the peg. Hasty marriages with boys who'd looked good in uniform. I even wondered about me and Walter, not that I didn't love him, but I'd had a grand war, all things considered, and he'd already started talking about "when we go back to Chatsworth."

Well, there was nothing for me at Chatsworth.

29

A Kennedy Poodle

President Roosevelt died in April. I couldn't believe it when we heard it on the wireless. Only sixty-three and we'd seen pictures of him when he went to Yalta with Mr. Churchill. He'd looked all right then. But Kick said her Daddy wasn't in the least surprised. He'd tried for years to get him to stop smoking, and anyway, according to Mr. K, the war had worn him to a shadow. So poor Mr. Roosevelt didn't live to see peace and Mr. Truman took over.

The last day of April they put the lights back up on Big Ben and Adolf Hitler ate his last bucket of swill at the Kew Garden Piggery. It was perfect timing. He was ready for eating by Victory Night. We had a great big juicy chop each and a baked apple and then we walked down the Mall to see the King and Queen waving from the balcony at Buckingham Palace. There were bonfires lit in Green Park and firecrackers set off. Kick was there too, with Cynthia Brough, though we didn't know it. I got separated from Walter and Hope in the crowd. There were people dancing all the way up the Mall, total strangers taking you by the arm and swinging you round. I kissed all sorts that night, I was so relieved to think it was over and there'd be no more bombs. But of course it wasn't really over. There were still the Japs to deal with.

Kick came to Carlton Gardens just after VE-night, put her head round the scullery door. We'd just cleared up from tea.

"Surprise visitor," she said.

And there behind her stood Jack, all skin and bone but cheeky as ever with his kisses. He was wearing civvies.

"The Navy let me go," he said. "They've got enough old crocks without keeping me on the muster list."

He'd come to England to watch what happened in the elections and report back to Mr. Kennedy. "Observing the postwar scene," he called it.

"I'm Dad's eyes and ears over here," he said. "He's grooming me for office, Nora. I'll be running for Congress in due course. Grandpa Kennedy's old district."

I said, "Then you'd better start polishing your shoes. And learn how to spell."

Kick said, "Congressmen don't need to know how to spell. They have secretaries. And after congressman he's going to be a senator and then president."

She was looking better than I'd seen her since Lord Billy died. Any Kennedy always looks happier when they've got another Kennedy on their arm.

I said, "Jack Kennedy for President! They'll fly a man to the moon more likely."

He said, "Hear that, Kick? Scratch Nora from the guest list. There'll be no White House invitations for her."

I said, "I've been to the White House, thank you very much. And I'm sure you'll do very well at whatever you go in for, but I wouldn't wish the president's job on a dog. Not when you see how it killed poor Mr. Roosevelt."

"Well," he said, "I think it'd be neat. Kick can run my press office. Euny can do all the brain work. And I'll have to find something for St. Bobby. And if you decide to write your memoirs, you know, *Jack Kennedy: The Nursery Years*, you'll have to run it past me first. I don't want the voters knowing everything."

Of course, with his Grandpa Fitz's connections and his Daddy's dollars to grease a few palms, I knew he was guaranteed to get somewhere in life and he could be quick with a wisecrack. If it came to making speeches to a hall full of smarty-pants, Jack could give them as good as he got. But I still didn't believe he had the staying power for anything big, and he doesn't take such a good photograph either, not like Joseph Patrick.

I said, "And how's my Rosie?"

"About the same," he said, "I guess."

I said, "Don't you visit with her?"

He said, "Mary Moore goes. And Euny went a couple of times, I think. There's not a lot of point though, Nora. That's the thing with a mental handicap. It's not like a head cold. It's not going to get better."

I said, "Is that what she's got now? A mental handicap?"

Kick said, "She always was slow."

Jack said, "It's nothing to be ashamed of. There's a lot of it out there. Mother and Euny are going to do something with it, start a charitable foundation or something. It'll be a real talking point."

I could just see it. Rosie getting dragged out of her nursing home for one of Mrs. Kennedy's show-and-tells.

I said, "You must leave the poor girl in peace, Jack. Haven't your Mammy and Daddy done enough harm?"

He said, "Dad and Mother did everything for the best and I'm not going to discuss it anymore. It's family business."

He went off to do his "observing," traveling around the country, asking people which way they were going to vote and why.

"Labour" was the answer to that, because people didn't need poor old Winnie Churchill anymore now he'd won the war for them. Clement Attlee promised them free doctors and jobs for all. Walter said Labour would have got in if they'd promised to paint the sky green. He was heartbroken for Mr. Churchill and he wrote and told him so.

"That's human nature for you," he kept saying. "No gratitude. No sense. All they want is novelty. And what's going to happen if you make doctors' visits free? I'll tell you. Folk'll get ill all the time."

Jack hadn't been in England long when he had another bout of his fevers. They told him it was the malaria come back and he was liable to get attacks at any time. They gave him some pills, but these made him feel sick all the time, and then his skin turned yellow. Mr. K sent him a cablegram, told him to get back to the States and see a proper American doctor. Said he'd send Eddie Moore to bring him back if necessary.

I went to the clinic to see him.

He said, "I have to go home, Nora, and I want Kick to come with me. Can you persuade her?"

She said, "Why would I do that? Mother's not even speaking to me."

Jack said time would heal all. He said Mr. K wanted the whole family involved when they started campaigning. Mr. K believed the voters would love to see how the Kennedys worked together, a bunch of good-looking youngsters and their glamorous Mammy as well, with their pictures all over the dailies. Mr. K said they'd be the talk of America, just like they had been when we came to London. But Kick wasn't convinced.

She said, "I don't know, Nora. I'd like to help Jack, but I'm sure Mother doesn't want me there. And the thing is, London feels like home now."

I couldn't advise her. I knew Mrs. K would nag her to a shadow if she got her back in her clutches. But Kick loved her Daddy more than anything. She always wanted to please him and she'd never allow that he had any faults.

She said, "You know Daddy really didn't mind about the church thing and Billy. He just hates to see Mother upset. And he says he'd find me something useful to do if I go back. He'd probably buy me a newspaper or something so I can write great things about Jack."

But she didn't go back. She got it into her head that she wanted to make a home in England, and it suited me. It bought me a bit of time. Walter had been up to Chatsworth already, to take a look over the gardens and inspect the damage to his camellia beds. All I heard day and night was how there'd be a nice little cottage waiting for us on the estate. I'd known all along it would come to it.

I said, "But what will I do? There's nothing for me up there."

He said, "How about being there in a nice clean pinny when I come in for my tea? Isn't that what wives do?"

I said, "How should I know? I've only ever been a war wife."

"That's what I'm saying," he said. "Nearly six years, Nora, and all I've seen of you is the back of you running out the door to your Women's Voluntary. It's time to settle down, pet. Make a proper home."

I said, "I'm fifty-one, Walter, and I've worked all my life. I can't sit idle."

He said, "You won't sit idle. There'll be the cooking and the cleaning and the mending. We'll have a little garden, grow our own potatoes and a few greens. And knitting. You like knitting. And then when Lord Andrew comes home I expect him and Her Ladyship will go in for more family. And Lady Anne'll get married and Lady Elizabeth. There'll always be nursery maids needed, if you must keep your hand in."

He knew perfectly well there wouldn't be a place for me. When families like the Devonshires have babies they bring their old nurses out of mothballs, and even if something was found for me, I couldn't have knuckled down, taking orders from another woman. I was accustomed to running things without interference. There were times with the Kennedys when we didn't see Herself for weeks on end. That was the kind of work that suited me.

Still, the time was coming when we had to decide. The ATS girls were gone. All we had were a few Canadian officers waiting for orders to the Pacific. Then the week before VJ-day Kick turned up with an offer. She'd taken a lease on a little house on Smith Square and Their Graces had suggested she take me and Walter as housekeeper and driver.

I'd have jumped at it. But that's one of the things about being married. You're supposed to jump together, and Walter wasn't at all smitten with the idea of staying in London. The more he thought about Derbyshire, the grimier London looked.

"See what I mean?" he'd say if there was a smell of traffic fumes or he found smut on his shirt. "You wouldn't get that in the country."

I didn't need anybody to tell me about country life. I lived eighteen years at Ballynagore. Shoes always muddy. Walking miles to catch a bus. And the same bored old faces week after week. If you put a new ribbon on your Sunday bonnet it'd get written up in the *Tullamore Reminder*.

I'd say, "You wouldn't get anything in the country."

And then Hope would chip in. The Vincent boy had come back from his war work, so her days on the milk cart were finished. She was ready to pack up her rolling pin and go north and she expected us to go with her.

"Chatsworth's not just country," she'd say. "Chatsworth's the finest house in England. Seventeen staircases, Nora. Thirty bathtubs. And I've had the highest people in the land eating my damson tarts."

I said, "And if we stay in London we'll have the best of both worlds. Walter'll be driving for Lady Kick, so he'll still go up to Chatsworth once in a while, and Compton Place. If they keep all those houses on. That's the other thing. Times are changing. We had a lot of girls at the Women's Voluntary that used to be in service and there's hardly a one of them going back to it. The big houses won't be the same, Hope. Dozens of people bowing and scraping, waiting, cap in hand, for a bit of a cottage or an attic over the stables. That's finished."

"Not for Stallybrasses it isn't," she said. "And how about if things go haywire down here? What if Her Ladyship changes her mind and goes home? All her people over there. Then you'll be out on the street."

Walter didn't say anything and neither did I. Two days I left it, though I did go to Farm Street and pray to St. Anthony. I don't know if he intercedes when there's a Protestant involved, but I don't suppose a prayer is ever really wasted. And in the end he said, "All right. I'll give it a try. As long as we can get out to Richmond Park on a Sunday. I shall go off my chump if I don't see a bit of green."

Walter loved the deer park. He knew the names of all the birds.

I said, "Have you told Hope?"

"No," he said. "I'd best put my tin helmet on before I do."

Hope said there'd be Stallybrasses turning in their graves if they knew he was staying in London when he could be back at Chatsworth.

"You'll be nothing but an odd-job man," she kept saying. "You'll be running errands, fetching her packages from Harvey Nichols. And you'll have no garden."

"Well, Hope," he said. "Here's the thing. If Nora's not happy I don't see how I can be. And I shall think of looking after Her Ladyship as doing something for Lord Billy. Do you remember when I come back from Flanders? He were out on the lawns with one of the nursery maids, just starting to toddle. We both thought we'd end our days working for him. I remember driving His Grace to Buxton one time with Lord Billy along for the ride. He couldn't have been more than four, asking me all about how the engine worked and where I lived and why. I thought I'd live long enough to see him Duke, but there we are. He's left behind a poor young widow and I'm sure he'd have wanted a Stallybrass to look after her."

I said, "Two Stallybrasses, Walter."

"Aye," he said. "Two. There's just one thing though, Nora. Will Her Ladyship be having all them Kennedys come to visit?"

I said, "I'm sure the youngsters will come. In time. But I don't think Herself will be troubling us. I believe she's given Kick up for lost."

He said, "Well, I hope that means the old bootlegger won't be visiting neither. The thought of driving him around fair makes my skin crawl."

Kick took the house unfurnished but she didn't need to buy a thing. Their Graces gave her everything she needed, some of it sent from the Dower house, some from the big house, and even a piece or two from Compton Place. She rushed around trying things out in different rooms, unpacking half a box then starting on another, till we looked like a fire sale. It reminded me of when we were at Naples Road and she and Rosie used to play with their dolly house out on the veranda.

Smith Square was a good house for her to start off in. It had just the one cozy little parlor and a dining room, three bedrooms, and then the top floor for me and Walter and a girl called Delia

Olvanie. She'd been a housemaid at Lismore and had let it be known she wanted a taste of London life, so Her Grace sent her to Kick. I wasn't very taken with Delia. She moved too slow, for one thing. She could make sweeping a staircase last half the morning, and if ever she dusted the side table that had Lord Billy's photo on it, then the waterworks would start and she'd have to sink into an armchair till she'd recovered. The only time you saw her stir herself was when it was her day off. Then she'd be running around, fleet as a whippet, with her hair in curling papers and her toenails painted. And she never locked the bathroom door.

Well, help like that is no help at all, but Kick would keep her. She said it comforted her to have people around who'd known His Lordship, though I don't know that Delia Olvanie saw Lord Billy more than half a dozen times in her whole life.

Life picked up gradually. People drifted back from their war. Kick went to Lady Astor's for the weekend and saw Ginny Balderston, as used to be Ginny Vigo. Her husband had lost an eye in Palestine but they had a baby on the way. Then she ran into Susie Finch-Johnstone and brought her home to tea. She'd been in North Africa and then in Italy with General Eisenhower.

She said, "I was with your lot, on the Order of Battle charts. I was one of those girls that pushed the little flags around. It's been such fun. I'm meant to be going home. Cosmo's pretty hot to get married, but I think it might be rather a bore after Africa."

She'd been engaged to Cosmo Snagge for years, but the wedding never did come off. She went to Australia instead, with one of her pals from the ATS. They're hoping to grow pineapples. Minnie Stubbs didn't go home either. She married a French airman she'd nursed down in Devon. Started off emptying his potty. As she said, after that, things could only look up. His people have a bread shop in Paris. Kick said it was a very superior bread shop, but the Stubbses still had a fit when they found out she'd already married him.

Cynthia Brough was the only one the end of the war didn't make much difference to. She carried on flying. She joined the Aviation Corps for a while till somebody objected to her taking her dog in the cockpit, so now she's a flying taxi driver, working for herself. Kick went up with her one time. She had to deliver blood to a hospital on the Isle of Man and then they stopped off for luncheon with Lady Cynthia's people in Cheshire. Kick came back very impressed.

She said, "I wish we could be like the Broughs. Cynthia doesn't get quizzed about where she's going or who she's seeing."

I said, "Neither do you. You're a grown woman now with a house of your own."

"I guess," she said. "But there's still Mother. Do you know what I mean?"

I did. When Mrs. K was put out, even that big Atlantic Ocean wasn't wide enough to stop you feeling it. Though I don't believe she gave much thought to her troubles with Kick the summer of '46. Jack was running in the primaries, up against nine other candidates, all older and savvier than him, so the whole tribe had gone to Boston to help him with his campaigning and Herself was in her element. They'd taken two hotel suites and His Honor was out with Jack every day, canvassing door to door, standing right behind him when he was on the stump. They reckon Mayor Fitzgerald could remember the names of every one of his voters, and the little favors he'd done them over the years.

I predicted Jack would take a drubbing, Grandpa Fitzgerald or no. I couldn't see why anybody would vote for a boy who looked fourteen years old, particularly a Kennedy who'd never done a proper day's work in his life, but they did. He strolled home ahead of the other nine, and once he'd gotten the nomination it was in the bag. The Eleventh District would never have sent a Republican to Congress.

October, Kick got a letter from her Daddy. A new altar was being made for St. Francis Xavier church in Hyannis, in memory of Joseph Patrick. It was to be dedicated just after the election and Mr. K expected all of them to be there.

She said, "You have to come with me, Nora. I can't face Mother again all on my own."

I said, "I can't go to America. I've Walter to consider."

She said, "Walter won't mind. Delia can cook for him."

I'd pity the man who had to depend on Delia Olvanie for his sustenance. But it wasn't that I was thinking of. Walter'd be quite happy to live on bread and dripping. It was just the very idea of me going somewhere and him staying home.

I said, "I'm your housekeeper, sweetheart. I'm not your nursery maid anymore."

She said, "You'll always be my nursery maid. And Joe would have wanted you to be there. You'll be able to visit your sisters and that cute nephew, and you'll see Teddy and Jean and the gang. It'll be fun. Don't worry about Walter. He won't mind, not when I explain how important it is."

I watched his face. He said, "When is it, this dedication?"

November, December. She didn't know exactly.

He said, "So how long are we talking about? A week to get there, a week to get back, three weeks all up?"

She said, "Gosh no, it's a long way to go just for a few days, and there'll be lots of people to see. A month or two, I guess. Nora wants to see her folks."

He said, "Do you, Nora? You've never said."

I said, "Walter, I've never thought of going back. But it'd be daft to go all that way and not see them."

He said, "And how will we be placed, Your Ladyship, if I don't agree?"

She turned to look at him and out jutted that Fitzgerald chin.

She said, "What do you mean, 'don't agree'?"

He said, "Well, I don't know as I want my wife gone for months on end. I don't think any husband would."

She said, "I do pay you."

For the briefest second it was as though Mrs. Kennedy herself was standing there.

"Aye," he said, "you do. Not very much, mind."

And he turned on his heel and walked out.

She said, "Why do people have to be so difficult?"

Then the doorbell rang. It was Lady Balderston with her car outside, looking for Kick to go shopping with her, so I was left to deal with Stallybrass, with Delia Olvanie pretending to burnish the fire irons and listening to every word we said.

I said, "You'd never speak like that to Their Graces."

He said, "I wouldn't need to. So what's happening? Are you going?"

I said, "I don't see what else I can do. I am supposed to look after her."

"No," he said, "you're supposed to look after the house and the house is here. If she wants a traveling maid, let her get one."

I said, "That's not the way it is. I was her lady's maid when we came down to Compton Place, and to Chatsworth. When you work for the Kennedys you turn your hand to whatever's needed."

He said, "You and your ruddy Kennedys. I knew this would happen. I've gave up thirty-five years of good standing and the chance of a cottage, and now you expect to go swanning off."

I said, "I don't expect to do any such thing. Swanning off! You make it sound like a cruise to Monte Carlo. I'd just be paying my respects to Joseph Patrick, see his altar dedicated. You get all misty-eyed about Lord Billy, well, young Joe took his first steps holding my hand. Why would I not want to be there? And

I know how Kick's feeling. Mrs. K's a holy terror when she's been crossed. You don't know what she's like. She'll have the other girls all toeing the line. Kick'll get no support from them. She just needs someone with her who'll take her part."

He said, "And that's you, is it? Every time she has to go over there, you'll be expected to tag along? Because she's frit of her mother? And all because she married Lord Billy, as laid down his life for King and country. What's wrong with the old battle-ax anyhow? Why can't she let it lie? You don't see Her Grace walking around with a prune face, and if anybody had cause to complain about that marriage, it were her. A fine old family like the Devonshires getting mixed up with a cowboy like Kennedy. But they took Lady Kick in and they treated her like one of their own."

I said, "We can't all be as perfect as your sainted Devonshires."

"Well, that's one thing you've got right," he said. "That's the trouble when people have got money and no breeding. No breeding, no consideration. And I'll tell you the next thing as'll be on the cards. Her Ladyship'll take up with one of her old admirers and we'll be out of a job. We could have had one of the Pilsley cottages, Nora, if I hadn't give way to you."

I said, "You didn't give way to me. You did it because Her Grace asked you."

He said, "We could have had our own bit of kitchen garden. Maybe gone in for a pig. We could have had security."

I said, "Nobody has security anymore, Walter. Not even poor Mr. Churchill."

He said, "I'll bet Tommy Marstin's been given the place that should rightly have been ours. He's not half the gardener I am. And he can't drive."

I said, "Then why don't you go up there and get your blasted cottage. If His Grace is all you've cracked him up to be, he'll find you something, and keep you in your dotage."

He said, "Hope said it'd never work out. I should have listened to her."

He put his cap on.

I said, "Where are you going?"

"To the Labor Exchange," he said. "See if they've got anything for a retired poodle."

He slammed the door so hard on his way out the barometer slipped sideways off its nail.

Delia Olvanie said, "I wouldn't mind going to America. If it'd be any help."

But it wasn't. Kick wanted her old Nora and nobody else would do.

"Uh-oh," she kept saying, when she got back from her shopping. It was her latest little catchphrase. "Uh-oh, what are we going to do about Walter?"

You could have billeted the Household Cavalry between us that night, the way we both slept clinging to the edge of the mattress, and when I woke up he was packing his valise.

I said, "Where are you going?"

"What's it to you?" he said.

I told him I didn't want him to go.

He said, "That's something, I suppose."

He was very calm.

He said, "Are you still set on this American jaunt?"

I said, "It's not a jaunt."

"Is it not?" he said. "Well, there we are then. They say English and Americans don't speak the same language. Over here, when a person goes off thousands of miles when there's no necessity, we call it a jaunt. I'm afraid I blame the war for this. Before the war the husband were head of the house and the wife went wherever he decided. Now everybody pleases theirselves. Well, I hope you won't regret it, Nora. I hope your Kennedys do the right thing by you."

He slipped away quietly before Kick was awake, but she soon knew about it when Delia Olvanie went in with her breakfast tray, shedding her crocodile tears over Walter, angling to go to America in my place so me and Walter could be reconciled.

She sent for me.

She said, "Has he really gone?"

I wasn't sure. He'd taken a bag. He hadn't kissed me on the back of my neck like he usually did to say "Good morning."

I said, "I don't think marriage is what he expected."

"Gosh," she said. "But isn't this a bit radical? We're only going on a little trip. Husbands and wives didn't see each other for years during the war."

I said, "Wartime was different. And Walter's old-fashioned. He thinks drivers should drive and housekeepers should house-keep, and wives should be at home when the hubby comes in at night."

She said, "I see. So should I take Delia instead? It wouldn't be the same, but I guess I could."

I had the choice. I stood there in that messy bedroom and it was left to me whether I ran after Stallybrass or did what I really wanted to do.

I said, "No. I'm going to come with you for Joe's dedication."

Well, then I was her Darling Nora, of course.

She said, "But what can we do about Walter?"

I said, "Nothing. He's in a monkey mood. But we do have to get a few things straight, sweetheart. I have to know where I stand. What if you decide to stay on in America? You know your Daddy'll start persuading you the minute you set foot. What if he makes you give up Smith Square? He won't pay for me to come back without you. He already thinks I owe him for staying behind when war broke out, and your Daddy never forgets a debt."

She said, "He won't persuade me, he won't. I'll definitely come back here and we'll make Walter come home and everything'll be fine. I'm going to telephone Dookie. I'll tell him what's happened and I'll ask him to absolutely not let Walter back on the estate."

I said, "Don't do that. He loves that place. Just leave him be. He'll go and stay with Hope and he'll simmer down eventually. This is likely what happens when old-timers get wed. It's like putting on a new pair of shoes when you've been shuffling around in the same comfy old barges for years. They're sure to pinch."

She said, "I didn't mean to upset him. Do I really not pay you much?"

I said, "No, not very much. We live in, of course. We don't have to find rent. But he worries about the future, you see. After fifty you have to think about these things, particularly when you've never had a place of your own."

"Do you?" she said. "I'm not much good about money. I don't really know how much I've got."

They were all like that. They could have whatever they wanted and Mr. Kennedy's office paid their bills, so they never kept track. And they'd money of their own too. I remembered Mr. K explaining it to me when they were still tiny tots. He said he was putting money in trust for them, so it'd be safe from spendthrift ways any of them might slide into and they'd always have enough to be able to do more important things in life than scrabble for a living. But none of them ever seemed to know what they were worth, or how much ordinary folk had to live on. Jack had touched me for ten shillings when he was over that summer, to save him rushing to the bank before it closed, and I knew I'd never see that again. It was forgotten the minute it was in his pocket.

She said, "Oh you mustn't worry about when you're old. I'll always look after you, Nora. Cross my heart and hope to die."

Perpetual Light

We stayed in New York, at the Biltmore, and a car was sent to bring us up to St. Francis Xavier for Joe's memorial. There was standing room only in the church. Half of Hyannis had turned out, not out of any great love for the Kennedys but I suppose they wanted to take a look at Congressman Jack, see if it was really the same hooligan that used to thieve gum from Scussett's store. All the children were there, except Rosie, and she was the one I'd have liked to see more than anyone else. It had been seven years since I'd seen the younger ones and I'd hardly have recognized Bobby or Jean or Teddy. The three Gargan cousins too, and Lem Billings, Mr. and Mrs. Moore, of course, and Danny Walsh, that I'd never have known either, he'd run so to fat. I sat with Gertie, and we had a lovely cry when they sang the *Lux aeterna*.

There was tea and sandwiches served at the house afterwards and Kick said I was to mingle with everybody else in the parlor, like a regular guest, but I could never have done that. I stayed in the kitchen with Gertie Ambler, and in the end I saw everybody I wanted to see. Lem was the first to come looking for me.

"Nurse Strict!" he said. "I'll bet you don't remember me."

I said, "I never forget anyone who's kept me awake at night with their giggling."

"Ah yes," he said. "The rap of Nurse Strict's shoe on the ceiling."

He was living in New York, writing advertisements for a living. He had a bit of shrapnel in his leg, but he said it only pained him if it got below freezing. No sweetheart, as yet. Too busy, he said.

Teddy appeared, looking for more sandwiches, and then Pattie. Teddy was only fifteen, but he'd already grown taller than Bobby and he'd bigger bosoms on him than Euny. If he'd been a girl Herself would have had him on one of her regimes, I'm sure, but she could never see any fault in her boys.

He said, "Why are you here? Do you still work for us?"

Pat said, "Why, Ted? Does your diaper need changing?"

Gertie said, "Is it cake you're looking for, Pat?"

"No," she said, "I'm looking for a drink. Do you have any rye down here?"

Teddy said, "Daddy says you shouldn't drink. I'm gonna tell."

"Go ahead and tell, Fat Boy," she said. "I really don't give a damn."

Pattie had grown into quite a beauty. Hard though. She'd no time for her old Nora. She was too busy searching for liquor.

Don't they say you should never go back?

Gertie said, "The best thing for Pattie would be if this was made a dry house."

I said, "I suppose it's the upset of the memorial service."

"Not really," she said. "Pat likes her rye whatever the occasion."

Mr. K didn't speak to me that day.

I'd heard him outside the church, talking up a storm about Jack's prospects and about Bobby going to Law School, but the sparkle was gone out of his eyes, and when Mrs. Moore told me exactly what had happened to Joseph Patrick I understood why.

She said, "You know he volunteered to fly one of those Liberators. They were packed with explosives and that first month they lost nearly every one they sent up. There was a problem with the electrics for one thing, but Joe insisted on flying his mission. Somebody should just have grounded him, but he'd already had two stand-downs because of bad weather, so they let him go up. You know what he was like. He was worried the war would be over before he did something to top Jack's little adventure. Such a stupid waste."

So it wasn't only the loss of his boy that was weighing on Mr. K. In his heart of hearts he knew he was the one at the root of it.

"I don't want to hear from runners-up," he always used to say. "If somebody beats you, go right back out and practice till you're good enough to beat him. And I don't want to hear any of that applesauce about it's trying that matters. That's bull. Winning is what matters."

He'd made them vie with each other as well as the rest of the world and that was why young Joe was dead. Danny Walsh said, "What I hear, you've done all right for yourself, Brennan, riding on Her Ladyship's coattails."

I said, "I don't ride on anybody's coattails. I've spent six years doing war work, and my husband likewise. How about you?"

"Too old for the forces," he said. "I'd have volunteered for the Coast Guard but Your Man kept me on. Driving, security, that kind of thing. When you're well known like they are, you need staff you can trust. And now with Jack going into public life. See, it's not just the driving. You have to know how to handle yourself."

Danny always was a big bag of hot air.

I said, "It's Jack I can't get over. I never thought he'd get elected."

He came over all confidential.

He said, "I'll tell you something, between you and me. The amount old man Kennedy's spent, he could have got a chimpanzee elected."

Gertie Ambler said, "There's nothing wrong with that. It's his to spend, and there's never been an election fought in Boston where money didn't change hands. And it's helped Mr. K get over his loss, keeping busy with the campaign."

She told me how the news had come about Joseph Patrick. How Mr. K had gone up for his nap after lunch and Mrs. K was on the porch reading the Sundays when two Navy chaplains came to the door. The children were meant to be racing in a regatta out of Osterville and Mr. K wouldn't allow them to cancel.

"Kennedys carry on," he'd said. "It's what Joe would have done and you must do the same." Then he'd gone to his quarters and Mrs. K had gone to hers.

Gertie said, "She must have wept. What mother wouldn't? But I never saw her, not that day nor since. I heard the Ambassador though. He made those children take their boats out onto the Sound as if nothing had happened, but he shut himself up in his room and there wasn't a corner of the house where you couldn't hear his sobbing."

I knew Mrs. K had noticed me at the church but she didn't speak to me till people were leaving.

"Nora, dear heart," she said, "wasn't it a wonderful memorial service? Everyone came."

I said, "I'm so sorry for your loss. He was a fine boy. One of the best."

"The very best," she said, "but life goes on. Jack will take over now. He'll do very well. You must see a great many changes here."

I didn't. It was eight years since I'd set foot at Hyannis but it felt like only yesterday. There wasn't a stick of furniture that had changed and there was a pair of rotten old sneakers slung behind the kitchen door I'd swear had been there since 1938. The whole place could have used a coat of paint and some new drapes.

And the children had just grown into the people they'd always been going to be. Euny doing everything at a sprint, Bobby wanting to be taken seriously, Jean trying to make elbow room for herself in the family picture.

First thing Jean said to me was "Nora, who do I look like? Not Bobby. Don't dare tell me I look like Bobby."

I said, "Darling girl, you look like Jean Ann Kennedy and there's only one of you in the world."

"Yes," she said. "But I look quite like Joe, don't you think? And by the way, I have the nicest legs of all the girls in my class." Sorry little mite.

I got the "dear heart" treatment from Mrs. K for five minutes. That tight little smile. Those hard, shiny eyes.

She said, "You did leave us in a fix, Nora. I could still be rather cross with you. When Mary Moore told me what you'd done I couldn't believe it. You were always so steady. I absolutely trusted you, you know? How could you run off like that?"

I said, "I didn't exactly run off, Mrs. Kennedy. I gave the Ambassador notice. And I went to Rosie's graduation. I went with Mrs. Moore, you know."

She started fiddling with her watchband when I said Rosie's name.

She said, "People do such silly things when war breaks out."

I said, "You still had Fidelma. I knew you'd be able to manage with her."

"Fidelma!" she said. "There's another one who abandoned her post. Well, I hope you married a good Catholic at least."

I said, "No, Walter's an Undecided. He doesn't really hold with the Church. But he's a good man."

"Oh," she said, "I don't see how that can be."

But if you ask me, Mr. K himself wasn't the kind of Catholic she made him out to be. He'd go to Mass but only because it was the done thing. He liked to be seen in the front pew, and it was an easy way of keeping Mrs. K sweet, but I reckon he just thought of Our Blessed Lady as someone worth having on his team, like Jimmy Roosevelt.

She said, "Of course we don't keep the staff we used to. Jean's boarding at Noroton and Teddy's going to Milton. The Ambassador and I have hotel suites now. It's so much more convenient. And are you back in the States to stay?"

I said, "No. I came with Kick, for the dedication."

She said, "How extravagant. Did Kathleen pay for you to come?"

I said, "I wouldn't be here if she hadn't. I do work for her, you know? I keep house for her at Smith Square."

"Oh yes," she said, "Smith Square. The Devonshires put her up to that, I'm sure. Another extravagance. Well, the sooner she gets London and that whole episode out of her system the better. She should come home and make herself useful. Euny and Pat have been the backbone of Jack's campaign, and this is only the start."

I said, "How's Rosie going on, Mrs. Kennedy? I'm hoping to visit with her while I'm here."

And her face snapped shut like the cover on a pocket watch. She said, "There's very little point. She won't know you."

I said, "Is there nothing can be done? If an operation caused it, can't another operation put it right?"

"No," she said. "Anyway it wasn't necessarily *caused* by the operation. Rosie became a very difficult girl after she came home from London. You weren't here. You don't know. We did everything we could for the best. She's very comfortable at Craig House and you know one very good thing that's come out of all this is Euny and Pat's interest in mental handicap. They're starting up some very worthwhile projects.

"It's something Kathleen should think of doing too. I must talk to her about it. It would do her far more good than languishing in London spending money on houses. It's a terribly good cause, and of course if the Kennedys become known for such things it can only help Jack."

There were still a few guests lingering in the house, but as far as she was concerned, the party was over. She went off down to the strand, to her cabin. She must have been glad of that hidey-hole. To look at her at the dedication you'd never have taken her for a woman who'd lost two beautiful children, she looked so bright and polished. The only way she managed it, I'm sure, was to save her heartache for when she was alone in her little white hut.

Me and Kick went our separate ways after Hyannis. She'd promised to visit Nancy Tenney, to see her baby girl, and then go down to Washington to catch up with her old crowd. I went to Boston, to see if my nephew had really turned out as peculiar as his brother said he had.

Margaret said, "Ray's not here. He's in New York. He works at Lord and Taylor in Footwear, doing ever so well."

Val wasn't there either. After he'd been demobilized he'd gone into the police department, to Albany. He had a girlfriend there. Margaret said he'd wanted to go into some line of work where he could still carry a gun.

The way things had worked out over the years, Margaret had grown bigger as Frankie had gotten smaller. There never was much of Frankie Mulcahy, but by 1946 he was like a wee goblin, bent over from all the coughing and wheezing and hawking. Still getting through three packs of smokes every day though.

He said, "I cut back. And these are mentholated. They're meant to be good for asthma."

Margaret worked evenings at a place that sold hot dogs and frozen custard and things like that. She got a discount, so soft-serve ice cream was pretty much what she lived on. Ray had bought them a Kelvinator and she had all the flavors.

She said, "I suppose you know Ursie's out of her mind?"

I said, "Val didn't say anything when I saw him."

"He wouldn't," she said. "She's been the same ever since he remembers. She asks you the same thing, over and over."

Ursie had retired, that was the trouble. She'd nothing to do all day, only dust under her lace doilies and heat up a can of soup. She came over on the bus.

Margaret said, "Whatever you do, don't mention Mr. Jauncey."

I didn't need to. Ursie walked in, a bit grayer on the temples than the last time I saw her but not much altered otherwise. First thing she said was "You know, Nora, I've never believed Mr. Jauncey had claudication of the arteries. I'm sure it was nothing but plain old charley horse, but you see his wife was determined to move to Marblehead. She'd been plotting it for years."

I said, "How are you, Ursie? It's been a while."

"It has, it has," she said. "And I'm glad to see you because I have a Belleek teapot bought for your wedding present. I didn't care to send it at the time in case it was sunk by a U-boat, but now you're here you shall have it."

Margaret said, "Give it to me, Ursie. It's too late for a wedding gift. He's upped and left her."

"Nora!" she said. "What a thing! Was it another woman?"

I said, "No, it wasn't. It was just us wanting different things."

It sounded a poor excuse when it was told to someone who didn't know how things were.

Margaret said, "What kind of things? Do you mean dining sets and that kind of thing?"

Ursie said, "It doesn't matter what things. Better she found out sooner than later, that's all. And I can't say I'm entirely surprised. You went into it with unseemly haste, Nora. You and Margaret have always been silly about men."

Margaret said, "What do you mean, 'silly about men'? I've been with Frankie twenty-seven years."

Ursie said, "Is that all it is? It's seemed longer. Well, at least Nora's free again, and wiser I hope."

I said, "Nora's not free again. I'm still married to Walter. It's just that he wants to live in the boondocks and I don't. But that's our business. Now why don't you give Margaret the teapot? I reckon she's earned it after twenty-seven years with Frankie."

"I will not," she said. "Look at the state of her cups. Margaret bangs about and chips everything she touches. I shall take it back to the store."

It was all the same to me. I don't care for Belleek.

"Now," she said, "I've been wanting to talk to you about the house. Our house. It was left between us, you'll remember. One-fifth shares each."

I said, "You're not going back?"

"No," she said, "of course not. Mr. Jauncey will be coming out of retirement momentarily and he'll need me back at my post. But the last I heard, Edmond had shifted to Tullamore with that wife, and if I know him he'll have gone off and left it with the door unlocked. You're in that part of the world, Nora. You might think of going to inspect the place when you have a minute."

I said, "Ursie, I live in London. I never set foot in Ireland. And anyway, what's to be done about the house? I don't give a tinker's about it. It was a hovel."

"It was not," she said. "It's a solid stone house and our birthright. And there's the land. We're entitled to it, and if you don't want your share, I'll take it. I'll hold it for Deirdre. If she ever goes home she'll need a roof over her head."

Margaret said, "Are you sure it still has a roof? The Clavin widow likely took the tiles with her when they quit."

I said, "And Deirdre's been thirty-five years in Africa. If she goes back to Ballynagore she'll be dead of the damp before she's unpacked her trunk. You have the house, Ursie, and welcome to it. But don't depend on me to find out if it's still standing."

"Well," she said, "I'd have to have that in writing. I'm sure Mr. Jauncey would be very happy to draft something for us. He didn't at all want to retire, you know, but his wife nagged and nagged him to do it."

Margaret said, "Sweet Jesus, not Mr. Jauncey again. The man must be eighty if he's a day."

I said, "I'm in service with Lady Hartington now, you know, Ursie? With Kathleen Kennedy as was? She won't ever be Duchess now because Lord Billy's dead and gone, but she still goes as Lady Hartington."

"Oh yes," she said, "it was in the dailies about her getting married. Not a big write-up, but I did cut it out to send to Deirdre. But I'm afraid we don't have such a high opinion of the Kennedys as we used to, not since Mr. Kennedy went for Ambassador. Mr. Jauncey said the man was an embarrassment to us in London and a thorn in the flesh of the poor President. I'm afraid we think them all rather vulgar."

Margaret said, "Speak for yourself. I went to one of those Meet the Kennedys coffee parties, for the election, and I thought they were grand. One of the Altar Guild ladies held it in her conservatory. It wasn't the boy, the one who was running, but two of the sisters came, lovely, tall, smiling girls, and then Mrs. Kennedy. She drove up in a big limousine car. Beautiful powder-blue costume and an ostrich feather hat. Honestly, Nora, it was like meeting the President. Better probably. She gave us a little talk, about being Mayor Fitzgerald's daughter, and how she's raised nine children, and all about visiting with the King and Queen at some castle in England."

I said, "That was Windsor. And the King and Queen were asked back. I saw them as close as that door."

She said, "I know. I remembered you writing about it. I told everybody there about you and I'd have mentioned you to Mrs. Kennedy only I never got near enough to speak. She asked were there any Gold Star Mothers present, which there were, Laura Checketts for one, lost her only boy in Burma. She had a special word with them. And then she said she hoped we'd vote for her Jack, because boys like him were America's great future. And I did vote for him."

I said, "Well, Jack's a fine lad. Though I can't say Mrs. K had much of a hand in raising him nor any of them. She knows how to put on a good show though. She learned that from the Queen of England. And you know your Val went dancing with Lady Kathleen when he was in London?"

Ursie said, "Yes. He wrote and told us all. He said she was a very pleasant girl. And now Val's in the police. We've that to be thankful for. One of Margaret's boys has turned out all right."

Margaret said, "Both of Margaret's boys have turned out all right. There's nothing wrong with shop work."

Ursie said, "Ray should have gone into something worthwhile, like insurance, or banking. You get no respect in shop work, but you see, Nora, all he's interested in is clothes. And New York! Well!"

Margaret said, "Will you take some ice cream, Nora? I've strawberry flavor and chocolate."

I said, "There's nothing wrong with New York. He'll have wanted to spread his wings, same as we did. You've got a short memory."

"Not the same thing at all," Ursie said. "I found a good position and stuck to it. And I saved for a rainy day. Ray spends every cent he earns. He's just like his father. And if he must work in retail he could have gone to Jordan Marsh. Mr. Jauncey always buys his shirts at Jordan Marsh."

Margaret said, "Here we go again."

And Ursie started right back in, like a broken phonograph record.

She said, "You know, Nora, I've never believed Mr. Jauncey had claudication of the arteries. I'm sure it was plain old charley horse, but you see his wife was determined to move to Marblehead. She'd been plotting it for years."

31

The Latest Thing for Diseases of the Mind

Fidelma Clery was on 230th Street, living over the brush with a man called Horace. He'd been kept out of the military because of brain seizures, so he'd spent the war doing paperwork, at the shipyard where she'd gone as a riveter.

She said, "He's all right, for a 4F. He's still got a bit of snap in his celery."

She was scandalized when she heard me and Walter were living apart.

I said, "It's not so easy, this marriage business. Especially when you go into it later in life. When you've been accustomed to pleasing yourself."

She said, "Pleasing yourself? Working for Queen Kennedy? One night off a week and a load of theatricals if you asked for a raise, is that what you call pleasing yourself? You want your bumps felt, Brennan. Given up the chance of a little house and a man with a job for life? For a Kennedy? I wouldn't depend on the

Kennedys for anything. If you ask me, they've had their day. We had the best of it when we were at Prince's Gate."

She wasn't the first I'd heard give that opinion. There were plenty who thought Mr. K had come off badly, that he'd put his shirt on the wrong horse, saying the Germans could never be beaten. But Joe Kennedy never put his shirt on anything. He was too canny for that. He was certainly all right for money. But he had stuck out, still arguing against the war when there were brave American boys volunteering, so in that respect the tide had turned against him. And that was what people remembered. They took him to be a sidestepper even though he'd lost his own son, who'd been the star in his crown.

I said, "Well, I know he won't be doing any more ambassadoring. Those days are over. But I'd still like to follow what the youngsters are up to and Kick surely needed somebody to come with her to face the music, especially now Joe's gone. You know he was the only one who really stood by her when she married Lord Billy. And Herself won't give her a minute's peace till she's back in the fold. Then she'll start campaigning for her to get an annulment, I'll bet you anything. She won't rest till she's wiped Lord Billy off the slate."

Fidelma said, "How is she?"

I said, "She's started going dancing again. I don't know. They only had two weeks together. They can hardly have known each other. But there are plenty of others in her shoes. She's gone to see Nancy Tenney while we're over. She's left on her own as well, and with a child to raise. I want to go to Craig House while I'm here. I want to see for myself what they've done to my darling Rosie. Do you know how to get there?"

"Yes," she said. "I do. Is Kick going with you?"

But Kick had never quite answered me about that. She'd said

she'd think about it. I'd asked Jean and Teddy if they'd like to write her a little note. Jean said I'd better not upset Mother talking about Rosie, and Teddy said only family was allowed to visit, but then he went scrambling off on his bicycle to Scussett's and came back with a box of Almond Joys for her. He went himself too, instead of sending Joey Gargan like he usually did when he couldn't be bothered, and his eyes filled up when he asked me to give them to Rosie.

Fidelma said, "Euny was at the nursing home one time when I went. She said they had thought of having her to Hyannis for a week in the summer but Mr. K had kiboshed that. He said it was too liable to unsettle her."

Horace came home and the whiskey bottle came out before he'd even hung up his cap. Not like my Walter. The first thing he looked for was a brew of tea. I felt a long way from home that moment, sitting in Fidelma Clery's walk-up, drinking liquor I didn't want with a man I hardly knew. I wasn't even sure where home was anymore.

We had cheese and crackers for our dinner and then Horace fell asleep.

Fidelma said, "You know what, Nora? When you go to see Rosie, I'll come with you. We'll take the bus."

It's a pleasant ride from the city up to Beacon. When a person needs caring for night and day you couldn't ask for a better-favored place than Craig House. It has beautiful lawns where the patients can be taken for walks, and seats set under the trees with a view down to the Fishkill Creek. And the inside is very fancy. They have parlors where they can sit with their visitors, and a chapel and a dining room. There's even a grand piano. Fidelma said there was another part, for the bad cases that need locking up, but we didn't see any of that. In fact, we hardly saw anyone, just a couple of poor souls shuffling along a corridor with their visitors.

Rosie has two Sisters who take care of her. I suppose Mr. K bungs them a bit extra, so they'll make sure she's all right. She has her own bedroom and bathroom and everything she needs. More like a hotel than a sanitarium really, with a few of her little bits and pieces to make her feel at home. There were cushions I remembered from the house in Bronxville and some of her dollies, and a painting of yachts racing on Nantucket Sound. No photographs though. Sister Bernadette asked us most particularly not to give her photographs, because they make her agitated.

She came walking towards us so fast and eager I thought she'd recognized me, but that's just the way she walks now. Going nowhere in a hurry. She was clean and tidy except for her hair.

I said, "Fetch me your comb, Rosie. Let me make your hair pretty."

But she just gazed at my shopping bag, as if she was wondering was there anything in it for her.

She'd put on weight of course, for they feed them a lot better at Craig House than at the Kennedys, and she's not forever getting hauled out to play football or do her daily gymnastics like she would have been at home. She has her own personal phonograph and a wireless, and plenty of magazines. Sister Barbara said she loves her magazines. She'll look at the same one over and over and never tire of it.

When it was decided to send her for the operation, Mr. K. told Fidelma it would calm her down and stop her from getting nervous tension. He said it was the very latest development, being done for all kinds of diseases of the mind, even things like Communism and men going with men. He said they were lucky to get her an appointment so quickly, because there was quite a waiting list, and that apart from a bit of bruising around her eyes and a patch where they shaved away her hair she'd be the same, the same old Rosie, only happier. Well, doctors can be wrong. It was the same old house she used to live in, you might say, only my Rosie wasn't at home.

She ripped open the candy Teddy had sent her and ate every last piece, though she'd only just had her luncheon, and then she sat, not looking at anything in particular. She has one arm that doesn't move. She carries it tucked tight against her bosoms. The other arm never stops. Up and down all the time, with her hand like a chubby little claw, as if there's something bothering her, as if she's trying to recall something, trying to catch hold of it and it keeps fluttering away.

We'd taken stale bread with us, because when Fidelma had visited with her before, the Sisters had said she loved to go out into the grounds and feed the birds. But all she did was dump out the whole lot onto the path and walk away. She seemed to have forgotten about feeding birds, and how to smile. She knew her name. If you said it she'd look at you, but it was an empty look.

We talked between ourselves, me and Fidelma, bringing up things she might remember, watching her to see if she caught on. About the day Teddy was christened and she was allowed to carry him into the church, proud as a queen. About the night she was presented at Buckingham Palace, her and Kick with Prince of Wales feathers pinned in their hair and Mrs. K dazzling us all with her diamonds. And the little club her and Kick got up with Nancy Tenney, to swap pictures of the film stars, and how Miss Swanson paid them a visit and signed her autograph.

Fidelma said, "Do you remember the first time the old goat brought Miss Swanson home? For afternoon tea, if you like! He's the brass front of the devil, that one. And Miss Swanson had on that gold cape and a cocktail gown, but Mrs. K was all buttoned up in a cardigan set, smiling and passing the cream. You know, I've often thought he could have diddled one of his sweeties right there on the parlor couch and Herself would have carried on smiling and pouring the tea."

It wasn't a nice thing to speak of in front of Rosie. I remembered Danny Walsh trying to see up Miss Swanson's skirt as she went up the ladder into the loft over Mr. Tenney's garage, but I wouldn't have talked about it in front of the children. Mrs. K was right though. Rosie didn't appear to understand anything. So I thought I could at least stop fretting about her, parked there while the family carried on without her. It didn't make her sad, because she didn't remember what had been. The way she kept rifling through the empty candy box, she didn't even seem to remember she'd eaten them all not half an hour before.

But then, when we'd put our hats on and it was time to go, she got me in such a bear hug with her arm that jiggled and clung to me and mewed such funny little sounds into my ear.

"Nor nor nor," she was saying. "Nor nor nor."

I believe she did remember me. Sister Bernadette came to take her to her room, and still she clung to me. I thought my heart should have broke.

Fidelma said, "You have to sing 'On the Lovely Banks of Laune.' She loves that. That used to calm her down if she got into one of her paddies."

Sister Bernadette said, "We don't get into paddies anymore, do we, Rose Marie? You have to realize, madam, she's not the person you knew. None of the old things apply anymore."

Fidelma sang it anyway,

> *In the green arbutus shadow*
> *On the lovely banks of Laune.*
> *I would rock my laughing lassie*
> *In her cradle, up and down . . .*

but Rosie just walked away with the Sister and never once looked back.

Neither of us spoke till we were on the bus.

I said, "We shouldn't have come. All we've done is upset her."

She said, "That wasn't upset. That was her remembering something. It was probably the smell of you when she gave you a hug. Well, I shall still come. It's a nice trip out and one of these days she might just come to, like waking up from a long sleep, and we'll have our old Rosie back. The only thing that bothers me, I wouldn't like to run into Herself. I suppose she'll be turning up one of these days."

Five years Rosie had been there and neither her Mammy nor her Daddy had visited.

Fidelma said, "When we were working for them, did old man Kennedy ever, you know? Did he ever try it on?"

I said, "What, with me? Hardly. He liked glamour-pusses, not nursery maids. I had my behind pinched a few times by Mayor Fitzgerald, but that was years back. In the end I learned to dodge him."

She said, "Your Man liked the glamour-pusses when he could get them but he'd settle for anything that was handy for a quickie. That's what happens when men are kept on short commons at home."

I said, "You're not telling me he tried anything with you?"

"Sure he did," she said. "At Beals Street. I'd only just started with them so I thought I'd better oblige. I thought it maybe went with the job. It does at some places, you know?"

You never could be sure with Fidelma. She was a bit of a romancer.

I said, "He never did. What if Mrs. Kennedy had walked in on you?"

"Oh," she said, "he wasn't that stupid and neither was I. It was when she'd run off home to her Daddy, remember? When she was expecting Kick?"

I said, "Did he come to your room?"

"God Almighty," she said. "I don't think he'd have known where my room was. No, he had me in the pantry. It was all over very fast. It was a bit like getting the smallpox shot."

I said, "Why did you never mention it before?"

"I don't know," she said. "To be honest, Brennan, you always struck me as a bit of a prude. I wonder he didn't try it on with you though. I reckon he'd have liked someone who put up a little fight. And you were better-looking than I was."

I said, "Well, he never tried a thing with me and just as well. You wouldn't have seen me for dust. I could never have looked Mrs. K in the face again."

"Oh," she said, "I thought that was the best part of it. Looking at her and thinking, 'Your old man might have a pot of money because he's nothing to write home about in the other department.'"

I said, "Was it just the once?"

"No," she said, "it was any time he thought of it, until Herself came home. Do you remember how she got the red-carpet treatment? Anything in the world she wanted. We know what her price was. A new car and a bigger house. So, when you married your man, Nora, you were still a virgin. That must have come as a shock, at your time of life."

I'd never said I was a virgin.

32

The Official Black Sheep

I went twice to Lord and Taylor looking for Margaret's boy Ray.
The first time the man I spoke to in Footwear said he'd never heard
of him, but I went back when the manager was there and he said
they had had a young Mr. Mulcahy and he believed he might now
be working at Saks. And that was where I found him, in Formal
Wear. He'd dropped the "Ray" and was going as "Ramon."

He's a good-looking lad, but stunted, like his father.

He said, "I haven't grown since thirteen. Malnourished. Any
seconds, Val always got first dibs. If you don't mind my saying,
Aunt Nora, you shouldn't bunch your scarf up like a piece of old
rag. Here, let me drape it for you."

I said, "When you've finished dressing me, can I take you for
a steak dinner?"

"No thank you," he said. "I don't eat animals that have dirty
bottoms. But an egg salad sandwich would be eminently okey-
dokey."

We went to Schrafft's just down Fifth Avenue. He was living in Brooklyn, one room but with its own hand basin. No girl-friend.

He said, "I don't really go for girls, Aunt Nora. Not that way. But I expect Aunt Ursie already warned you."

I said, "I'm not interested in stories like that."

As a matter of fact, I thought it might be a fashion he was going through. I'm sure things like that never existed before the war. But he's going on twenty-four now and still not courting, so maybe it is just the way he is.

I said, "As long as you're not lonely. New York's a big place to be on your own. Have you made any pals?"

"Sure," he said, "I pal around with a crowd of the girls from the store. I'm doing okay. It'd be great to get a bigger room but I wouldn't want to live with anyone. People are so messy. Mom's messy. And Val loves all that jock bunkhouse stuff. I tell you, if you'd had to share with Val you'd have left home too. So you're the one who got away. I remember you visited us one time. You brought a friend with you who smiled all the time."

I said, "That was Rosie Kennedy. I was her nursery maid."

"Oh yes," he said, "Mom tells everyone you work for the Kennedys. They're rolling in it, aren't they? Do they eat off gold plates and everything?"

I said, "No, they eat off Fiestaware."

"Oh," he said, "I see. They're that kind of rich. Mrs. Kennedy looks kinda spiffy though in her pictures. Her clothes always look good. What is it with their teeth though? They got shares in Pepsodent? There's a couple of those Kennedy girls got way too many teeth in their mouth. More isn't always best. You should tell them."

I walked back with him to the store.

He said, "I can't believe you came looking for me. It was so sweet of you. And just to think, when I got up this morning I thought it was going to be an ordinary old day. I'm going to take you to meet my friends in Fragrances. Show them I'm not a poor pathetic orphan after all."

He got a "Hello, Ramon" from all the salesgirls.

He said, "This is my aunt Nora. She works for those toothy Kennedys and she's come all the way from London, England, to see me. Isn't that something! Aunt Nora, name your perfume."

I said, "I can't afford to buy scent."

"Perfume," he said. "Call it perfume. It sounds nicer. And I'm buying. I get a discount. We'll take your smallest Arpège, Doreen, gift-wrapped."

I went into St. Patrick's after I left him, and lit four candles. One for the soul of Joseph Patrick, one for poor Rosie, one for Ramon Novarro Mulcahy, that he have a long and happy life and not fall into sinful New York ways, and one for Walter Stally-brass, who doesn't hold with candles, but I've never allowed that to stop me lighting them for him.

Me and Kick were on our way back to London by the end of April, though there were times I'd thought I'd be sailing on my own. They'd done everything they could to get her to stay. Mr. K had offered to get her a good position with a newspaper, so she could write up everything Jack did and keep the family in the limelight. Mrs. K wanted her to go shopping with her sisters and pray the Nine Fridays and then start walking out with Tom Allen or some other nice Catholic boy. But she held out against them.

She said, "I love Pat and Euny and everybody. And I still like all the gang down in Washington. It's just that we don't have a lot to talk about. I guess the war changed everything. I've disappointed them though, Nora. I really hate to disappoint Daddy. And Mother's word used to be law, but I don't see things that way anymore. I'm the Kennedys' official Black Sheep. Next time I go to a costume party, that's what I'll go as."

She had no plans. No driver either. The Devonshires were more than willing to send Gardener Stallybrass down to drive for Her Ladyship again but Gardener Stallybrass declined to be sent. He said if it was all the same to Their Graces he'd prefer to stay and get his camellias back up to standard. Kick said if that was the case she'd manage without a driver.

She said, "I'll use taxicabs. It'll be something else to scandalize Mother. Or maybe I'll ride a bike. Wouldn't that be wild? I wonder what happened to my old Red Cross bike. I'd just love to turn up to Ginny Balderston's on that."

Lady Balderston, Ginny Vigo as was, had roped her in for a ball they were organizing, in aid of veterans from the Commando Corps. It was to be held at the Savoy and they were having committee meetings all the time. It was nice to see Kick with a good reason to get out of bed in the morning. But it was through the Ball Committee that she got to know Obby Fitzwilliam, and that wasn't such a good thing. Lady Fitzwilliam ran with a very fast set. Nothing but parties and drinking and slamming car doors in the middle of the night. Kick brought a crowd of them back a few times after they'd all been out dancing, but I think I made it clear that it wasn't convenient. It's one thing for people to carry on like that when they've a great big place like Chatsworth to get lost in, or the Fitzwilliams' place up in Yorkshire. It's one thing to spill liquor and leave ring marks and cigarette burns when you've help by the hundred, but not when all you have is a housekeeper and one apology for a housemaid.

I went down in my nightdress and wrap one time when I heard glass breaking and there they all were, lounging around in our nice little parlor, drunk as lords, and Lady Obby was standing on a chair singing "Somewhere Over the Rainbow." Most of them were older than Kick, old enough to know better. I know for a fact Lady Obby had a child at home. Sissy Ormsby-Gore didn't approve of her at all. "An old lush," she called her. She said she couldn't understand why Kick gave them the time of day.

But she didn't see them all the time. She had quite a number of admirers that summer. Lord Billy was in his grave two years already, so there was nothing wrong in it. She went sailing with Barrington Addy, and to a cricket match, and then there was Hugh Fraser that she liked, and Tony Rosslyn and Richard Wood. He was Lord Halifax's youngest boy. He'd been keen on Kick before the war but he'd bowed out when he knew Lord Billy was serious. Another real gentleman, Captain Wood. He'd come back from El Alamein on walking sticks and two tin legs but he was still a fine figure of a man and I believe he'd have gone a very long way to win Kick's heart. He wasn't Catholic, of course, but as Kick said, the kind of Catholic boy Mrs. K had in mind likely wouldn't want a bride who'd already been married to the enemy and denied the sacraments.

She said, "I do like Richard. I just don't think I could love him."

I said, "You said that about Lord Billy once upon a time."

"Did I?" she said. "Well, we'll see."

But then the Veterans Ball took place. Viscount Addy picked her up in his roadster. She went off in her pink satin, pretty as a picture, like a girl again, and she came home a changed person. Four o'clock in the morning she woke me up clattering up the stairs in her dance shoes. She dropped her little mink bolero on the floor and fell asleep still wearing her stockings. Twelve noon she had a gentleman caller on the front step, looking to take her to lunch. Lord Fitzwilliam. She didn't go. She hardly got her head off the pillow, too tired from all the dancing, but she saw him the next day and the next and the next. Three luncheons in a row.

I said, "I see his game. He has to go home to Her Ladyship

at night. That'll be why we never see him of an evening. But of course she'll never be up early enough to know what he's up to at lunchtime."

"Oh Nora," she said. "It's nothing like that. Obby doesn't do lunch. And anyway, Peter and I are only friends. I'm allowed to have friends aren't I? I'm allowed to eat?"

Well, there's eating and there's eating. How long can a ham salad take? One afternoon when Ginny Balderston came looking for her she still wasn't home at five.

She said, "Is she out with Fitzwilliam?"

It isn't a maid's place to do anything, only take a visitor's coat and packages, but Delia Olvanie had such a trap on her.

"Oh yes," she said. "Gone to lunch. Her Ladyship's out with him every day practically."

Lady Ginny pulled a face.

She said, "Well, tell her we were supposed to have tea. Tell her to call me would you?"

I don't know if she did. She neglected all her nice friends that summer, running around with Blood Fitzwilliam. Eventually it was dinners too. Lady Obby was in Ireland apparently, visiting with her people.

Kick hadn't told me that part. It was Sissy Ormsby-Gore who spilled those beans.

"Oh yes," she said, "she left directly after the Veterans' Ball. And she probably knows what's going on anyway. The Fitzwilliams are rather modern about things. I'm really shocked at Kick though. I thought she was a Sacred Heart girl through and through." And so did I, but Lord Fitzwilliam had turned her head. People would invite her out but she turned everything down, sitting by the telephone until she got his call. She'd be out till all hours and I couldn't sleep till I knew she was safe in her bed. I'd lie awake listening for His Lordship's motor squealing to a halt outside.

Three, four o'clock, night after night. Then in the morning neither one of us was fit for anything.

I said, "If you didn't come home so late you wouldn't be too tired to wipe off your face powder. Look at the state of your pillowslip."

"Soooorry," she'd say. "Soooorry."

I said, "Half past three you banged that door. And I'll bet you didn't say your prayers."

She swore she did.

She said, "Nora, don't be cross. I'm having such a lovely summer. Aren't I allowed a nice time?"

I said, "He's married."

"Not for much longer," she said. "He and Obby are kind of separated. Like you and Walter."

I said, "You leave me and Walter out of this. We're not the ones carrying on. What do you mean by separated? They didn't look separated when they were here carousing night after night."

She said, "They were just keeping up appearances, till after the ball. But they've actually been living apart for ages and they're going to get divorced. And then Blood and I'll get married."

I said, "That's nice. Then the family'll never speak to you again as long as you live. It was a hard enough frost set in when you married Lord Billy, and except for his church they couldn't have asked for a nicer boy. They'll wash their hands of you, and if you ask me, Lord Fitzwilliam isn't worth it."

She said, "You don't know him. And Jack'll still talk to me. He doesn't have to listen to Mother anymore."

I said, "And when is this divorce coming off?"

"Next year, probably," she said. "The thing is, Obby's quite tricky. Some days she's all for getting on with things and then she goes on one of her benders and starts throwing things. Blood has to handle her carefully. So it's up to him."

I said, "Don't you think you should stay out of it? Why don't you go out with Captain Wood or one of those other nice boys? Let Lord and Lady Fitzwilliam make their own arrangements? If he's really the one for you, you'll still be here when all the nastiness is over."

I was worried she'd be named in the divorce proceedings.

She said, "But I don't want to date some nice boy. I love Blood."

There was no reasoning with her, even when Christmas was coming and His Lordship told her he'd have to go to Yorkshire to spend the holiday with Lady Obby.

She said, "He doesn't want to go. He's only going for the child's sake."

I said, "If you say so, sweetheart."

She said, "Don't look at me like that. And don't be so grouchy every time Blood's name comes up. We're going to have a wonderful Christmas, I've decided. Now listen."

She put on her "pretty, please" face.

She said, "I ordered you a very special Christmas present but now I'm not sure if you're going to like it."

I said, "I don't need Christmas presents. I need you to behave."

"No, no," she said. She was jumping about in her bare feet. "You do need a present. Just promise you won't get mad when I tell you."

We were to go to Chatsworth from Christmas Eve until the New Year.

She was trying her hand at matchmaking, or "patch-up-making," as she called it, throwing me back in the path of Walter Stallybrass.

I said, "I'm not going up there. He'll think he's won. Take Delia. She can maid for you. I'll stay here."

"No," she said, "Delia won't do. It has to be you, Nora, so I hope you're not going to disobey orders. I hope I'm not going to have to dismiss you for insurrection."

Her intentions were good, but Kick never thought things through.

I said, "Nothing's changed, you see. Walter's been all his life with the Devonshires and I've been thirty years of my life with you Kennedys. We're both too set in our ways to change."

She said, "But you were so adorable together. I loved watching you, even when you got cross with each other."

I said, "And we got cross with each other far too much. We only got married because we thought the world was going to end. A lot of people did in 1939."

She said, "But I feel so terrible every time I think about your being apart. If Billy hadn't been killed we'd have been up and down to Derbyshire all the time and we could all have lived happily ever after. Walter's such a dear. Please don't be cross. Please come and maid for me over Christmas and talk to him at least."

I managed to finish a striped muffler for him on the ride north, white and black, until I ran out of the black yarn. I had to do the last few stripes in blue. It wasn't my best effort, but there was no heating on the train and you can't knit well when you've lost the feeling in your fingers. I quite thought he'd be there to meet us when we got to Bakewell. My guts were all churned up and I don't know for why, because he was only my husband. But they'd sent old Barker from the stables to pick us up and not even in livery.

He said, "I'm sorry it's the shooting brake, my lady, but we can't get the parts for the sedan."

Kick sat up front with him. She never played the ladyship, I will say.

I said, "The last time I was up here we had a driver called Wildgoose. A young lad."

He said, "That must have been before the war. He were a POW with the Japs. Come home looking like a skellington."

I said, "Will he be all right?"

"Who can say?" he said. "He's gone for a lathe operator at a factory in Chesterfield. There's a lot of them not coming back to the estate, one way or another. Bloody war. Things'll never be the same."

The big house had been used for a school while the war was on, and they were still putting it to rights. There were rooms where everything was still under dust sheets and rooms that stood empty, ready to be cleaned and painted, but there was a Christmas tree dressed in the front hall and a small fire burning. Kick could have been at Palm Beach, warm enough to go swimming and drive around in an open-top car, but I could see why she was happier to be at Lord Billy's home. She could have his sisters for company and mull over her memories. I even thought it might bring her to her senses about that chancer Fitzwilliam before it was the scandal of the year. I'm sure if Their Graces had had wind of what had been going on they never would have made her so welcome.

I was nervous as a housemaid starting on her first day. Every corner I turned I expected to bump into Walter. I didn't go down to the servants' hall till the very last minute and when I did walk in, everything went quiet. Hope saw me and turned her back, banging her saucepans and chivvying the girl to get the plates out of the warmer. There were a lot of new faces, but it was obvious they knew all about me.

I said, "Hello, Hope. How are you? I've a Christmas card for you, from Vincent's Dairy."

"Oh aye?" she said.

One of the maids said, "Walter not in tonight, Mrs. Stallybrass?" and that fool footman Cleaver said, "Which Mrs. Stallybrass are you addressing, Florrie?" and the others all started tittering.

I said, "If that's me you're hinting at, I'll be known as Hartington while I'm here, as you should know. I believe that's how things are done."

Hope said, "He'll come in when he can. He's got a lot on, bringing in the blooms for the dining room. You know Walter. He doesn't desert his post till his duty's done."

She whacked out a ladleful of soup so hard it spilled over the side of the plate. I got all broth and no leeks.

There was an empty place at Hope's end of the table, far away from where I was told to sit. She intended keeping him out of my way. She was carving the silverside when he walked in. I got a nod and then down went his eyes and he didn't look up again until he'd finished his sago pudding and pushed his dish away.

He said, "There's snow forecast. Boiler in the lily house is playing up. Well, I'd best press on."

And he scraped back his chair and walked out without giving me another glance. Everybody had been watching us.

I said, "I brought a few bonbons for you, Hope. It's funny, we still can't get bananas for love nor money, but I managed to get you some of those violet creams you like."

She said, "We make our own bonbons up here, thank you very much. Walnut brittle, peppermint creams. We don't need shop-bought bonbons nor anything else from down south."

The scullery maid said, "If they're going spare I'll have them. I've never had anything from down south."

Footman Cleaver said, "That's not what I heard. How about that sapper from the Royal Engineers?"

I said, "You've changed your tune, Hope Stallybrass. I remember when you'd have done anything for a violet cream. Well, I'll bring them to the table tomorrow and anyone who likes to can help themselves. And don't feel obliged to make my life a misery. I'm only here as Lady Hartington's maid. Anything else is between me and Walter."

She said, "Just don't think you can waltz back in, that's all. He's nicely settled now so don't go causing upset. He's nothing to say to you."

But when I went upstairs there was one of those striped camellias floating in a saucer on my washstand and a note. It said, *There's no juice to spare for a motor but I'll gladly walk you to Hassop in the morning if you want to go to your Mass. As you may recall, this one's called Yours Truly.*

I could smell the snow before I opened my eyes. Before I lived in Boston I'd never seen the stuff, but we had plenty my first winter there and I've had a nose for it ever since. I went in to Kick, to see if she intended coming to Mass.

"No," she said, "I think I'll sleep in a bit longer. I'll just say my rosary later."

I said, "Well, I'm going."

"Are you?" she said. "I wonder who'll drive you to Hassop?" and she gave me such a cheeky grin.

I said, "Did you put him up to this?"

"Me?" she said. "Gosh, no, I haven't even seen him."

The kitchens had been humming since seven, getting the Christmas dinner ready, but everywhere else was quiet. There was only one set of footprints that had broken the snow down to the kitchen gardens.

He started singing "In Her Master's Steps She Trod" when he saw me picking my way. I gave him his muffler.

I said, "Black and white's not very cheery, I know. I'd have done red but I couldn't get the yarn."

"Red?" he said. "Nay, Nora, I wouldn't wear red. Black and white's Derby County colors. Just the ticket."

I said, "And then I ran out of the black, that's why the last stripe's blue but if you tuck it inside your jacket it'll never be noticed."

"Even better," he said. "Blue for Chesterfield. A scarf for all footballing occasions. Now take my arm. I don't want you taking a tumble. If you break your leg we could be stuck with you up here while Easter. You don't want that."

We never got as far as the church. It was hard enough getting to Baslow, and we saw an old boy at the crossroads who said the snow had drifted three feet deep on the lane to Hassop and we'd be fools to try and get through. Walter knocked on the side door of the Square and Compasses and they opened up and we sat in the snug and had two ginger wines apiece. Then we trudged to his cottage and he ended up getting a kiss and a cuddle for Christmas, as well as his scarf, so that's alcohol for you.

He said, "I'm fifty-five, Nora. And I didn't wait all them years to let go of you five minutes after I found you. So I've been thinking."

It wasn't a bad little place he had. The ceilings were low but the fireplace didn't smoke and he'd been promised piped water in the near future.

I said, "Walter, I don't want another fight. I know this is home to you. But there'd be nothing for me to do here all the day long and I'm not cut out for idleness."

He said, "I know that and I know you don't want to let Her Ladyship down. Of course, whether she feels the same way is another matter. She could get her mind changed for her and you'll be left in the lurch. But here's the thing. We've been talked about, you and me."

I said, "That was pretty clear when I walked into the lion's den last night. All those kitchen maids giggling. Hope giving me the evil eye."

"Nay," he said, "I don't mean that. I mean we've been talked about Upstairs. Her Grace came to the glasshouse, said she wanted to talk about camellias but she never did. She said she knew how well the Stallybrasses had served the Devonshires over the years and Her and His Grace didn't like to think of a man parted from his wife in the line of duty, not when there wasn't a war on. She said they want me to come to London, Nora, to drive for Lady Kathleen and be with my wife, and not to worry about losing my place up here. She said when the time comes as Her Ladyship remarries and we're not required, which you can bet we won't be, there'll be a place found for us back here, and work for you, if that's what you want. That's what I'd call a compromise, Nora, and I don't think you'll get a better offer if you live to be ninety."

I said, "What did Her Grace say exactly? Did she actually mention Kick getting married again?"

It wouldn't have surprised me if they'd heard about Blood Fitzwilliam, even in Derbyshire. There was plenty of talk in London.

"No," he said. "She just said that the time would come. It stands to reason. She's a bonny young lass. Why? Is she courting?"

I said, "She's very popular. You know Kick."

"That's right," he said. "She's too young for widow's weeds. And Their Graces'd be happy to see her settled again, I'm sure."

Indeed. Settled the other side of the ocean with a nice quiet millionaire, not running around England with another woman's husband.

He said, "So what do you think? Shall I come? Do you want me back? Or have you got yourself a fancy man?"

I said, "Nobody's interested in me, at my time of life."

"I'm interested in you," he said. "I'm so interested in you I'm willing to leave my camellias in the horny hands of Tommy Marstin. I've missed you, Nora."

I said, "You'll never hear the end of it from Hope. I've not had a civil word out of her since I got here."

He said, "Bugger Hope. She's never happier than when she's got something to moan about."

The sun was shining when we came out, so bright the snow dazzled the eyes.

He said, "Before we go up to dinner, come round the back. There's somebody I want you to meet."

He'd got a young Berkshire, rooting around in a pen next to the privy, black with three white socks.

"Not so much a pig," he said, "as a machine for turning Jerusalem artichokes into sausages. Nora, meet Emperor Hirohito."

33

The Irish Card

We hadn't been back at Smith Square five minutes before Blood Fitzwilliam was on the doorstep wanting to take her to lunch. Walter had been expecting to drive her to Lady Balderston's to see the new baby but that was all out the window as soon as she saw His Lordship standing there, trilby hat tipped forward over his eyes. They went roaring off in his little two-seater.

Walter said, "No need to tell me who that was. Flash Harry. Did you see how fast he pulled away? Never checked his mirror, never signaled. I wouldn't want any daughter of mine riding with him."

But Kick loved it. All the Kennedys drove like crazies, except for Mrs. K, and when she took the wheel, which she did once in a blue moon, she took it steady, because she could hardly see over the steering wheel.

I said, "She reckons he's the one for her. Can you believe it? The only thing is, I'm sure he's the restless type. It's a terrible thing to say, but I hope he hurries up and breaks her heart, then we can all get back on track."

Most of her old friends had faded from the scene because of Lord Fitzwilliam. Cynthia Brough had told her to her face she was a fool. Ginny Balderston and Sissy Ormsby-Gore were the only ones who persevered, and there were times I thought she'd lose them too. His Lordship only had to snap his fingers and off she'd go, didn't matter if she'd arranged to go shopping or visiting with somebody else. There were his friends, of course, hard-drinking types they knew from the racetrack, but they didn't come to Smith Square so much, especially after Walter was back on the scene.

She said, "Why does Walter have to look so fierce? He frightens people off."

I said, "He's doing no more than your Daddy would do if he could see you. He wouldn't allow carousing and carrying on till three in the morning. He'd send them packing. Wouldn't he tell them to do something gainful with their lives?"

"Uh-oh," she said. "If I wanted a lecture I'd apply to Mother."

The one comfort I took was that His Lordship seemed to like going around with a crowd, so at least he didn't have an opportunity to take advantage of her. But then came the night when she didn't come home. I didn't get a minute's sleep and when I heard the milk cart at five and she still wasn't in, I woke Walter.

He said, "I'll drive around Grosvenor Square. See what's what."

Grosvenor Square was where Blood Fitzwilliam's mother had a house. He stayed there when he was in town. Walter wasn't gone half an hour.

He said, "His Nibs's motorcar's parked outside the house and the curtains are all shut tight, so I'd say he's took her home and had his way with her."

It was nearly eleven when she showed her face, hair not brushed, bags under her eyes.

She said, "I am wrecked. I'm going to soak in the tub and then sleep, sleep, sleep."

I said, "Have you not been to bed? Well, no more have I. I was out of my wits thinking you'd met with an accident."

"Oh Nora," she said, "I'm sorry. But I've told you not to wait up. We closed Frisco's and a party sort of happened at Blood's and I just kind of stayed."

I said, "Oh well then. And was old Lady Fitzwilliam at home? Or Lady Obby?"

"No," she said. "But so what?"

A fine thing.

I said, "So you're sleeping with him now, is it?"

She laughed. Not a happy laugh though.

She said, "What if I did? I'm going to marry him, Nora, just as soon as he's free, and what's a few months? I don't believe in all that stuff the nuns say anymore. Obby doesn't love him and I do, so there's nothing wrong in it."

All those years I'd looked after her, it was the first time we'd ever talked without her looking me in the eye.

It was just before Easter when she received a letter from Mrs. K, asking had she made a retreat for Lent like she was expected to and to say that Lady Dellie Cavendish had invited the family to Lismore during the summer. Mr. K wasn't feeling up to traveling, but Mrs. K was going to bring Pat and Jean and Jack hoped to go too, if he could get away.

Kick said, "See? I knew Mother would come round. I'll bet Jack's been putting in a good word for me."

I said, "If it's an olive branch, take it. And don't go spoiling everything, bringing up Lord Fitzwilliam's name."

"'Course not," she said. "Not till the time is right. I'm gonna get Jack on my side first. They'll hit it off, both being war heroes and everything. Then Jack can work on Daddy and Daddy can work on Mother."

We went to Lismore towards the end of June. Herself was already installed by the time we got there, holding court, especially with the pols. She monopolized that handsome Mr. Eden something terrible. The Duchess of Kent was there and Fred Astaire, visiting with his sister. There was a real jolly houseful and there was nothing grand about Lismore. If you're obliged to keep a castle in the family you couldn't ask for a more comfortable little place. Pat and Jean and Kick went horseback riding every day with Lady Anne and Lady Elizabeth, and Mrs. K played a bit of golf, but it was the fishing Jack loved. He went out in a boat from Dungarvan, hoping to catch blue shark and came back empty-handed, but then he took two beautiful salmon the day he fished on the Blackwater, fifteen-pounders. One was sent up to the kitchens for baking and the other went to the smokehouse. Jack was looking fitter than I'd seen him in years.

I said, "The politicking suits you."

"Yes," he said, "I like it better than I thought I would. Mother says I was fed on it. She reckons it was in that Fitzgerald gold-top mother's milk she gave me."

I said, "And are you really going for president?"

"That's the plan," he said. "Eventually. Senator first. Then the White House. And you'll come to my inauguration, of course. Guest of honor."

I said, "But I don't need to pick out my hat just yet?"

"No," he said, "I'd say you have fifteen years at least."

I said, "And do you have a sweetheart?"

He laughed. "You know me," he said.

I said, "Well, you may as well enjoy your oats. You won't be able to chase after girls once you're a senator. You'll need a nice, suitable wife."

"I guess," he said. "We're thinking about that. She's got to be somebody the ladies'll like. You know? Somebody they'll feel like they could chat to about the drapes and the baby's new tooth. Nice-looking, for the cameras, but not stacked or anything common. Dad's working on it."

I said, "So your Daddy's running the show? What does His Honor think about that?"

He said, "He's okay. I probably wouldn't have won that primary without him. He worked so damned hard. The only thing with Grandpa is he's a bit behind the times. He thinks I should play the Irish card, but voters aren't like that anymore. They want to know what you'll do about the Communists, not whether you can play a tin whistle. I'm going to humor him though. I'm going to go over into Wexford, see if I can rustle up a few Kennedy cousins. Get some photos. You never know when they might be useful."

He quite thought Kick and Pat would go with him, but they weren't interested. They'd got up a tennis tournament.

I said to Kick, "Why ever don't you go? Spend a bit of time with your brother. You haven't seen him in long enough."

There was a time when Kick would have done anything for Jack, and if she didn't do it willingly Mrs. K would have made her do it anyway, but at Lismore Mrs. K was minding her Ps and Qs. As long as she had the Devonshires watching her she played at Happy Families.

Kick said, "It'll be boring. It's the kind of thing Jack has to do these days but that's his hard cheese. Anyway, I don't need any more relations. And the tennis is all arranged. You go if you think it'll be so fascinating."

So I did. I sat up front, beside Walter, and Pamela Digby

Churchill rode in the back with Jack. She'd been married to Mr. Churchill's boy, Randolph, but it hadn't lasted. The ink was still wet on her divorce papers, but she was back on the prowl already. Always a Jezebel, that one. I remember how she used to flirt with Mr. K when we were at Prince's Gate, and she couldn't have been more than nineteen at the time. I think she'd been hoping for a romantic ride out into the countryside, but Jack wasn't interested in her. His mind was on finding the place his granduncles had farmed.

He had an address from his aunt Loretta Kennedy, who'd visited years back and found some cousins in a house near Dunganstown. We stopped and asked directions of a red-faced old boy. He had his pants held up with string.

He said, "Well now, let me think. It must be Jimmy Kennedy's you want. You go away down here and then left, only not left where you might think. After the turn you don't want there's another bit of a lane. It's a pity you've come this way. It would have been easier to tell you if you'd been coming from New Ross."

He was peering into our beautiful shiny motor. He must have thought we had Mr. de Valera himself in the back.

We found the house belonging to James and Kitty Kennedy, and they had us all in for a cup of tea and a photograph, but they must have wondered what in the world was going on, because they were no more related to Jack than they were to the King of Siam. In the end it was their wee lad who piped up.

He said, "You got the wrong house, mister. It's Mr. Ryan's you want only Mammy doesn't like to say so."

Mrs. Mary Ryan was a Kennedy by birth, they said.

It was only another mile down the track, a muddy yard and a little crouched-down cottage. Jimmy Kennedy followed behind us on a bicycle, with his boy on the crossbar, to make sure we found it. There were three children ran squealing into the house when they saw our motor stop at the gate, but Mrs. Ryan, née Kennedy, didn't look so thrilled to see us. She came out wiping her hands on her apron.

Mrs. Churchill said, "Heavens, Jack! They got these people from Central Casting. I'm sorry. This isn't really my kind of thing. I'll just stay in the car."

Jack was already out, trying to give Mrs. Ryan the Congressman's big handshake.

"Jack Kennedy," he said, "Boston, Massachusetts. I think we're family."

"Are we so?" she said. "Mary Ann, run and fetch your Dadda."

She had that washed-out look of a woman who's on the go from dawn till late, and up from her childbed after three days. My own Mammy looked just the same, and all her sisters.

Walter said, "This gentleman's come all the way from America."

She said, "I suppose I'll make a pot of tea."

I heard Mrs. Churchill say, "Please, no more tea. I could use a whiskey but then where would one go to tinkle?"

James Kennedy said, "Your man here's a politico, Mary, in the United States of America."

She said, "He looks like he's only just out of short trousers."

I said, "He's old enough to have won a medal in the war."

But she was already on her way into the house.

Walter shouted, "He's drove all the way from Lismore Castle to see you. He's the guest of the Duke and Duchess of Devonshire."

Jimmy Kennedy cut right across him.

He said, "I'd pipe down about dukes and duchesses in front of Mary Ryan if I was you, driver. She's a fearsome Fenian, that one. She's like one of the lads."

A lot of the Nationalist women were. Our Aunt Flighty was

married to a Home Ruler, and she always said if there were guns to be moved the women would do it because they weren't so likely to get searched.

Mammy used to say, "I don't want to hear about it, Flighty. Children getting their schooling is what'll change Ireland, not women hiding guns under the eiderdown so one mother's son can shoot another."

That's why we were never kept out of school, no matter how much work there was to do at home, and Edmond was made to stay on till he was fully fourteen, though God knows there wasn't much inside his skull for the masters to work on.

I went into the Ryan cottage with Jack. Walter stayed outside with Mrs. Churchill. The children all sat around and studied us and then Mr. Ryan came in from the field. He said he recalled hearing something about Kennedys in America. Jack loved it. He doesn't have the same patter Joseph Patrick had, or Mr. K's way of bowling you over, but he's more natural. He was teasing the little ones how they'd the same freckles he did, telling them the names of his brothers and sisters. All except Rosie. He didn't say anything about her even after I reminded him. They've everything worked out, my Kennedys, except what story to tell about what's become of Rosie.

Jack took a snapshot before we left, but first the Ryan girls wanted their Sunday ribbons put in their hair and then the neighbors came nosing, to see who belonged to the limousine. Half of Dunganstown was in that picture before we were finished.

I felt sorry for Jack. He was so thrilled to have found his folks, but all Mrs. Churchill would say was that she had flea bites. They would have been from the cat she'd picked up and dandled.

He kept saying, "If Great-grandpa hadn't left, that's where I'd have been born. Except I wouldn't have been. I just wouldn't exist. You realize they don't have a telephone? They don't even have electricity."

I said, "We none of us had the electric light. Now I think back, it's a wonder we're not half blind the way we used to knit by candlelight."

He said, "Nora, I always thought you were from Boston."

He had no idea.

I said, "I came from Westmeath, you noodle, eighteen years old with nothing but a cardboard valise and two sisters waiting for me. Fidelma Clery the same, she was from Tralee, Danny Walsh was from Limerick, Gabe Nolan was from Kerry."

He didn't remember Gabe Nolan.

I said, "He used to drive your Daddy, way back, before we went to England. We were all from the Old Country in those days, apart from Mrs. Ambler. All from wee houses like the ones you were in today."

He said, "Well, let's go see yours. Where's Westmeath? Let's go tomorrow."

I said it was likely too far. Walter said he didn't mind an early start. I said I hadn't been back in thirty-five years, had never wanted to, and I didn't even know if the house was still standing. Jack said all the more reason to go find out.

Mrs. Churchill said, "Count me out. It's all been just too Tobacco Road for me."

Wherever Tobacco Road is it obviously isn't a good enough address for an Honorable Mrs.

Kick was fuming when we got back.

She said, "You're late, Jack. People are having drinks, dinner's ready and you don't even have time to change."

He said, "I had a great day though. Found our folks. Got pictures and everything. Wait till you see."

She said, "Well, Pamela didn't have a great day. She says it's been boring and beastly. Why couldn't you be nice to her? And you smell of dogs or something. Tomorrow I want you to be especially nice to her. Play golf with her. She's so sweet."

"Sorry, Sis," he said, "no can do. Tomorrow we're going to look for Nora's roots."

34

The Trouble with Blood

We left at seven, with soda bread and thermos flasks of tea, and went up through Kilkenny and Port Laoise. Jack was in the mood to love every beck and horse and cart he saw and even Walter allowed that the hills were nearly as bonny as Derbyshire, but I couldn't look at any scenery. I was too worried about what we were going to find. Just before we got into Tullamore I smelled that hot, biscuity smell of the distillery and I knew I was nearly home.

We were past the cottage before I realized. Things are always smaller than you remember and it seemed set lower from the road. Walter had to back up. And we were no sooner out of the car than there was a face at Donnellys' window across the way. A woman came out.

She said, "You'll find nobody there. It was Mrs. Clavin's house but she left."

I said, "It was Mr. Brennan's house. Did he die?"

"Don't know," she said. "I'm from Mullingar. Was he an old man?"

Hardly. In his sixties, but younger than Ursie.

I said, "Are you one of the Donnellys?"

"Yes," she said. "I'm married to Sylvester."

I said, "And who's Sylvester?"

He was Martin Donnelly's boy.

I said, "Martin had two sisters went to America, Bridget and Marimichael. Marimichael was my friend. We sailed the same time."

"Oh yes?" she said.

I said, "Marimichael's been dead years, of course. Did you ever hear speak of her?"

"Don't think so," she said. "There's an awful lot of the Donnellys dead. It's hard to keep track. You don't sound American."

She'd followed us down the path.

I said, "Mr. Brennan was my brother. He was married to Mrs. Clavin."

Jack said, "Any idea where we'd find her?"

"Tullamore," she said. "She went to a row house in Tullamore. You sound American, so. Are you a film star?"

"No," he said, "I'm a congressman. I'm Jack Kennedy."

She said, "You look like a film star. What do you want with Mrs. Clavin? Has she come into money?"

The door was hanging off its hinges. We could walk right in. There was nothing much left inside except Mammy's picture of the Sermon on the Mount and some old shelf paper Ursie put up with thumbtacks.

I said, "You know what, Edmond must have passed away and that Clavin woman never thought to let Ursie know. All that driving for nothing. Well, now you've seen it. Now you know why we all left."

Jack said, "But it's cute. I'm glad we came. Let's go back to Tullamore, try some of that whiskey. What do you reckon, Walter?"

Walter said, "I never touch the stuff, sir. But I'd be happy to keep you company with a pint."

The Donnelly woman said there were row houses next to Daly's malt barn.

She said, "What did your man say his name is?"

I said, "He's Jack Kennedy. He's a very important young man. You listen out for that name in years to come."

"I will," she said. "I've a friend in Mullingar gets *Silver Screen* magazine sent her. I'll look out for him."

We walked along to the graveyard and I picked dog roses. There was a blackbird singing on Nellie's headstone. It was the only time the sun broke through all that day. *Helen Mary Brennan 1898–1902.* She'd have been nearly fifty if she'd lived. We split up when we got back to Tullamore. Jack and Walter went to the pub while I knocked on doors in Daly Street. One woman said she knew everybody and there were no Clavins or Brennans.

Another woman said, "There is an Edmond. An old feller. I don't know his other name. He'll be drinking in Larrissey's this time of day. Will I send my boy to fetch him out for you?"

But Jack and Walter had already found him. There were the three of them walking up the middle of the street like Larry, Moe, and Curly.

Edmond said, "Is it you, Deirdre? Have you come home?"

He had all his hair still, but not a tooth in his head. He showed us his dentures when we went in for a brew of tea, still in their box, because they'd pained him so much he couldn't wear them. He said he kept meaning to put an advertisement in Magennis's window, to see if he couldn't sell them. The Clavin woman was gone. She'd died of bad headaches and was buried at Ardnorcher, and Edmond was left on his own in a fine little house with an inside toilet and electric light.

He kept saying, "Where are you staying, Deirdre? You can stay here."

And I kept saying, "It's not Deirdre, it's Nora. Do you not remember? I went to America."

He'd seem to catch on for a minute. He said, "I do remember. And you sent Mammy a handbag. We've got it still."

He went off and found it, that beautiful leather bag Ursie sent to Mammy, must have been 1910, never been used. I'd have had it from him, only it was so old-fashioned-looking.

I said, "It was Ursie sent this bag. Remember Ursie? She's the one always writes to you. She went first, to Boston, and then Margaret and then me. I'm Nora."

"That's right," he said. "I remember now. It'd be worth something, that bag. I could sell it."

I said, "Are you hurting for money?"

"No, no," he said. "Annie Clavin left me all right. I can have anything I want. And we've the two rooms. You could stay here. We'd be company for each other."

I said, "I can't stay with you, Edmond. This here is my husband. We've a home in England. I just came by to see how you're doing. Take a look at the old place."

He said, "I'm doing just grand. England, so? You're not with the Sisters anymore then?"

I said, "It's Deirdre who's with the Sisters. And Ursie was saying, about the old house. That Deirdre might be glad of it if she ever comes home from Africa."

"Oh," he said, "you wouldn't want to live there. It's terrible damp. Tell Ursie she can stop with me. Tell her I've got a wireless set. I'll bet she doesn't have one of them in Africa."

Poor Edmond. The few wits he ever had were gone. I felt terrible walking away from him. He shouldn't have been living there like that, all alone.

I said to Walter, "It's true what they say about ignorance being bliss. Now I'll be worrying about him. He needs looking after."

"Nay, Nora," he said. "He's all right. They seem very fond of him in that pub. They give him his dinner every day."

Well, I still felt bad. Typical of that Clavin woman, to have had her pleasure and then upped and died.

Directly the holiday at Lismore was over, Mrs. Kennedy and Pat and Jean went home. There was a new Navy destroyer ready for launching. It was to be called the *Joseph P. Kennedy* and Jean had been chosen to name it. But Jack traveled back with us to London and the minute she had him to herself Kick spilled the beans about her new sweetheart. She thought that because Joe had sided with her when she wanted to marry Lord Billy, Jack would do the same, that he'd step up to the mark now she needed a friend again. I wasn't so sure. There was a very big difference between Billy Hartington and Blood Fitzwilliam, and anyhow, Jack refused even to meet him. Her face fell.

He said, "I'll do just one thing for you, Kick. I won't call Dad and warn him what's going on, like I should do. But you have to wake up and face facts. I'm trusting you to do the right thing before Mother hears about it."

She said, "Go ahead and call Daddy. I don't care. You don't even know Blood, so why are you so down on him? You'd like him if you met him. He's got war stories and stuff. He plays golf."

Jack said, "Listen, a guy might be okay for a round of golf, but that doesn't mean I'd want him marrying my sister. A married man? You're dreaming if you think this'll ever work out, so don't even bring it up at home. You'll break Dad's heart for one thing, and Mother'll run off to the nursing home again, which'll rebound on Teddy and Jean. It's just not fair. I'm going to give you time to come to your senses, so don't go firing off any dumb letters. Hell, Kick, what is it with you? You meet plenty of nice guys. Why can't you fall in love with somebody who fits the bill?"

She said, "Well, that's pretty rich considering the mess Daddy had to get you out of down in Florida, Mr. Whiter-Than-Snow Congressman."

His face turned to thunder.

He said, "Don't you ever speak of that. You hear me? You don't have any goddamned business knowing about it. Who told you about that anyhow?"

"Joe did," she shouted. "He told me everything. And he wouldn't be such a hypocrite if he was here. And don't use bad words in front of Nora."

But he'd already slammed out. It was a rare thing for those two to quarrel.

She sat biting her nails to the quick.

I said, "Do I have to bring out the mustard again?"

"I miss Joe," she said. "He'd have known what to do."

I said, "And how do you think he'd have advised you?"

"Don't know," she said. "But he couldn't have said much, could he? That girl he was seeing was married."

I said, "That was wartime. A lot of things went on then. But you know fine your Mammy and Daddy would never have given him their blessing, and he wouldn't have expected it. And it's not only that His Lordship has a wife and a child. He's in the wrong church, he's too old for you, and if you ask me, it's your money he's after."

"That's not true," she said. "Blood's got money of his own."

His wife's money, according to Lady Ginny. And he ran through it like a hot knife through butter, paying for his cars and his racehorses.

I said, "I don't like to see you fighting with Jack. You see little enough of each other."

"Well," she said. "Isn't he the sanctimonious one all of a sudden. He must be pretty cocksure that embarrassing little secret of his is buried where no one can find it."

I said, "And what is the secret? Did he get a girl in trouble?"

"A girl!" she said. "Hardly a girl! Picked-over goods, I'd say. Oh Nora, you remember! When we were living at Prince's Gate and Jack didn't come over for Christmas? And Daddy went home too because he had to see his stomach doctor, so Grandpa and Grandma Fitzgerald came to stay. You remember how Grandpa Fitz had to keep going to the telephone."

I said, "I remember all the telephoning. I thought Jack had had a mishap in his motor."

"Ha!" she said. "Mishap in a city hall, more like. He went to New Jersey and married this really gruesome woman, divorced twice at least and much older than him. She was obviously a gold-digger. Daddy was furious. It wasn't easy to fix something like that I don't imagine."

I said, "Jack wasn't married. I don't believe that."

"Yes he was," she said. "Wild, isn't it? What a fool. I guess he did it for a dare."

I said, "Well, then he had to get divorced. How did he manage that?"

"Well," she said, "not divorced exactly. They were only married for about five minutes, so I guess it was a kind of annulment. Anyway, Grandpa made some calls and Mr. Timilty went down there and took care of everything."

I said, "And did your Mammy know about it?"

"I don't think so," she said. "I mean we just absolutely never talk about it. But I don't see why I should have Jack lecturing me about Blood, considering his history. Gee, he's getting as pi as little St. Bobby."

I didn't know what to make of it. If it was right, what she

said, it could only have happened in drink, like boys sometimes get a tattoo or go to a whorehouse. Kick and Jack patched things up before he flew home, but only because he had to be rushed to the hospital, which gave us all a fright. He collapsed with terrible pains in his belly, and when they got him to the clinic they said he was jaundiced, so it was very likely the malaria had come back. Then Herself started bombarding the doctors with letters, explaining how he'd had a very hectic year and all he needed was rest. But it was plain to see, looking at the snapshots he'd had taken in Ireland, how the weight had dropped off him. He stayed cheerful though.

"Tell you what, Nora," he said. "I reckon this jaundice suits me. It gives me a kind of tanned, movie-star look. I should have signed my autograph for that girl in Ballynagore."

He didn't look like any movie star to me. He looked like a scarecrow with an orange face. And then we got the verdict from the doctors. It wasn't malaria at all but a disease of the glands and very serious indeed. But they had a brand-new medicine for it, injections that had only just been invented. They said he was practically the first person they'd be trying it out on and it might mean the difference between life and death. I think Our Lady must have been watching over him. And over those inventors.

So they started him on the injections and the pains calmed down and he didn't feel so weak. The only drawback was his face ballooned out. People started saying how well he looked, but he's been a bag of bones all the years I've known him. I couldn't get used to him looking like the Man in the Moon.

They taught him how to give himself the injections before he sailed home. Walter nearly fainted when he saw him jab that needle in.

"Nay, sir," he said, "can't they give you a pill?"

"Not yet," he said. "They will, in time. Candy-coated and

everything. But they'll be for whiners. Kennedys take their shots like men."

He'd been a very sick lad, that I do know, but Herself declined to believe it was anything that a plain diet and a dose of Poland Spring water wouldn't cure. She's a card, that one. Shut herself away in a clinic when Kick married Lord Billy, and yet I've seen her soldier on with sprains and cuts and women's pains and all sorts. Keeping the Kennedy bandwagon rolling, that's always her first idea.

As soon as Jack arrived home she had him whisked up to Boston to see a top gland doctor, and she had a shock. The Boston doctor agreed with what the London doctors had said. He'd to continue with the injections, and get his blood tested regular.

Kick heard from him.

Personally I think you should come home, he wrote.

Take time out. See how things look from this side of the ocean. Above all, don't do anything crazy about this Fitzwilliam guy. Maybe you should talk to Dad. You know you can always trust him to give you good advice. Remember, you're a Kennedy and we all love you a million.

She said, "I had a nightmare, Nora. I think we were at Hyannis. It was a house by the ocean, and we were all dressed up in sailor suits, lined up in a row to have our photo taken, but every time the photographer was ready somebody was missing. Jack was gone, then Pat, then Rosie and Jean. The funny thing was though, Joe was still there. I saw him clear as anything."

I'd had a bad dream myself. I was in a room with hundreds of babies, all Kennedys, but I didn't know any of their names and they all had the same little face. I was searching and searching through them for Rosie, only I could never find her.

Kick said, "Maybe I should talk to Daddy. Maybe I should write or go see him. What do you think?"

I could see what was coming.

I said, "I don't think it makes any difference what you do. You're not going to get your Mammy's blessing, and if she won't give hers, your Daddy won't give you his. And as for trailing back to America, you know I can't do it again. If that's the way it's going to be, me and Walter'll have to give you our notice."

Out came the pet lip.

She said, "Don't say that. Walter can come to America too."

I said, "Walter doesn't want to come to America, and neither do I. Take Delia Olvanie. Sure she'd jump at it."

And she did. I got no more work out of Delia till her bags were packed.

"Palm Beach, Florida," she said. "That's where we're going for Christmas. They say it's nothing but millionaires and mansions."

I said, "But you can leave your mink in storage. All you'll be doing is shaking the sand out of Lady Kathleen's clothes and going to bed hungry. There's not an ounce of comfort to be had in a Kennedy house."

She said, "You're just jealous."

"Oh I am," I said to her. "Just what I want. Living out of trunks again. Getting yapped at by Mrs. K. You're welcome, Delia Olvanie. And I'll give you a word of warning. If Lady Kathleen lets slip a word about Lord Fitzwilliam the balloon will go up. They'll have her bundled off to St. Gertrude's or somewhere, kept under lock and key till she repents, and then we'll all be out of a job. So you watch out. Any letters come for her, any telephone calls, don't go shouting it from the rooftops."

As it turned out there weren't likely to be any letters nor calls, because Blood Fitzwilliam went off to Equatorial Africa to shoot elephants. Kick took along Lord Billy's sister, Lady Elizabeth, and they had a quiet Christmas down at Palm Beach. She waited till their very last day there to bring up Fitzwilliam's name. I had it blow by blow from Delia.

She said, "Mr. K hardly said a word. But Mrs. K said if she marries any divorced man she'll see her cut off without a penny. And her sisters were yelling at her too, especially that Euny, about leaving the church. They sent a monsignor chasing after us when we got to New York, but Lady Kathleen wouldn't see him. She told me she's never, never going back to America, Nora. It's a terrible shame. I thought it was grand place. Then when we got on the boat she was trying to get through to Lord Fitzwilliam, but she never got him. Every day she tried. She was in a right old state, but I don't see how anybody could make a telephone call from the middle of the ocean. There's not wires long enough. So anyway, now I don't know what's going to happen. We could all be out on the street if Mr. Kennedy stops her money."

Kick was subdued.

She said, "I knew there'd be a fuss but it was much worse than I expected. Mother's really on the warpath. Euny's not speaking to me. Bobby's not speaking to me. Jack's keeping his distance. My only hope now is Daddy."

There was a time when her Daddy could have fixed anything for her, and Herself would just go lie down, wear her frownies for an hour, then put on a smile and learn to live with it. But it seemed it wasn't like that anymore. Since Joseph Patrick was killed, it seemed that Mrs. K had started trying on the pants.

35

A Day of Tears

They came before it was light, ringing and ringing on the door-bell. Walter went down. Two constables were on the front step. They said a plane had crashed in France and papers had been found belonging to a Lady Hartington. Walter had shown them into the drawing room by the time I came down. It was only the older one did any talking, but I suppose they always send two.

He said, "Is Lady Hartington away from home?"

I said, "She went yesterday. To France."

He said, "Was she traveling alone?"

Walter said, "We wouldn't know."

"Well," he said, "a passport was found. That's all I can tell you at present."

Kick wasn't the only Lady Hartington, of course. When Lord Billy died the title passed on to Lady Debo, but she was already accounted for. Kick was the one flying in airplanes with another woman's husband.

I said, "Was it an American passport?"

"Couldn't say, madam," he said.

Her Grace came on the telephone from Chatsworth to say they'd had a visit from the police too and she very much feared another tragedy had occurred. They'd told her the plane had crashed into a mountain in very bad weather.

I told Delia to keep the curtains closed. Then I went to Kick's room, to smell her scent, and see if the place felt any different. It didn't. I sat on her bed and I thought, She can't be dead. Joe died and then Lord Billy, so we've had our tragedies. It's somebody else's turn now.

I don't know how long Walter had been standing in the doorway watching me.

He said, "You'll be wanting to go to church."

I said, "I can't. I shall have to be here."

"What for?" he said.

I said, "Well, there might be further information."

"Sweetheart," he said, "you go. Take Delia and some of them candles. Light one for me too. I'll be here if there's any news. It'll be the family they tell first though."

Mr. Kennedy was in Paris on business. He was expecting to see Kick on her way back from her jaunt, to meet Lord Fitzwilliam and see if anything could be done about them marrying. It was the American newspaper people who tracked him down to his hotel and Joey Timilty who had to break the news to him. They said the place where the plane had crashed was the back of beyond, so they'd have to bring the bodies down off the mountain on oxcarts. All that day we kept hoping there'd been some mistake but then Mr. K went down there on the train and saw them in their coffins. After that there was no denying it, but as me and Delia were walking back from the cathedral we saw Lord Balderston drive by in a fancy-looking motor with no roof and the first thing I thought was, I must tell Kick.

They brought her body back to Croydon and Walter drove me to the aerodrome to meet her.

I said, "She was the closest I ever came to having a wean of my own. Her and Rosie. And now one way or another they're both gone."

"Aye," he said, "I know. I grew very fond of her myself."

Mr. K had come with her, and after they carried the casket off the plane, he didn't seem to know what to do next. All the spark had gone out of him, and no wonder. You don't expect to bury your children.

I said, "There's a bed for you at Smith Square."

But he had Joey Timilty with him and he said a hotel would be better.

Mr. K said, "I don't know why I brought her here. I should have had the funeral in Paris. I could have done."

He was like a sleepwalker.

I said, "What does Mrs. Kennedy want?"

He said, "She's in Hyannis. She'll be going to Mass. She'll leave it up to me what to do."

Kick lay at the American Embassy that night. I'd have liked to sit with her, but Mr. K said it was a father's place to do it. And so it was. Just so long as somebody waked her I didn't mind who. Then Lord Billy's mother stepped in about the funeral. She said, "Bring her to Derbyshire. Let her be buried in the family plot. She was Billy's widow, after all."

There was a Requiem Mass said for her at Farm Street. It was packed to the doors with her friends, even the ones she'd neglected since Fitzwilliam came on the scene, and all the Devonshires came too. But her Daddy was the only Kennedy there. I suppose they were lighting candles for her in Hyannis, but not a one of them crossed the ocean to see her laid to rest. Not even Jack, who loved her so. Not even her own mother.

Then we went to St. Pancras station, still a good crowd of us, and caught the train to Bakewell. Me and Walter rode with the casket in the guard's van. There were two bicycles in there with us, and a basket full of racing pigeons. The hearse went directly to Edinsor and she was buried in the churchyard there in the plot that had been intended for Lord Billy someday. Little Kathleen Kennedy laid to rest among the Dukes of Devonshire. I saw her into the world and I saw her out of it. Mr. K looked such a poor old man all of a sudden. When it was over he came looking for me.

He said, "Nora, there are things at Smith Square, some furniture Billy's folks loaned her, and jewelry? Have it all sent back, would you?"

And then he walked away, him and Joey Timilty, looking for a car to take them back to the rail station. It was His Grace who paid the priest.

The facts are getting rearranged already. Lady Astor's going round saying it wasn't an accident at all but a plot, with the Pope behind it. She thinks Mrs. K wrote to the Holy Father, and the Holy Father had the airplane tampered with, to stop Kick marrying Fitzwilliam and going to Hell. Well, I've thought for the longest time that Lady Astor has a screw loose.

Then one of the newspapers said that Lady Hartington had been on her way to Paris to see her father, even though it was plain as a pikestaff that the plane was flying *away* from Paris. Another paper said she was a family friend of Lord Fitzwilliam and he'd offered her a lift seeing as he was on his way to inspect his horses in the south of France. Nobody appears to have noticed that he didn't have any horses in the south of France. Walter reckons Mr. Kennedy will have gotten his newspaper friends to tidy up the facts, to spare the feelings of the family. To save Jack and the other boys from any scandal and messiness, seeing as how they're all going to be president of the United States. I don't know why he'd go to the trouble. Those boys can create messiness enough of their own. A little story about Kick isn't going to make them or break them. Anyway, there are people enough who know what really happened.

The first thing was Fitzwilliam was late. He was always very slipshod about time and she'd been ready more than an hour, fidgeting around, watching out the window for his car. Then he telephoned to say his motor wouldn't start, so Walter would have to drive them to Croydon. His Lordship arrived in a hackney cab and off they bundled. She looked radiant, I must say. Like a bride going away. She was in her new blue suit and her pearls. No hat.

Walter came home tight-lipped. All the way to the aerodrome Lord Fitzwilliam had kept telling him to step on the gas.

He said, "More than thirty years I've been driving and never a mishap. Telling me my business. I said to him, 'My job is to get Her Ladyship safe to her destination.' You should have heard him then. Barrack-room language. Lady Kathleen were embarrassed, I could tell. Lord Billy must be turning in his grave to see her walking out with a man like that."

When they got to the aerodrome the pilot said as they were so late there'd have to be a change of plan. There were storms forecast for the afternoon, so he said he'd only take them as far as Paris until the weather improved, but Fitzwilliam wouldn't listen.

Walter heard him say, "You're chartered to take us to Cannes and you'll bloody well take us to Cannes."

And the pilot said, "If you'd been here for a timely departure, sir, the weather wouldn't have been a problem."

It's haunting Walter, I can tell. He keeps saying, "Perhaps if I'd gone a bit faster and got them there sooner."

But he has nothing to blame himself for. Minnie Stubbs came to the Mass at Farm Street and she told me exactly what happened. When they got to Paris they were meant to be meeting Minnie and her husband and some friends of Lord Fitzwilliam, to go to a restaurant. The pilot said if they insisted on flying on to Cannes they must do it immediately and hope to beat the weather, but Fitzwilliam wouldn't hear of it. He said he'd gone to great trouble to get a table so the pilot would just have to wait. So they had their luncheon and Minnie rode back with them in a taxi to wave them off from the airfield. She said the pilot was fit to be tied. He said they were more than four hours behind schedule and they'd be flying straight into storms, so they were going nowhere. He told them they'd all have to stay the night in Paris and carry on next morning.

Minnie said it was something to see how Fitzwilliam got his way. He told the pilot there'd be a nice bonus in it for him. Told him he'd come highly recommended as a pilot who could fly through anything and that neither he nor Kick would be bothered by a bumpy ride. He persuaded him, though that pilot should never have agreed to it. It's the kind of stunt Joseph Patrick would have pulled. Fitzwilliam had that side to him. He wouldn't be bested. He thought the bad things that happened to ordinary people couldn't happen to him. Maybe that's why Kick fell for him. He had a touch of the Kennedys about him.

I got a card in the post, from Herself, a Mass card for Kick, with a prayer for a soul in purgatory. What a thing! I threw it on the fire. Kick was a good girl, that's all I know and hardly more than a child. She loved her family and she said her prayers every day, and if that devil Fitzwilliam hadn't addled her head she'd be here still.

Walter said I shouldn't take what Mrs. K does so much to heart.

He said, "She doesn't tick like thee and me. You know she doesn't. From what I've heard she's had a rum life altogether, and enough sadness lately to turn a person's mind. That's what it'll be. Her mind's gone. You'll have to make allowances. Now I'm not a betting man and I'm not a pew-kisser neither, but if I had to choose between you and Rose Kennedy to say prayers for me, my money'd be on you, Nora Stallybrass. And another thing, I don't know much about womenfolk, but I reckon you had more joy of that girl than her own mother ever did."

Well, I don't know about that, though she did bring me joy. They say there's nothing in the world like a mother's love.

36

The View from Stalin's Sty

I take camellias for her, when they're in flower, and Their Graces
used to lay a holly garland at Christmas, but I don't know if that'll
be kept up now we've a new Duke and Duchess. So many changes
they never expected to see at Chatsworth. First Lord Billy mowed
down in his prime, and then last year his father. He was out saw-
ing firewood down at Compton Place and dropped like a stone,
only fifty-five. So now Lord Andrew and Lady Debo have had
to step up to the plate and Kick has a new neighbor in Edinsor graveyard. I hope His Grace doesn't find her too noisy. The
day she married Lord Billy I remember the old Duchess saying,
"Cavendishes rarely speak and Kennedys apparently never stop. I
wonder what their children will be like."

It's been three years since Kick died and Herself still hasn't
visited. Mr. K hasn't been back either. So far Jack's the only one
who's paid his respects. When it came time for the headstone
to be raised Her Grace wrote and asked them what inscription
they'd like, but they say she never got a reply. Perhaps it was too

much for them to bear. Hard enough to bury one child, let alone three.

Kick's the only one laid under the earth, of course. Joseph Patrick went out like a shooting star. He's everywhere and nowhere, you might say. But Rosie's as good as buried. They've moved her from Craig House to St. Coletta's in Jefferson, Wisconsin. She has her own chalet bungalow, with a Sister to watch over her and one of those television machines for company, but it's a long, long way from the family. It's too far for Fidelma to ride up on an afternoon and bring her a magazine and a box of candy. If Kick and Lord Billy had only lived, she could have come here. She could have helped with the babies and gone for nice walks around the estate. She'd have been as right as ninepence.

Mrs. K appears to be thriving though. Lady Debo clipped me a photograph from a magazine when Bobby married the Skakel girl. It looked like a big fancy affair, and Herself was in a hat the size of a cartwheel, all eyes and teeth for the cameras.

Well, she never was one to sit around and mope. "Pray for the dead, work for the living" is her motto, and she'll never have an idle moment, the way they have Bobby and Teddy lined up for high office behind Jack. Out on the stump she'll be, shaking hands and banging the drum for her boys. That's more up her alley than visiting graves. Anyway, I'm here to do that.

Hope still grumbles.

"That's the Cavendish section," she says. "They had no business putting an outsider in there. No offense, but they should have put her up the other end or took her home."

Walter says, "Nay, Hope. She is home. Her people live in hotel rooms. Nora'll tell you. And she's only in the spot Lord Billy should have had so she's not putting anybody out."

When you have charge of a nursery you grow eyes in the back of your head and ears that can hear a bat squeak. You know where they all are and what mischief they're up to before they've hardly thought of it themselves. That's why I like the Easter Morn blooms best, or the Ave Marias. They're pale, like coconut ice, easy to pick out from a distance. So even from here I can see where she lies. Every time I take the pig bucket down for Stalin, I say to her, "I see you, Kick Kennedy. Your old Nora's got her eye on you."

DATE			